JO-ANNE

Heléna

Ark House Press
PO Box 163
North Sydney, NSW, 2059
Telephone: (02) 8437 3541; Facsimile (02) 9999 2053
International: +612 8437 3541; Facsimile +612 9999 2053
www.arkhousepress.com

All rights reserved. No part of this publication may be reproduced, stored in a retrieval system or transmitted in any form or by any means electronic, mechanical, photocopying, recording or otherwise without the prior written permission of the publisher. Short extracts maybe used for review purposes.

Unless otherwise noted, Scripture quotations are from the Holy Bible, New International Version, Copyright 1973, 1978, 1984, 1998 by International Bible Society

© 2006 Jo-Anne Berthelsen

Cataloguing in Publication Data:

1st Edition

ISBN 978 0 9775671 4 0

Berthelsen, Jo-Anne
Helena

1. Music students – Fiction. 2. World War, 1939-1945 – Czechoslovakia – Fiction.
3. Immigrants – Australia – Fiction. 4. Czechs – Australia – Fiction.
5. Czechoslovakia – Fiction. I. Title.

A823.4

Printed and bound in Australia
Cover design by Media Inc

For

Joy Crawford – my 'lifesaver'

and

in loving memory of a special young woman

Emily Chapman

1985 – 2006

PART I

"For I know the plans I have for you,"
declares the Lord,
"plans to prosper you and not to harm you,
plans to give you hope
and a future."

Jeremiah 29:11

Chapter One

'Father, we thank you for your love and care, and your constant provision for us. We thank you for our friend Stefan, and his presence with us. May he be encouraged by our fellowship, and strengthened for the work you have given him to do. Bless us now as we share this meal together. Amen.'

Heléna never tired of hearing her father's beautiful voice, so full of depth and sincerity, as he said grace before a meal. It was part of their family tradition, an expression of their deep faith and trust in God that remained firm, whatever was happening around them. Now more than ever, she treasured these moments, since her father was away so often on business. She opened her eyes, and glanced lovingly across at him, as he raised his bowed head, his silvering hair glinting in the light of the candles positioned nearby on the dinner table. He smiled warmly at her, some of the weariness apparent in his face lifting as he did. She was glad he was home again – and she was glad he had arranged for his friend Stefan to join them.

'It's wonderful to have you both here,' her mother commented, putting Heléna's own thoughts into words. 'Of course, Heléna looks after me well while you're away, Václav, but we've missed you so much! And it's so good to have you here again, Stefan. If I remember rightly, Heléna was at school in Prague last time you were here, so I'm pleased you can finally meet.'

'I'm very happy to be here, Anezka, and especially pleased to meet the daughter I've heard so much about,' Stefan responded, the sincerity in his voice unmistakeable, as his eyes rested for a moment on Heléna's flushed face.

Heléna's eyes met his, and then quickly fell. Her head was spinning a little, with the effort of processing the gamut of unaccustomed emotions that had risen in her ever since Stefan's handshake, when Václav had first introduced them. She remained silent now, helping herself to the meal Berta had brought them, listening to the exchanges that soon flowed around her again, seeking some inner equilibrium as she did so.

Anezka, always particularly observant where her daughter was concerned, had noticed the momentary loss of her usual poise, acquired through the years of helping her entertain Václav's many business guests.

'I hope you approve of the celebrations we've planned for your birthday, Václav,' she commented brightly, endeavouring to divert attention away from Heléna. 'We've invited just a few close friends and neighbours, and Berta and I are looking forward to preparing the food over the next two days. I know you men will be well occupied with all your business matters. Heléna will help too, so it won't be a burden at all.'

Václav noticed the rather anxious, imploring glance directed at him, as Anezka finished speaking. No doubt she had seen the concern in his eyes that she would not overdo it, he thought. He carefully searched his wife's face, looking for the telltale signs of weariness or ill health he had seen there all too frequently over the years since their little son Andrej's death. It had been a bitter blow to them indeed, and one from which Anezka had had difficulty recovering, both physically and emotionally. God had brought her through, however, and obviously this past year that Heléna had been able to spend at home had helped keep her spirits high. Now his face softened, as he gently responded to her unspoken plea.

'I'd be honoured, my dear – one doesn't turn fifty too often! But you're right,' he continued. 'Stefan and I do have work to do together. He's a big help to me right now, and knows much more about current political issues in our homeland than I do, which I fear will impact not only our businesses, but all of us very soon. I thank God we met when we did – it must have been over a year ago now, wasn't it, Stefan, at the conference in Brno? Anyway, enough of all that. I'm sure there are much more interesting matters to discuss over dinner! How are your music studies going, Heléna? We heard you practising hard when we first arrived today.'

Heléna felt herself relax a little. This was safe ground for her, any constraints being swept away in her desire to share about her music.

'I'm working hard on a Beethoven concerto at present, and also some Tschaikovsky – two of my favourite composers, as you know. There are some difficult sections yet to master, but I'm enjoying the challenge. Uncle Erik's been a wonderful help. I've been walking to the village twice a week for my lessons with him, but sometimes he comes here, so he can hear me play on our beautiful piano. I think he's pleased with my progress, but he's rather sparing with his praise, and always challenging me to do better! I love him though. He's a dear man, so talented and experienced – and so willing to share all he knows with me. He must certainly have been worth hearing in his heyday.'

'He was, I can assure you,' Anezka quickly agreed. 'Of course, he'd become famous more as an organist, by the time we met, but he was always helpful to me in my own career. And then, of course, he met you, Václav, and the two of you got on so well, that we're all still friends to this day!'

'Do you still play, Anezka?' Stefan asked. 'I'd love to hear you, as I know you had quite a following yourself as a concert pianist.'

A slight shadow passed over Anezka's face as she replied.

'No... no, not any more. I used to play a little, especially for our frequent guests, after we were first married and moved here to Tábor, but that was a long time ago. I'm afraid I haven't been in the best of health for some years now – my heart's a little weak – so I didn't have the energy to put in the hours of practice needed to play really well. I'd rather not play at all than play shabbily, and disappoint both myself and my audience, whether that audience is two people or two thousand! I think my daughter has inherited some of my perfectionist tendencies – I often admire her perseverance, whenever I hear her practising certain passages over and over again!'

'Did you teach her yourself at the beginning?' Stefan enquired.

'Only for a very short while,' Anezka laughed. 'I'm afraid I've always disliked the idea of teaching – I was definitely a performer! Also, as she grew older, we became such good friends that I didn't want to complicate our relationship by trying to be her teacher as well! Fortunately, Uncle Erik came to our rescue, so I'm very thankful for that. I think my main role with Heléna is to encourage her in whatever way I can and to be an understanding and most appreciative audience! It's the least I can do for the time she has given this past year to care for me and keep me company. But hopefully things will change for her next year – she's currently practising hard for the auditions at the Prague Conservatorium in a few weeks' time. Both Uncle Erik and I feel she has a very good chance of succeeding, but it's in God's hands. We'll trust him, whatever the outcome.'

'Perhaps Stefan's tired of all this musical talk,' Heléna interrupted, a little embarrassed at having become the main topic of conversation.

'Not in the least,' he responded quickly. 'In fact, it's one of my passions too. I have my family's baby grand piano in my apartment in Prague, but unfortunately I don't play it very well. When time permits, however, I love playing my cello – again not well, but passably, I hope. These days, like Václav, I'm afraid that managing the family business, with its factories spread across a number of cities, and also greater involvement, by necessity, in the political future of our country, keep me fully occupied. But while I'm here, Heléna, I'd count it a privilege to hear you play. Perhaps later this evening?'

'Excellent idea, Stefan! Of course Heléna will play for us, I'm sure – I'd love that too. Shall we adjourn to the music room, then, if that suits you both?' Václav suggested, rising to his feet.

For an instant, Heléna found herself slightly panic stricken. She realised, with a shock, how very badly she wanted to make a good first impression on Stefan, how important it seemed for him to like her and to enjoy her playing. She was about to open her mouth to suggest that they leave it until the following evening, when they heard someone knocking loudly on the front door. Václav went to answer it, and soon was ushering their young neighbour, Emil, into the dining room.

'Good to see you again, Emil! I hope your parents are well?'

Turning to Stefan, Václav introduced them, explaining that Emil's parents' estate ran alongside their own property.

'Our families have been friends for years, and over that time, Heléna and Emil have certainly managed to get themselves into a decent number of scrapes together, including capsizing our boat on the Luznice, just a short distance from here, and setting the horses at too high a fence somewhere!' he laughed. 'They still love going for long cross-country rides on occasions – it's wonderful country around here to explore, Stefan. Too bad we have no time for such things these days,' he sighed.

'Actually, I came over here this evening for two reasons,' Emil responded a little awkwardly, his eyes flicking constantly to Heléna. 'Firstly, my parents asked me to let you know that we'll all be able to come to your birthday celebration on Saturday, Mr Kovar, and to thank you for the invitation. And secondly, I was wondering if I could have a word with you, Heléna – but I didn't realise you had guests,' he concluded, looking somewhat disgruntled, and obviously disappointed.

There was a short silence, during which Heléna could feel her face redden with a mixture of anger and embarrassment. Eventually Stefan spoke quietly but with firmness.

'Please don't worry about me. Václav and I have a lot of work to get through while we're here, and we really should make a start tonight. This is merely a postponement of the pleasure of hearing you, Heléna – make sure you practise hard for your special recital for us tomorrow evening!'

Heléna pulled herself together, grateful to him for handing her a way out of the situation.

'I'll be pleased to. I'm playing for our guests at Táta's party, so you can be my critics before my next public performance.'

Václav and Stefan soon disappeared into the study, while Anezka went to find Berta and organise for coffee to be brought to them there. Emil and Heléna were left alone in the dining room, where they were soon seated facing each other.

'Heléna, I'm sorry if I interrupted anything tonight, but I wanted to ask you to come riding with me tomorrow. It's ages since we've done something together like that – you always seem too busy practising or going to your lessons or helping your mother. I know those things are important to you, but surely I'm important too! Surely our long friendship and all the plans we've made together for our future mean something to you!'

Emil had not meant the words to come out in such an angry, frustrated way, but they had been spoken now, and could not be taken back. Agitated, he brushed his fingers through his dark, wavy hair, and leaned forward to take Heléna's hands in his. Before he could, however, she placed them firmly in her lap, drawing herself upright as she sat opposite him, her colour still heightened, and her eyes dangerously bright. For a moment, she bit her lip, trying to calm herself. She did not want to hurt Emil, but was determined he would hear and understand how she was feeling. Silently she prayed for wisdom to respond in the right way.

'I'm sorry to have to disappoint you again, Emil,' she said evenly at last, 'but tomorrow I have to help Máma and Berta with some of the preparations for the weekend, and also I have another lesson with Uncle Erik, as well as more practice to do. I'm afraid my time is rather at a premium at present – as you know, the auditions for the conservatorium are coming up soon. I'm not sure when I'll be free to go out with you again over the next little while, Emil. You know yourself on the farm that there are seasons when you're too busy to ride and explore as we used to – and things change too. Of course I value your friendship, but my music's also important to me, and I believe God would want me to use the gifts he's given me to the best of my ability.'

Emil was silent for some time, as he stared almost unseeingly at Heléna, his fingers forming into tight fists where they rested on the table. Heléna in turn gazed back at her childhood friend, scenes from their many escapades together flitting through her mind in quick succession as she did. Emil's strong, sturdy frame holding their boat while she clambered in, dripping wet, after a quick swim, his laughter as his horse flew past her in the race for home, the excitement in his voice, as he talked and dreamed of plans to develop the family farm. Her heart constricted within her, but some inner prompting held her back from any compromise. Eventually Emil stood abruptly, and spoke in a shaky voice.

'There's no more to be said then – for now at least. I'll see you on Saturday night at the party. Surely after that you'll find time somewhere to spend with me! Goodbye for now, Heléna!'

Emil moved quickly to the front door, closing it rather roughly after himself, so that it banged loudly. Heléna stood alone in the hall, hoping the noise had not disturbed Stefan and her father. Slowly, she turned and, as if drawn by an invisible magnet, made her way to the music room, her mind in turmoil. Seating herself at the grand piano, she rested her hands on the keys for a moment before launching with great deliberation into her Beethoven concerto.

She played with verve and passion, as if to exorcise any demons of doubt and confusion within her, attacking the more difficult sections with a vigour that Anezka, who was passing through the hallway at that point, had not heard before. She stood still, listening intently. Then unobtrusively, so as not to disturb Heléna, she entered the music room, seating herself at an angle some distance from the piano, so that she could observe her daughter as she played.

Such an expressive face, Anezka always felt – so full of character and determination, yet with that special softness apparent in the curve of her mouth and the sensitivity of those unusual grey-green eyes inherited from her father. This evening her shining blonde hair hung loose to her shoulders, rippling in the light from the chandelier above with every slight movement she made. From time to time she hastily brushed aside an errant tendril of the finer, curly hair that grew around her temples and occasionally escaped onto her forehead, obscuring her vision a little. Yet this quick unconscious movement did not break her concentration or interrupt the flow of exquisite sound that filled the room and spilled out into the hallway and beyond. Heléna seemed oblivious to her physical surroundings, her whole being suffused with the passion of the music, her mind and spirit transported, as it were, to another dimension. Anezka watched, and listened, and prayed.

Heléna came to the end of her concerto, and sat still, as if all emotion had been drained from her. She rested her hands in her lap, before slowly lifting them to begin playing again. This time the tender, haunting sound of Schubert's 'Träumerei' filled the room, followed by one of Mendelssohn's more sombre 'Songs Without Words'. As the last notes died away, Anezka slowly moved to stand beside Heléna, resting her hand lightly on her shoulder. Heléna's choice of music told her all she needed to know.

'What is it, Heléna?' she asked gently.

Heléna lifted troubled grey-green eyes to Anezka's face. For a while she was silent, toying absently with a long blonde strand of hair, her hand shaking slightly, and her beautiful creamy skin flushed in confusion. Eventually, words tumbled from her lips.

'Sometimes after I spend time with Emil I feel so restless and angry, and somehow so ... so ... pressed into a mould!' she finally blurted out. 'It's like he takes it for granted that I'll always be here for him ... his little Heléna! He's been saying for some time now that we belong together, that God has always meant us for each other, and I used to think so too ... but I don't know any more! I don't know what to think, or how to say things to him even. It seems that nothing's easy between us any more!'

As she spoke, the tears, held back as she had played, rolled down her flushed cheeks.

'Maybe we've been seeing too much of each other. Maybe if we didn't meet for a while, then we'd see things more clearly. I love Emil – I don't want to hurt him, but sometimes lately I've felt so ... trapped! I love being here with you, I love Tábor, but I want to do things with my life – I want to travel, I want to study more, I want to play in all the best venues in Prague just as you did! I don't want to waste my life, doing less than what God intended me to do! And I don't want to be successful just for selfish reasons either – which is what I feel Emil has been suggesting lately! Is it being selfish to want to do our best for God, to want others to enjoy and be blessed by the gifts we've been given? It's more selfish, I believe, to want to keep people close, when it's time to let them go, and to stop them from being all God wants them to be!'

She was crying in earnest now – tears of pain and confusion, but also tears of relief, as she shared what she was really feeling. Anezka had listened and soothed her, and now sat thinking deeply.

'Heléna, I have a suggestion to make. What would you say to a few days together in Prague? Maybe some shopping – or a concert or two? I'll need to rest up a little after our weekend celebrations, but we could travel with Táta when he returns to his office. What do you think?'

Heléna swallowed hard, eventually finding enough voice to respond. 'I... I... I don't know what to say! Are you sure it wouldn't be too much for you?'

She had quietened a little by now, and sat scanning her mother's face for signs of tiredness or pain. What she saw there was reassuring.

'I'd love that so much! Maybe all I need is a break and change of scene...'

Even to her own ears she sounded less than convincing. With a soft sigh, she continued.

'Things change I know – but it's painful, isn't it, this growing up, this finding out who you are? I don't want Emil to be unhappy, but I feel I must do what God wants me to do, above everything else – whether that includes Emil or not!'

Anezka hugged her warmly for a long while.

'It's through the hard times and difficult decisions that we grow the most, dear. Be at peace! I know you have so much inside you from God to offer to the world. Just listen to your heart, and to his heart for you – always!'

Chapter Two

Heléna woke earlier than usual the next morning, aware immediately of a feeling of anticipation, but also a sense of moving into uncharted waters. For a moment, as she looked out her window at the beautiful blue sky and warm sunshine, she remembered with a pang Emil's invitation that she had turned down. She had made her decision, however. No turning back, she reminded herself, as she dressed and made her way down to breakfast.

She found the others waiting for her in the little outdoor eating area in a corner of the rose garden, where Anezka loved to sit on summer mornings.

'How's my little girl this morning?' her father greeted her warmly. 'Looking beautiful as always – what it is to be young, eh, Stefan?'

The sight of his daughter always gave Václav great pleasure. This morning, as she seated herself at the table, he reflected once again how much like Anezka she was when they had first met. Yet there was something different too in her beautiful features – a subtle strength and determination that he felt belonged more to his side of the family and that he had occasionally noticed in his own mother.

'Not so little any more!' Heléna laughed. 'Remember, I'm almost twenty – and you'll be fifty tomorrow!'

She glanced briefly at Stefan as she greeted him, their eyes meeting momentarily. Now he was smiling at her, aware, she felt, of her slight embarrassment, as she responded to her father's teasing banter, but also her affection for him. He poured some coffee for her, and she noticed, as yesterday, the smile lines around his mouth, the wide, intelligent forehead, and the warmth in those clear blue eyes, as they again met hers – observant eyes that seemed to ascertain quickly every small detail, yet also to convey a deep sensitivity and gentleness. The early morning sun highlighted occasional flecks of silver in his thick, black hair, causing her to wonder idly how old he was. Perhaps her mother knew.

'What are your plans for today, Heléna?' Anezka asked, breaking into her reverie. 'I know these gentlemen can't get away soon enough back to the study, where no doubt they'll stay buried all day!'

She spoke lightly, but her heart was heavy. Václav had come to bed late the previous evening, sharing little with her about the issues he and Stefan were discussing, and the plans they were making. She sensed he did not want to worry her unduly, so had not questioned him further, but she could see how tired he was – tired, and somewhat troubled in his spirit. Silently she had prayed for him, and for Stefan, and for wisdom for the work in which they were both involved. She was sure that something more than mutual business interests had drawn them together over the past months. Both employed a large number of people, and were responsible for the oversight of their companies in Prague and elsewhere, but Stefan's biscuit factories and their subsidiaries had little in common with Václav's farm machinery companies, or his management of the large farming estates he had inherited in the early years of their marriage. She trusted Václav, however, and knew he would tell her when the time was right.

'I have a lesson with Uncle Erik later this morning, but I plan to help you and Berta with some of the preparations before I go,' Heléna responded brightly. 'Then I want to spend this afternoon practising, if I can – I want to make Uncle Erik especially proud of me when I play for your guests on Saturday evening, Táta !'

'I know you'll make us all very proud, my dear,' Václav assured her. 'God has given you a wonderful gift, and I know Uncle Erik feels very privileged to be able to help you develop it. And yes, you're right, Anezka, and as perceptive as always,' he said, turning to his wife and smiling. 'Stefan and I do have much to discuss today, and we're eager to begin, so we can relax this evening and enjoy your company, along with some of Heléna's special music. We'll look forward to it!'

Václav and Stefan stood then and made their way to the study. As they settled down to work, Stefan found to his surprise that he was uncharacteristically distracted at first, despite the weighty matters to be considered. Heléna's beautiful face swam before his eyes as she had looked this morning – young and vibrant, full of love for her parents and her music. For Emil too, he wondered idly? Before he realised, he found himself speaking his thoughts aloud.

'You must feel very blessed to have a daughter like Heléna, Václav! So gifted and attractive – the whole world before her really. She certainly seems to want to succeed in her music career, doesn't she?'

Václav regarded his friend somewhat thoughtfully before responding.

'Yes, we thank God for her every day. She's been a big comfort and help to Anezka this past year, when I've been away so much, but I believe it's time for her to move on and pursue the next step God has for her. I hope and pray my wife won't miss her too much, but Anezka's health has been much better lately, for which I'm profoundly thankful. She took a long time to recover from the death of our son, Heléna's older brother, years ago now, and still has a weak heart, as she mentioned last night, but God continues to heal and strengthen her. And I fear we'll all need every bit of strength he can provide in the days ahead, Stefan, if our homeland and our businesses and our families are going to survive!'

The two bowed their heads then and there and committed their work to God, asking for his wisdom and grace for the day ahead, and for the future as well. Then with diaries ready and maps spread out, they began their planning.

Anezka, Heléna and Berta, their long time housekeeper and family friend, spent a pleasant morning in the kitchen, immersed in advance preparations for the birthday celebrations, making final decisions about the special menu. However, Anezka soon noted Heléna's mind was elsewhere.

'Why don't you leave the rest of these arrangements to the two of us, dear?' she smilingly suggested, as they shared a coffee break. 'Berta and I can manage here, so consider yourself free for the rest of the day! Besides, it's almost time for your lesson with Uncle Erik, isn't it?'

Heléna always enjoyed the brisk walk to Uncle Erik's home on the outskirts of the village, and the warm greeting she received from her teacher and his sister Edita, who kept house for him. She played well that day, she knew, and Uncle Erik, while few with his words, was satisfied. After checking that they were coming to the birthday celebrations the following evening, Heléna left, allowing her thoughts to wander on the way home, as she mulled over her recent conversation with Emil. In her mind's eye, she could see him riding across the fields alone, his thick wavy hair tousled, the sun tanning his olive skin to an even deeper brown, revelling in the open spaces he so loved. Yet even as she did so, intruding ever so gently on her thoughts were a pair of clear blue eyes, so full of understanding that they seemed to be seeing into her very soul.

Later that afternoon, as Heléna practised on her beloved grand piano, she sensed an extra intensity and depth to her playing, an edge of excitement that enabled her fingers to navigate the difficult Beethoven passages with agility and accuracy. It was almost as if something had come to life deep inside her – something that had lain dormant, waiting for that word or signal that would bring it to birth. She left the music room to tidy herself before dinner, aware of feeling unusually nervous. Yet she was looking forward to the evening ahead, to observing Stefan more, and taking part in the conversation around the dinner table. In her room, she changed her clothes, dressing with care, but at the same time aware that Stefan was, in essence, the type of person who would look beyond any surface appearance to the inner character that lay beneath.

Anezka and Heléna were seated at the table by the time the men arrived. Heléna could not help noticing, as they entered the room, how Stefan's broad shoulders and solid build caused her father to appear quite slight in comparison, despite being around the same height. Both were still deep in discussion, the expression on their faces serious, but paused immediately when they became aware of their presence.

'Our apologies, Anezka,' Václav said swiftly. 'We've been working through some difficult problems all afternoon, and lost sight of the time. Stefan, would you do us the honour of saying grace?'

Stefan responded readily, delighted to be included in the family circle in this way. Even in the rather subdued lighting from the flickering candles on the table and the elegant lamp in the corner of the room, both Heléna and Anezka noticed lines of tension and tiredness on the men's faces, as they bowed their heads. Thankfully, it was not long before the good wine Václav poured for them, the excellent meal, and Anezka's knack of turning minds from the preoccupations of the day, combined to lift their spirits and enable them to relax.

As the conversation gathered momentum, it was obvious to Heléna that her parents held Stefan in the highest regard, and that that feeling was reciprocated. She felt a deep peace, as she watched and listened – as if they were all being held in God's hands, despite the heavy issues confronting Stefan and her father. She relaxed, responding easily when questioned about her day.

Stefan noted the warm glow that suffused Heléna's beautiful young face, as she shared her delight in the music she planned to perform. As he did, something stirred deep within him, something new and different. He could not put a name to it, but he was aware of a strong fascination for Heléna, of wanting to find out more, and a fierce desire to protect her from anything that would dampen or quench that warmth and vitality which exuded from her. This desire, almost overwhelming in its strength and suddenness, deeply surprised him. Here he was, twenty-nine, almost thirty years of age. He had met many beautiful women in his life, had admired their intelligence and enjoyed their company. Yet he had never felt drawn to consider a lifelong commitment to any of them. Always there had been this inner voice, the Spirit of God within him, Stefan believed, urging him to wait, assuring him that somewhere there was someone for him, and that when he saw her, he would know. Now, sitting opposite Heléna, he wondered, with a sudden leap of his heart, if what he now felt was indeed that very 'knowing', despite their having been acquainted for such a short time.

After the meal, the pleasant conversation continued, as they drank their coffee in the music room. Finally, Heléna moved to the piano, to perform the music she had chosen for their guests the following evening. As she played, she occasionally looked towards the corner of the room where her parents and Stefan sat, the lamplight gently illuminating their faces. Stefan sat very still and observant, his eyes fixed on her, his whole body appearing relaxed and at ease, yet also intent and alert, as if listening to every note. Sensing the deep appreciation flowing from them all, Heléna soon gave herself over to her music, glancing up from time to time to meet Stefan's steady gaze and fleetingly return his smile.

'Bravo! Bravo!' they chorused, when she finished playing, and joined them again.

'How privileged our guests are to be hearing you, my dear!' her father added. 'Uncle Erik will be so proud of you! But now, much as we love the company and your beautiful music, Heléna, I'm afraid we need to get back to work. We have to make some decisions that will enable important plans to be set in motion, so that we can work out final details tomorrow. Please excuse us.'

Disappointed, Heléna glanced at her mother with a questioning look on her face, as the men left the room.

'I'm afraid I can't shed much light on the exact issues they're discussing yet, dear. Obviously it's to do with the current political state of affairs, and how that will impact their respective companies, but somehow I feel there's more to it than that. Let's trust God in it all, Heléna, and trust the men to make good and right decisions.'

Heléna was silent for some time, lost in thought. Even as she sat there that evening, she had a strong sense that in some way both she and Anezka would be deeply involved in the outworking of these decisions, and that it would be costly for them. O God, she prayed silently, watch over us all. Keep us safe in your care!

Soon both of them headed for bed. Tomorrow was Václav's fiftieth birthday, and it would be a busy day.

Václav and Stefan were not at breakfast the next morning. They had apparently risen early, and walked to Uncle Erik's, before returning to work in the study. The morning sped by for Heléna and Anezka in a flurry of preparations for the party, which around twenty of their close friends and neighbours were expected to attend. Heléna saw nothing of her father and Stefan all day, except a brief glimpse through the open door of the study, as Berta carried their midday meal to them. In the afternoon, as her mother rested, Heléna again practised the Brahms and Schubert works she had selected to play later in the evening. Finally, it was time to dress for the festivities, and then to help her parents welcome their guests.

Heléna, who had known most of them since she was a child, moved with ease amongst them, keenly aware of wishing to avoid extended contact with only one – Emil. As the guests moved to the dining room, and the younger members of the party congregated at one end of the table, Heléna was not surprised, however, to find him seated on her immediate right, with his sister, Maria, to her left. She stifled a sigh, but was determined to greet him pleasantly.

'Hello, Emil – and Maria! I'm glad your whole family could come tonight. I hope you all enjoy yourselves!'

After that, Maria fortunately kept up a steady flow of chatter, and this, along with Heléna's efforts to include the other younger ones in their conversation, helped to avert the need for any particularly personal exchange with Emil.

The fact that Emil felt keenly the sense of distance and discomfort that currently existed between Heléna and himself was obvious to two people that evening – Anezka, alert, as always, on her daughter's behalf, and Stefan. Despite being seated at the other end of the large dining table, he had read the situation well, and, with that keen observant sense that benefited him so greatly in business and other arenas, saw much more than Heléna was even aware of herself. Certainly she and Emil still spoke to each other, but there was a stiffness and a reserve in her manner that warned Emil to keep his distance, rather than press matters further that evening. Nevertheless, when the guests eventually moved to the music room for the coffee and birthday cake, Emil could not help hovering as close to her as possible, even standing next to her in a rather proprietorial manner, as she seated herself at the piano.

'If I could ask you all to be quiet for a few moments, we have a treat for you!' Václav announced, when everyone was finally seated. 'Heléna has agreed to play a selection of music especially prepared for the occasion, and I'm proud and honoured to be able to hand over to her now!'

In that instant, Heléna found herself seeking out not Emil's eyes for encouragement and reassurance, as on other occasions, but rather those clear blue eyes that had met hers as she played the previous night. And Stefan did not fail her. He smiled directly at her, his warm gaze steadying and strengthening her, so that she soon felt calm and confident. She began playing then, the music flowing effortlessly and joyously from her fingertips.

Heléna emerged as if from another world, as she came to the end of her performance, and was greeted with enthusiastic applause and cries of 'Well done!' and 'Encore!' She obliged once more, and then laughingly asked that the party continue. Anezka proposed a toast to Václav, the enormous birthday cake was cut with due ceremony, and soon the conversation flowed again. Heléna saw Uncle Erik deep in discussion with Stefan, their gaze on her from time to time, but soon her attention was claimed by Emil, unable to keep himself from her side for long.

'So will you come riding along the river with me tomorrow, Heléna, as we planned?' he asked rather abruptly, feeling strangely unsure of himself for the first time in any conversation with her.

'I think you mean as *you* planned,' Heléna said gently but firmly, after a short pause.

'I did tell you, remember, that I may not be available, and now that's definitely the case. Tomorrow my mother and I plan to travel to Prague with my father. We'll be away for a few days – I'm not exactly sure how many – and then when I return, I'll be very busy preparing for my audition at the Conservatorium next month, as you know.'

Emil was silent for some time. As the awkward pause grew longer and longer, Heléna found herself becoming more and more uncomfortable, and at the same time increasingly resentful that Emil could make her feel this way. Eventually he drew a long uneven breath, and spoke with considerable heat and passion.

'I'm getting the distinct feeling, Heléna, that lately you've been making up excuses as to why we can't spend time together any more. I don't want to play games with you. Either we belong together, or we don't! You know what I wish it to be, and what everyone else is expecting too. Can't you see that you could still continue with your music, even if you gave up this idea of going on to the Conservatorium? You could still learn here in Tábor with Uncle Erik, and play at so many places and events, like you have tonight. I beg you, Heléna, if you really love me, don't make plans to go to Prague! Certainly go with your mother this week, but come back quickly! Come back, so we can be together like we're meant to be!'

By now Emil had gripped Heléna's arm, holding her firmly and speaking quite forcefully, so that she felt everyone in the room must be noticing, curious to know what was being said. Hot tears stung her eyes, as she impatiently removed his hand from her arm and stood poised for flight, speaking to him rather unevenly, as he made to follow her.

'Please, Emil, don't let's talk now! Let's just leave it be! I know you mean well – and I do love you. But I think of you these days more as a brother to me than anything else. I value you so much as a good friend. Can you please accept how I feel and leave it at that? I'm so sorry, Emil!'

Heléna left hurriedly, making her way to her room, where the tears flowed unchecked. After a while, she managed to pull herself together, washing her tearstained cheeks, and repairing any telltale damage to her appearance. For a moment, she stood quietly, calming herself, and praying for God's wisdom and peace. Then, squaring her shoulders, she hurried downstairs, keenly aware of not wanting to worry her mother, and also of her responsibility to see to the welfare of the guests.

As she entered the music room again, no one seemed to have noticed her absence. The animated discussions continued as before, interspersed with laughter, and the sounds of coffee and cake being served by Berta and her mother. She went to help them, noticing as she did, that Emil was nowhere in sight. As she took over pouring the coffee from Anezka, Maria came to join her.

'Heléna, Emil asked me to tell you that he had to go – he's needed early in the morning to help a friend build their new barn. He said to say he's sorry, and he'll try to see you tomorrow.'

Heléna thanked her, reasonably sure that Maria, with her rather bubbly, scatterbrained personality, was unaware of the undercurrents between her brother and herself. Anezka, for once, did not seem to have noticed anything amiss, being preoccupied with seeing to the wellbeing of their visitors. Eventually Heléna relaxed a little, and began to circulate among the guests, relieved to find that no one commented on Emil's sudden departure. Her heart was warmed and comforted by many further words of congratulation in the process – even from Uncle Erik, her sternest critic, but also, when praise was indeed due, her greatest supporter.

At last the guests began to realise the lateness of the hour and take their leave. Heléna stayed on in the music room, slowly clearing up and putting things to rights, conscious of an overwhelming tiredness, but also great turmoil within her. As she turned to close the piano, she hesitated, finally sitting down and letting her fingers relax on the keys. Soon, almost unbidden, the haunting strains of Tschaikovsky's *'Nur wer die Sehnsucht kennt'*[1] filled the room, and Heléna became lost to the world again as she played, allowing the healing comfort of the beautiful melody to wash over her and touch her deep in her spirit. The music ended, but she did not move.

Eventually, she became aware of the presence of another, standing quietly just inside the door. The person moved slowly towards the piano, and Heléna saw it was Stefan.

He spoke gently, not wishing to break the spell of the beautiful music.

'One of my favourites too,' he said quietly. 'Such a simple melody, and yet one that captures so much of what one feels when times of parting come, don't you think?'

Heléna could only look mutely up at him.

'Be at peace, little one,' he eventually continued. 'As one of the great Christian mystics said a long time ago: "All shall be well, and all manner of things shall be well."'

And with that, he left the room, closing the door gently behind him.

Heléna sat where she was for some time, not moving at all, but simply allowing her whole body to be bathed in the deep peace that seemed to descend on her and fill every part of her. She sensed it even on her skin, and felt it giving strength to her limbs, as she straightened her back and sat erect. In her heart, she knew that the words Stefan had quoted were indeed true. Surely, whatever happened to her, wherever God would lead her, all would be well, and all manner of things would be well.

---

[1] *'None but the lonely heart'* - lit. *'Only those who know longing'*

Chapter Three

By mid-afternoon the following day, everything seemed ready for their departure for Prague. As was their usual custom, the family had attended the morning service in the little village church, joined this time by Stefan. Whenever Václav was home on Sundays, he loved to sit with Anezka and Heléna in the beautiful centuries-old chapel, allowing Uncle Erik's brilliant organ playing to stir his spirit. Somehow this gave him deep comfort in a world that seemed to be changing at an alarming rate, a world growing more and more insecure as the months passed. O God, he had silently prayed that morning, as he sat between the two women he held most dear, please keep them safe, and protect us all! May your kingdom come and your will be done in our land, and may peace and justice reign!

Anezka, sensing Václav's heart-cry that morning, had gently placed her hand over his, as they sat next to each other. Silently she whispered her own prayer for his safety, and for godly wisdom for the major decisions she knew he was making.

The four of them walked home afterwards without haste. Václav stopped from time to time to point out features of the familiar landscape to Stefan. Occasionally, they paused to admire tiny flowers nestling half hidden under the hedges bordering the laneway that skirted the family's extensive gardens, and led on down to the nearby river. For some unknown reason, Václav sensed that this opportunity to share and enjoy this special corner of his beloved homeland might never come again. In fact, each one of them seemed aware of the uniqueness of the occasion. They completed their walk in nable silence, but a silence tinged with an indefinable sense of loss, feeling as d around them that this moment in history needed to be etched indelibly on their memory. They eventually arrived home, pausing on the entrance steps to gaze out over the serene countryside, the summer breeze swirling the leaves around their feet and ruffling their hair as they stood there together.

'Beautiful, isn't it?' Václav finally commented. 'God grant we may all continue to live in peace here and enjoy his goodness to us for many years to come!'

After lunch, and a further brief time closeted with Václav, Stefan was the first to leave for Prague.

'Thank you very much for having me again, Anezka! I'm so glad I was able to make it here on my way home from the south in time for Václav's birthday. We've achieved a great deal in the hours we've spent working together, and I pray it will all bear fruit in the months ahead. If you can manage it, I'd like to return the hospitality, and invite you all to dinner tomorrow evening at my apartment! It would be no trouble at all – I'd be delighted to have you!'

They accepted readily. Stefan farewelled them warmly, kissing them all on both cheeks, and then he was gone.

As they stood on the steps waving goodbye, Heléna felt a profound sense of relief that she would be seeing him again so soon. Turning to go indoors again, she suddenly caught sight of Emil making his way up the driveway towards them on his favourite grey mare.

As Emil saw her standing with her parents, dressed for travel rather than riding, he slowed to a trot, and his shoulders slumped markedly. Obviously Heléna had meant what she said. There would be no riding today, and none the following day – or the next. She looked so grown up and beautiful, with the wind whipping her fair hair about her face, and her cheeks pinker than usual. Emil, at times somewhat slow to pick up unspoken messages and subtle nuances, nevertheless knew in his heart of hearts that for him there would in fact be no more days together with his Heléna as before. No more carefree rides across the countryside, no more times of idly trailing their fingers in the river, as they let their old boat drift lazily along, no more talking of what they would do together in the years to come.

He halted his horse, but did not bother to dismount. Anezka was the first to break the rather strained silence.

'Hello, Emil! As you can see, we've just farewelled one visitor, and now we can welcome you! We're off to Prague soon, but there's time for a drink together before we leave.'

She spoke in her customary warm manner, conscious, at the same time, of a stiffening in Heléna, standing next to her. Anezka knew of Heléna and Emil's exchange the previous evening, yet felt it polite to welcome him as usual.

Fortunately, she was not called on to extend that welcome any further. Emil tried to respond equally politely, but his deep sense of rejection showed itself clearly in the curtness and abruptness of his words.

'Thanks, but I'd better be on my way. I merely called to see if Heléna had changed her mind about riding out with me this afternoon, but I can see she hasn't.'

With that, he turned to Heléna, and, looking directly down into her eyes from his position astride his horse, spoke firmly and with finality.

'Goodbye, Heléna. I think today our journeys really are taking us our own separate ways. I hope everything works out well for you – have a good time!'

He wheeled his horse, and was soon out of sight. Heléna moved quickly inside, obviously wanting to be left alone for a few moments. Anezka, respecting her daughter's need for solitude, gently guided Václav to the kitchen to join Berta for a final warm drink together.

'Somehow I don't think we'll see Emil here much more, Václav. It seems to be a time of change for all of us,' she observed, not without a little regret.

They drank their coffee in silence, Václav's mind soon preoccupied with the business issues awaiting him in Prague. Eventually, Anezka put her concerns about Heléna firmly aside, secure in the knowledge that God's hand was on her, whatever changes were occurring, and began to plan their special few days together in Prague.

During the drive, nothing was said about Emil, but Heléna knew, without anything needing to be put into words, that her parents understood. She loved them for it, and was looking forward to these few days together. She was glad her father had elected to join them at Uncle Tomas and Aunt Eva's house, rather than staying, as usual, in his small apartment attached to his office. It would be a special time of family reunion for them, with her aunt and uncle due to return from sabbatical leave in England in two days' time. Anezka had been under strict instructions from her sister to make use of their home whenever they needed to, and Heléna was delighted that her mother felt well enough to take up their invitation at last, and to be able to welcome them home.

They reached the city in good time for dinner, and spent a quiet evening together, followed by an early night. As Heléna lay in bed, listening to the bells of the old cathedral nearby pealing out over the city, it was as if they were heralding a new era for her – the closing of one stage in her life, and the beginning of another. While part of her felt a sense of great loss and regret at the prospect of a Tábor without Emil, another part was gripped with a refreshing feeling of freedom, and an anticipation of exciting possibilities, not only in relationships, but also in terms of her musical career. For what seemed a long time, she lay there in the dark, ready for sleep, but also buoyed by the many pleasant thoughts and dreams that occupied her mind.

Heléna's final waking memory that night, before drifting off into a soundless sleep, was the image of Stefan moving towards her across the music room the previous evening, his eyes so full of understanding and compassion, and his words giving her such comfort and peace.

The following day, Václav left early for the office. Anezka and Heléna ate a leisurely breakfast, eventually agreeing, after much discussion and laughter, on a starting point for the day's shopping excursion. As Anezka finished getting ready, Heléna moved to the sitting room, where an old upright piano, which her aunt and uncle had kept for her sake, stood against one wall. She had spent many hours practising on its yellowed keys while boarding with them during term time, attempting to master the music she was required to play for both her school and national music exams, and also to reach Uncle Erik's exacting standards, when she returned home for weekends and school holidays. Now, in these waiting moments, she ran her fingers over the familiar keys, playing scale after scale, in order to keep her fingers nimble and supple. Heléna was not overly concerned about these few days away from her usual practice schedule. She had worked hard all year under Uncle Erik's guidance, preparing for the upcoming Conservatorium auditions, and knew that these few days of relaxation with her mother were more likely to help rather than hinder her preparation. Already she felt the benefit of the change of surroundings and the new experiences awaiting her. Her spirits lifted, and, as was her custom, she quietly committed her day to God, seeing it as a special gift from him.

Anezka and Heléna made their way directly to the heart of the city, chatting and laughing together, and began strolling through their favourite stores and arcades, and investigating tiny boutiques. They tried on clothes and made purchases, but did not hurry over any of it. They enjoyed lengthy coffee breaks, and a special luncheon at one of their favourite cafes, where an excellent pianist entertained the customers, eventually returning home in the late afternoon, in time for Anezka to rest before their dinner with Stefan.

Despite a busy schedule since returning to the city, Stefan had made time to buy all that was necessary to prepare an excellent meal for his visitors. He approached the task with vigour and a sense of anticipation. He enjoyed cooking, a legacy of many hours spent in the kitchen with his parents' housekeeper during his growing up years – and besides, on this occasion, he freely admitted to a strong desire to create a truly memorable meal. Today, he had left his office early, in order to allow sufficient time to prepare everything just as he wanted it, so that he was free to greet his guests in a relaxed, unruffled manner, and to enjoy this special evening with them. Now, as the moment of their arrival approached, he checked his appearance again, aware of wishing, as never before in his almost thirty years, to make as excellent an impression as possible in every way.

Presently he heard a car pull up in the square below, and then Václav's voice directing the women to the correct apartment. I'm like a moonstruck teenager, Stefan thought wryly to himself, as the doorbell rang. He went to greet his guests, attempting to quell within him an inordinate desire to see even the smallest spark of interest or admiration appear in Heléna's beautiful grey-green eyes.

He was not disappointed. As he opened the door, for an instant, in the midst of the flurry of greetings, their glances locked, and, in that moment, each saw delight at being together again written clearly in the eyes of the other. Stefan quickly strove to collect himself, welcoming his guests and making them comfortable, and then, after a short while, excusing himself to serve dinner. The food was delicious, the wine excellent, and the conversation flowed with ease. Anezka and Heléna gave a lively account of their day together, Václav delighting to see more spark and energy in his wife than he had observed for some time.

'Wonderful meal, Stefan!' Václav commented for all of them, as they finished eating, and moved to the sitting room. 'I'm afraid your culinary skills far surpass mine!'

'But then you probably weren't left largely in the company of your housekeeper during your growing up years, as I was!' Stefan responded laughingly. 'I learnt so much by watching her, and she very patiently used to let me help. My father had no choice, you see, since my mother died when I was very young. Fortunately his business was by then a success, so he could afford to engage someone to look after us. I still employ the same housekeeper to clean, and to cook my meals, but she's quite old now, so if I'm having guests for dinner, then I do the cooking. Besides, I enjoy it!'

Stefan's baby grand piano, inherited some years earlier on the death of his father, took pride of place in the sitting room, while his cello stood in a corner, beside bookshelves laden with beautifully bound copies of many of the old classics.

'And here you can see the other pastimes fostered in my growing up years as an only child with hours to spend by myself, when my father was busy with his work,' he smiled. 'I'm not complaining, however – I thank God now for the rich discoveries I made in those times, and I know my father did his best.'

After drinking their coffee and talking together for some time, Anezka asked the question she had wanted to put to Stefan ever since they had moved to the sitting room.

'Stefan, will you play your cello for us?' she asked hesitantly. 'I know what it feels like to be out of practice and yet to have to perform, but I for one would love to hear you! I'm equally out of practice, but I'll even offer to accompany you – so how could you possibly refuse?'

Stefan gave in graciously, choosing to play for them Saint-Säens' poignant melody 'The Swan'. As Heléna listened that evening, watching Stefan's hands as he played, and the varying emotions that flitted across his face, she felt both moved and blessed. The beautiful music stirred her soul so deeply that she could not prevent tears springing to her eyes. Soon Stefan finished playing, and immediately looked towards her, strangely aware that his music had somehow drawn them together in a unique way, firmly intertwining their very spirits.

No one wanted to break the silence that followed. At last, Anezka rose from the piano to resume her seat beside Václav, and Stefan gently replaced his cello in its stand.

'Beautiful ... so beautiful!' Václav eventually said with great feeling.
'Congratulations to both of you!'

Soon after, the striking of the clock in the old town hall tower across the square reminded them that time was passing. Reluctantly, Anezka began their leave taking, knowing that another full day lay ahead for Heléna and herself, while Václav always had more than enough to do whenever he was in Prague. She had enjoyed the visit immensely, but she was tired.

Stefan would have liked to prolong the evening a little further, but after exchanging glances with Václav, decided to leave any more discussion until another time. Instead, he asked them all to dine with him again that Friday evening.

'I know it will be your last night in Prague, for this visit at least, but it's wonderful to be able to return your hospitality to me! Perhaps we'll have more time to talk then – and maybe Heléna will play for us!'

They agreed, and Stefan was heartened by the pleased look on Heléna's face. After the farewells had taken place on the steps outside, and Václav was helping Anezka into the car, Stefan took his courage in both hands, seizing the moment to speak to Heléna alone.

'I'll be tied up tomorrow night, and I know you'll be welcoming your aunt and uncle home, but may I telephone you tomorrow to arrange dinner for just the two of us the following evening?'

Heléna could only nod her agreement, as Stefan helped her into the car, giving her hand a brief squeeze in the process. She was surprised and flattered – and very happy indeed. Later that night, as she lay in bed looking back on their evening, she began to wonder if she had perhaps misheard his invitation. Then another thought came to her. What would her parents think about it all? All I can do is discuss it with them tomorrow morning, she decided eventually, as she drifted off to sleep amidst a tumble of pleasant thoughts, and a delicious sense of anticipation about the days ahead.

In the end, Heléna slept in, as did her mother. Václav had already left for the office by the time they came down to breakfast. As Heléna and Anezka finished eating, and sat drinking their coffee together and planning the day's activities, Heléna took the opportunity to bring up the issue of Stefan's invitation.

'Máma, how would you feel if Stefan and I were to spend some time together while I'm here in Prague – just the two of us? He wants to take me to dinner tomorrow night, but I'll say no if you're unhappy about it.'

For a moment Anezka was silent. It was not so much the request itself, but its swift occurrence that had surprised her. She had not been unaware of the warm relationship that seemed to have sprung up so quickly and naturally between Stefan and Heléna. She had wondered, however, if the affectionate kindness and gallantry she had observed in him was how he would act towards any woman of Heléna's age, rather than the beginnings of any serious attraction. Now as she looked at her daughter's flushed face across the breakfast table, and saw the pleading expression in those grey-green eyes so like her father's, her own heart skipped a beat, and her breath caught in her throat. Was there indeed a future ahead together for Stefan and Heléna? She reflected a moment longer before speaking, aware of wanting to say yes immediately, but also wishing to shield Heléna from any unnecessary hurt.

'Heléna, nothing would give me more pleasure than to have you enjoy yourself in Stefan's company. I know he's completely trustworthy, and one of your father's most valued friends – but please take things slowly, my dear! Stefan is a good few years older than you, and has seen and learnt quite a bit in his life, particularly in recent times.'

Heléna reached across the table and grasped her mother's hand tightly.

'Thank you so much! You always say such wise things to me, and I love you for it! Hopefully one day I'll be able to give my own children the support and understanding you always give me!'

She rose then to finish getting ready for the day's outing, as well as fit in a little piano practice before leaving. For Heléna, her musical career was certainly first and foremost, and all that she could clearly envisage at that stage for her immediate future.

They enjoyed another special morning together. Heléna concentrated on clothes shopping, knowing she would need to dress differently from how she did at home in Tábor, should she succeed in her upcoming audition. Anezka, who came to the city so infrequently these days, was relishing the opportunity to replenish her own wardrobe, as well as buy Christmas gifts and other small items. They returned home soon after lunch, since Anezka needed to rest in readiness for Tomas and Eva's arrival from England, while Heléna was anxious not to miss Stefan's phone call.

With dinner preparations safely in the housekeeper's hands, Heléna put in some valuable practice, until interrupted by the sound of the doorbell, heralding the arrival of her aunt and uncle. Then, even as she was greeting them warmly, the telephone rang.

Heléna took the call in the study. If it was for her, she wanted to be private.

'Heléna, this is Stefan – how are you?'

'I'm fine, thank you,' she responded rather breathlessly.

'I need to leave for a meeting soon, but could I pick you up around seven tomorrow evening for dinner? I know a special restaurant I think you'd enjoy not far from your aunt and uncle's home. That's fine with you? … Good! Till tomorrow evening then!'

Heléna sat where she was for a short while, remembering the sound of his deep voice, picturing his smile as he rang off. She was glad she had a whole day in which to savour the special privilege of being invited to share an evening with him.

In the mean time, it was wonderful to be able to welcome Tomas and Eva back home, Anezka because Eva was her only sister, and Heléna because her aunt had been like a second mother to her throughout her high school years, and a strong support when her own mother had been so unwell.

Václav was particularly looking forward to talking with Tomas that evening on many key issues, and gleaning from his insights. He had always deeply admired him, not only for his intimate knowledge of politics, but also for the integrity he had always shown in bringing the truth of history to light, whether these opinions were shared by the powers-that-be or not.

'Welcome home, Tomas!' he greeted him warmly. 'Ready to stir things up in the world of political history again and cause some more debate in that university of yours? I'm sure there's plenty of scope for that right now, even in your staid old department!'

'If things at home are in anywhere near the same state of upheaval as they are in some other parts of Europe we've visited, then all of us are certainly in for a challenging time – not just me!' Tomas responded rather grimly. 'Nevertheless, I'm glad to be back, Václav, despite the welcome I may or may not receive from some of my colleagues, and others with differing views. Nothing like one's own homeland, even though one may not agree with the way things are heading!'

'You're right, Tomas. Actually, there's so much I want to talk about with you, but perhaps it might be wise to keep such things until later, rather than spoil the mood of this first evening together, don't you think? Better not to worry the others unduly just yet.'

'Yes, let's enjoy the moment,' Tomas readily agreed. 'Who knows how many more such opportunities we'll have in the days to come?'

Václav looked at his friend with a worried frown, and a feeling of dread in his heart, but Tomas smiled, and put his arm around Václav's shoulder.

'There's always hope, my friend – hope that we'll learn from the past, but above all, hope in God. Let's leave it with him for now, shall we?'

Heléna certainly joined in all the conversation and laughter that evening, but at the same time, her mind was filled with eager anticipation of her next meeting with Stefan. The following day could not go quickly enough, even though it was spent very pleasantly, shopping again, and helping her aunt unpack. Eventually it was time for her to get ready – a task she undertook with great care, choosing a dress of soft sea-green material that matched her eyes exactly. Anezka, greeting Stefan at the door when he called for Heléna, could not help but notice his quick intake of breath, and the sincere admiration in his eyes, as she descended the stairs and walked towards them.

'Have a wonderful evening, both of you,' she said gently, kissing Heléna goodbye.

And as Anezka watched Stefan help her daughter carefully into his car, she was surprised to feel a deep sense of peace and rightness stealing over her.

That night, Stefan parked the car a short distance from the ancient Charles Bridge, one of many spanning the Vltava River, on the edge of the picturesque 'Little Quarter' of the old city. Together they walked unhurriedly a short distance along narrow cobbled streets, until they came to a quiet cul-de-sac, where Heléna discovered, hidden away, a little German restaurant. A good friend of his owned it, Stefan explained, and soon they were greeted warmly, and seated alone in a quiet corner.

After they had ordered their meal, Stefan told her how he had met the owner's son, Axel, during his university days in Prague.

'We were both studying economics and business management, and Axel was also a fine musician. We joined a music society at university – he played the violin like his father Wilhelm does – and we began performing together in a quartet. Soon I was invited to spend weekends at his home, and straight away found myself warmly welcomed by his family. Fortunately I can speak German, so there was no problem communicating with his parents. They were particularly important to me when my father passed away, just as I was finishing my studies – so perhaps you can understand now why I still love coming here.'

Soon the conversation flowed easily between them. As they enjoyed the fine food, they exchanged views on all sorts of topics, including their mutual commitment to God. Stefan had been aware of Heléna's strong faith from his time in the family home, and now could not help but be impressed, once again, with the depth and maturity of her insights. She was so young, and yet possessed a passion for God and a quiet strength that was rare even among his own contemporaries, he felt. And that appealed to him immensely.

As the night wore on, and the remaining patrons were happy to stay on drinking coffee, Wilhelm emerged from the kitchen cradling an old violin, which he began to play with great expertise, the incredible beauty of his music touching Heléna deeply. Eventually, he paused beside their table and played, especially for them, Schumann's beautiful and haunting 'Träumerei'. As he finished, Stefan placed his hand over Heléna's on the table, and grasped it firmly. Each of them knew what the other was feeling, without any words needing to be said.

They sat for some time, neither wishing to spoil the magic of the moment. At last Stefan rose to pay the bill, and they emerged into the night air, strolling hand in hand down to the river, and eventually making their way back to Stefan's car. They drove home in silence, and Stefan saw her to the door.

'Would you be free again tomorrow evening, Heléna?' he asked quietly.

'Of course – I'll make sure I am!' she responded, without hesitation.

That second evening, they ate at a little Italian restaurant Stefan had discovered some years earlier. It was another warm and wonderful experience, and a further opportunity to learn so much more about the other. In particular, Stefan told her about his own family background.

'There aren't too many of us left now, but I do have some interesting ancestors! Some centuries back, they were among the original Hussites, so I come from a long line of Czech patriots, all with a reputation for having a firm faith in God and the truth of his Word, and also a very deep love of their homeland. I think all those things were there, deep in my blood, ready to be tapped into, as I grew up. I read a lot, since I spent so much time by myself, and my father and I had many long talks whenever he could, but it was in my university days here in Prague that I began to investigate so much more for myself, and come to grips with what I believed. Strange that my own ancestors studied at the same university so many years earlier, and gave their very lives for what they believed in so passionately.'

Heléna was fascinated. She loved the sound of his voice, and yearned to hear more of his personal journey.

The following evening, their last together in Prague, the whole family dined as planned with Stefan. Throughout the meal, he and Heléna found it difficult, and in truth, impossible, to hide their growing feelings for each other. Eventually, as they were all seated enjoying their after dinner coffee, Stefan took a deep breath and, taking Heléna's hand in his as she sat beside him, decided it was the moment to speak.

'Václav and Anezka, before we go any further, I need to ask you something that means very much to me, and to Heléna. I want to ask your permission to see Heléna as often as possible in the days and weeks ahead! I know I'm considerably older than she is, and therefore I'll respect your wishes, if you're not happy about it. Also, I don't wish to presume on my friendship with you especially, Václav, or take advantage of it in any way. But both of us would be very relieved if you gave us your blessing, and were happy to have us get to know each other much better in the days to come! Please don't feel you have to give an answer now, if you'd prefer to discuss it with each other. On the other hand, if you have no objection, then that would be wonderful news for us to hear right now!'

Heléna, taken by surprise at Stefan's forthrightness, and with face aflame, simply clasped his hand tightly and looked down. Her agony did not last long, however.

'Of course we give our permission!' Václav and Anezka chorused almost in unison. 'We'd be delighted!'

'As long as you feel you can manage your studies at the same time, Heléna, we'd be very happy about it!' Anezka added.

'And Stefan, thank you for considering our feelings,' Václav said warmly. 'You acted with integrity, as always – and we know we can trust you!'

It seemed obvious to Heléna that Anezka had spoken to Václav about the developing relationship, in their brief moments together during the last two days, so that Stefan's request had not come as a complete surprise to him. She was very grateful to her mother, and relieved also.

'I'm so glad you're pleased for us! Of course Stefan and I want to spend as much time together as we can, but I won't neglect my music,' she assured her parents. 'We both know it's important for me to do my best at the auditions, so Stefan will be supporting me in every way. We both believe we're in God's hands – and I'm sure his timing for us will be perfect!'

'Yes, it's good to know that you both look to him for guidance. We'll all need to be doing just that more and more, I believe, in the weeks ahead,' Václav responded gravely. 'Last night, Tomas and Eva shared with us many things about what they had seen and heard over the past months of their sabbatical. They had opportunity to meet with a number of Tomas' colleagues from different parts of Europe, and it seems they all feel that recent events in Germany, in particular, certainly do not augur well for our own nation.'

Václav paused for a moment, as his eyes met Stefan's. Slowly Stefan nodded his assent, and Václav continued.

'I wish I didn't have to say what I'm about to tell you – especially after this delightful news we've had! However, Stefan and I both feel it's time to explain something that, up until now, we've kept to ourselves, in order to protect you, and also not to worry you. But you know, Anezka, how uncomfortable I am in withholding anything from you especially! We need to tell you that, while Stefan and I did meet some years back now through our mutual interest in progressive business management, that's not all we talk about during our discussions. I think you're aware of that much. In recent months, we've both independently seen the need to become more pro-active in the political future of our nation – through what at present is known as our underground partisan movement. With our extensive business interests in different cities, Stefan and I are able to provide not only financial help, but also good networks and safe cover for partisans across our country. Currently, Stefan is active in leading meetings and training new partisan recruits, while I myself function in a more advisory capacity. We don't want you to worry unduly, and we trust that God will protect us and bless our land with peace and prosperity – but there may be some difficult days ahead. Our German neighbours are becoming very restless, and while we're not looking for unnecessary trouble, we feel we must plan and act for the protection of our nation and way of life. There may even be times when it will be better for you both if we don't tell you where we're going or why. As far as you're aware, if anyone ever asks you, we're away on business – that will be sufficient for you to say. Please ask us any questions you want to about this now, and we'll answer as best we can – but after that, for your own sake, we feel it would be wiser not to give you any further information. Let's pray that you'll never have to give account for us, but better to be prepared, should it happen – and also better to know nothing!'

Silence followed Václav's announcement, during which Stefan continued to hold

Heléna's hand firmly. He could feel the slight tremors that passed through her body, as she digested their news. Anezka, sitting opposite him, was pale, but seemed remarkably calm, he thought.

Then a clamour of questions rose from both Anezka and Heléna at once, which the men endeavoured to answer as satisfactorily as possible.

'Well, I can't pretend, Václav, to be greatly surprised by all this!' Anezka finally said, as their questions came to an end. 'After all, we've been married for twenty-four years now, and I think I've learnt to recognise beyond a shadow of a doubt when something's troubling you, and when there are matters heavy on your heart that you choose not share with me, for one reason or another. I'm aware it's often because you wish to protect me, and that in time you'll share these things with me, if you feel that's what God wants. Now all I can say is that I'm so very proud of you both! Speaking for myself, I feel I can trust you to make wise decisions and to know when to take risks, and when to leave well alone. I'll pray to God that you'll have his mind and his protection in everything you undertake. But please let us know if there's any way we can support you, and we'll do it! We love you so much – and our nation too, of course!'

Anezka spoke bravely, but her voice shook, as she choked back the tears.

Heléna sat quietly, nodding in agreement, most of her fears allayed, for the moment at least. If possible, she loved her father more than ever. She had always admired his integrity and sense of fair play, demonstrated time and time again in his sincere personal concern for many of the employees in his factories, and the workers on his farms. Now this evening she had caught a small glimpse of the same characteristics in Stefan. She gazed at his profile, as he sat beside her on the couch, and thought she saw etched there something of the firm commitment and determination of his Hussite ancestors whom he had described the previous evening. There were depths within him, she sensed, that would take a lifetime to fathom and appreciate, even if then. She prayed silently that God would give her the opportunity to do just that – that Stefan would be kept safe, and that this relationship between them, so new but already so deep, would continue to grow, and in time reach full bloom. And even though the information she had just heard from her father cast a shadow over their lives and future, nothing could take away from her the excitement and wonder she felt at spending time in the days ahead with this man seated beside her, who had already begun to become such an integral part of her life.

Chapter Four

The next day Václav, Anezka and Heléna returned to Tábor. For Václav, this was only a brief reprieve before another extensive business trip involving many government level discussions, both in his own homeland and also in other parts of Europe to which his farm machinery was currently exported. What other meetings would eventuate, and with whom these would occur, remained unknown to Anezka, as had been decided.

Heléna returned to her routine of lessons with Uncle Erik, and many long hours at the piano. She missed Stefan so much, despite their times together having been so few, although their frequent phone calls to each other somewhat alleviated the situation. Letters arrived too – sometimes serious, sometimes funny – each adding to the picture Heléna began to piece together in her mind of exactly who Stefan was.

Three weeks passed, and then late one evening, Václav phoned from Prague.

'Anezka, it's so good to be phoning you again from our apartment here at last – and I plan to be home with you in two days' time! I'm very pleased to have completed most of what I had to do satisfactorily – even in Germany and Austria. I need to tie up a few loose ends here in Prague, and then I'll be home for the weekend!'

They chatted for some time, and then, as if as an innocent afterthought, and with a teasing note in his voice, Václav asked one final question.

'Oh, I almost forgot, Anezka – I've invited Stefan to join us, if that's all right with you! Could you please check with Heléna whether she'd mind if he spent the weekend with us again?'

Anezka, noting the joy that lit up Heléna's face as she gave her the news, assured Václav gravely that she didn't seem to mind at all.

The next day passed in a fever of anticipation for Heléna. She tried to discipline her mind and immerse herself in her music, since the Conservatorium auditions were now only days away. She was determined to give her all to fulfil her dream of studying there, not just for her own sake, but also for her family's, and Uncle Erik's too. They believed in her so completely – she did not want to let them down. When she was away from the music room, however, thoughts of Stefan occupied her mind almost exclusively, so that, on occasions, even Anezka had to speak twice before being heard.

It was with great excitement then, that the two of them heard first one car and then another pull up outside late on the Friday afternoon, and rushed to greet the new arrivals. The fact that they knew Václav and Stefan had most likely been engaged in secret and even dangerous meetings since last seeing them added to their joy and relief.

Václav mounted the steps first, and on seeing Anezka, put down his cases and held her close, before turning to greet Heléna. While Heléna lovingly returned his hugs, her eyes nevertheless searched beyond him to Stefan, as he came slowly up the stairs towards them. After courteously greeting Anezka, Stefan turned to Heléna and, taking her hands in his, kissed her gently on both cheeks.

'I've missed you so much!' he said softly, as he smiled deep into her eyes, holding her hands as if he would never let them go.

That weekend became another golden memory for Heléna. After the men had completed some necessary planning and discussions the next day, she and Stefan were free to wander the nearby lanes and riverbank, stopping occasionally to take in the beautiful scenery around them, deeply enjoying each other's company, and growing closer together as the hours passed. In the evening, Heléna again practised for her audition, with Stefan content to sit nearby and listen, watching her beautiful profile as she played. Heléna loved to have him there. His presence somehow relaxed her and caused her to give of her best, since she knew he deeply enjoyed her music and truly appreciated the results of her long hours of practice. By Sunday evening, when Stefan was due to return to Prague, both were extremely reluctant to say goodbye.

'I don't want to leave, Heléna, but I have to. Just remember we'll see each other again in a few days' time, and by then your audition will be over! It must seem rather daunting, to have to perform before such a select panel of judges, but I know you'll do brilliantly!'

'It helps to know you have such faith in me, but I know I'm up against students from all over the country and beyond. I can only do my best – and I'll spend every minute I can before then practising hard! The thought of having a special dinner with you afterwards will keep me going!'

Václav, Heléna and Anezka travelled together to Prague the day before the audition. When the time came for Heléna to leave for the Conservatorium, however, she chose to go alone.

'I feel this is something I have to do for myself,' she explained to Anezka. 'I do hope you don't mind! It's just that ... well, people are bound to recognise you at the Conservatorium. The music world has not completely forgotten you, you can be sure!'

But Anezka knew it was more than that. Being a professional pianist, she understood how important it was to have one's own space in which to prepare mentally for a performance.

'Bless you, Heléna – go with God!' was all she said.

Heléna arrived early, and tried to remain calm and focused, as she waited her turn. Finally she heard her name called, and entered the room with her head held high. Dear God, keep your hand on me, she breathed. Help me to do my best for you – and for my family and Uncle Erik! She seated herself at the piano, and as she began to play, it seemed to her that, even more than normal, all the passion deep within her was flowing through her fingers and on into the music, finding such freedom and full, satisfying expression. She played on, only dimly aware of the selection panel at the far end of the room, and of their stillness and absorption in the music. Eventually she finished her repertoire, having continued on when no comment or instruction to do otherwise was forthcoming from the judges. After she had stopped playing, the room remained quiet for some time. Then, as she stood, one of the judges, an older woman, walked across to her, and, putting her hands gently on her shoulders, kissed both her cheeks, before addressing her in a voice that shook with emotion.

'Thank you so much, my dear!' she said sincerely, almost as if the words were wrung from her. 'You'll hear from us soon, be assured of that! I can't say anything more until my colleagues and I have conferred, but be encouraged – you have a very special gift indeed!'

Heléna left the room in a daze, still gripped by the emotion of her performance. She decided to walk home, allowing herself time to return slowly to reality. Around her, the bustle of every day life in the streets restored some measure of normality at least. She knew she had performed well. She simply knew that deep within her, and the effect her playing seemed to have had on the woman who spoke to her also confirmed it to her. So it was with a light heart that she eventually knocked on the door of Tomas and Eva's house, and regaled her mother and aunt with an account of the day's events.

From the moment Stefan called for her that evening to the moment she waved goodbye to him some hours later, Heléna felt she was floating in a haze of happiness. After a special dinner together, they walked again by the Vltava, and onto the Charles Bridge a little way, gazing down in awe at the shimmering pathway created by the moon on the surface of the water. Eventually Stefan took her in his arms, kissing her gently at first, and then somewhat more fiercely, finally holding her so tightly to himself that she could clearly hear his heartbeat through his warm jacket. When he could finally trust himself to speak, Stefan spoke quietly, yet in a voice full of emotion.

'I know it's only early days yet in our relationship, Heléna – and I know this will sound like such a cliché – yet I feel like I've known you for years! I'm so much older than you, and I don't want to rush you in any way, but I love you so much! These past three weeks I've felt so alive, so full of excitement, and yet so at peace – as if I've found something that's been missing for a long time. I don't expect you to say anything right now – I only wanted you to understand exactly how I feel. Let's take all the time we need in the weeks ahead to get to know each other better, and to be really sure about our relationship, but I have to say that I believe with all my heart that God has brought us together – and just at the right time for both of us!'

Heléna stayed quietly in his arms, enjoying the security and love she felt there, overwhelmed by God's grace in giving her a glimpse of the beautiful future opening up for her. It was too vast, too much to express in words – she was so thankful that Stefan was giving her time to come to grips not only with his feelings for her, but with her own feelings for him. Eventually, again as if mutually knowing each other's heart, they turned and made their way home, secure in the knowledge that a deep understanding and firm trust existed between them. They parted reluctantly, Stefan promising to phone her before she and Anezka left for Tábor the next day, and before he himself went away again. Václav, with more pressing business issues to attend to, unfortunately also needed to remain in Prague.

It seemed strange for Heléna to be back home, without the immediate pressure of piano lessons and her usual hours of practice. She enjoyed so much the freedom of wandering into the music room when she felt like it, and sitting down to play whatever music took her fancy. She was quiet, Anezka noticed, as they shared meal times together, or relaxed in the evenings, a fact that her mother attributed to the strain involved in waiting for her audition results. At the same time, there was a warm glow and a quiet happiness about her that seemed to counteract any tension she might be feeling. Anezka said nothing. Better to stay quiet and see how events unfolded, she decided.

Then late one afternoon, around a week after the auditions, the phone call Heléna had been waiting for finally came. She held her breath as she listened. It was the older woman from the panel, who had spoken to her so kindly after she had played. She was happy to inform Heléna that she had indeed been successful in gaining a full time place in the Conservatorium's student intake for the coming year.

'Congratulations, my dear – I'm delighted for you! I felt your performance was quite outstanding – and happily the others agreed! You'll receive notification of your acceptance by mail, along with further details about your study course, but you'll need to begin organising things immediately, as classes are due to commence on the first day of September. In fact, in just a week's time, you're required to be in Prague for a further interview, to finalise your study program. Hopefully then you'll also be able to meet your new piano teacher! Again, my congratulations – I look forward with great interest to observing your progress!'

Heléna stood by the phone after the conversation had ended, too stunned to move at first, but then filled with such wild elation that she felt she wanted to shout out her news to the world. Eventually she hurried to the kitchen, where her mother was helping Berta set the small table at which they often ate when Václav was away. Anezka looked up, and, having heard the telephone ring earlier, knew even before any words were said, that Heléna had been accepted. Soon the three of them were hugging and kissing, crying and laughing all at once.

'I'm so proud of you, Heléna – so very proud! I know what it feels like, and I'm so delighted for you!' Anezka said, when she was able to speak. 'I'm sure you'll want to share this fantastic news with your father and Uncle Erik as quickly as possible, so go ahead, dear! But come and join us again when you've finished.'

Fortunately, Václav was in his office, and available to take her call. His response was simple but sincere, with more than a dash of fatherly pride.

'Of course I didn't doubt for a moment that you'd get in!' he said, in a voice that clearly showed his great pleasure and delight. 'Everything seems to be unfolding so quickly and wonderfully for you, my dear! I'd love to be there with you and your mother right now, but let's all celebrate together when you come up to town next week! Perhaps Stefan will be home by then too.'

Later that evening, Stefan phoned Heléna from Pilsen, where one of his larger subsidiary companies was located.

'Have you heard anything yet? … You have? … Oh, that's wonderful – I'm so happy for you, Heléna! Very, very happy indeed – congratulations, from the bottom of my heart! This is so frustrating, not being able to see you face to face right now!'

'I know – but I can hear from your voice, Stefan, that you truly are so pleased for me. I have to be in Prague again in a week's time. Will you be home by then?'

Stefan immediately decided to expedite his remaining business meetings over the next few days, and be back in time to celebrate with the family the following week. He wanted nothing to keep him away from being with Heléna on such an occasion. It took his breath away when he remembered how he had met Heléna only a matter of five weeks previously, and yet how deep his feelings for her had grown.

'I'll do my best to be there – I love you, Heléna!'

'I love you too, Stefan – with all my heart!'

Soon after breakfast the next morning, Heléna walked the short distance to Uncle Erik's home on the edge of the village. He had been such a large part of her success – she was so looking forward to giving him the news. As soon as she greeted him, he guessed what she had come to tell him, but waited for her to say it in her own words. She needed to savour the moment – and she deserved to be able to. They had worked hard, both of them, but Heléna had worked the harder by far, and her talent was undoubtedly exceptional. He would have indeed been surprised if she had not succeeded, yet when she finally told him, he found tears welling up in his eyes. He could not trust himself to speak for a few moments, but eventually, with his old hands shaking, he reached out and held hers, tears coursing freely down his cheeks.

'Heléna, you've made an old man so proud! I count it such a privilege to have been part of your journey! I've watched you mature not only musically, but deep in your soul and spirit also. You're young yet, but God has given you a maturity way beyond your years. I believe he's done this for a purpose, knowing there will be many challenges ahead of you. Whatever happens, Heléna, keep believing in yourself, keep drawing on that inner strength I know you have, and above all, keep trusting in God! Keep the faith, my dear, keep the faith!'

When Uncle Erik had regained his composure a little, and Edita had brought coffee and biscuits for them all, he went on to talk of his own time at the Conservatorium, and of some of the great churches where he had given organ recitals over the years.

'Unfortunately, I fear those days are gone now, Heléna. Times change, our country has changed, and soon our government will no longer really be ours, if what I hear is correct. We must prepare for some difficult days ahead, even those of my generation, who've already seen much trouble in this world. But I do feel reassured when I see people like your father and his friend Stefan standing for what is true and right, and fighting for what's best for our homeland. I've heard them speak at meetings, and the three of us have also met together to discuss possible ways ahead when we have to act. May God strengthen and protect them in the days to come! I'll do what I can as an old man, but we need faithful leaders like these ones, whose strength comes not only from within themselves, but also from our God.'

Uncle Erik spoke with such passion, that his voice had begun to shake again. A cold chill struck Heléna – not Uncle Erik, as well as Stefan and her father! She was silent, unsure how to respond. She concentrated on drinking her coffee to give herself time to think, finally deciding to question him further, but as she looked up to speak, she intercepted a warning glance between Edita and her brother. She remembered her father's words on the night he had shared about his own underground involvement, and his request not to ask further questions, so now out of respect for him, and for the safety of them all, she chose to take the conversation in another direction. Deliberately, she turned to Edita, and began chatting happily about her arrangements to live in Prague again with her aunt and uncle.

'I'll come home on weekends as often as I can, I'm sure – and when I do, Uncle Erik, I promise I'll come and play for you!

Uncle Erik had managed to regain a little more composure, while Heléna was speaking.

'I'll be waiting, my dear,' he said, with a twinkle in his eye and a teasing note in his voice, 'but soon you'll be much in demand for concerts, I know. And soon, I'm sure, there'll be many young friends in your life in Prague – young men in particular! Whatever happens for you, I hope you'll never forget your old friend Uncle Erik back here in Tábor. God has given you a wonderful opportunity, Heléna. I'll be praying you'll work hard and give of your best, but also that you'll be able to relax and enjoy the many new friendships and exciting experiences ahead. God bless you – I'm very proud of you!'

Václav drove home from Prague the following weekend, delighted to be with them again. Yet, while he joined fully in the animated discussion concerning arrangements for Heléna's immediate future, Anezka noticed that he did so with an effort, and that, often, when he was unaware of being observed, his face wore an unusually grave expression. The only insight into whatever was troubling him came as they glanced briefly at the newspaper together at one point, while sharing a leisurely cup of coffee. Václav sighed heavily, as he read the reports indicating that soon Czechoslovakia would come under the political oversight of Germany. Anezka laid her hand over his on the table, and met his eyes, a troubled look in her own.

'There are difficult days ahead, Anezka, I'm afraid,' he responded eventually. 'Nothing but trouble can come from this political expediency. I'm glad our Heléna can begin her studies and prepare herself for her chosen career, but I pray to God she'll be able to complete them, and fulfil her calling in freedom in her own homeland!'

They sat together in silence, each preoccupied with thoughts of a future that seemed increasingly uncertain. At last Václav put his free hand over Anezka's, as it lay on his, and squeezed it gently, letting her know that he appreciated her quiet presence, and her unspoken encouragement. Earlier that day they had talked at length about her own health concerns, and how she would fare without Heléna's presence at Tábor during the weeks when Václav was away. She had reassured both him and Heléna that she was much stronger now, and that this was indeed an opportunity Heléna must not miss.

'Besides, Heléna will come home as often as she can on weekends, I'm sure,' Anezka had continued determinedly, 'and these days I do feel much more able to make the trip to Prague, especially now that Eva's back.'

Despite Anezka's assertions, Václav determined to work for longer periods from his study at Tábor whenever possible, and also to find others on his staff who could travel on his behalf. And although neither spoke of it, both Václav and Anezka wondered exactly how and where Stefan would fit into their lives in the weeks and months ahead. Only time would tell. Better to leave it unfold under God's hand, and trust Stefan and Heléna to make their own decisions about their future.

Late on the Sunday, all three travelled back to Prague, where Tomas and Eva greeted them with open arms once again. Although Heléna tried to contain her impatience, she found herself on tenterhooks, as she waited for Stefan's return. She was aware that the business in which he was engaged undoubtedly involved more than company matters, but did her best to put him to one side in her mind, and focus on the various tasks awaiting her attention. In the end, her days were fully occupied, firstly with a further interview at the Conservatorium, and secondly with more clothes shopping, now that she knew what the coming year would hold for her.

And then at last Stefan was there, phoning her from his apartment, arranging dinner together that night. The following evening was to be a special family celebration at Tomas and Eva's home, to which Stefan was also invited – but this first night was for them alone. They drove again to the old part of the city, Stefan having booked a table at an elegant restaurant overlooking the river, and sat listening together to the cathedral bells. Heléna's face was glowing with childlike delight.

'I love the sound of the bells, don't you, Stefan? Somehow they make me feel that God's own heart is bursting with joy and happiness for us, and that he really is delighted to be blessing us tonight!'

Stefan smiled and nodded in agreement, again aware that she had voiced his own thoughts exactly. Each time they were together, he realised more and more how much they had in common, despite the age difference. As he looked at Heléna across the table that evening, he saw her youthful excitement and joyful anticipation of all that life could possibly hold, but he saw also a maturity and gentle sensitivity, especially in the way she curbed her own excitement, taking time to observe where he was at and listen to his heart. He loved her for that, and for so many other things that were part and parcel of who she was. Stefan knew he had found his life partner – he had never been surer of anything in his life – but he did not want to rush her either. Yet, like Václav, he knew of the troubled times ahead for his country, and wondered with a stab of pain how much all the upheaval would impinge on Heléna's future in particular. He wanted to be there for her, to walk beside her and encourage her, to protect her, but he also knew he was called to fulfil a vital role for his country at this time.

Oh God, let me know your priorities, let me make the right choices, he prayed silently.

The celebration the next evening was a special experience for Stefan, after having been without close family of his own for some years. Tomas already knew Stefan slightly from his student days at Charles University, and now he and Eva welcomed him warmly into their home. Soon he was at ease amongst them, as if he naturally belonged there, joining in the fun and laughter, as well as the more serious conversations around the dinner table.

'I remember hearing you give some public lectures years ago, Tomas, on the rise and fall of political and religious movements. I very much enjoyed your insights and agreed with your perspectives then, so could you tell us something more about your recent experiences overseas, and elsewhere in Europe? What do you believe the future holds for our country in the current political situation?'

'I'm happy to answer your questions, Stefan. Only last week I gave a public lecture on recent political changes we observed in the countries surrounding us. The Anschluss, it appears to me, has certainly not lost its momentum, and we need to remember as a nation the annexation of Austria last March. I believe that the Sudetenland will be next – and then where does that leave us? We have much to ponder and to prepare ourselves for, I fear.'

The others agreed. Stefan and Václav, in particular, had believed this for some time. Now Tomas' knowledge and insights further confirmed their views.

The next week, Heléna moved what possessions she needed back to her 'second home' with her aunt and uncle in Prague, ready for the commencement of her classes. From the very beginning, she was at ease with her new piano teacher. Alexandr Veverka was Jewish, slightly built and quietly spoken, and a few years older than Stefan. She loved his gentle sensitivity, and the warm smile that lit up his kind but usually rather sad eyes whenever he was pleased with her playing. She treasured the opportunity to explore so many different musical works, both old and new, and to receive input not only from him, but also from the other dedicated and talented musicians who comprised the Conservatorium staff at that time.

She also loved, from the outset, the camaraderie of the other students, who, despite their strong determination to achieve their dreams in their chosen field of music, still found time to laugh and relax together, as well as occasionally discuss more serious issues. She enjoyed forming friendships again with those of her own age, particularly one shy and lonely German girl from Domažlice, close to the Bavarian border, with the most amazing soprano voice she had ever heard. Heléna enjoyed too the easy banter and teasing of the male students, having missed so much the company of her own brother as she was growing up.

Yet in the midst of all this change and excitement, Stefan was her rock and her special confidante, the one with whom she shared her uncertainties about herself in the face of so much musical talent around her, and the one who spoke deeply and indelibly into her life. With him she could relax completely and share the many new ideas and challenges confronting her, knowing he would listen patiently, but wisely allow her to come to her own conclusions. Alongside this, she valued the loving support of her parents, not only on the weekends when they could all be together at Tábor, but also on the occasions when her father would make time in his busy schedule to take her out for coffee or share a meal with her. Her aunt and uncle too, though leading full lives, were always there for her. But it was Stefan with whom she wanted to share above all, and whom, she had come to realise without a doubt, she loved with all her heart.

Unfortunately for Heléna, these days more than ever, Stefan was away, ostensibly dealing with business matters, but in reality doing much to help organise the underground movement. The very month she had started her studies in Prague, things had gone from bad to worse for their homeland, with Hitler having his way, and Britain and France signing over the Sudetenland into his control under the Munich Agreement, without even consulting the Czechoslovak government. Days later, President Beneš had resigned and left the country, while soon after, hundreds of German troops had marched into the Sudetenland. Enormous events were beginning to unfold one after the other in the political arena.

Yet in the midst of it all, despite heavy burdens on his spirit, Stefan tried to be there for Heléna, phoning her whenever he could, and returning to Prague as often as possible. For Heléna, things quickly came to rights again when Stefan was with her. Somehow she simply felt complete. As for Stefan, his whole world seemed different, and everything so much more bearable when he was with Heléna.

One evening in mid-November, when Stefan had returned from a particularly taxing trip, he and Heléna walked hand in hand through the cool night air to a nearby restaurant. Stefan was quieter than usual during their meal, but Heléna was content just to be with him, watching his face and thinking how much she loved him. Later, they wandered through the streets of the old part of the city, eventually finding their way onto the Charles Bridge. They stood with arms around each other, in the shelter of one of the beautiful statues that had watched over so many lovers during past centuries, hearing each other's heartbeat and comforted by each other's warmth. Eventually, Heléna heard Stefan's voice from above her head.

'Heléna, I think it's time we came to a decision. Not long after we met, I told you how much I love you and how important you are to me. The only thing that's changed is that my love has deepened, so that I find it almost impossible to be away from you! I know I said I wanted to give you time – and I'm very aware you've just begun your studies. You have so much to fill your life right now, but I believe we're meant to be together – forever. And I'd love that forever to start as soon as possible!'

Heléna was silent for some time, so that Stefan began to wonder if in fact he had spoken too soon. Eventually she pulled away a little and lifted her head, and he saw the tears spilling out of her beautiful eyes.

'I want that with all my heart too, Stefan,' she whispered shakily. 'I want us to be together, every moment we can! So much is happening, not only in our own lives, but all around us! I think the right time for us is now – and that this is God's time for us too, Stefan. And you haven't rushed me. I've never been more certain of anything in my life than this!'

They kissed and cried and embraced for a long time. Stefan could not seem to let her go. Each time he kissed her, he wondered if he were dreaming, if something would come to snatch away this beautiful gift he had been given. She was so precious, that he did not want to let her out of his sight, yet he knew they would indeed soon be constantly separated. He wanted nothing of that to touch this moment, however – this magical moment, as they leaned together on the stone parapet, watching the moonlight dance on the water below.

'I'll speak to your father as soon as possible,' Stefan said softly, as they eventually began to head home.

The next evening, after both men had attended another of the many partisan meetings taking place in the city at that time, Stefan invited Václav back to his apartment for a coffee. They drank in silence for a while, before Václav, sensing his friend had something on his heart to share, took pity on him.

'I've been wondering, Stefan – is everything working out well with you and Heléna?'

Stefan looked at the older man with his direct gaze, and answered him simply and honestly.

'Last night Heléna agreed to marry me, and we'd like to announce our engagement as soon as possible. I love her with all my heart, and she feels the same. I'm aware she's still so young, and that for her, life is just beginning to open up, but I know I need her, and I sense she'll need me very much in the days to come. I believe in her totally, and want to honour the many gifts God has given her, Václav, so I promise you I'll encourage her to pursue all that God has ahead for her to do and be. I know I should have spoken to you first before I said anything to Heléna – I apologise for that. I do value your friendship highly, and would very much like to know we have your continued support and blessing.'

Václav felt his eyes grow moist, as he looked into Stefan's earnest face.

'There's no one I'd prefer to trust with my daughter's future more than you, my dear Stefan,' he declared, with deep feeling. 'I wish for your sakes that the times were less turbulent, but I agree now it would be best for you to marry sooner rather than later. I know you, Stefan, and I know you would give your life for Helena, just as Anezka and I would. I pray God's richest blessings on you both, as you prepare for your marriage, and through all the years ahead!'

That weekend all three of them travelled to Tábor to share the news with Anezka face to face. Anezka immediately observed how close Stefan and Heléna had become, so it was no real surprise when they told her, as they were relaxing around the warm fire in the sitting room after dinner. Like Václav, tears of joy filled her eyes, as she warmly hugged both Heléna and Stefan.

'This is such wonderful news! As soon as I saw you both, I could see how very happy you were, and now I know exactly why! I couldn't be more delighted! Have you thought about when you might marry? I hope you don't plan to have too long an engagement!'

'I'm so glad to hear you say that!' Heléna responded in a relieved voice. 'I think I have the most wonderful parents in the world! I know I'm young, and just beginning my studies, but I really believe that being with Stefan will help me to focus and do my best, rather than hinder. Whenever we're together, I somehow feel so complete – so happy and secure! Stefan encourages me so much, I end up believing nothing is too difficult for me!'

'And from my perspective, there's no reason to delay, particularly given the current uncertain times,' Stefan added. 'I obviously don't want to wait long, and I have the resources to support Heléna. Also we both believe God has brought us together, and is in this with us.'

'Actually, we wondered if New Year's Day might be a good day for our wedding,' Heléna continued excitedly. 'We know it's an unusual choice, but it would be a special new beginning for us – the start of a new year and a new life together! Also, my short holiday break falls then. We'd love to be married in the village chapel, with just an informal gathering of family and friends here afterwards. There'll only be time for a short honeymoon, because of the pressures of Stefan's business commitments, as well as my studies, but we can take a trip together somewhere later. Besides, with such unrest around us, it doesn't seem wise to be away anywhere for too long.'

On their wedding day, the snow was still thick on the ground, but the skies above were clear and blue. Heléna's beautiful close-fitting dress of fine white wool, with its matching cape, kept her warm and snug, and the sound of Uncle Erik's wonderful organ music greeted her, as she entered the chapel on her father's arm. And there waiting, looking serious, but also so proud and happy, was Stefan. He held her hand firmly as they exchanged their vows, standing tall beside her – Stefan, her strong tower, her beloved gift from God, her friend and partner forever.

Heléna had no wedding attendants – only family, friends and neighbours around her, as she had wanted it to be, and also a few of Stefan's good friends, plus an aunt and uncle and two cousins, his only living relatives. The service was simple, the music superb, and Stefan and Heléna spoke their vows to each other with such firm conviction, that Anezka's heart skipped a beat, as she glimpsed with even greater clarity the depth of commitment between them. The majority of those present had also been invited to the informal luncheon afterwards, catered for by dear Berta, Aunty Eva and Anezka herself. Around Stefan and Heléna, there was a vibrant glow of deep happiness that could not fail to lift everyone's spirits and, for the moment at least, lessen the burden on the hearts and minds of those like Václav and Tomas, who held such deep concerns for their country's future.

Shortly before darkness set in, farewells were said, a proud Uncle Erik prayed for the happy couple, and a final blessing was given by Václav. As they drove away, Heléna looked back, smiling at the little crowd still waving on the front steps. Silently she asked God to etch this scene on her memory. Suddenly she knew with great certainty, even in the midst of such happiness, that she would never see all of these special people together again.

PART II

*Even though I walk
through the valley of the shadow of death,
I will fear no evil, for you are with me;
your rod and your staff,
they comfort me.*

Psalm 23:4

Chapter Five

For Stefan and Heléna, their three-day honeymoon in a little cottage on a friend's farm in the hills south of Tábor was truly magical. The weather remained very cold, with light snowfalls, but Stefan's friend had ensured they would be comfortable, with a log fire blazing in the tiny sitting room when they arrived, and fresh bread and other provisions on hand in the warm kitchen. The absolute stillness of the countryside around them, as it lay blanketed in snow, was exactly what they needed, after the bustle and pressure of the past weeks. They lay for hours contentedly in each other's arms, snuggled together in front of the warm fire, sometimes talking animatedly, sometimes simply enjoying the quietness together, neither saying a word. And at other times, after they had made love, Stefan held Heléna tightly to him, stroking her gently and kissing her softly, still hardly able to believe that he had been entrusted with such a precious gift, such a wonderful companion with whom to share every part of his life.

Heléna clung tightly to him in those times also.

'I love you so much, Stefan! I feel like I could burst with thankfulness – I wish I could shout out my happiness to the whole world! But then, another part of me wants to keep our precious relationship to ourselves, hidden away from everyone, in case it's snatched away from us somehow! Perhaps it's the isolation of this place that's making me feel like that – almost like we're in our own little dreamlike world!'

'Yet we can't ignore the challenges and responsibilities waiting for us out there in the big world, Heléna – not even for one more day, I'm afraid!' Stefan sighed. 'The business world awaits, as does my partisan work – and for you, Heléna, lots of study and practice! At least I've been able to avoid having any business commitments away from home in the next month, but I can't be so sure there'll be no partisan work to do in that time. I've arranged for others to do some of the training instead of me, as well as lead meetings, but there's a limit to the personnel available to do such things.'

'I know, Stefan, and I'm very grateful you've tried to be home as much as you can. None of us can be certain what will unfold in the next few weeks or even days, and I understand you have to be ready at a moment's notice to organise the emergency safety networks, if things get worse.'

'Not if, but when, I'm afraid, Heléna – but let's trust God in it all! He's brought us together and given us these things to do, and I believe he'll give us the strength to do them well.'

Back in Prague, Heléna soon found her time fully occupied. While the academic side of her course was challenging, involving studies in harmony and composition, music history, and analysis of various works by the great masters, the practical components were by far the most demanding and rigorous. Each student was required to reach a high standard in his or her major performance area, as well as become adept in a second. For the latter, Heléna had chosen to work on her voice – a light, lilting soprano, which Stefan always felt seemed to float effortlessly in the air. Her lessons with her singing teacher Gina, a jolly, rotund, ex-opera singer of Italian descent, were filled with much fun and laughter, particularly when Gina, with her wonderful contralto voice, could be induced to join her student in singing some of the haunting old Czech folk songs Heléna loved. Heléna gave of her best in everything, including her singing lessons, but it was for her beloved piano teacher, Alexandr, that she worked the hardest.

'Somehow,' she explained to Stefan, 'I can't find it in my heart to disappoint him in any way! He believes I can perform at a level far beyond my years, so I feel I have to do justice to his faith in me and my ability to scale the heights he envisages!'

This fact, coupled with her own innate desire to achieve her dreams, inspired her, enabling her to remain focused and determined throughout her long hours of practice at Stefan's beautiful old Bechstein piano. She put her heart and soul into these times, much to the apparent enjoyment of their neighbour in the apartment below, an elderly school teacher who loved music, and remembered attending many of Heléna's own mother's performances.

After they had been married for just over a month, Stefan could no longer ignore his business responsibilities in a number of the larger cities. Also, while he had on occasions met with other key underground workers during this time, usually just before dawn, when Heléna was still asleep, he could no longer avoid their urgent pleas for him to attend top-level meetings elsewhere. His expertise was needed to bring about a major reorganisation and strategic deployment of those involved in the partisan movement across their homeland.

'Heléna, you know I don't want to leave you alone, but these meetings are vital just now,' Stefan explained. 'Why not move back to your aunt and uncle's while I'm gone? You might feel safer there, and it would mean I could go away with an easier mind about you.'

Heléna considered his suggestion for a while before answering. She was not afraid to be by herself, but realised that perhaps Stefan knew of dangers that she was unaware of. In the end, she decided to agree, and not ask any further questions.

'Yes, I'm happy to do that, Stefan. It should work fine – I'm used to studying there. I know Aunty Eva will be pleased to have me.'

He was away for around a fortnight, and although he phoned Heléna as often as he could, she missed him terribly. When he returned, neither he nor Heléna relished the idea of being separated again. Yet each of them knew that this would be inevitable in the weeks and months to come.

Two more weeks passed before Stefan needed to make another trip, this time again because of his underground work, rather than any actual business reasons. By then, he and Heléna had come to the decision that because of the strong possibility of further similar trips in the weeks to come, it was impractical for her always to be moving back and forth to her aunt and uncle's.

'We could ask your mother to come and stay, Heléna,' Stefan suggested at first. 'Do you think she'd be well enough?'

Heléna hesitated, her face clouding over a little.

'I doubt it,' she said eventually. 'She really is better at home, where she can rest and be quiet. I don't like to trouble her, and if I ask her, she won't want to say no, for my sake. Stefan, how would you feel if I stayed here by myself this time?'

'I'm not sure … . How *you'd* feel is more the question!'

'I truly believe I'd be fine. I'm not afraid at all to be by myself. And I know God will look after me. Besides, I do have a lot of assignments and practice to do, so if I'm alone, I can more easily devote my time fully to it all. Not that I won't miss you every minute!' she added, as she saw the expression on his face. 'You know how much I hate our being apart! It's like a gaping hole that nothing could fill – not even the most beautiful music ever!'

By the time another month had elapsed, things had begun to escalate at an alarming rate on the political front, until, on 15th March, the German army finally invaded and occupied their homeland. And because of the fear of war, and of Hitler in particular, there was little protest from inside or outside the country. The Nazi Protectorate of Bohemia and Moravia came into being, Slovakia declared its independence, and Ruthenia in the south disappeared under Hungarian control.

Thus the proud and independent Second Republic of Czechoslovakia ceased to exist.

While Stefan and Heléna, along with a large percentage of the Czech population, had expected this to happen ever since the Sudetenland had been handed over to the Germans, the speed with which it occurred took their breath away. At first, most people were able to go about their business as usual, except that now there were German officials everywhere, determined to run the country much more efficiently, but in the process, of course, focusing on the wellbeing of Germans and the German economy, rather than that of the Czechs. For others, business most certainly did not proceed as usual, including Stefan and Heléna, and many close to them.

At first, Stefan had no choice but to stay put in Prague, since his company, along with many others involved in food production, was of great interest to the German government authorities. The German armed forces, both those already occupying Czech lands and those mobilised in their own homeland, needed to be fed, after all. Alongside this, with German industry becoming more and more focused on an almost certain war effort, food soon became a precious commodity for both Germans and Czechs. After several lengthy attempts at negotiation with the authorities, Stefan found that in reality he had no choice but to forego the current marketing strategies of his main biscuit factory in Prague and its subsidiaries elsewhere, and to accede to their demands to gear production more towards supplying a variety of food items for the German armed forces. As the weeks and months passed, and the prospect of war became imminent, the factories were required to operate almost round the clock, resulting in huge personnel and management issues for Stefan to resolve. By this time, food rationing was in place for the general population, but this did little to offset the greatly increased level of production needed from factories like Stefan's.

In the midst of all the emotional pressure involved in these drastic changes, and with his physical and mental energy depleted, Stefan continued to work tirelessly, often late into the night. Heléna saw little of him, even when he was home in Prague. Occasionally the two of them were able to get away for a weekend with Heléna's parents at Tábor, but even then, Stefan and Václav often had so much to discuss, that Anezka and Heléna were largely left to their own devices.

It was not only issues to do with their partisan work that occupied the two men on these occasions. Even more urgent a topic was the immediate future of Václav's companies. Both knew it was only a matter of time before German authorities would show intense interest in these, not only because of the farm produce involved, but also because of the heavy equipment his factories were able to manufacture. While Václav was prepared to acquiesce, as Stefan had, with demands placed by the Germans on the produce from his farming estates, his factories were a different matter.

'Stefan, you need to know that I'll never agree to anything else being produced by my factories other than farm machinery! If the Germans want that, then I may concede to their demands – I may have to. But should they direct me to supply army equipment, or weapons of any description, I'll have to refuse. I could never agree to such demands, whatever the consequences! Never!' Václav asserted strenuously.

At first, Stefan disagreed with this decision, believing it would achieve little.

'Václav, it's not only possible this will happen. I believe it's highly likely – and sooner rather than later! Surely there's some room at least for compromise? Think of the consequences, if you don't give in to such demands!'

They debated the issue back and forth, until Stefan saw that nothing would induce his friend to change his mind.

'I can understand your position, Václav,' Stefan finally said, with a sigh. 'I can see that such an action would be a violation for you of all God's given you, and everything you've worked for. Let's hope and pray that, despite what I've said, you'll never have to make such a decision!'

Anezka looked frailer these days, the deep concerns she felt for their country and, more personally, for Stefan and Heléna, as well as Václav himself, taking its toll on her heart. Václav tried to shelter her from most of the issues concerning his business interests, choosing rather to discuss these with Stefan, but she realised, without needing to be told, the pressures that may soon be brought to bear on him. She spent hours alone, praying fervently for great wisdom for him, and for them all. Some of these concerns she discussed with Heléna, but other deeper ones she kept to herself.

'I know there are big issues facing Václav, and all of us,' she would say to Heléna, 'but I want to remain calm for his sake, and not add to his concerns – or yours! Only God can really hold us in these troubled times, Heléna. Only he, I know, can give me peace, and the strength I need to support your father as I want to.'

Both she and Heléna knew too that neither Stefan nor Václav had lessened their involvement in the underground movement, despite the presence of the Gestapo everywhere, even in Tábor. The partisans were indeed working feverishly, not only to coordinate personnel and gather resources for the various activities aimed at opposing the German occupation, but also to provide certain contingency measures, including places of safety and escape routes, for any who might need them. By mutual agreement, each time Stefan and Heléna left Tábor now after spending the weekend there, all four of them would stand together in a small circle in the hallway, hands clasped tightly, and heads bowed, as they asked for God's guidance and protection in all decisions made and every activity undertaken.

During term time, there never seemed to be enough hours in Heléna's day, whether Stefan was at home or away, for all she felt she needed to do. It seemed as if almost everyone at the Conservatorium, both teachers and students, had redoubled their efforts to give of their best and perform at their highest level. They seemed determined to keep the soul and spirit of the nation strong in the midst of uncertainty, and driven to explore and pass on the rich cultural heritage that was theirs. Yet even within the walls of the Prague Conservatorium, the political turmoil within the country as a whole was beginning to have its effect. For Heléna's beloved piano teacher Alexandr, this was an anxious time, as he watched his fellow Jews being dismissed one by one from key government positions, and various areas of the civil service. Alexandr had always worked hard, giving of himself to all his students. Now he focused even more on his work, sensing that time for him might also be short. Heléna likewise redoubled her efforts to please him with her playing, but her heart ached for him, as she saw the lines become more firmly etched on his clever, sensitive face, and the sadness already present in his eyes deepen.

For many of the teachers and students of German origin too, the political situation brought deep confusion. Particular sensitivity was often needed on their part, as they joined in the inevitable discussions in the staff room or student café. Among them was Heléna's special friend Helga, from Domažlice, torn between her commitment to her family, with their deeply ingrained loyalty to their own homeland, and her own growing love and respect for her friend Heléna, for her Czech singing teacher, and indeed for the beautiful old city of Prague and its people in general.

Meanwhile, for Tomas and Eva, this was also proving to be a critical period, with their outspoken political views, which were widely known on campus and beyond. Whenever Stefan's work commitments and Heléna's studies permitted, they would spend an evening with her aunt and uncle, either at their home, or in one of the small, secluded restaurants in the old part of the city. As the weeks progressed, Tomas and Eva's concern was palpable, their conversations becoming more and more impassioned each time they met with Stefan and Heléna.

'Now it seems I can't even give my normal history lectures in peace!' Tomas said indignantly one evening. 'Recently, I'm sure there've been some different faces in my classes, but because I have such large numbers, it's difficult to say for sure. I have wanted to confront them, and find out exactly who they are, but often many students want to talk with me at the end of my lectures, and their questions are important. Then just this week, good friends of mine in one class engaged some of these strangers in conversation, and they're sure these people are plants, closely linked with the Gestapo. They're not going to discourage me that easily, however! Perhaps they may even learn something valuable, if they stay long enough!'

Tomas continued to lecture on fearlessly, maintaining his own deeply held political perspectives with integrity. But eventually, students connected with the partisans warned that, according to their sources, the situation was becoming very grave, and his position at the university in jeopardy, along with Eva's also.

'It may be a wise move, Tomas, if you were to take some more study leave, for a short while at least,' Stefan suggested to him one evening. 'I have contacts in Poland who'd be glad to have you visit. Perhaps by the time you return, the Gestapo will have lost interest in you, and have more important things to do!'

Tomas agreed to think about it. As he talked with a small group of students after his lecture the following day, however, several Gestapo members entered the room, with Eva in tow. She had already been arrested in the midst of a tutorial, and now it was Tomas' turn. He knew he could not resist, since, apart from anything else, he feared Eva might be harmed if he did.

'Tell Stefan!' was all he had time to say to a student he knew was a partisan, as they were driven away. Eventually it was ascertained that they were to be taken as forced labour, along with others, to a new iron and steel factory near the coalmines of northern Moravia.

At first Stefan's connections across the country were able to keep Heléna and her family informed of their welfare, but as this became increasingly difficult, concern mounted for them. Anezka, in particular, grieved deeply for her sister and brother-in-law, spending many hours sitting quietly in the garden at Tábor, praying for their safety and protection, wherever they were and whatever was happening for them.

The events that had overtaken Tomas and Eva grieved Heléna deeply also, but for her, as with others in similar situations, life had to go on. Her first year at the Conservatorium was rapidly drawing to a close, and the added pressure of written exams and practical performances was upon her.

'What has happened to Aunty Eva and Uncle Tomas makes me more determined than ever to do well,' she explained to Stefan. 'Not only to make up for the grief that Máma's feeling, but somehow also to honour the faith that my aunt and uncle always showed in me.'

Her hard work and determination paid off. Heléna finished the year with flying colours, excelling in particular in her practical performances – both piano and singing. It delighted her to see the pride and joy on her parents' faces, and of course Stefan's, when she was awarded top marks amongst the first year students, and was chosen to perform at the Conservatorium's final recital for the year.

As the summer break came, and the weeks passed, things seemed to settle a little on the political front, with the Czech government continuing to be reorganised as the German authorities wished. It concerned Stefan, however, that throughout this time, no further news was received of Tomas and Eva. He was not surprised when, early in July, he eventually discovered, through his network of contacts, that Tomas and Eva had been sent to the Ruhr area in Germany to work on armaments production.

Then in August, the blow finally fell that Heléna had been dreading, and that Václav and Anezka themselves had suspected in their heart of hearts would one day be inevitable. The past few months had been difficult ones of reorganisation for Václav, with much of the production from his farming estates gradually commandeered to feed German troops and personnel. Now, the German authorities, as expected, were demanding that his factories cease production of heavy farm machinery for the foreseeable future, and instead switch to the production of large machine guns and other field weapons, along with new model tanks, sorely needed to re-equip the German army. Václav had been given a week to comply.

He called the family together, despite knowing there was little left to discuss. He had made his position clear, and was determined to honour God by staying true to what he felt was right. Yet how could he put Anezka, in particular, through the trauma that would inevitably follow for her? His heart was heavy, but he knew he had to remain firm.

'What do you intend to do, Václav?' Stefan asked quietly. 'Is there any possible compromise, or other course of action open to you?'

Both he and Heléna knew what his answer would be, but dreaded hearing it.

'You know I sympathise with your strong stand, Václav, but surely there must be some middle ground, some way of apparently complying, while still maintaining our integrity!' Anezka burst out, her voice trembling, and her face agitated.

Václav was silent, his face marked with pain and grief, but also with firm resolution.

'I will state my case again to the Germans, but remain adamant that none of our companies will ever be involved in producing weapons or military equipment, and certainly never for the German armed forces,' he eventually responded, quietly and grimly. 'May God help us all!'

In the end, the Gestapo offered no compromise. Václav emphatically refused to comply, and was immediately arrested and driven away.

Again through underground contacts, it was discovered days later that, having long been suspected of partisan involvement, he was at first interrogated at length in Prague by the Gestapo with their usual thoroughness, but had refused to speak. He, along with others, had been sighted being roughly bundled into a van, which had been followed to a holding place on the German border. Their likely fate, it was believed, was to provide forced labour for a large armaments factory in the south, near Munich. Václav's own factories were taken over by German personnel, while his farming interests continued to function as well as they could under the supervision of his own loyal staff, who tried their best, but inevitably suffered greatly from the loss of his wise oversight.

Anezka, bowed down with grief, and extremely fearful for Václav's health and safety, almost gave in to despair, staying in her room for hours on end, or wandering alone through the gardens around their home. Heléna was initially able to be with her, since it was her summer break, but could not stay indefinitely. Even though she had no lectures to attend, there was so much to do in preparation for the year ahead, as well as concerts in which she was scheduled to take part. Anezka understood and accepted this.

'I know Václav wouldn't want this to affect your studies any more than it has, dear,' she said softly, her face sad. 'So please, go home to Stefan! You mustn't be separated from him any more than you already are because of his own work commitments.'

No sooner had Heléna returned to Prague, than she heard the not wholly unexpected news of the invasion of Poland by German troops, against the wishes of Britain and France, as well as the Polish people themselves.

War was finally declared.

Weeks passed, during which Anezka slowly regained her emotional and spiritual strength, if not physical, under the watchful eye of their faithful old housekeeper, Berta. Stefan and Heléna travelled down on weekends whenever possible, seeking to help in any way they could.

'It's no trouble,' Heléna quickly assured Anezka, when she voiced her concern. 'In fact, it's wonderful to enjoy the tranquillity of Tábor, after the upheaval in Prague. It seems to be getting worse each day.'

And now there was a further reason that made it advisable for Stefan to visit Tábor regularly. Some months earlier, Václav had told him of a network of underground tunnels that existed beneath the old part of the town – over half a kilometre of them, built during the fifteenth century as places of refuge from the enemy or from natural disasters. Apparently Uncle Erik had known of them for years, and had suggested them as soon as Václav mentioned to him one day the need for suitable hiding places for partisans.

'I can take you there now, if you like,' Uncle Erik had told Václav, becoming more excited by the moment. 'One of the best entrances is via some stairs behind a panel right next to our organ in the village church! I discovered it many years ago, when I was just a young boy playing with my brother one day, while my father practised the organ. We vowed to keep it a secret between us, and I've never shared it with anyone until now!'

At Uncle Erik's suggestion, he and Václav had invited Jiří, one of their old friends, to accompany them. Jiří, also a staunch supporter of the partisans, lived just across the laneway from the church, and that day the three of them had explored the tunnels together.

'Parts of the tunnels are currently used for storage purposes, but from what I saw of them that day, they seemed ideal for any partisans in need of a place to hide. Are you interested in seeing them, Stefan?' Václav had then asked, with a twinkle in his eye.

Stefan was more than interested, as Václav had known he would be. He had only just been told of their existence, but already he was convinced they would prove to be the difference between life and death for many. That afternoon, Václav had taken him to see them, and immediately their potential was obvious to him. After that, whenever they could, he and Václav had explored the tunnels further, managing over time, and through conversations with underground sympathisers who owned businesses in the area, to draw a reasonable map of the tunnel network, and any known exits. Much work still remained to be done, however. Now, aware that Václav had felt this to be his most important contribution towards the underground work and the freedom of his homeland, Stefan was determined to complete the project, working hard on it whenever he was in Tábor.

He missed Václav deeply, almost as much as Anezka and Heléna did, and continued to pursue every avenue and contact he knew in Germany to discover his whereabouts. Then towards the end of September, news finally reached them, in the form of a short note written by Václav himself, and passed faithfully along a trusted chain of partisans and sympathisers stretching from the German border to Prague.

To my dear Anezka, Heléna and Stefan
I am sending this from our camp near the armaments factory where we are forced to work, outside of Munich. I was ill for some time, because of injuries sustained during interrogation, but have now regained strength, although the long hours of work make me very tired. Conditions here are passable, but I miss you all so much! I hope you are well, Anezka. I pray for the day to come soon when I will be able to see you again. May God watch over you and bless you all! Much love,
Václav

Anezka, heartened by his note, and by others received intermittently in the weeks that followed, spent most of the remaining days of summer in a shady corner of their garden waiting and praying – for her beloved Václav, for Tomas and Eva, but also for continued protection for Stefan and Heléna. She aged a great deal, and to Heléna's eyes seemed to have lost even more weight each time they visited, her face and hands appearing almost translucent at times. Yet in the midst of the pain and uncertainty, the strength and fire of her faith continued to hold firm. There was a peace about her, too. It showed in her eyes and on her face – a peace that could only come from her God.

In those first weeks and months after Václav's arrest, Stefan did his best to take work home, and to be away from Prague as little as possible, but eventually he could not ignore the need to attend to business matters elsewhere in the country. During this trip, Heléna's friend Helga from the Conservatorium was invited to keep her company.

'Yes, it's working quite well,' Heléna replied, when Stefan managed to phone her from his hotel.

'You sound a little hesitant – what is it, Heléna?'

'It's nothing to do with Helga's being German, Stefan – she's a true friend, and it's been good to have her company and support, especially because I'm still missing Táta so much. It's just that, while we can usually study well together, it's difficult for both of us to put in the long hours of practice we need. Next time you're away, I think I'll try being by myself again. I'll be fine – I know God will watch over me!'

During the weeks that followed, Heléna soon found this to be true. When Stefan was away, she came to love the quietness, and the healing and release it brought her. Over time, she learnt how to sit still, reflecting in particular on the things of God, until she became deeply conscious of his loving, comforting presence all around her. Often she would reach for her bible and read a passage several times over, sometimes aloud, until it seemed to her that the words were spoken directly into her heart. She would pray earnestly too – for her father in Germany, for her aunt and uncle, for her mother at Tabór, for others she knew of so far from their families, for her homeland, for an end to this whole terrible war. Then eventually, when she sensed the time was right, she would move to the piano, to immerse herself again in her music. Most evenings, she would play Stefan's beautiful piano for around two hours, often including some singing practice as well. Then afterwards, she would drift into a more relaxed mode, playing and singing favourite melodies as they came to mind. Sometimes she would select something light and carefree, or perhaps something dreamy and floating. At other times she preferred something more solid and reflective, even sad or melancholy. Often when Stefan was away, she would find herself concluding with a piece of music she knew they both loved – Tschaikovsky's 'Nur wer die Sehnsucht kennt'. She usually sang it in its original German, feeling the deep passion in the words.

Nur wer die Sehnsucht kennt, weiß, was ich leide!
Allein und abgetrennt von aller Freude ...[2]

The music itself, even apart from the lyrics, appealed very much to her. She loved how, at times, the beautiful melody line wove its way intricately among the powerful chords, yet, at others, flowed along softly and gracefully with quiet dignity, proclaiming its simple message from the heart. She remembered how she had played it at Tábor the night she and Emil had argued, and how Stefan had reached out to her, quietly offering her simple but profound words of comfort.

One evening, as she was again playing this special song, Stefan returned home a little earlier than usual. He entered the study, motioning to her to continue playing, and picked up his cello. Together they played on, neither needing to utter a word. They completed it for the second time, and then sat in silence, heads bowed and lost in the emotion of the moment. Eventually Stefan stirred, put his cello aside, and moved to stand behind Heléna at the piano, putting his hands gently on her shoulders and bending

---

[2] *Only those who know longing, are aware of what I suffer, alone and separated from all joy...*

to kiss her head. Heléna leant back against him, gripping his hands and drawing them down over her heart, as she held them between her own.

'Stefan, this is our special piece of music, isn't it? It's my heart speaking to your heart, and yours speaking to mine, of everything that's within us. Thank you for playing it with me tonight. I can never play it now, or even hear it, without thinking of you.'

For some reason tears began to flow down Heléna's cheeks, as she sat quietly leaning against him. Eventually Stefan felt them fall onto his hands, which Heléna still held tightly. He could feel too the uneven beating of her heart, and the deep emotion stirring within her.

'I love you so much, Heléna!' he responded softly. 'Let's agree now that we'll never play this special music of ours unless we can play it together, just as we did tonight! That way, if I ever hear you playing it by yourself, or if you hear me, then we'll know that something's wrong!'

He moved his hands then, lifting her to her feet and turning her to face him. They clung to each other, and Stefan spoke gently but urgently.

'Heléna, I mean that seriously! If ever there comes a time when I'm home, and for some reason I feel it's unsafe for you to be here, I'll try to play our special music! I believe we're safe, but it's better to have a plan in mind. You know about my involvement with the underground, and that so much is being planned for the days ahead. I pray to God the Germans will never suspect me and come to interrogate me, but we must be prepared! If that ever happens, Heléna – if you ever hear me playing our special music – then don't come up to the apartment! Go home to Tábor as quickly as possible!'

Heléna quivered in his arms. In her heart, she felt Stefan was possibly keeping information from her that he did not wish her to know at this point. She knew him well enough not to question him, but she could not hold back the anguished little cry that escaped her lips, or the tears that began to flow even more.

'I pray that will never happen, Stefan!' she cried, her voice trembling with emotion. 'I love you so much! And I promise I'll do the same for you. If I'm ever here by myself, and the Germans come looking for you, I'll warn you in the same way! And when you hear …'

She could not continue. Stefan hushed her and tried to comfort her.

'Heléna, if the Gestapo ever do come while I'm not home, they'd be unlikely to stay long. Anyway, let's hope and pray it will never happen – that we'll only ever play that piece when we're together!'

When she had settled a little and stopped trembling, they sat together on the lounge for a long time, quietly talking matters over. Eventually, as tiredness engulfed them both, they moved to the bedroom and prepared for a good night of rest and refreshment. But as they lay in each other's arms, their longing for complete union soon took over, banishing any thought of sleep. They made love with a deeper intimacy than ever before, each feeling an urgent need to bring complete fulfilment to the other. Heléna's body ached with desire, as she responded with every fibre of her being to Stefan's lovemaking, returning his kisses with fervent passion. Stefan stroked her and held her close, filled with almost excruciating love for her, marvelling again that such a beautiful, warm human being was his and his alone – such an amazing gift to him! For a brief moment, he contemplated with horror the thought of life without Heléna, of how empty and colourless and devastatingly lonely it would be. With a slight shudder, he quickly pushed such thoughts to the back of his mind. Instead, he chose to savour the present moment with every part of himself – body, soul and spirit.

Chapter Six

As October came, and with it the traditional anniversary celebrations of Czechoslovakia's independence as a nation, Stefan knew he needed to be doubly alert in his underground work. The Germans had deployed extra troops to the capital, to quell any demonstrations or possible uprising, especially as the 28th of that month approached, which they knew was an important National Day for all Czechs. Stefan had been disturbed by proposals made by some of the younger partisans, arguing for a show of force on that day, to wrest control of the country from the Germans, and return it to the Czech people. He had therefore addressed them firmly, but also with sensitivity, knowing that feelings were running high.

'Please know that I do understand how you feel, but I believe nothing will be achieved if we act rashly! Our sources are reliable, and they all tell us we'll easily be overwhelmed!'

'But we can't sit by and do nothing!' many of them, mostly students from Prague University, had argued vehemently. 'Our nation had suffered too much already, with so much of our resources siphoned off for the German war effort! And are we supposed to ignore it when many of our best lecturers are also disappearing before our eyes? It's not only those who've spoken out against the German authorities either who've been removed, but anyone with Jewish blood – the cream of our scholars and teachers! Lately too, anyone supporting communism is quickly silenced by the Gestapo. Where is it all going to end, unless we do something radical – and soon? We think our National

Day would be the perfect time to act!'

Stefan was highly respected as a leader among the partisans, but this time his pleas fell on deaf ears. Later, Heléna and he discussed the situation at length.

'Of course I want to support our underground workers, but this time I really feel it's far too dangerous to take part in any public demonstrations,' Stefan concluded. 'I think the way I can best help is by travelling to Tábor, and stocking the underground tunnels with equipment and food supplies, in readiness for any partisans who may need a safe hiding place. The only problem is ...'

Stefan became silent. An idea had occurred to him, but he was unwilling to put Heléna in any danger.

'The only problem is ... what?' Heléna asked, sensing it was something to do with her.

'I think it will be almost impossible, given the extra troops around, for any partisans to make it to Tábor undetected on the actual day,' he said slowly, in the end. 'However, they might be able to make it here to our apartment, if they're in extreme danger, which would mean you'd need to let them in and look after them for a short time. Then, when it's safe – probably during the night – I could make sure they get safely down to the tunnels, and from there to freedom! But Heléna, this is dangerous business! I really didn't want you involved in any way!'

For some time, Heléna had wanted to help Stefan and his co-workers in what they were doing, despite not being an official member of the underground movement herself, but she had held back, aware that Stefan had wanted her to know as little as possible about the work. Also, she knew the main task God had for her at this time was to focus on her studies and performances. Yet now she clearly sensed God's hand in Stefan's suggestion.

'Stefan, listen to me!' she responded. 'I know it's no light thing to hide anyone from the Gestapo – but it seems so right that I help in this way! In fact, I feel it's the least I can do, given the situation. I know there are risks involved, but I believe God will keep me safe! And in my heart, I feel this would be something Táta would have wanted me to do. He would have been proud to help, so let's begin making plans!'

Stefan held her close, feeling her heart beating fast.

'I love you so much, Heléna!' was all he said.

As well as his work in the tunnels, Stefan's role involved passing on very careful instructions to other key partisan leaders concerning how and where to find him in Tábor if needed, and also how to approach Heléna for help. He had always felt that they could never be completely sure of their neighbours, in the midst of a fairly shifting population in the city, and determined to take extra care, since Heléna would be alone. Code words were arranged, so that anyone greeting Heléna at their door would sound completely natural. As October 28th dawned, Stefan left for Tábor, still with preparations to complete there, and also anxious to avoid any of the violence he felt would inevitably erupt later.

'I must go now, Heléna,' he whispered to her, as she struggled to wake from a deep sleep. 'Be at peace, dear – remember that any partisans who come to the door will know exactly what to say and do. Please don't leave the apartment at all, will you, Heléna, until I get back! Who knows what the mood will be in the streets, and exactly how the Germans will react after today? Promise me you'll stay here quietly, and just be ready to help any partisans who need it! Our country has a big place in my heart, Heléna, but you're more important to me than the whole world!'

He held her close in a long, firm embrace, not wanting to let her go, but knowing it was more than time to leave. Heléna clung to him fiercely in turn, so proud of him, but also wanting so much to protect him and keep him safely with her.

'Stefan, what you're doing today is so important for our people! I'm very proud of you – I love you so much! I'll pray that God will watch over you. Go in his strength! I'll be here when you come back – I love you!'

They parted with heavy hearts. For a while Heléna wandered aimlessly about the apartment, unable to concentrate on her music or on the essay she was currently writing. Finally, she sat down at the piano. Without thinking, her fingers began to play the familiar notes of 'Nur wer die Sehnsucht kennt', until she remembered the agreement she had made with Stefan. Hastily she stopped playing, and a little shiver ran down her spine. She got up and moved restlessly over to where Stefan's cello stood in the corner. Placing her hand on it, the turmoil within her gradually settled, and as she gently smoothed the beautiful wood beneath her fingers, she felt not only Stefan's quiet presence, but also the beautiful, calming reassurance of God around her and within her. She stood still, drinking in the strength that flowed into her, and allowing the peace she felt to settle deep down inside her. Refreshed and renewed, she eventually moved to the piano again and began to attack aggressively the magnificent yet difficult chords of the Chopin Polonaise she was soon due to perform.

The hours passed, as she gravitated from Chopin to Tschaikovsky and from there to her beloved Beethoven. Later, she moved to her desk, soon becoming engrossed in creating interesting harmonies for a folksong melody she dimly remembered from childhood. At one stage in the early afternoon, she thought she heard gunfire in the distance, followed by screams and shouts closer to home, but then all was silent again. Darkness finally fell, and as she sat and ate her solitary dinner, she planned her evening in her mind. Firstly some singing practice, she decided, and then a time of quietness and prayer, followed by some reading, after which she fully expected to fall into a soundless sleep, ready for another busy day of classes.

None of this eventuated, in the end. Soon after nine o'clock, just as Heléna had settled down to read, she heard hurried footsteps on the stairs leading up to their apartment, followed by a loud knocking.

'Who is it?' she asked cautiously, remembering Stefan's instructions.

Immediately two or three voices responded almost in unison, sounding distinctly frightened, but also somewhat defiant.

'It's us – your cousins from Kladno! Sorry we're so late!'

These were the words Heléna had been told to expect. Carefully opening the door, she was greeted by the sight of two obviously exhausted girls, accompanied by a dishevelled young man who appeared to be injured. Quickly Heléna ushered them in, motioning them to be quiet, so as not to disturb the neighbours, particularly the old lady downstairs. As she seated them in the study and provided them with cool drinks, the students briefly introduced themselves, the two girls speaking over the top of each other at times, as they related the day's events in short, jerky sentences.

'We didn't know what to do – it all happened so quickly!' the older one began. 'It started off well this morning, but more and more students kept turning up, and wanted to join in the demonstrations. It just escalated before our eyes! Soon there were ugly confrontations between some of our partisan leaders and the Gestapo. Then violence broke out, and there were injuries on both sides. Even though so many partisans and supporters turned out, it was obvious we were outnumbered, like Stefan warned us we'd be! After a while, we could see that nothing more would be achieved, so we tried to disperse, but the authorities wouldn't let us! We had made our point loud and clear, and they didn't like it one bit! They tried to round us all up, and were determined to teach us all a lesson. They were in no mood to show mercy to anyone, particularly any partisan leaders! We tried to rush them and make a break for it, but they chased us all! We ran as fast as we could, but my brother, Karel, was caught in the middle of the stampede, and twisted his ankle. The windows of some government buildings were smashed, as people tried to get away, and Karel cut himself on broken glass when he fell. When we saw that he was injured, we knew we'd never make it to Tábor without being caught. So we decided to come here!'

'We don't want to bother you in any way, or put you in any more danger than we have already,' the second girl added anxiously. 'We just want to fix up Karel's wounds somehow, and maybe have a shower, and then rest for a few hours. Then we can be on our way to Tábor before dawn tomorrow – that is, if Karel's okay.'

All three were partisan leaders, Heléna discovered, despite their youthful appearance. She did her best to clean and bandage the cuts on Karel's arm, but there was little she could do for his ankle, now bruised and swollen, except to bandage it tightly. The second girl held Karel's hand tightly, as Heléna did her best to treat him. Heléna noticed tears in her eyes, and saw in them the same deep love she felt for Stefan. O God, she prayed silently, keep them safe. Keep us all safe!

Soon the three of them fell into an exhausted sleep. Heléna, determined to give them the best chance of escaping, roused them before dawn with coffee and a simple breakfast. It was not easy for them to slip quietly out of the apartment building in the dark, with Karel trying to keep the weight off his injured foot, but Heléna consoled herself with the thought that most people would still be sleeping soundly at this hour. She closed the door silently after them, pleased she had been able to help, but relieved too that her role was now over. She wondered what Stefan was doing at this hour. She imagined him awake, quietly sending other partisans on their way from Tábor to the next safe place, or perhaps making further preparations to help them lie low in the tunnels until the danger was past. She stood at the window for a while, praying for him, for those whom she had just farewelled, and also for her beloved homeland, caught in the midst of such political madness. She yawned then, suddenly feeling exhausted. The whole experience had drained her, and she had slept for only an hour or two before her alarm had woken her just before dawn. She curled up on their bed, falling asleep again until well into the morning.

When she woke, she endeavoured to continue working as she had the previous day, but found it hard to settle. Then in the early evening, as she was eating dinner, the telephone rang. Heléna breathed a sigh of relief on hearing Stefan's deep voice.

'I'm so glad you're okay, Helena! I can't talk for long, but I wanted to let you know that our cousins from Kladno arrived here safely! I'll be home tomorrow evening, all being well. Take care, Heléna – I love you!'

As he rang off, Heléna moved to the piano again, her spirit singing with mingled joy and relief. Her fingers seemed to fly over the keys, as she embarked upon a particularly exciting and explosive Chopin Mazurka, for the sheer joy of expressing the feelings deep within her. Neither of them knew what the days ahead would hold, but it was enough to know that both of them had made it through, and would soon be together again.

That next evening was a precious, golden time, as they lay in each other's arms once again.

'Heléna, what you did for those three partisans was so valuable,' Stefan said softly. 'I'm so proud of you – and I know your father would be too! He would love to know, I'm sure, how useful the tunnels proved as a hiding place. Everything worked really well, thanks in no small part to Uncle Erik and Jiří's expert knowledge of the area, and their deep commitment to our cause. I hope and pray we get to tell him soon!'

Unfortunately, it was not long before the tunnels were again needed, and the whole emergency process put in place for 28th October had to be repeated. In mid-November, a popular student leader died from wounds he had sustained during the violence in Prague the previous month, and immediately this became the catalyst for even larger demonstrations. The German authorities were ready for them, however, acting quickly and decisively. Hundreds of students and teachers were arrested, along with a large number of politicians unhappy with the German takeover of their government. Many were forced to flee, some again via Stefan and Heléna's apartment.

The most devastating immediate result of this mass cry for justice and freedom was the closure of places of higher learning by the German authorities. Students and teachers from universities and colleges across the country were instead forced to work in factories, mines, or forests, or on farms, either in their homeland or in Germany. Fortunately for Heléna, the doors of the Prague Conservatorium remained open, for the time being at least, largely because political issues were rarely discussed or debated there, either by staff or students. For the most part, music was their whole world, and preparing for their careers paramount in their thoughts, despite the political turmoil around them.

While Heléna endeavoured to continue her studies as usual, Stefan's schedule was even more demanding and chaotic. Not only did he have to deal with more management and personnel issues, given the increased student workforce in some of his factories, but there was also an immediate upsurge in his partisan responsibilities. He worked tirelessly night and day, often travelling to Tábor and beyond after dark, to ensure safe passage for key partisan leaders and others out of the country. He was most concerned, however, in these early weeks of turmoil, at the increasing need to involve Heléna.

'You know I wouldn't wish you to take any part in this underground work, but we seem to have little choice, Heléna! These ones whose lives are in danger need somewhere closer to hide, even if only for a few hours. The Germans are everywhere now, always on a sharp lookout for partisan leaders, or anyone opposing the war effort. And they can be brutal, Heléna – very brutal! So we must be careful, and alert at all times.'

Certainly many who came to the apartment at that time were often traumatised and deeply frightened, despite their outward displays of courage. During their few hours with Heléna, she tried to provide a safe, quiet oasis where they could be refreshed and renewed in their spirits as well as their bodies, at least for a short time. She often played and sang for her visitors, and also prayed for their protection, sometimes aloud as they clasped hands together, in the same way that she and Stefan had prayed with her parents so long ago now, it seemed.

For almost two months, there had been no contact with Václav, and no first hand news of Tomas and Eva. Anezka remained strong in her spirit, and at peace, even in the midst of sadness and loneliness, yet it was apparent to Heléna that she was becoming more and more frail, despite Berta's faithful and loving care. The delicate bone structure of her face and beautiful hands seemed more pronounced, each time she saw her, and Heléna grieved deeply for her.

Christmas came, and with it a brief respite from studies. Stefan's schedule had also become somewhat less frantic, with the completion of the initial reorganisation of his factories, and the momentary lessening of the need for escape routes. He and Heléna travelled to Tábor, each sensing the precious nature of these days together with Anezka and Berta, and other family members and friends. The strict food rationing in force across the country had certainly curtailed the festive menus that Berta had been accustomed to prepare over the years, and the circle of family and friends able to share in their celebrations was noticeably smaller. Nevertheless, their fellowship was as warm and as strong as ever, and even more meaningful, given the turbulence of the times. At the beginning of their special dinner on Christmas evening, Anezka asked Stefan to say grace, and to remember those unable to be present with them. As Stefan prayed, mentioning in particular Václav, and Tomas and Eva, Heléna laid her hand over her mother's, feeling her tremble, and aching to comfort her. Anezka smiled into her daughter's eyes after Stefan had finished, and gently squeezed her hand.

'I know your father would wish this time to be as festive as possible,' she said firmly to Heléna, before turning to the others seated around the table, and continuing bravely. 'So let's enjoy this special evening, and be glad that God has enabled us all to share it together!'

After dinner, they gathered around the grand piano and sang carols, a family tradition for as long as Heléna could remember. They sorely missed Václav's beautiful, rich tenor voice, but Stefan and Uncle Erik endeavoured to make up for that by extending their baritone voices to the limit. Then Heléna played for them. She put her whole heart and soul into giving of her best for these ones who meant so much to her, especially Uncle Erik, sitting so erect as she played, still so proud of his star pupil. She could not help thinking how much older he looked, and wondered if this was the result of the extra responsibilities and interrupted nights of the previous weeks spent helping Stefan. Suddenly, anger fuelled her emotions as she played, her fingers attacking the difficult Beethoven chords with unusual ferocity. She was aware of a great rage within her, that such weariness and suffering should have to be borne by these ones so close to her. And then, even as she came to a calmer, quieter section of the music, her rage dissipated, replaced instead by a deep sadness that was not lost on those listening.

As Heléna finished playing, there was a lengthy silence. She looked around, and noticed a number of their guests surreptitiously wiping away tears, while others were letting them flow unchecked.

'That is the best I've ever heard you play, my dear!' Uncle Erik said gruffly, his own eyes decidedly moist. 'May God protect and preserve the precious gift he's given you, to be able to express through your music the things that are in your heart!'

Stefan moved over to the piano and stood beside her, his arm around her shoulders.

'Wonderful, Heléna!' he said softly, as he bent to kiss her, before turning and addressing the guests. 'Let's drink one last toast together to Heléna and her future career, to our hostess Anezka, and especially to Václav, wherever he may be this evening. May

God bring you home soon, my friend!'

On New Year's Day, Stefan and Heléna celebrated their first wedding anniversary. They had been with Anezka since Christmas, but had decided to return, just for two nights, to the cottage where they had spent their idyllic honeymoon. While the farm itself had been under much more intense cultivation during the past year, because of the food needed for the war effort, the cottage was still just as cosy and welcoming. Stefan and Heléna revelled in being able to relax together in their quiet, snow-covered surroundings, far removed from the pressures of the outside world.

'God has been so gracious to us this past year, don't you think, Stefan?' Heléna reflected, as they sat curled up together in front of the crackling fire, on their second evening away. 'He's sustained us both through some stretching times, but I feel I've grown so much in the process!'

'I know I have,' Stefan agreed, 'and I think it's also brought us so much closer as a couple. No doubt our next year of marriage will contain as many, if not more challenges, whether the war ends soon or not, but I know we can still continue to trust God, whatever happens. Let's agree to commit ourselves fully to him again, Heléna, and to each other – forever!'

That night, as Stefan gazed at Heléna, he was deeply stirred again by her beauty and intelligence, and amazing giftedness. Yet there, shining in her eyes, he clearly saw her love for him, and was filled afresh with great gratitude to God.

For Heléna, she knew without a doubt that Stefan was her hero, her rock, so courageous and upright, so capable himself, and yet so humbly supportive of her in all her endeavours. She felt so blessed – so very blessed and happy. Suddenly she thought of Anezka, separated from Václav, the man she loved with all her heart. She could not envisage such a separation from her beloved Stefan – she did not want even to think about it. At that moment, she felt her mother's pain as never before – the deep pain of not knowing how her father was, of being unable to communicate with him.

Stefan noticed the shadow that passed across her face, and the sudden clouding in her eyes.

'What is it, dear?' he asked gently, drawing her to him. 'Are you thinking of your father and mother?'

As always, Heléna was amazed at how deeply Stefan understood her and sensed what was happening for her. She nodded, holding him fiercely to her as if she would never let go. Stefan felt the fear in her – fear, he knew, that they too would be separated, as her parents had. Quietly he suggested, after a little while, that they pray together.

'O God, grant us your peace, as we face the year ahead. We ask for your hand of protection upon us, and for wisdom for us both. Above all, we ask for an end to this war that has brought so much pain to so many. We commit Václav and Anezka to you especially at this time. Bring your healing to them both, Lord. Comfort and strengthen them, and may your peace be upon them. Amen.'

Soon after, they reluctantly left the cottage, intending to return for one final meal with Anezka and Berta before heading back to Prague. As they arrived at the house, Berta came to greet them, a worried look on her face.

'Heléna, I'm so sorry, but your mother is not at all well. The doctor came yesterday, but he says there's nothing more we can do! He'll be coming back soon – perhaps you can see her for a little while before he arrives. I'm so sorry!'

Stefan stopped to comfort the distraught old lady, while Heléna hurried immediately to Anezka's bedroom. She found her mother sitting half propped up in bed, her breathing quite laboured and her skin grey in colour. Her eyes were dull, but when she saw Heléna, a small spark of life returned to them, and she smiled her usual beautiful smile. Heléna moved swiftly across to her, wanting to know what was happening, but also aware that it was probably better for Anezka not to talk much. She kissed her mother and grasped her hand, feeling the cold clamminess of her skin beneath her own warm fingers.

'I'm so sorry we weren't here,' Heléna whispered brokenly to her mother. 'Berta says the doctor will be coming again soon. Don't talk – just rest! I'll stay right beside you here.'

Minutes passed, during which Heléna felt she could hardly bear the agony of hearing Anezka struggle for breath. Little beads of perspiration gathered on her mother's upper lip, so Heléna gently sponged her face and hands. She could not have been more relieved when the doctor at last entered the room, accompanied by Stefan and Berta. Dr Novak, a tall, thin man in his late fifties, with slightly stooped shoulders and sparse greying hair, had attended the family for years, and his medical knowledge and experience were second to none. Now he looked searchingly at Anezka as he took her pulse, catching Stefan's eye briefly before turning to Heléna.

'My dear, I'm sorry, but there's nothing more we can do for your mother here in Tábor. I did suggest yesterday that it might be possible for her to be admitted to a good hospital I know in Prague, but she was quite emphatic that she wished to stay here. I fear it might be somewhat overcrowded there now, since I understand it has largely been taken over by the German authorities to treat their own wounded, but they do at least have equipment that could make your mother a little more comfortable. My good friend is still the senior medical officer there, and I can contact him, should you be able to persuade her to change her mind. At the same time, I do understand fully her wish to remain here quietly at home.'

The doctor then took Stefan aside to explain further details of Anezka's condition to him, while Heléna again sat close to her mother, willing her to breathe more easily, and wanting to hear any slight whisper she may make. Eventually she seemed to drift off into a rather restless sleep, and Heléna moved to join the two men.

'Of course, moving her at this point does have its dangers,' the doctor was in the process of explaining, 'and then the treatment hopefully available to her at the hospital would simply delay the inevitable, I'm afraid – probably by only a matter of days.'

Stefan gripped Heléna's hand tightly as she began to comprehend fully what Dr Novak had just said. He hated to see the stricken look in her eyes, and guessed what was uppermost in her mind, before she even spoke.

'If only my father were here!' she finally burst out in an anguished voice, as tears welled up in her eyes and began to course down her cheeks. 'They were so close! It's been so very difficult for her these past few months, being separated from him, and not knowing exactly how he is!'

Stefan held her to him, feeling the tremors run through her body. He knew and shared at least something of the anguish inside her, having lost both parents, and had also come to love and respect Anezka and Václav deeply himself. Many times he had contemplated attempting to make his way into Germany to where Václav was most likely being held, and, with the help of partisan friends, trying to bring him home. But even as it entered his mind again, he knew it was impossible. Border crossings were extremely difficult, especially for someone as well known to the Gestapo as Václav, and also, Stefan suspected, as he himself by now. And it would no doubt be very difficult, if not impossible, to penetrate the labour camp where he was being held. It was only as Václav and the others with him were marched each day to the nearby munitions factory that there had ever been opportunity for the partisans to receive notes from the Czech prisoners. Even that was extremely dangerous, having to be carried out right under the watchful eye of the ever-present guards. Besides, Stefan was deeply concerned at this point about Václav's own state of health. Nothing had been heard from him for some time, and Stefan's underground connections had not sighted him at all in recent days.

Soon the doctor left them to make their decision together, and to attend to other calls. Stefan and Heléna returned to sit quietly by Anezka's bedside. They did not speak, but simply prayed silently for her, and for wisdom to know what was best.

In the end, the decision was made for them. Towards the middle of the afternoon, Anezka stirred, and opened her eyes, recognising them immediately, and smiling her sweet smile again. As Heléna tried to offer her some of the soup Berta had brought, she shook her head slightly, and then seemed to lapse into semi-consciousness. Her breathing was less laboured now, probably as a result of the medication given her by the doctor. It was so quiet that Heléna could not keep herself from checking to see the slight rise and fall of Anezka's chest, as she lay on her side now, curled up like a little child. Eventually her eyes opened again, and she looked straight into Heléna's, as she sat nearby holding her hand. Suddenly she began speaking quite urgently, her voice soft, but surprisingly clear.

'Heléna, I've just had such a wonderful dream! I was playing some of my special

Mozart pieces on our piano, thinking I was by myself. And then when I looked around, there was Václav – and someone else beside him with the most beautiful face, and their faces were shining with happiness and with love for me! They were both applauding loudly, and then I saw that there were beautiful angels all around them – row upon row of them! They were clapping and were all so joyful, as if they were welcoming me somehow. And then the man with Václav stood up and walked towards me – and I saw it was Jesus! Heléna, I so much want to go with him now!'

At that moment her face lit up with joy and her hand tightened as it clasped Heléna's, and then suddenly relaxed its grip. As Heléna cried out, a look of absolute peace and relief came over Anezka's face, and Stefan and Heléna knew immediately that she was gone.

They sat together in silence for some time, each unwilling to move from what seemed to them a holy place, a place which God had touched in a special way, as he had welcomed Anezka into his eternal presence. They felt his peace around them, but also incredible sadness and loss in their hearts. Eventually Stefan stirred and slowly stood up.

'I'll go and get Berta, Heléna,' he whispered softly. 'She'll know what to do for your mother. I'll also let Dr Novak know. Stay here a while, if you wish, dear.'

Heléna sat quietly in her parents' bedroom, letting the tears flow freely. So many long forgotten memories began to surface in her mind. Memories of her mother looking so young and beautiful, playing for her brother Andrej and her, as they sat beside her on the piano stool. The sound of her mother's broken-hearted sobbing, when Andrej's short life had finally ebbed away, her arms around his little white coffin, unwilling to let it go. Her mother's hand holding hers when, as a little girl, she had skipped along beside them to church on a Sunday morning. The many wonderful gatherings of family and friends she had presided over in their home. And the most frequent picture of all, her mother sitting quietly in an armchair in the far corner of the music room, listening as Heléna played the piano, always smiling her encouragement, always gently putting her arm around Heléna's shoulders afterwards, and saying to her: 'So beautiful!'

Two days later, Anezka's funeral took place in the old village church, with many friends attending, despite the difficult times. Uncle Erik again played the organ, but even in the midst of her own grief, Heléna could not help noticing the added stoop to his shoulders, and the tears that he did not even bother to hide as he played. He remembered Anezka as he had first met her, so young and talented and vibrant, thrilling audiences in Prague with her beautiful playing, in the days before she fell in love with Václav. And then as he played he thought of Václav, at that moment somewhere near Munich, unaware of his wife's death, exhausted and unwell. Perhaps the only thing keeping his friend going was the hope of soon being reunited with his beloved Anezka, his special life partner, the one who had always been waiting for him whenever he returned to Tábor. But she would not be there this time, when he eventually came home. Or was it *if* he came home? He did not want to think about such a possibility, however. Tears blurred his vision, so that he could barely see the keyboard in front of him as he played.

The following week, after Stefan and Heléna had done all they could at Tábor for the moment, in the way of finalising matters, sorting through Anezka's personal possessions, and, in general, giving themselves time to come to grips with their grief, they returned to Prague, leaving Berta in charge of the family home. Soon, her daughter, Simona, and young child would be joining her, while Simona's husband was away, having been conscripted to work for the German army. For Stefan, there was much to attend to at his factories, as well as in his underground work. And for Heléna too, life had to go on. She grieved deeply, but knew that her mother would want her to continue to give of her best in her studies and performances. Anezka had believed in her daughter implicitly, and Heléna would endeavour, with all her heart, to honour the faith she had shown in her.

Then, while Stefan was attending a meeting late on the Saturday evening, a small package with a note attached from an underground member across the border near Munich was passed on to him. Stefan opened it with a feeling of dread.

To Stefan

I am sorry, but I have to tell you that it appears your friend Václav is now dead. For weeks, I looked out for him but did not see him. Then I enquired as discreetly as possible, but the other Czech labourers all told me the same thing. It seems he never really recovered from wounds received when he was first arrested, and died one night in his sleep. Apparently he knew he did not have long, and asked one of the other workers to try to get a note home to his wife. I have enclosed this, along with his watch and family photo. I have done my best – I am sorry.   *Viktor*

Sick at heart, Stefan returned home in the early hours of Sunday morning, not to sleep, but to sit and watch Heléna as she slept, and to pray for her. Finally, when the first rays of the sun shone in at their bedroom window, he gently woke her to tell her the news of her father's death.

In the midst of her grief, as Heléna lay in Stefan's arms, her head cradled over his heart, she whispered brokenly to him.

'Now at least I understand what that dream really meant – why Máma saw Táta sitting with Jesus, so enjoying her music, so happy to welcome her. He truly was there already, Stefan – he was there waiting for her!'

Torrents of tears followed, but along with the grief eventually came comfort and assurance from God for Heléna that her parents were indeed together, and that their suffering was over. They were now whole. They were free in every way. Heléna determined deep in her heart that the life each of these beautiful people had given her would be pursued with courage and strength in God, and that the things they had taught her and the many opportunities they had given her to develop her gifts, would not be wasted. Together with Stefan, she would make a difference in a world that was broken, beginning in their beloved homeland, where right now freedom was denied to so many.

Chapter Seven

Three weeks passed – weeks during which Heléna chose to skip lectures, and one or two rehearsals, preferring to stay at home alone with her grief, playing the piano whenever she felt able. At first, studying and writing were beyond her – she could not summon the energy to fight her way through the fog that seemed to cloud her brain and dull her mind. Even prayer was difficult, despite the fact that she knew God was with her, and understood her pain. Stefan did his best to be home early each evening, sitting for hours with her in front of the fire, holding her, praying for her. Her friend Helga visited, bringing flowers and little treats, eventually sharing with her any interesting pieces of news that she felt Heléna would enjoy hearing about her fellow students. Other friends came too, some from partisan circles, some from the church fellowship where she and Stefan met each Sunday, when they were at home in Prague. And gradually, through the care shown by those around her, and through the loving-kindness and comfort of God, the light began to break through the fog, and she felt her spirit slowly coming to life again. By the fourth week, Heléna knew it was time to try to pick up the threads of her life, in some measure at least, despite her deep sadness, and to try to move on in God's strength.

She was not alone in experiencing such grief, she knew. So many families were being torn apart at this time, so many were in pain throughout their homeland. Some students at the Conservatorium had had to curtail their studies and return home, because of the death or arrest of a parent, and others, because their families could no longer support them financially. Heléna recognised God's hand of mercy and healing on her, even in the challenge of having to apply herself once again to her studies, and she was thankful – thankful to be continuing, and thankful for the focus her studies gave her, in the midst of the sadness and loss all around. And as she immersed herself again in her music, pouring her energies into producing almost flawless performances, her grief gradually became a little more bearable.

She was glad too when the winter months ended. With the coming of spring, all around her she could see the promise of new life, even in the midst of death and the chaos of war. The window boxes of many of the old apartment buildings near where they lived were soon filled with a riot of colour, and children began to venture outside a little more, as the weather became milder. And a busy concert season was soon in progress, despite wartime restrictions. Most of the public concerts were well attended, not only by the many music lovers of Prague, but also by the German armed forces occupying the country. Stefan made it a priority to attend whenever he could, always so proud of Heléna, as he watched her walk gracefully onto the platform, and listened to her play so passionately and exquisitely.

'Your parents would have been so proud of you tonight, Heléna!' Stefan said without thinking, after one very memorable performance. 'Your mother in particular would have so enjoyed witnessing the success you're beginning to have!'

Tears filled Heléna's eyes at his words. Stefan, immediately apologetic, reached out to comfort her, but Heléna smiled at him, despite the tears.

'It's all right, Stefan – it's good to talk about it, and I realise you miss them too. You know, this may sound strange, but lately, at the end of each performance, somehow I've felt that Máma is indeed right there beside me, with her arm around my shoulders, just as she used to do at home in Tábor. Sometimes I think I even hear her speaking softly to me, saying "So beautiful!" – just as she so often did! And sometimes too, when I finish playing, I see Táta's face, smiling and nodding with such pride and enjoyment! I think it's God's doing, Stefan – I know he understands and wants to comfort me.'

Heléna was indeed beginning to gain recognition and acclaim. She was still only a student, with much to learn, but her city had now begun to embrace her as a bright star of the future. While around her in the world chaos reigned, Heléna could feel a glimmer of hope that she and Stefan would see it through, under God's hand, and that better days would come. Now, as she neared the end of the second year of her course, she worked even harder, supported strongly by Stefan each step of the way, secure in his love, and strengthened so much by his faith in her, as well as their mutual faith in God.

Stefan continued to spend most of his days trying to solve personnel and production problems at many of his factories across the country. Although under strong pressure from the German authorities, with increasingly impossible levels of output expected, and no choice but to comply, he worked tirelessly to keep staff morale high, personally meeting with many of his people, and encouraging them as best he could. Underground work continued to place demands on his time also, with escape routes constantly needing to be activated for any who fell foul of the Gestapo. There had been something of a lull in arrests of underground members and other dissidents since the November riots, but the German authorities remained alert for any who might cause trouble.

At regular intervals, Stefan and Heléna's apartment was still required as a halfway house, for those who could not quickly make it out of the city. These ones who were wanted by the Gestapo, both young and old, courageous even as they fled, yet also often exhausted and traumatised, always received a warm and compassionate welcome. Then, usually in the small hours of the morning, they would be off again, silently creeping down the stairs to make their way to the tunnels at Tábor, and from there travel further south, and eventually to Switzerland. Stefan did all he could to avoid using their apartment, often choosing instead to drive or at least accompany those needing help in getting to Tábor, returning home exhausted in the early hours of the morning. Anything, rather than endanger Heléna.

The work was risky, he was well aware, and becoming more and more so, as the days went by. In the past, other partisans had been available to undertake such tasks for him, but now, as the war continued to escalate through the summer months and then on into autumn, their numbers had gradually dwindled. By Christmas of 1940, many of Stefan's most able partisan colleagues had been arrested and transported to distant destinations as forced labour. Yet always there were new recruits volunteering to take their place – young men and women whose study plans had been put on hold by the closure of the universities, and who were now eager to resist those who had enforced such unwanted changes in their lives. Training these new partisans had now become Stefan's main task. The responsibility he carried was enormous, and his workload huge, but he was a natural leader, regarding obstacles as challenges to be overcome, rather than insurmountable difficulties. Besides, he was determined to see things through to the very end, giving it every ounce of energy he had.

That Christmas, with both needing at least a few days' break, Stefan and Heléna decided, albeit with mixed feelings, to drive to Tábor and celebrate this time quietly with Berta and her daughter Simona and her family. As they stood in the little church on Christmas morning, singing the familiar old carols, Heléna felt deeply sad, despite the joyful music around her. She remembered how they had stood in that very same place two years before, with Václav nearby joining in with his beautiful harmonies. Last year he had been missing from his usual place next to Anezka, and they had all prayed for him, that somehow his Christmas Day would hold some special moments, even though they were apart. Now this year, there was no Václav, and no Anezka. The tears flowed, and Stefan, noticing this, placed his arm around her and held her firmly against him. She rested her head on his shoulder, a great wave of sadness engulfing her, as the sound of the voices around her swelled. Through her tears, her eyes caught a glimpse of the dark wooden cross on the chapel wall, standing out starkly against its white background. Here they were together, she reflected, celebrating the birth of the one who had come down from heaven to be born in human form. He had given away the glory that was his, and taken the form of a servant, experiencing the deepest pain and grief possible, the sinless one dying for the sinful.

'Dear Jesus,' her heart cried out, 'you know what this pain in me is like! You endured so much grief and agony! And even now your heart is bleeding, as you see the suffering in your broken world, in your children who've turned their faces from you! Jesus, I choose to walk with you through my pain – I choose to trust you, even when I can't understand, because I know you've walked this way before, and you choose to walk beside me now, comforting me and strengthening me!'

Even as her eyes remained gazing at the cross, her ears began to take in the words being sung around her.

Hail, the heav'n born Prince of Peace! Hail, the Sun of Righteousness!
Light and life to all He brings, ris'n with healing in His wings...

Silently she stood breathing in the life of God and his healing power, taking it deep into her very soul. She felt she had climbed an incredibly high mountain during the past year, but also that she been strengthened beyond measure, shaped through these experiences for whatever lay ahead. As the carol ended, she smiled mistily at Stefan and squeezed his hand, letting him know that, despite everything, all was well, as he had once told her, and all manner of things would indeed be well.

They had invited a small number of friends and relatives for Christmas dinner that evening. While Berta was again unable to prepare her usual festive food, given the increased wartime rationing, her ingenuity and hard work still produced a truly delicious meal. It was a special delight to welcome Simona's husband, Jan, who had managed to obtain a few days' leave from the mechanical work he had been conscripted to do, servicing German army vehicles. Jan was overjoyed to be there, not only because it was Christmas, but also because he was able to hold his new baby daughter Kristina, now two months old, for the very first time. Alongside Jan and his wife, Simona, and their elder daughter, Anna, at the dinner table were Uncle Erik and his sister, Edita, and also his old friend, Jiří, with whom Stefan had played chess on many evenings, while mapping the underground tunnels. Jiří's cottage was well positioned, being so close to the church, and their games of chess had provided the perfect cover for such activity.

This year, Heléna's cousin, Edvard, Tomas and Eva's son, and his wife, Judith, had also joined them, an unusual occurrence even in peacetime, since Edvard worked as an engineer for a mining exploration company and was often stationed in remote places.

Recently, however, his company had recalled him to oversee the search for alternate fuel supplies closer to home. Heléna was especially glad they had been able to come, since she had not seen him for so long, and had never met his English wife. At the same time, their presence was a strong reminder of Tomas and Eva's absence, and that no news of them had been received for some time.

As the meal progressed, conversation soon turned to issues related to the war. Everyone hoped that hostilities would end soon, but were extremely sceptical, fearing that the nation would be milked dry of resources, before Germany and its allies would either be victorious or surrender. Edvard, having seen much of what was happening worldwide in previous months, was particularly negative about the future for their homeland.

'I don't want to depress you on this festive day, of all days,' he commented, 'but Judith and I plan to migrate after the war, and raise a family somewhere far away from Europe. I love my homeland, but things will be very difficult here over the next few years, I believe. We've seen many different parts of the world, and certainly wouldn't want to settle in some places we've visited! However, there are others where we feel there'd be great opportunity to build a new and better life. We're thinking of Canada or America, or maybe even Australia – who knows as yet? Perhaps my parents may join us too, when this is all over. It would mean a new start for them late in life, but they're adventurous! Or maybe they'll prefer to go to my sister, Maria, in New Zealand. She tells us that some parts of the South Island aren't so different from our mountain regions here, although not quite as cold.'

There was a moment's surprised silence, followed by a babble of conversation, as each responded in different ways. Jan was the first to comment.

'We're of one mind, then, Edvard – I heartily agree with all you've said! Of course, unlike you, Simona and I have no first hand knowledge of anywhere else, since we've had no opportunity to travel. We've discussed this together, and also with Berta, and we feel that we too will make a fresh start somewhere else when the war's over. Hopefully others we know from here will join us, and we can make a new beginning together. As you say, who knows what the future will hold? Even yet some of us may have no choice in the matter, if we value our lives and those of our families. A speedy escape may be our only option!'

While Jan smiled ruefully as he uttered these words, everyone knew he was not joking. At first, being a committed partisan like Stefan, his conversations that evening with Edvard and Judith had been somewhat guarded, since he was unsure how sympathetic they were towards the underground movement. He had soon been reassured, however, by a word from Stefan, that Edvard held similar views to his freethinking parents, and was totally sympathetic to the partisans. Jan's final comments, then, did not surprise any of those present.

On the other hand, the bulk of what both he and Edvard had said did indeed raise some eyebrows. Uncle Erik, for one, seemed distinctly shocked and disapproving.

'I'm surprised you can talk so lightly of leaving your homeland!' he said vehemently, glaring at them from under his bushy eyebrows. 'This is my country, I am Czech, I have lived here for a long time, and I will die here! I have performed in many of our best concert halls and our grandest churches, and the history of this place is part of me – it's who I am! I would never want to live out my life anywhere else but in my homeland!'

His eyes had filled with tears, and he raised a shaky hand to his face to wipe them away with his handkerchief. His sister Edita, while placing a hand on her brother's arm to soothe him, nodded her agreement, as did his old friend, Jiří. Eventually Berta spoke up.

'I understand how you feel. I'm only a little younger than you are, Erik, and I've lived here all my life, never travelling anywhere else. I love this place with all my heart, but things have changed so much! Should it become even more different, and we can't live as we would choose, then I'm prepared to follow my children and grandchildren wherever they feel God is leading them!'

Heléna's eyes met Stefan's, and he knew immediately, by her pleading expression, that she felt enough had been said on the subject. They themselves had talked about similar things only recently, but Heléna had become very emotional, feeling she did not want to experience any more loss at that point. Now Stefan nodded reassuringly at Heléna, quickly intervening in the lively discussion that had followed Berta's comment.

'Heléna and I have also talked recently about our future, but we feel that while we can dream about what might lie ahead, for us our lives here and now demand all the energy and commitment we have! We pray that God will continue to give us the strength to do what he has called us to do, and that we'll hear his voice, as he guides us day by day. Should he want to lead us out from this place, I believe he'll show us clearly at the right time. Remember what he said a long time ago – *'there is a time for everything, and a season for every activity under heaven: a time to be born and a time to die, a time to plant and a time to uproot ...'*? So let's be thankful that tonight we can be together and share this special evening, even though there may be uncertainty ahead!'

Everyone seemed to relax then, each agreeing with Stefan, and each happy to enjoy this moment given to them. And while Uncle Erik was a little quieter for the rest of the meal, he nevertheless joined in the singing and the general fun and laughter with goodwill, after they had moved to the music room. Heléna again treated their guests to a special performance, playing selections from works she was currently practising for a New Year concert in Prague. Much later, when farewells were finally being said, she felt compelled to give Uncle Erik an especially warm hug and kiss.

'We love you so much, Uncle Erik! Thank you again for all you've done for me! People like you have made our country as strong and resilient as it is. It would take a lot to persuade me to call somewhere else home!'

On New Year's Day, the first day of 1941, Stefan and Heléna chose to celebrate their second wedding anniversary with a quiet dinner at the little restaurant near the Charles Bridge owned by Stefan's old friend, Wilhelm. They had no time to go away, since Heléna was in the midst of preparations for the Conservatorium's special concert series featuring its most gifted students, while Stefan was occupied with strategic planning for the year ahead. That evening, they found the restaurant quieter than usual. Rationing had seriously affected such businesses, they knew, but soon after being greeted warmly by Wilhelm, they discovered a further reason.

'I'm sorry to have to tell you this, on such a happy occasion for both of you, but around four months ago, Axel was conscripted into the German army. We would have let you know, Stefan, as you and he were so close at university, but he told us not to tell you. I think he felt ashamed that he'd be fighting against friends like you. Then a month ago, we received news that he's been listed as missing in action, after a British bombing raid on the town where he was stationed. Unfortunately we've heard nothing since, and my wife isn't coping well, so I haven't been able to open my restaurant as much. But it's so good to see you here tonight! I hope you have a very enjoyable evening!'

Heléna noticed the lines of worry and grief that had appeared on Wilhelm's face since they had last seen him, and felt deeply sorry for him. She felt even sadder when, later in the evening, she noticed tears in his eyes, as he played his violin for them. As the beautiful notes of his favourite 'Träumerei' died away, he lifted his head, looked directly at them, the only customers in his restaurant by then, and spoke with difficulty.

'My son loved the violin, so I feel close to him when I play, even though it's hard. If he's dead, then I play my best in honour of him. And if, please God, he's still alive, then somehow I feel that my playing will comfort him and make him strong – and bring him back to us!'

He wept openly then, and Heléna could hardly swallow because of the lump in her throat. Stefan put his arm around the man's shoulders, gently comforting him.

'It is a very hard time for you – a hard time for us all, whether we're Czech or German. Let's all pray that this madness will soon end, and that we can live together in peace, as the brothers and sisters we truly are! You always treated me like your own son and welcomed me into your family, and I'll never forget that. Please know that we'll continue to pray for Axel's safety, and for you all!'

Stefan hugged him close, and he and Heléna then left the restaurant. As they walked beside the river before returning to their apartment, they could not help reflecting on Wilhelm's pain and grief.

'So many lives, on both sides of this war, will have been changed forever, won't they, Stefan?' Heléna said with a deep sigh, as they leant together on a wall overlooking the river below. 'So much heartache, so much unnecessary pain and loss!'

'Yes – and I believe there's more to come yet, unfortunately. That's why, Heléna, you must continue playing your music, touching and healing people's hearts with its beauty. It's a wonderful gift from God, and our world needs it so desperately! It's like a language that goes beyond the mind and speaks into our very souls. Whatever happens to me, you must continue – promise me that!'

They clung to each other for a long moment, each feeling a strange mixture of love and pain deep within them. Finally Heléna spoke in a muffled voice, as she rested her head on Stefan's coat.

'I can only promise I'll try my best, Stefan, but I need you beside me so much! So don't let's even think of anything happening to you!'

She lifted her head then, and, looking up into his eyes, strove for a lighter tone in her voice, in an effort to dispel the rather melancholy mood that had engulfed them both. Kissing him lightly, she continued on a more teasing note.

'After all, where would I be without you to tell me all the time that I'm the most beautiful and talented woman in the whole world?'

As the snow began to fall lightly around them, they made their way arm in arm to their car, and back to their warm apartment. Stefan put some soft music on their old gramophone, and they were soon in each other's arms, the love on their faces clearly evident in the soft glow of the candles Heléna had lit. Presently, as the romantic mood of the evening began to envelope them totally, the reality of the outside world, and the sadness that had touched them earlier receded, and they moved slowly towards the bedroom, lost in each other's love. Nothing could take that from them this night, as they marked the end of their second year together.

Later, Stefan lay awake for some time, looking down at Heléna, asleep in his arms. He wondered what the next year would contain for them both. Much hard work, no doubt, much growth through the difficult times in which they were living, but also much fulfilment – for Heléna in particular, he felt. They had decided that they would not start a family until Heléna had finished her studies, and had made at least some inroads into trying to establish herself as a concert artist. As Stefan lay there, he quietly breathed a prayer in his heart for her. Lord, whatever happens to me this year, please protect her and keep her close to you! Be to her both father and mother, providing, comforting, caring for her in every way. Please help her to be all you have purposed her to be, in your way and in your time!

Stefan knew he could trust God, and entrust Heléna to him. He felt he was ready to step out into the year ahead, fully committed to do the things God had for him to do. Yet as he lay in the dark, he felt that he would need every ounce of courage that God could supply. Better not to imagine what might happen, he told himself. Better not to think too far ahead, but rather to take one day at a time. As Heléna stirred, he kissed her gently, and rolled over himself. Help me to keep my eyes on you, Lord, he whispered, more as a reminder to himself than as a prayer. A moment later, he was asleep, as if already aware how much he needed to conserve his strength for the months ahead.

For some weeks, Stefan had been unable to discover any further news of Tomas and Eva, via his underground sources. By the end of February, he was beginning to suspect the worst, but did not convey this to Heléna, since he was reluctant to burden her unnecessarily. She, along with her fellow students, had been so focused on preparing for their concert series, that she had not realised what this silence might mean. Then late one evening, after a particularly successful concert, she and Stefan had returned home to find Edvard waiting for them.

'I wanted to come and break our news personally to you, Heléna, rather than telephone,' he began immediately. 'For some time after Máma and Táta were arrested and taken to Germany, I received news of them through engineering contacts of mine. I hadn't heard anything for weeks, and wondered what was happening. Then, only today, I discovered that they both died over a month ago!'

Eduard's voice faltered at that point, but he continued bravely.

'They were killed while asleep one night in their quarters near the munitions factory. The Ruhr area is obviously now a prime target, and this night, there was apparently a particularly daring and successful bombing raid by the British, ironically enough. Unfortunately, many innocent people like my parents have now lost their lives,' he concluded bitterly, his shoulders now shaking with sobs, as he buried he face in his hands.

Stefan tried to comfort, but Heléna was devastated. Two such intelligent, beautiful people, so dear to her, and with so much still to give, now gone – wiped out in a moment, in a place where they had not deserved to be! In the days ahead, Heléna grieved deeply, but knew at the same time, that she had to remain focused on her final concerts. Edvard had told them that he and Judith wanted to leave his parents' home as it was, at least until they decided where they themselves would live after the war, so as soon as Helena was able, she went alone to the empty house to say her own special goodbyes.

She quietly let herself in, wandering slowly from room to room. Eventually she reached the sitting room, where she and her aunt and uncle had held so many lively discussions on all sorts of topics. She walked over to the old piano that she had played so often, gently touching the keys, as the memories came flooding back. Then finally she climbed the stairs to the small bedroom that had been hers during her school terms – the place where she had dreamed many dreams, and studied for so many hours. At last, sensing she had completed what she needed to do, she stood in the hallway, saying a mental goodbye to Tomas and Eva, thanking God for all they had meant to her, and for the rich times spent in their home. She knew her visit had been significant, yet as she closed the front door, a great wave of devastation swept over her. Oh God, her heart cried out, how many more times am I going to have to say goodbye to those I love? How many more of the relationships that mean so much to me will be destroyed?

As spring arrived once again, Heléna barely had time to notice the flowers coming into bloom in the window boxes nearby, and neither she nor Stefan could spare any weekends from their busy schedule to visit to her old home at Tábor. Stefan was often away, reorganising production in his factories, as greater pressure was put on him by the Germans. More and more, he was forced to consult with German government supervisors before any changes could be put into effect, so that his patience was tested to the limit. Then, as the summer months arrived, his underground work also increased significantly, as their homeland became even more politically unstable. Key government leaders known to him began fearing not only loss of power and position, but also loss of their very lives.

The situation also worsened in the capital's cultural circles, with difficulties surfacing even at the Conservatorium. While Heléna still greatly enjoyed her course, despite the challenges and long hours involved, she found herself looking forward to finishing at the end of June. These days, her beloved piano teacher Alexandr, fearful for his future, had redoubled his efforts to teach his best students all he could, but this was obviously taking its toll. He rarely slept much at nights, and hardly ever sat still, often pacing the floor as Heléna played, his slight frame almost reduced to skin and bone.

'We've heard in our synagogue meetings about new policies that will mean disaster for my people,' he explained to Heléna one day. 'I never thought such things could possibly happen – never! At first, I thought the rumours might not be true, but now I'm not sure at all. So let's work extra hard, you and I, because our time together might be cut short!'

As Alexandr listened to his favourite pupil play so beautifully and with such depth of feeling, he was aware, despite his worries, of a deep sense of pride. Pride in her and her accomplishments, in himself, that he had played some part in her development as an artist, and also in his people, who had so enriched the culture of this his homeland, as well as that of so many others. Mingled with this pride now, however, was great fear. It was like a vice gripping his very soul. He was afraid for himself, his little family, and his people – but also, for some inexplicable reason, very much for Heléna.

On the last day of June, the graduating students staged their final concert, albeit to a noticeably smaller audience, with many gaps now in the ranks of family and friends. The most warmly acclaimed performances, without a doubt, belonged to Heléna and her friend Helga. All students had to wait until the end of the long summer break before results could be finalised and their degrees conferred, but they chose to hold their concert now, before dispersing in different directions. While some were preparing to take up teaching posts in schools, others wondered whether there would be any music career available to them. Some wanted to teach privately, but in wartime, few families could afford such luxuries for their children. Others, like Heléna and Helga, were first and foremost performers, many looking to join symphony orchestras and music ensembles across the country. Some took any job they could while waiting for results, while others busied themselves preparing for auditions for the few orchestral places available. For a select number, however, there were firm offers of further paid solo performances, Heléna herself being one of these. All of the students hoped to come together for their formal graduation in September, but even as they promised to attend, many knew it would be almost impossible. Among these was Helga, who, despite offers of a summer concert series and a likely operatic contract, had no choice but to turn these down and return to her family's farm near Domažlice. All three of her brothers had been drafted into the German army, like many of their fellow Germans in the Sudetenland area and elsewhere, and recently even her father had been called up as a border guard. With no one to help her mother on the farm, Helga felt she had to put her career on hold, and return home.

Heléna and Helga's parting was a tearful one.

'Heléna, when will we ever see each other again?' Helga wept. 'You know it's highly unlikely I'll be able to attend our graduation. I'll miss you so much – you've been such a loyal and loving friend! Take care, Heléna – and please keep in touch!'

Heléna's heart was heavy for her friend. She knew what it had cost Helga to turn down the career opportunities offered to her, and wondered in her heart if she would ever again be given the chance to succeed that she so richly deserved.

'I will, Helga! Goodbye – God bless you!'

As they warmly embraced, Helga suddenly pleaded with Heléna to contact her, should she ever need help. Like Alexandr, she somehow feared for her friend's future, despite her obvious giftedness, and the fact that Stefan was there to protect her.

'I can't explain it, Heléna – it's just a feeling I have! Please know you'd be welcome to stay with us any time!'

Heléna's first truly professional concert tour to some of the other big cities across the country was to begin in September, the day after her graduation. She knew she needed a good break from the pressures of the past year, however, before embarking on her final preparations. Initially she was happy staying at home in their apartment, listening to music, reading, cooking, and relaxing in the evenings with Stefan. Then, as August approached, the hottest time of the year in Prague, Stefan drove her down to Tábor, so that she could spend the remaining weeks walking or riding across the countryside, exploring the banks of the river, as she had as a child, or relaxing with Berta's family. Heléna loved the garden around her home. She revelled in the beauty and intricacy of God's creation, as she gazed at the climbing roses cascading over walls and trellises, or the tiny faces of the pansies that bordered the pathways. Stefan was able to stay for only a few days, before business matters called, and Heléna then spent most evenings chatting with Berta and Simona, playing with little Anna and Kristina, or visiting Uncle Erik and his sister. This was a special time of true re-creation – the strengthening she needed, she realised later, for the days to follow.

Heléna continued a modified practice schedule at Tábor, but by the middle of August, she knew she had to return to Prague and prepare in earnest for her concert tour. This entailed not only hours of practice at home, but also rehearsals with the small orchestra with whom she was touring. Stefan was also back in Prague, but, with the constantly increasing demands of his underground work, it was rare for them both to be home in the evenings. Their most precious time together was usually Sundays, a day they each tried to keep free in order to share fellowship with a small group of friends who held the same deep commitment to God as they did. Later in the afternoon, the two of them often walked or drove somewhere, ending the day at home together, preparing for the week ahead, but in a way that still allowed time for each other.

It was very early one Monday morning in late September, after a particularly sweet Sunday of sharing rich times with each other and with their friends, that Stefan received a sudden urgent call for help. He was needed immediately, to extricate some partisans from a dangerous situation near the German border. He hurriedly kissed Heléna goodbye, promising to do his best to be home for her graduation in two days' time, and also the beginning of her concert tour.

The very next day, disaster struck in Prague and across the whole nation. In one sudden but well planned move, the Third Reich appointed Reinhard Heydrich as Protector of Bohemia and Moravia, arrested the current Prime Minister, and took complete control of the Czech government. A wave of brutal arrests and executions by the Gestapo followed, causing Czech citizens, particularly those in positions of authority, to fear for their lives. Worst off were the country's Jewish population, who, having already been stripped of legal rights, were now herded together and eventually deported to unknown destinations in Poland, after a period in the 'ghetto' town of Terezin. Added to this, all cultural organisations across the country, including the Conservatorium, were immediately shut down, as had the universities before them.

These events of course had a devastating impact on Heléna. Without warning, the much anticipated graduation ceremony was postponed, her concert tour was cancelled, and the lives of many of her musician friends thrown into complete chaos. And overnight, her beloved teacher Alexandr disappeared, along with his little family.

Heléna, making her way to rehearsals that morning, had heard gunshots in the distance, followed by the roar of German army vehicles coming closer. At one point, just metres ahead of her, she witnessed the arrest of a prominent Jewish professor, and the rough treatment meted out to him, as he was bundled into a waiting van. Eventually arriving at the door of the Conservatorium, she was told the news by the Director, who, although looking pale and drawn, spoke calmly, under the watchful eye of a Gestapo lieutenant. After this information had sunk in, and realising nothing could be done, she knew she had no choice but to leave. She quickly returned home, closed the door and leant against it, legs shaking and heart pounding. She stayed quietly in the apartment that day and the next, barely sleeping during the night, and hoping upon hope that Stefan would come home, or at least phone.

Very late on the second night, just as Heléna was finally drifting into an exhausted sleep, there was a loud knocking at the door. She had not heard a car pull up, so she knew it was not Stefan. Anyway, of course he had a key – or at least he should have. Thinking that it might be more partisans in trouble, Heléna made her way to the door.

'Who is it?' she asked cautiously, her voice trembling a little.

There was silence, and then suddenly the knocking became even more urgent. Still Heléna hesitated to open the door. Stefan had not warned her about anyone needing somewhere safe for a few hours. Besides, whoever was outside had not even tried to use any of the pre-arranged passwords. And yet, she reasoned, given the events of the past two days, and with everything in chaos, details like this would possibly be forgotten. In fact, whoever was waiting outside their door might be in very grave danger.

Eventually, judging it the best action to take in the circumstances, Heléna slowly opened the door.

Outside, staring at her, eyes alert and darting everywhere, with guns drawn, stood three members of the Gestapo. And behind them, for a brief instant, she glimpsed the triumphant face of her elderly neighbour from the apartment below.

Chapter Eight

For a moment Heléna stood as if turned to stone. The Gestapo hurriedly pushed past her and proceeded to search every room, opening wardrobe doors and looking behind and under everything. Eventually, one of them, obviously a higher ranked officer, addressed Heléna.

'Madam, I presume you're Frau Marek. We've received information that you might perhaps be hiding members of the underground, but in particular, we're searching for your husband. We've had him under surveillance for some time, and now that our people have control of the government, we have much greater authority to carry out our investigations. We can arrest anyone we wish – do you understand?'

The officer had spoken to Heléna in fairly basic Czech, with a sprinkling of German, as he stood between her and the closed front door, to prevent her escape. Fortunately, Heléna understood German reasonably well, having begun learning it from childhood friends who had grown up in the Sudetenland. Later, her father and Stefan, who were both fluent in the language, had taught her more – and besides, these days she and Helga used it often, when speaking and singing, since it was her friend's heart language. Somehow, however, she sensed that she did not need to let these men know this as yet. As the other officers returned from their search empty-handed, Heléna, still in her dressing gown, was ushered into the sitting room and ordered to sit down.

Eventually, the officer who had already addressed her spoke again.

'Your husband – where is he?'

Heléna could only give him vague answers, because she honestly did not know exactly where Stefan was. She was thankful she was not faced with the dilemma, at that point at least, of whether to lie to protect him, or to choose to tell the truth.

'I think he's somewhere near the German border – Pilsen probably. He had to sort out some difficulties at his factory there. He said he hoped to be home today, or at the latest, this evening. He usually phones if he's delayed, but I can't phone him, as I never know exactly where he'll be and when. Sometimes these business matters take much longer than one expects, so I gave up waiting for him, and went to bed. I'm assuming he'll phone tomorrow. Or is it today now?' she smiled ruefully, looking at Stefan's old grandfather clock in the corner, which showed it was now almost one.

The Gestapo were unmoved at the lateness of the hour. The same officer continued to question her.

'We have reason to believe, Frau Marek, that your husband is one of the key partisan leaders in Prague, and indeed the whole country,' he said heavily, staring intently at her, wanting to gauge her response.

Heléna, endeavouring to appear shocked and incredulous, asked the officer questioning her in his broken Czech to repeat what he had said, pretending she might possibly have misunderstood him. After a short pause, she managed to respond in what she hoped was an extremely offended tone.

'I can tell you that would be extremely unlikely! Why would someone like my husband, a successful businessman, who's worked so hard to build a good reputation, risk all he's achieved in such a way?' she argued vehemently.

'We know he goes away a lot – often on short trips, and often leaving at night. We're not stupid!' the officer replied, equally vehemently.

'Of course my husband goes away a lot!' she agreed, in a slightly exasperated tone, still careful, however, to keep her voice and words polite. 'He has a number of factories and subsidiary companies in the western part of the country, and others to the north and south. These are simply business trips, and have indeed become more frequent recently, since the factories have had to produce so much more for the war effort,' she insisted.

'And you never go with him on these trips – a lovely young wife like you?' the officer sneered, obviously hinting that there must be a good reason why Stefan would not want her by his side.

'I rarely go with him,' she replied firmly, not liking the tone in his voice. 'I know very little about his business interests, because I've been studying hard at the Conservatorium these past three years. In fact, today my first concert tour was scheduled to begin! I'm a pianist, and I was to have performed with a small orchestra in various cities across the country.'

Heléna was in no doubt by now that they were aware of this. The officer did not comment, but merely continued his questioning.

'Perhaps you're a partisan in your own right?' he said softly, again watching her carefully.

'My career means too much to me for that,' she quickly replied. 'Because you're German, you may not be aware that my mother was a well-known concert pianist here in our country. She passed away last January, not long before my father. I want to keep my mother's memory alive, and to succeed for both my parents' sake, but, more than that even, I have a strong faith in God, and want to honour him by playing my best, and doing what he's called me to do.'

Heléna thought she noticed a softening in the face of one of the other officers – an older, heavily built man, with rather kindly blue eyes, edged with a myriad of smile lines. Her voice had quivered, despite herself, as she answered. The older man spoke in German to the one questioning her, suggesting that, because of the lateness of the hour, they could perhaps let her rest, but his words were cut short by a stern look and raised hand.

On and on the questions continued. How long had she known Stefan? How long had they been married? Where was she from? How had she and Stefan met? At that point, from glances that passed between the officers, Heléna sensed that they knew of Stefan's prior link with her father, and also that they at least suspected Václav's involvement in the underground movement. Heléna continued to answer their questions calmly, not hiding the fact that her father had introduced her to Stefan, but pointing out it was through their mutual interests in good business management, that Stefan's friendship with her father had developed.

'We have been given information, Frau Marek,' the officer maintained with a smirk, 'that your husband has been meeting secretly with your father for some years, as far back as when you were still at school here in Prague!'

'My father preferred to work from home as much as he could, to be near my mother,' she stated quietly. 'Perhaps you're also aware that she had been unwell for some years. He was often in the habit of entertaining business associates in our home.'

Eventually, the questions returned to more current issues.

'We're aware through our contacts,' her interrogator declared in a now strongly accusatory tone, 'that Czech partisans and others wishing to flee this country have been observed entering, and later leaving this apartment, often at unusual times of the day. How do you explain that?'

Heléna had anticipated this question, so did not hesitate in her answer.

'I'm not surprised that you, or any of our neighbours, have seen people coming and going at different times! As I've said, my husband is frequently away, returning home at odd hours, since he often has to drive long distances, and sometimes he brings his associates back with him. Sometimes they stay with us for a short time, while they observe how things are managed in the company's main factory here, and then return home. Often, if they do, they have to leave very early in the morning, in order to begin work that same day. They usually travel by train then, in which case my husband, or one of his senior employees, takes them to the station. No doubt on occasions our neighbours have heard one of these men knocking early on our door in order to wake us and take our guest to the station on time. I often study late, so am not good at getting up early!'

By the sceptical look on the face of her questioner, Heléna was aware that he had great difficulty believing her. After clarifying her explanation for the other two men, the three conferred as to their next move. As Heléna waited and listened to their conversation, she prayed silently. Lord, please protect Stefan! Lord, watch over me! Give me strength and wisdom, to know how you would want me to respond to these men!

Presently, she realised that the older of the other two officers wanted to leave, and return later in the morning, after checking with their sources in Pilsen to see if Stefan were still there. His younger partner appeared uncaring and remote, bored with the whole proceedings. He seemed to want action – sitting talking in the early hours of the morning was obviously not what he would choose. The senior of the three officers, however, thought otherwise, overruling them both.

'We'll stay,' he said in a voice that she knew would brook no argument, as did his fellow officers. 'We'll wait for as long as it takes, Frau Marek, to see if your story is true! Perhaps your husband will come home soon. If so, we'll be ready for him! You may go to your room and rest. We'll wait right here for Herr Marek!'

Heléna went to the bedroom, but not to rest. Every part of her was alert, her mind groping for possible ways to warn Stefan of the Gestapo's presence. She dressed, feeling uncomfortable in her nightwear with the Germans in the apartment. Lying on the bed fully clothed, and holding her bible to her, she prayed with all her heart that somehow Stefan would be aware of what was happening in their apartment, that something would prevent him from returning home that day. Wherever he was in the country, he would know of the Prime Minister's arrest, and the other political events that had occurred two days previously. These had been officially broadcast across the nation, she knew. And he would also be aware of the terrible arrests and executions that were happening in Prague, especially to their Jewish friends, even if these things had not been officially reported. Such shocking news travels fast, and Stefan certainly had his contacts. Would this cause him to be more careful, and stay away until things hopefully settled down – or would he try to get home to her as soon as possible?

Suddenly she realised that he might not as yet be aware that cultural organisations across the country, including the Conservatorium, and the very orchestra with whom she had been scheduled to travel, had also been shut down. He might in fact believe that her planned tour had still gone ahead! Tonight they were to have given the first of their concerts in a town not far from Prague, which Stefan had hoped to attend, since he could drive there and still easily be back in Prague the following day to see to any pressing business matters. He had definitely wanted to be home in Prague the previous evening for her graduation, and to wish her well before she left. But he had also told her that if for some reason he did not make it, he would link up with her wherever she was on the tour as soon as possible – he knew her itinerary, and where she would be staying in each town. He might in fact believe she was out of Prague by now, and thus in a somewhat less dangerous place. Heléna hoped and prayed that, if this were so, he would head directly for wherever she was supposed to be staying, and not travel via their apartment.

As daylight came, she got up, knowing she needed to function as normally as possible, while at the same time staying alert for the sound of Stefan's car pulling up in the square below, and his feet on the steps leading to their floor. She felt now that if he did know about the closure of the Conservatorium and the cancellation of her concert tour, he might try to phone her to check if she were safe. When he did, she needed to have a plan in place to warn him of the situation in the apartment, without letting the Gestapo know what she was doing. They were in the same room as the phone, and would inevitably listen in on any conversation. All she could do then, was to pray that if and when Stefan rang, it would be at just the right time, and that she would be given the words to say.

Helena opened her bedroom door and moved towards the kitchen, planning to prepare some breakfast. As she glanced in the sitting room door, she noticed that, while two of the men were apparently asleep, the older one of the three was awake and alert. She smiled at him, motioning that she was going to make some coffee. Quickly she set out four cups on a tray, and prepared a pot of strong coffee for them all, carrying it to the sitting room. By this time, all three were awake and watchful. They accepted her coffee, although somewhat awkwardly, she felt. Obviously the Gestapo would not be used to being served coffee as they waited to arrest someone! Soon she returned to the kitchen to prepare breakfast, but because she and Stefan had expected to be away, there was not a great deal on hand from which to choose. Carefully she arranged some rye bread and cheeses on a plate, along with a few slices of sausage and tomato, and carried these back to the sitting room.

'Put the food here, madam, and then please leave us!' the senior officer ordered abruptly.

Heléna obeyed, eating hers alone in the kitchen. She wished she could hear what they were saying, and determined to rectify that. She wanted to know, and thus be forewarned about their actions, and any further questions they might be planning on asking.

The problem was soon solved, since, even as she was wondering what her next move should be, the telephone rang. She hurried back to the sitting room, and moved to answer it. As she did, she was aware that the men had moved close by, listening intently for the voice on the other end of the line, as well as trying to observe any emotion she might show.

It was not Stefan. Heléna almost dropped the receiver, as a mixture of relief and deep disappointment swept over her, causing her whole body to feel weak. She sat down on the nearest chair, not caring whether this pleased the Gestapo officers or not. It was in fact Andela, one of her friends from the orchestra with whom she had been meant to be touring.

'Heléna, how are you? I'm sure you're even more disappointed that I am, so you must be very upset! Do you feel like talking? I need someone to help me think through what I should do now.'

Usually they talked for ages. Andela was also a member of the fellowship where Stefan and Heléna met on Sundays, so they had much in common. This time, however, Heléna quickly explained that she could not talk for long, as she had visitors staying. Andela felt that was a little strange, since Heléna had planned to be away, but she was aware, through things her friend had said in the past, that Stefan was a partisan leader. These visitors, she suspected immediately, might in fact be underground workers needing to escape from the danger surrounding them in Prague. She decided not to ask any further questions.

'I'll go, Heléna, and let you care for your guests, but when you expect Stefan back?'

Something in Heléna's tone at that point, and the brief, dismissive way she answered her final question, told her that Heléna was worried and distracted, that all was not well with her, despite her assurances otherwise. As soon as Andela hung up, she prayed for her friend and for Stefan. She also determined to check on Heléna in person in the next day or two.

As Heléna put the phone down, the senior officer spoke abruptly again, obviously very annoyed.

'Frau Marek, please remember that if the phone rings again, you must try to speak in German! Otherwise, we'll stop the conversation! Do you hear me?'

It was impossible for Heléna not to have heard him, since he was almost shouting at her. Suddenly she realised that, as she had spoken quite quickly in Czech, he, with his limited knowledge of the language, had been unable to keep up with all she had said, although he had understood the general drift of the conversation. If the caller had indeed been Stefan, Heléna could probably have warned him away, before the German had realised what was being said, and cut them off. The officer continued to shout at her, obviously not wanting to lose face with his men by having to admit that he was not as fluent in Czech as he had led them to believe. Eventually he calmed down a little, asking her directly in Czech if she did indeed speak German. To her surprise, her voice sounded completely calm, as she answered him.

'Yes, I do speak a little German,' she admitted, still speaking in Czech. 'My music studies have required me to sing a little in the language, as well as read parts of the diaries and manuscript notes written by some of your great composers. I'm not fluent, but I'll endeavour to do what you've asked.'

'Tell your friends when they call, or your husband, that you need to practise your German then, that the Germans are now in charge here in Prague, and you must speak to them only in our language!' he commanded again.

After that, they sat in silence. Heléna's mind was whirling, wondering what she would say if Stefan phoned. She realised now that it was clearly wiser not to alarm the Gestapo in any way through her phone conversations, be it with Stefan or anyone. If she spoke in Czech, then she would be disconnected, and she would not have time to warn Stefan about anything. If she spoke in German, then he would think it very strange, but at least somehow she might be able to convey to him what was happening. By the very fact of her not speaking in Czech, she knew he would be alerted to some degree. She had to leave it at that, and trust God that she would be given the right words to say.

The minutes turned into hours, with the Gestapo becoming increasingly restless. Eventually, as lunchtime approached, the youngest officer was sent out to buy food – more to give him something to do, Heléna suspected, than anything else. Heléna ate her own meal alone in the kitchen, although, as they day wore on, she found it difficult to swallow anything. In the afternoon, she again lay down and dozed a little, eventually being woken with a start from a rather disturbing dream by the shrill ring of the telephone once again. At first she let it ring, unable to surface from her sleep to think clearly enough. She soon realised, however, that if it were Stefan and she did not answer, then he might well assume she was indeed on tour, and try to join her, as they had previously arranged. Not to answer then might well save him! On the other hand, if he did indeed know the tour had been cancelled, the fact that she did not answer might well cause him to worry about her and come straight home.

Eventually, unable to bear the ringing any longer, she hurried to the sitting room. With the officers' eyes upon her, she lifted the receiver and slowly put it to her ear.

It was her friend Helga this time, phoning long distance from her farm near Domažlice. Helga spoke quickly and agitatedly in her native German, knowing her friend would understand, since they often conversed in German.

'Heléna, I can't speak for long, as the lines are really bad, but I couldn't sleep last night for worrying about you. We heard rumours yesterday about the things that have happened in the past few days – about the closure of the Conservatorium, and the postponement of the graduation ceremony. Obviously the fact that you're there and not on tour means it must be true! Heléna, I'm so sorry! Are you okay?'

Heléna knew that Helga, above all people, would understand her deep disappointment in being prevented from setting out on her concert tour and from sharing the gifts she had been given and that she had worked so hard to develop. This had, after all, been Helga's own very disappointing experience. Before Heléna had time to murmur more than a few words of explanation in German, however, Helga continued.

'Heléna, remember that if you need any help, please come to us! It's quiet here – all the men are off fighting and working elsewhere. We could practise together, and then we'll be ready to perform when the world comes to rights again! Take care, Heléna – I miss you so much!'

Helga rang off, and Heléna sat for a moment, warmed by her friend's generosity. She had often felt that Helga had guessed at Stefan's involvement in the underground movement, but she had asked no questions, simply remaining her staunch friend. Now here they were, a German family, offering her shelter in their own home!

At last, becoming aware of the heavy silence in the room, Heléna turned and explained who the caller had been. The officer nearest to her had detected that the voice was female, however, and had already relayed this to the others. The men continued to stay where they were, simply waiting, until eventually, as it neared dinnertime, Heléna asked if she could get them anything. She knew that because of this dreadful war, these men were her enemies, but something in her still clamoured to offer them hospitality. Again the senior officer brusquely refused her offer, arranging instead to send the youngest one out for food again. The older of the remaining two, the one with the kind eyes and smile lines, gave Heléna what she interpreted as a sympathetic glance, as if to convey that they were not all so hard and inhuman. *Perhaps, unbeknownst to me, I could even be entertaining an angel, like the bible talks about somewhere*, she mused to herself, as she went to the kitchen for another small and lonely meal.

After dinner, Heléna served them coffee again, which they accepted, possibly because the senior officer at least was aware he needed to stay alert. Unwilling to sit in silence with them, or to listen in to their desultory conversation that contained nothing of importance – especially given the fact that they were now aware she understood German – Heléna moved to the piano and seated herself on the long padded stool. But she had no sooner done so, than the phone rang again. Before she had time even to put the receiver to her ear, she heard a man's voice, as did the senior Gestapo officer nearby.

It was Stefan.

'Heléna, I'm so relieved to be able to get through to you! Are you all right? I wanted to call you hours ago, but couldn't get to a phone. I've been with Jiří, playing chess! I heard the news this morning about the Conservatorium and the orchestras and

'... Heléna, are you there?'

Stefan sounded exhausted, as if he had been running for hours. She could hear him breathing heavily even as he talked, and was alarmed at what he had said. She knew exactly what he meant. They had discussed how, if he ever had to hide in the tunnels, he would let her know where he was by telling her he was playing chess with Jiří. If he had to hide, Stefan had reasoned, then they would probably need to talk in some sort of code, since his phone line could be tapped.

Heléna pulled herself together, not only for Stefan's sake, but also because she was very conscious of three pairs of eyes upon her at that moment.

'Hello, Stefan, it's so wonderful to hear from you!' she said, speaking slowly in German. 'Yes, I'm fine, though of course very disappointed, not only about our tour, but also the graduation ceremony. At least I'm safe. Stefan, if you're wondering why I'm speaking in German, it's because the Germans are now in charge here in Prague! I believe that if I want to continue with my career, then it's important I befriend them, so I'm practising it at every opportunity. When will you be home?'

There was a brief silence on the other end of the line. Heléna could almost feel the puzzlement her words must be creating in Stefan's mind. Despite the difficulties of the past few hours on the run, and the exhaustion that was rapidly overtaking him, he tried to imagine why Heléna would suddenly decide to speak in German. Not for a moment did he believe the reason she gave.

Eventually he managed to collect his scattered thoughts enough to answer her.

'Heléna, I can't tell you that exactly. There are some business matters that have come up, but I'll join you as soon as I can, now that I know you didn't set out on your tour at all. I wasn't exactly sure when the orchestra would have been given the news. Heléna, I want you to know I love you so much! It's so good to hear your voice! Please stay right where you are – don't go out unless you really have to! Promise me that, Heléna!'

His voice was extremely urgent, conveying to Heléna that he seemed to have a good idea of what was happening in the streets and across their city at that moment. With a wry smile, she assured him, still in German, that she would not be going out until he came home.

'Stefan, can't you give me any idea when that will be?' she pleaded. 'I miss you so much!'

'I'll be there soon, Heléna – as soon as I can, I promise! Heléna, I have to go, but remember, I love you so much!'

'Ich liebe Sie auch!'

As Stefan listened, those four short German words Heléna had uttered assured him of her deep love, but also brought a terrible fear to his heart. Even in his exhausted state, they rang like warning bells in his mind. He knew Heléna, and he knew that, in reality, she spoke German extremely well. Why then had she used 'Sie', the polite form of 'you', instead of the more familiar 'dich', to tell him she loved him? They always used the more intimate 'du' form, whenever they spoke German together, as any husband and wife would. He knew it had not been a mere slip of the tongue. For some reason, she had said it deliberately, he was sure.

Stefan put down the phone, and sat in a daze, trying to fit the pieces together in his tired brain. It was vaguely possible that Heléna wanted to be seen and heard speaking German as often as she could, in order to be on good terms with the authorities for the sake of her career. But who was there to overhear the conversation that had just taken place, apart from someone tapping into the phone line?

Suddenly he knew, beyond the shadow of a doubt, that there must be some German official, or even several, with her in their apartment. Clearly, she had wanted to warn him of this, without their realising it!

Horror engulfed him, as he sat, unable to move, in the tiny front room of Jiří's cottage. He had been on the run himself now for almost three days, unable to stop for any real rest, ever since he had walked into a trap set for the partisans in Pilsen. Someone had blown the whistle on them, with the result that two of their best men had been shot dead, and another arrested. He and a young female worker, Ivana, had managed to escape, eventually making their way undetected to Tábor. Once there, he had safely delivered Ivana into the care of Uncle Erik and his sister Edita, until she could be nursed back to health from the gunshot wound received as they fled. She had lost a lot of blood, and Stefan had had to carry her part of the journey, as they had made their way across country in the dark, running through fields and along ditches until they had reached Milevsko. There they had managed to hide under a tarpaulin in a half empty compartment of a goods train, finally arriving in Tábor around lunchtime. It had been a risky business, firstly to find someone to treat Ivana, and then to get her to Uncle Erik's without raising suspicion. All through the hazardous journey, every time Stefan had helped Ivana in any way, by carrying her or trying to bandage her wound, he had thought of his Heléna. If Heléna had been in this situation, he had reasoned, he would want someone to protect her and care for her, as he was doing for this girl. Now, his mission complete, he had returned to Jiří's cottage, and had sunk exhausted into a chair in his front room, determined to try to get through to Heléna before he hid in the tunnels, for a few days at least. Now he had discovered that, while he had been helping someone else, he had not been there for his own beautiful Heléna when she needed him.

As the fog in his brain began to clear, it occurred to him that Heléna's voice had not sounded troubled or wavering when she had spoken to him a moment ago. She had sounded in good health – he had to be thankful for that at least. He had always been careful to shield her from virtually any knowledge of the details of his underground work, even to the extent of not telling her exactly where he would be, because of just such a situation as this. If the German authorities – and that would mean the Gestapo – were indeed there with her, then she had nothing to hide, because she knew so little. Nor would they find any evidence of his activities in their apartment. The occasions when they had hidden partisans and others fleeing the country had caused him some qualms, since that of necessity had involved Heléna, but he had tried his best to move them on quickly and quietly, and thus attract as little attention as possible. Perhaps he was wrong – perhaps after all, nothing untoward was happening in their apartment. Yet he could not shake the foreboding feeling that had crept over him, and now lay on him like a ton weight, as he sat gazing unseeingly at old Jiří, who had appeared at the door. After he briefly told him what had occurred, Jiří was adamant that before Stefan did anything, he needed to get some sleep – whatever was really happening in their apartment.

'Stefan, listen to me! Even if the Gestapo are with Heléna, she's probably in no immediate danger,' he reasoned. 'After all, they'd be after you – not her! If I know anything about the way they work, they'll simply wait it out, until you're either captured elsewhere, or return to your apartment!'

Stefan heard the wisdom of Jiří's words, but his whole being rebelled at the thought of possibly leaving Heléna alone with the Gestapo for any length of time. Yet he knew that he truly could not help in his current state. Right then he could scarcely raise himself from his chair to make his way into the nearby church, and down to the tunnels. With a superhuman effort he eventually did so, however, leaning heavily on Jiří, so much older and shorter than he was. He fumbled his way in the dark into the old church, sliding rather than climbing down the steps leading into the tunnels, where he fell exhausted onto the nearest stretcher.

Oh God, he prayed in his final few waking moments before sinking into an exhausted sleep, forgive me – you know I can't go any further! Please look after her for me, I beg you!

Chapter Nine

Heléna put the phone down, and instinctively moved back to the piano, mentally trying to collect herself. She was ready when the senior officer began firing questions at her again.

'Obviously that was your husband,' he said with a slight sneer, 'although it puzzles me why you didn't use 'dich' rather than 'Sie' when you spoke to him! A little more German practice will obviously not go astray for you. Where is your husband now?'

Heléna, remembering the phone might have been bugged, felt it wisest to stay as close to the truth as possible.

'He didn't say exactly,' she replied, 'but he's been having a break, playing chess with a friend today. These games sometimes take hours, as I'm sure you can imagine!'

The officer appeared very sceptical, but then continued his questioning.

'And when will he be back?'

'He's not sure. Some more business matters have come up, so these may occupy him for a few more days. Now that he knows I didn't begin my tour, then it's no doubt better for him to attend to these matters before he returns.'

Heléna was determined not to sound concerned, and also to convey to them that it might be some time before Stefan returned. Perhaps that way, they would decide not to wait around, or be ordered to do more strategic or pressing work elsewhere. The young one at least would infinitely prefer that, she felt. The oldest of the three still seemed somewhat sympathetic towards her – she was not so concerned about him. But it was the senior officer, her questioner, whom she knew she needed to convince. He seemed equally as determined to stay put, however, as she was to see them go.

'We'll stay here, I think – tonight and tomorrow at least!' was his eventual reply.

Heléna heard the implacable tone in his voice, and knew once again there was no point in arguing. She stayed seated at the piano, wondering what she should say or do next. For some time, there was no sound in the room, apart from the loud ticking of Stefan's old grandfather clock in the corner, and the occasional flicking of pages, as the senior officer idly thumbed through a notebook he carried. Eventually, Heléna took her courage in both hands.

'I wonder if you gentlemen would mind if I played the piano for a little while?' she finally asked. 'I need to practise for when we're able to tour again. And if we can't tour, then I'll have to begin taking students as soon as possible, so I must keep my hand in.'

The one in charge seemed to consider her request for a long time. Then he spoke abruptly, as if it pained him to give in to her in any way.

'I see no reason why you shouldn't play, except that we need to know if a car pulls up, or if someone comes up the stairs. We'll open the window and keep watch there – and you will play!' he said, at the same time ordering the youngest officer to stand at the window.

Heléna sighed inwardly with relief, but was careful not to show him how much his decision meant to her. She needed to play for her own sake, because, in doing so, she could forget the world around her and immerse herself in her music. Much more importantly, however, she remembered the promise she and Stefan had made to each other, so long ago now it seemed, concerning their special song 'Nur wer die Sehnsucht kennt'. Here she was, in exactly the situation Stefan had foreseen then. She could recall the moment clearly, remembering the horror she had felt at the idea that Stefan might ever need to use this song to warn her of danger. She remembered how he had made her promise not to come near the apartment, if and when this happened. And she also remembered how, when she had promised to do the same for him, he had hugged her close, maintaining that the Germans would not stay long when they did not find him there, but would soon search elsewhere.

Now she knew otherwise. Perhaps Stefan had underestimated his importance to the Gestapo even then, or the past months had caused him to be regarded as a much more strategic fish to catch. They would wait, she suspected. Not just tonight and tomorrow, but until the net had been drawn tight around Stefan, either there or elsewhere.

Heléna played. She practised for over two hours, running through the entire repertoire she had prepared for the tour. She noticed at one stage the Germans talking amongst themselves, and momentarily wished she could hear their conversation, but the music had taken hold of her. Besides, she could hardly stop suddenly without making her purpose for doing so very obvious. As it turned out, they were apparently only changing guard, since now the youngest of the three was sprawled in one of the armchairs, eyes half closed, while the one with the kindly eyes stood at the open window. Heléna played on, until tiredness overtook her. Even if Stefan had intended to come home immediately after their phone conversation, despite what he had said to her, she realised it would take some time for him to do so. He would have to be particularly careful – much more careful than he had been even before the catastrophic events of the last three days. She felt in her heart that he had heard her warning and knew something was not right at their apartment, but whether this would cause him to try to reach her immediately, or to hold off for a while, she could not guess. There were so many factors involved, not the least being Stefan's energy levels at that point, which to her had sounded low in the extreme. Yet despite all these thoughts and questions in her mind, Heléna decided to conclude her practice session with their special piece of music. As she began playing the beautiful melody, she prayed silently. Lord, if Stefan is nearby, let him hear this, and take heed of the warning! Lead him by the hand – let him escape! But Lord, if he is not nearby, then let him know I am thinking of him and praying for his safety!

As the last notes died away, Heléna sat still for a moment. Then she rose, explaining that she needed to rest. As she passed the older officer on watch at the window, their glances locked. To her surprise, she noticed tears in his eyes, before he turned abruptly to look down once more at the square below, as if ashamed of his weakness.

'One of my favourites!' he muttered to Heléna in a low voice, as he did so.

Heléna lay awake for a long time, despite her tiredness. She prayed earnestly for Stefan, wherever he was. She prayed he would stay safe in the tunnels for as long as he could, and that when he did eventually come to the apartment, he would hear their special music, and leave quickly, not returning until the coast was clear. As she closed her eyes to try to sleep, the kindly face of the older Gestapo officer, and his look of deep sadness as he had turned away, kept coming back to her. She wondered what it was about their special piece that had stirred him so much. Was he simply a lover of beautiful music, like them? Was he also feeling the pain of separation and the loneliness of war? Or did he sense Heléna's grief somehow and feel for her in her situation? Perhaps it was all three, she mused. Perhaps he even loved God, just as she and Stefan did. If so, then he was her brother in a special way – part of the same family. Yet how could this be? How could two human beings with so much in common find themselves enemies? Everything was so confused, so distorted.

Heléna's mind, unable to grapple any longer with these heavy questions, finally gave up. Still fully clothed, ready for whatever would happen, she fell into a deep sleep for several hours, only waking when daylight came.

For a while she wondered why she was lying fully clothed on top of the covers. Then the memory of Stefan's phone conversation flooded back, and she sat up abruptly. Now fully awake and alert, she nevertheless stayed in her room, unable at first to make out any movement or noise from elsewhere in the apartment. She waited and prayed, hoping beyond hope, as she had the previous morning, that she would not hear the sound of Stefan's feet on the stairs, or his key in the lock. Eventually she heard voices coming from the sitting room, and ventured out to make coffee again, and what breakfast she could find.

As it turned out, she was too late, since one of them had already purchased fresh bread and more cheese and sausage, the remains of which were now spread untidily across the kitchen bench. As Heléna again brought coffee to them, the senior officer, she noticed, was in the middle of a rather intense phone conversation, obviously with one of his superiors. Impatiently he motioned for Heléna to put the coffee down and leave the room. This she did, but not before overhearing enough to deduce that, while the three officers were eager to leave, someone ranked above them was equally eager for them to stay on until Stefan was finally caught.

Heléna forced herself to drink her coffee and eat some bread and cheese. She needed all her wits about her for the day ahead, as well as energy to practise as much as possible. She prayed the officers would not tire of her music, and stop her playing. She wanted ample opportunity to warn Stefan, though she suspected that, if he did try to come home, it would more likely be under cover of darkness.

She was right. Very early that morning, waking suddenly from the deep sleep into which he had fallen as soon as he had lain down the previous evening, Stefan sat bolt upright. He was ready for immediate action, such was his training as a partisan leader. From the dim light of the one lantern in his section of the tunnels, he managed to make out the hands of his watch pointing to just after one o'clock. He knew immediately that he needed to leave as soon as possible. He had to try to get to Heléna that day, and the best time to start the journey was now, while it was still dark. God willing, he would at least get part of the way before daylight. Jiří had promised to come back at dawn with Uncle Erik, and then together, he had said, they would decide how best to help him, and whether it would be wise to try to reach Heléna at all. Stefan knew, however, that he could not find it within himself to stay where he was one moment longer. Each time he thought of Heléna, he could feel again that sense of deep foreboding that had come over him the previous night, and had now settled like a huge knot in the pit of his stomach.

As he sat eating an apple from the small store of fruit he had found on some shelves nearby, he tried to pull back, and see things more in perspective. God had watched over Heléna and him in the past, and had protected him throughout that long journey by train and on foot from Pilsen with Ivana, when there was danger all around. He was alive, when so many of his fellow underground workers had been killed. And so was Heléna. And last night, knowing that he could not go a step further, he remembered praying that God would again look after her. God, he knew, was trustworthy, and was much more able to care for Heléna than he would ever be. And yet, everything within him screamed to be with Heléna, to go to her, whatever the risk. Someone had obviously been present with her yesterday, during that strange conversation in German, and Heléna had wanted to let him know that. He knew that their conversation had held a warning to stay away, rather than being the plea to come home that it had purported to be on the surface, but Stefan could not find it within himself to stay away. He loved her too much for that. He could not rest until he found out exactly what was happening in their apartment.

He pulled a small notebook out of his shirt pocket and a pen, and hurriedly wrote a note for Jiří, which he placed on top of his stretcher. Then he made his way out of the tunnel through the panel inside the church, quietly slipping by Jiří's cottage in the darkness. Negotiating his way carefully to the main railway station, he found the same hole in the fence that he and Ivana had used the previous day, slipping through it into the shadows of the old, disused carriages that lined the perimeter of the station yard. Several trains passed through Tábor at regular intervals during the night, since it was on the main line between Vienna and Prague, as well as one to České Budějovice. Fortunately for Stefan, a goods train was not long in coming, and as it slowed to pass through the station, he managed to scramble through the partly open door of an empty storage van, curling up on a pile of old potato sacks and flattened cardboard cartons. Soon, the rhythmic swaying of the train had done its work, and Stefan, still worn out from the experiences of the past few days, slept for most of the time it took to reach the outskirts of Prague. He eased his way to the door, trying to assess exactly where they were, and hoping that the train would slow down enough for him to jump clear at one of the stations some distance from the city centre. This was not to be, so, as the train approached the centre of Prague, Stefan quickly jumped out and rolled into a small culvert beside the track. He scrambled to his feet immediately, unhurt, and intent on trying to reach the apartment before dawn.

This soon proved difficult, with so many soldiers in the streets, including Gestapo, even at such an early hour of the morning. Stefan had become very experienced in the past year, however, at passing undetected through many of the main cities across the country, making use of side streets and dingy alleyways learned from local underground workers. The old part of Prague, in particular, was a maze of such thoroughfares, with which Stefan was by now well acquainted. He nevertheless made is way very cautiously, never taking risks, but slowly and surely moving closer to his destination.

Finally, just as the sun was rising, he reached the square where their apartment was situated, and quickly made his way through a small unlocked side door in the old church opposite and a little to the right of the entrance to their building. He knew he would not be disturbed there at this time of the morning, and probably not at all the whole day, since the church was now used only on Sundays. Carefully positioning himself near one of the stained glass windows, from which he could easily see anyone entering or leaving their apartment block, he settled himself for two or three hours of boring but necessary surveillance work. It would be foolish, he knew, to rush this last part of his journey. Better to watch for a while to see if the Gestapo really were in the vicinity. By that time, however, he realised it would be broad daylight, and probably difficult, and foolhardy, to enter the building. Stefan resigned himself to a lengthy stay in the church – so near to Heléna, yet so far.

That morning, with no objection from the Gestapo, Heléna practised for around two hours, ending by playing their special song several times. In the afternoon, yet another Gestapo officer arrived, this time one apparently more senior than those already in the apartment. After questioning Heléna again in German, speaking very slowly and loudly, and eliciting the same answers the other officer had already obtained, he turned to the three men, speaking in very fast German.

'This man Herr Marek somehow slipped through our net at Pilsen, and then again two nights ago near Tábor. He's very cunning – a very experienced underground worker indeed – but we'll catch him – and soon! Be patient, just for one more night and day! We believe he's still in the Tábor area and will probably try to leave this evening. Call me if you find out anything more. We'll also keep you notified.'

Their visitor left, taking with him the youngest of the three Gestapo members. Heléna practised again then, beginning with their special piece, and returning to it once more after she had finished her concert repertoire. She played it several times, stopping at various spots, as if to correct some mistake, or to interpret it better. As she finished, the older of the two remaining officers addressed her, almost as if he could not hold back the question.

'Tell me, Frau Marek, why do you play that piece so often?'

Heléna's heart skipped a beat, thinking he had perhaps guessed something of its significance for Stefan and her. Then she realised that he could not possibly know – it was their secret, and theirs alone. She looked at the man, noticing again the kindly eyes surrounded by smile lines, but also the sadness that he seemed to feel when she played.

'It's one my husband's favourites, and mine also,' she answered truthfully. 'Whenever I play it, I feel close to him. That's why I like playing it.'

'I understand,' he replied. 'My wife used to play it often, but she was killed ….'.

He hesitated, stopping in mid-sentence, as he noticed the cold glance the senior officer was giving him from his position near the window, his hand slightly raised, as if to warn him not to say anything further. The older man swallowed hard, and then lapsed into silence, nodding to her one more time before turning away.

After dinner, which Heléna again ate alone in the kitchen, the senior officer made a number of phone calls, during which she was obliged to remain where she was. When he had finished, she asked if she could practise a little more, but this time her request was refused. The reason soon became obvious, when he took from his pocket a small pack of cards, and proceeded to deal them out. Neither apparently wanted to keep watch at the window, so needed the silence to hear any sound from outside. Heléna was very much aware that while they may have appeared to be relaxing, in reality they were extremely alert. From time to time, whenever some unusual noise occurred, Heléna noticed their hands go immediately to their guns, ready for whatever might happen next. Soon they tired of their game, and after the older man had resumed his post near the window, the officer who had refused Heléna permission to play earlier, now motioned for her to go ahead.

She began with some delicate Mozart sonatas, and from there moved to the brighter tones of her favourite Chopin mazurkas, following this with some quieter and more reflective music. Finally, just as she had launched once again into the plaintive melody of 'Nur wer die Sehnsucht kennt', she was aware of the officer at the window suddenly calling the other one over. It seemed to her from where she was sitting, that they were glancing across the square at a light flashing from a window in the building opposite. Immediately, the senior officer motioned for Heléna to stop playing. Breaking off abruptly in mid-phrase, she listened intently, straining her ears for any sounds on the stairs leading to their door. At first she could hear nothing, and neither, it appeared, could the two men. All three of them sat completely still, as if frozen in time. Then the officers began to move out silently into the hallway and towards the door of the apartment. Again they stood still, listening intently for any sound that may indicate the presence of someone – in all probability Stefan – on the stairs leading to their front door. There was only one other apartment on the same level as Stefan and Heléna's, but its occupants, a couple in their sixties, were away caring for their grandchildren.

Suddenly, just for a moment, Heléna heard an unmistakeable creak, as if a foot had been carefully placed on one of the stairs. Then nothing. Silence. Again it was as if time stood still. Heléna held her breath, willing Stefan, if he really were there, to turn around and leave as fast as he could. Then came another sound – the sound of something or someone momentarily brushing against a wall. Again silence. By now the two Gestapo were standing just inside the door, ready if anyone tried to enter. When Heléna saw that one had his gun drawn, she began to tremble, wanting to scream out to warn Stefan, or whoever it was. The thought had come to her that it might possibly be a partisan seeking help to escape, someone about whose arrival Stefan had been unable to warn her. If so, surely he or she needed to be warned too? But what would happen to her if she called out? The Gestapo would not let her off lightly, she knew, and then, if anything happened to her, who would warn Stefan? All these thoughts tumbled through her brain in a split second, as she opened her mouth almost involuntarily, ready to scream.

At that precise moment, there was a soft click – the sound of a key turning in the lock. Heléna could stand it no longer. It had to be Stefan. Careless of any repercussions, she heard herself cry out at the top of her voice.

'No, Stefan! I'm fine! Run! Oh, please run!'

In that instant the door opened, and there stood Stefan, only centimetres from the Gestapo.

. . . .

Almost the whole day, Stefan had stayed at his spot in the church, watching the door of the apartment block and the one window of their own apartment that he was able to see. He noticed that it was open, and, as the morning progressed, he thought he heard, above the noise in the square and the surrounding streets, as the city came to life again, the sound of a piano, his piano, and Heléna playing it. Soon he was sure of it – yes, there it was again! The music was definitely coming from the direction of their apartment window. As he listened intently, he realised that Heléna was playing her concert repertoire – a mixture of Mozart, Chopin and Beethoven classics. He had heard them many times, and could not mistake the brilliant nuances and the fresh, original touches that Heléna brought to these works. As the morning wore on, and the movement of people in the square lessened, Stefan could hear Heléna's playing even more clearly. The stirring and intricate melodies floated across the square, as if at times for his ears alone, he felt. Surely she's safe and well, he thought to himself – she's playing so beautifully! Perhaps there was some other reason she had spoken as she had during their conversation the previous evening.

Just as he had almost convinced himself that that was the case, suddenly he realised that Heléna was now playing Tschaikovsky – but not just any Tschaikovsky. It was their special piece of music, their 'Nur wer die Sehnsucht kennt'!

Again, in an instant, cold fear gripped Stefan. For a moment he tried to rationalise, telling himself that the piece was merely part of Heléna's repertoire for her concert tour, and, as he heard her playing it again, and then several times more, he was almost convinced that this could be so. But not quite. Stefan knew that this music was too precious to her, too intimate to share with any audience other than each other. Soon the music ended, and it was all Stefan could do to stay where he was. He wanted to go to her, to hold her close, just as he had on the evening when they had first played their special piece together. Yet something restrained him – an inner voice, cautioning him to stop and to consider. If Heléna really were playing their music to warn him of danger, then surely he needed to respect her judgment! Surely ignoring this wordless message to him was flying in the face of the promise made to each other on that evening all those months ago! He would wait, he decided, in the end – just a little longer, to see if there were any comings and goings to or from their apartment.

He did not have to wait long. In the early afternoon, Stefan saw a German army vehicle pull up, and a Gestapo officer get out. His heart stood still, hoping against hope that the officer perhaps had business in one of the other apartments. The next thirty minutes or so were, Stefan felt, the most agonising of his life. He watched and prayed, wondering whether he should have tried to follow the officer into the building, despite the presence of the young driver in German uniform leaning nonchalantly against the vehicle, smoking a cigarette. Then, just as Stefan felt he could leave it no longer, the officer emerged from the building, not, he was relieved to see, accompanied by Heléna, but rather by a younger Gestapo officer. For a moment the two of them surveyed the square and the buildings surrounding it, and then, while the senior officer eventually was driven away, the younger one walked slowly across the square and out of Stefan's line of vision. Did that mean, Stefan wondered, that these two had been the only Gestapo in the vicinity, that there were no more of them in the building, or possibly in their actual apartment? Was the coast really clear now for him to try to reach Heléna? And where had the younger officer gone? Was he still somewhere nearby, possibly getting food or other supplies?

At the thought of food, Stefan realised how hungry he was. Yet he did not dare leave his post for that reason only. Soon, he prayed to God, he would be inside his own apartment with Heléna, and together they could celebrate with whatever was at hand.

As these thoughts raced through in his mind, again he heard the sound of Heléna's playing. This time she began with their song – surely a warning to him that he should not venture near the apartment! He stayed where he was, listening again to her beautiful playing, outstanding in its brilliance and the emotion it expressed, despite, or maybe because of, whatever turmoil was taking place within her. And then later, much later, he heard again the haunting tones of their music – not once or twice, but several times in succession. Sometimes Heléna even stopped after a particular phrase, playing it over and over again until she was apparently satisfied with her execution of it. Surely, Stefan thought, she was not playing it simply to perfect her performance, which to his finely attuned ear, was already flawless! Surely this was a message straight from Heléna's heart to his!

Soon darkness came, and with that, Stefan's spirits rose a little. At night, he was able to risk much more. He stayed where he was, until the ranks of those hurrying home from work thinned, and until he saw lights come on in their apartment. Through their window Stefan thought he could see more than one person moving around – there was at least someone present with Heléna, it seemed. Maybe it was one of her friends from the orchestra – perhaps that was why she had been practising as she had? Stefan's brain had begun to reel a little, as much from tiredness and hunger as well as confusion. Now he was struggling to weigh up the various possibilities and courses of action. Oh God, he prayed again, you who know and see all things, give me your wisdom! Let me see with your eyes!

For an hour or more, Stefan sat looking up at the apartment. All was silent now, and in that silence, Stefan envisaged Heléna, hopefully eating dinner, reading, possibly talking with a friend, or listening to music. Heléna, such a beautiful, vibrant young woman, so talented, with so much to offer the world! As he waited, involuntarily his mind wandered back to his first meeting with her at the family home in Tábor. Heléna had come quickly to the door to greet her father, and he had immediately been captured by her beautiful, flushed young face, and by everything about her. He remembered the feel of her small hand in his, as he was introduced to her, and the stirrings within him, as their eyes had met and held for the first time. That had been three years ago now – not long really. They had journeyed so far together since that first meeting, he reflected, through wonderful and exhilarating times, as well as through many difficult ones, full of heartbreak and sadness. Stefan silently thanked God for Heléna once again – he longed for her so much. Surely this was the moment now for him to make his move?

As he stood and stretched his tired limbs, he heard Heléna playing again – the gentle, delicate music of Mozart first of all, followed eventually by her favourite Chopin mazurkas. In his mind's eye, Stefan could see her beautiful golden hair rippling over her shoulders, as her whole body moved with the gay rhythm of the music. Scarcely able to contain himself now, he hurriedly made his way outside, and, thankful for the cover of darkness, darted across the narrow alleyway beside the church and crept carefully along the edge of the adjacent building, keeping close to the few shrubs that grew there. He remembered hearing Heléna's music change from Chopin to something more sober and melancholy, as he slowly made his way around the perimeter of the square. Finally he came to the door of their apartment block, left open, as it usually was, in the warmer months. Slipping inside, he quickly mounted the stairs leading to the first landing. He paused there, aware of sudden flashes of light that penetrated the darkness of the stairwell for a moment and seemed to come from the building opposite. He thought nothing more of it then. All that gripped him was his overwhelming desire to be with Heléna. If any Gestapo were still with her, then he would fight, and fight hard, but he would not let Heléna be hurt in any way for his sake! He felt an incredible strength surge up within him – strength from outside of himself to continue on up those remaining stairs, strength to face whatever was waiting for him inside their apartment. He hoped with all his heart that he would find only Heléna, and perhaps one or more of her friends. Deep down, he sensed it was otherwise – but he was ready. Now was the time!

Still trying to move carefully, to give himself maximum opportunity to surprise any enemy who might confront him when the door opened, Stefan slowly crept up the remaining old wooden stairs, keeping close to the wall. He knew, from past experience at guiding partisans quietly out of the apartment, that this way he could avoid the worst of the loud creaks that he would inevitably make. Now Heléna was playing their special music again, but suddenly she broke off – and there was silence. Silence, that is, except for another loud creak that came from under his left foot, as his body reacted with a start to the sudden conclusion of the music. He leant against the wall to steady himself, and then with one final quick movement, reached the little hallway leading to their front door. In the moonlight filtering through the nearby window, Stefan could see the lock clearly. Quietly, he inserted his key and pushed gently. Just as he did so, he heard Heléna scream at the top of her voice.

'No, Stefan! Run! I'm fine! Oh, please run!'

From that point on, everything seemed to happen in slow motion. Stefan, quickly sizing up the situation, stepped forward, leaving the door open behind him. Ignoring the guns pointed straight at him, he moved swiftly towards Heléna, pulling her close. For a moment they stood locked together, bodies trembling and hearts beating so fast. Then Stefan kissed Heléna desperately, cradling her head with his hand, and holding her firmly against him with the other, as if he would never let her go. Finally he broke the silence, looking searchingly into Heléna's face as he spoke.

'Heléna, I love you so much! They haven't hurt you, have they?'

Heléna shook her head against him.

'I'm all right, Stefan. Oh Stefan, I love you so much too – I tried so hard to warn you!' she whispered brokenly.

'I heard our music!' Stefan whispered back. 'I'm so proud of you, Heléna! I love you so much!'

Behind him, Stefan was aware of the sound of the front door closing, preventing any possible escape that way at least. He turned, and caught sight of a third Gestapo member standing just inside the door – one of the two he had seen leaving the building earlier. From the way the more senior officer of the three now in the apartment congratulated this man, Stefan suddenly realised that his task must have been to keep the approach to the apartment under surveillance from the building opposite. As soon as he had seen Stefan making his way around to the entrance, he must have signalled the two in the apartment, and then followed him inside.

At that point the senior officer sprang into action. Waving his gun at Stefan and Heléna, he ordered them both into the sitting room.

'You've caused us a lot of trouble, Herr Marek,' he snarled at Stefan. 'Now we'll trouble you for some information!'

For the next hour, the officer bombarded Stefan with question after question about the underground movement. Who were its leaders in Prague? What was his role? Where had he been hiding since he left Pilsen? Who had helped him return to Prague? What did he know about the escape routes to Switzerland? On and on the questions went, and each time, Stefan refused to answer. It was only when the officer finally began asking about Heléna's involvement in the movement that Stefan found himself forced to speak.

'Gentlemen, I need you to know that I won't be answering any of your questions except this one. This one I must answer – and I assure you, with God as my witness, and in whom I believe with all my heart, that Heléna knows nothing about what I've done while I've been away, apart from a few of my business commitments!' he stated flatly and firmly. 'And even those she knows very little about. She's been extremely occupied with her own studies and career, and has had no time for anything else. Whatever you might want to accuse me of doing, I tell you truthfully, Heléna has had no part in it!'

Heléna had been sitting close by Stefan on the divan, as the officer questioned him. Throughout, Stefan had held her hand tightly. Now, as she started involuntarily at his strong denial of any underground involvement on her part, he grasped her hand even more firmly. She wanted to be with Stefan. She wanted to stay right beside him, whatever happened – but here he was, protesting her innocence vehemently, attempting to put as much space as possible between them. After he had finished, there was a long silence. Eventually the older officer with the kindly face spoke up.

'Mein Herr, I think this man is speaking the truth about his wife! She's devoted to her career – that's all that matters to her, I believe. Look how she practised and practised in these days that we've been here! Of course she'd do all she could to save her husband, but I don't believe she'd risk her career. Let's arrest him by all means, but let her go!'

At first, the officer in charge glared angrily at him, and the older man lapsed into silence. Even he himself was unsure why he had spoken as he had. It had seemed to him something he simply had to do – and besides that, he had so loved her music! Every note she played had sounded beautiful to him – so beautiful! Especially the song she had played over and over again. Now the younger officer at the door began laughing, ridiculing him and making crude suggestions as to why the older man would want to let Heléna go. Eventually the senior officer stood up abruptly.

'Enough! I'm tired of this whole exercise!' he said with finality. 'We've waited and waited. Why waste our time any further? Let's go – and take him with us. Leave her, if you wish, but bring him now! He'll talk before the night's out!'

Roughly the younger officer separated Stefan from Heléna, and pulled him to his feet. Placing a gun to Stefan's head, he began marching him towards the front door, followed by his superior officer. The older of the three held on to Heléna, pulling her back as she sprang up and tried to follow Stefan.

'No, no, Frau Marek, stay here! You must stay!' he said to her firmly, but not unkindly. 'Who knows? If your husband's innocent, he'll come back to you!'

Stefan knew that any attempt at resistance or escape now would be foolish, and might endanger Heléna's life. For one brief moment, as he was being roughly bundled out the door, Stefan looked into Heléna's eyes, and in a strong and vibrant voice full of love, called out urgently to her.

'Stand tall, little one – stand tall! Remember, you belong to God!'

Heléna stood motionless in the hallway. This was not happening, she told herself – it was as if she were watching a movie in slow motion. And yet there before her was the older Gestapo officer, looking back somewhat sorrowfully, as he hurried after the others. And as all four of them made their way downstairs, Heléna could hear Stefan's voice pleading to God on her behalf.

'Oh Lord, keep her safe! Oh Lord, please protect her! Oh Lord, put your angels around her!'

Eventually Heléna found the strength to move. Calling out Stefan's name over and over again, she stumbled down the stairs to the front door of the building and out into the square. She was just in time to see a German army vehicle pull out from the kerb, its chrome trimmings glinting in the moonlight, and its taillights glowing what seemed to her a malevolent red. Through the rear window, she fleetingly caught sight of Stefan's face, white and agonised, as he turned for one last glimpse of his Heléna.

The car sped off, and she was left standing alone in the empty square.

Chapter Ten

Heléna stayed rooted to the spot, the tears coursing down her cheeks. At that moment she was oddly aware of various sounds around her – the slight scraping of the autumn leaves blowing across the cobblestones, the creak of the churchyard gate, as it flapped back and forth in the breeze on its rusty hinges, and, somewhere in the distance, the crying of a baby. Above all, she was aware of a feeling of absolute horror, and a strange sense of unreality – as if the ground were shifting under her feet and she could find nowhere safe to stand. Suddenly she felt very cold, and trembled all over, her legs almost giving way beneath her. Perhaps if she were able to stand there long enough, she thought wildly, peering into the darkness, the car would return and Stefan would be there, greeting her with that special smile of his that she loved so much.

Finally, after what seemed an eternity of waiting, she staggered numbly inside, somehow managing to drag herself back up the stairs to their apartment. On the way, she noticed the slightly open door of the apartment below theirs, and the accusing eyes of the elderly woman she thought had been their friend staring out at her. Heléna turned her back, too numb to respond in any way.

The door of their apartment was still open, and Heléna stumbled inside, locking it behind her with shaking hands. She stood leaning against it for some time, trying to gather herself together, endeavouring to focus on the next thing Stefan would want her to do. She forced her still trembling legs to carry her along the hall to the sitting room, where she almost fell into the chair nearest the phone. Before she tried to contact anyone, she leaned back and pressed her shaking body into the soft upholstery, unconsciously drawing her feet up underneath her and holding one of the cushions pressed closely to her for comfort. At first, all she could think of was Stefan himself. Where were they taking him? What was happening to him right now? She needed to contact someone in the underground movement who may have an idea where he would have been taken. Perhaps it was not too late – perhaps they could still help him escape somehow! Even in her confused state, however, she realised that any phone conversation she might have could possibly be used against Stefan or her, if the line really were tapped, as they suspected. Equally possible, Heléna realised, was that she might inadvertently incriminate anyone she phoned, in her quest to get help for Stefan.

For a long time she sat immobilised, feeling so afraid and alone. Her mind lurched this way and that, groping for a way out of the endless black pit into which she seemed to be falling, swirling and twirling as she went – a pit filled with pain, overwhelming and shattering in its intensity, like nothing she had ever experienced before.

It was very late now, but still she did not move. All strength seemed to have drained out of her. Then, deep in this whirling vortex of pain and confusion, Heléna became aware of two things in quick succession. The first was the memory of Stefan's voice, as he called out his final words to her.

'Stand tall, little one – stand tall! Remember, you belong to God!'

Even as she heard them again in her mind, it was as if a strength flowed from outside of her and filled her, pushing away the darkness that was threatening to engulf her totally. Then quickly following on from this, she distinctly heard her mother's voice, speaking softly and gently to her. It was as if she, Heléna, were a child again, distressed and calling out in the night as she sometimes had, frightened for some reason, and unable to sleep. Always her mother would come to her, hold her close and reassure her with calm and loving words, soothing her by stroking her forehead, as she laid her down on the pillow again. Then, as she gently rested her hand on her head, as if in blessing, she would repeat some words spoken to God's people long ago.

'You're safe, Heléna! Remember, "the eternal God is your refuge, and underneath are the everlasting arms"!'

As Heléna registered these words again now, she was aware of the close presence of God, holding her in the midst of her overwhelming grief, cushioning her fall into that dark, frightening abyss of pain. They were such strong arms – arms that she knew would never grow tired and loosen their hold on her. Heléna lay there, letting them take her weight, sad and grieving, yet aware too of the loving security around and about her.

Eventually, she fell into a deep sleep where she was. At one stage, as dawn was approaching, she dreamt of Stefan. In her dream, he was in a small room, pacing up and down, up and down, obviously in a dilemma, unsure what he should do. After some time, he knelt on the bare floor, head bowed and hands covering his face, as if he were crying out in anguish to God. Heléna could see tears forcing their way through his fingers as he prayed, and running down over his wrists. Presently she became aware that he was praying aloud, but she could not understand what he was praying, until the final few sentences. Then she heard again the prayer that he had prayed for her as he was being led away from their apartment, the words pouring forth in even greater intensity from the depths of his heart.

'Oh Lord, keep her safe! Oh Lord, please protect her! Oh Lord, put your angels around her!'

In her dream, as soon as he had prayed those words, the door of the small room in which he was praying burst open, and two Gestapo officers roughly pulled him to his feet and marched him outside. Heléna woke with a start, knowing immediately that she needed to pray that very same prayer for Stefan, whatever was happening to him and wherever he had been taken.

'Oh Lord, keep him safe! Oh Lord, please protect him! Oh Lord, put your angels around him!'

Unable to go back to sleep, Heléna remained curled up in the armchair, as the first weak rays of sunlight shone through the window, praying her simple prayer for Stefan over and over again. She knew that she must contact some of their friends as soon as possible, but it was too early to disturb them yet. She sat, her eyes focused on nothing in particular, barely conscious of her surroundings. Thoughts of Stefan consumed her, and all she could see before her was his face – the warmth of his smile, the grey flecks that added such a distinguished touch to his dark hair, and his eyes – his beautiful, clear, blue eyes, full of kindness and sensitivity, and great intelligence. She would not let herself begin to think of the time ahead without him, however long that might be. Better to remain positive, to look forward to his walking into their apartment again any moment, to focus on the next things they planned to do together. Again she prayed fervently for him, so caught up with pleading for his safety that for one moment, when she heard the telephone ring loudly beside her, she had difficulty in identifying its insistent tone. In the few seconds that elapsed before she answered it, she was aware of her hands shaking again and her heart thumping wildly. Perhaps it would be Stefan – perhaps he had been able to escape, and was letting her know where he was!

She lifted the receiver, only to hear the slightly worried voice of her friend Andela greeting her again.

'Heléna, I know it's still quite early, but you were very much on my mind. Are you okay? After we talked the day before yesterday, I felt really concerned about you. I wanted to come over to see you yesterday, but couldn't make it. Are you free today, or do you still have visitors?'

Heléna, while almost sick with disappointment that it had not been Stefan, nevertheless felt relieved that the decision concerning whom to phone and what to do next had been taken from her hands. After a moment's pause, she found enough strength in her voice to reply to Andela's question.

'Hello Andela! Yes, I'm free today. Our visitors have gone now. When could you come over?'

Aware that others might be listening in, Heléna was anxious to leave any explanations until she and Andela could speak face to face. Her unusually abrupt manner and the rather flat tone of her voice, however, conveyed clearly to Andela that something was wrong.

'I can leave right now, Heléna – I'll be there as soon as possible. Then we can have the whole day to ourselves to talk, and maybe to practise a little – although who knows what we'd be practising for? I'll bring my violin and some music anyway. I presume Stefan is at work, is he?'

There was a slight pause before Heléna answered, but then, deciding to avoid Andela's final question entirely, she responded as normally as possible.

'Yes, please do bring your violin. See you soon then!'

Andela, like Heléna, was a very promising young performer, having been taught by her father, who until the war had taught music at a school in Prague. Although a little older than Heléna, she had begun her studies at the Conservatorium the same year as her friend, determined to succeed in her dream to be a concert violinist and travel the world. Normally, she was a bright-eyed, bubbly girl, full of enthusiasm for life, and ready to tackle new challenges. Yet beneath the chatter and frequent laughter, there lay hidden depths, unusual sensitivity, and a keen intelligence, all of which Heléna responded to warmly. In recent months, Andela had become somewhat quieter in general, ever since her father had lost his teaching position, and had subsequently been removed to a forced labour camp near the German border. Nevertheless, she was a resilient young woman, with a strong, positive faith in God and his goodness, and a great encourager of others.

Heléna loved Andela, aware that the latter's more outgoing, gregarious nature complimented and balanced her own quieter and more introverted one, and kept her from retreating too much inside herself. She also saw in her friend other qualities that she herself wanted to emulate, such as her rock solid faith, and her determination to see things in a positive light. Silently she thanked God that the very person she needed – someone warm and steadfast and real, to whom she could pour out her story – would soon be there for her.

Suddenly realising she was still in the same clothes she had been wearing when the Gestapo took Stefan away the previous evening, Heléna quickly showered and changed, in an attempt to look and feel somewhat more normal, for her friend's sake as well as her own. Soon after, she heard Andela's footsteps on the stairs, and her light tap on the front door. Steeling herself, Heléna opened the door and quickly ushered her inside. One swift look at her face was enough to show Andela that something was drastically wrong. She was sure that it was not just that their concert tour had been cancelled. Hastily putting her violin and music case down in the hallway, Andela put her hand on her friend's arm, her concern showing in her face.

'Heléna, what's happened? What's wrong?' she blurted out, unable to stop herself. 'You look so pale and tired. Has something happened to Stefan?'

Even before she had asked that last question, Andela knew what the answer was. Something had indeed gone very wrong for Stefan. Not even waiting for Heléna's reply, she put her arms round her friend and held her, feeling the coldness of her skin and the tension in her body. For some time they stood clinging to each other, as Andela felt her friend's pain, and as Heléna in turn felt the empathy and comfort that flowed from Andela.

Eventually Heléna stepped back a little, and, gazing numbly at her friend, spoke four simple words.

'The Gestapo came, Andela!'

That was as much as she was able to say, before the dam burst, and the tears began to flow. Quickly Andela helped Heléna to the lounge in the sitting room, where huge sobs racked her body. She continued to hold her and comfort her, the sobbing eventually subsiding enough for Heléna to be able to explain what had happened. Andela listened carefully, outwardly calm, her admiration for her friend, and for Stefan, growing by the minute. Inwardly, dismay gripped her. These days in particular, the Gestapo did not play around. If they had waited as long as they had, to find and arrest Stefan, then they would not let him go lightly. His only hope, Andela felt, was to be rescued by the partisans as quickly as possible. Knowing little herself as to how the organisation worked and whom to contact, Andela had to rely on Heléna's judgment, and encourage her to act immediately, without conveying any greater sense of urgency than she no doubt already felt.

'Heléna, do you know anyone in the underground whom you could contact? If we move quickly, then maybe someone can find out where Stefan was taken!'

Andela tried to question her friend calmly, but she knew she had still spoken in a very urgent tone. Recently her two brothers had talked with friends in positions of authority in the Czech police, and discovered something at least of how the Gestapo treated anyone suspected of involvement with partisan work. She was aware that they had not told her half of what they had heard, but from what she did know, she could well imagine what sort of treatment might await someone like Stefan. He was not only an active member of the underground, but one of its most experienced leaders.

Heléna explained to Andela that Stefan had never shared details about his underground work with her, and certainly nothing about who was involved or what their roles were.

She knew she could trust Andela and speak freely about such matters, because of the many times during which they had shared heart to heart.

'Stefan used to say he wouldn't tell me any more because he wanted to protect me, so that in the event of my ever being questioned by the Germans, I'd have nothing to tell them. He would have known that the Gestapo have ways of making people talk. At times, as you know already, we did have to shelter partisans here, and others whose lives were in danger, but for Stefan it was always a last resort, and he himself ensured they left as quickly as possible.'

Heléna was quiet for a little while after that, and then she spoke again, with great urgency, as if the words were being torn from her.

'Andela, I know Stefan's in great danger – I saw how much the Gestapo wanted him, and I know they'll do everything in their power to find out details of his underground work. It's too horrible for me even to contemplate that right now Stefan might be being threatened or tortured in some way! I tried so hard, Andela – I tried so hard to warn him, but he came anyway! He gave himself up for me! He couldn't bear to think I might be in trouble – Andela, I can't just let him do that without at least attempting to find him and help him escape!'

The two friends sat in silence, trying to think clearly, Andela holding Heléna's hands in her own. Eventually, she spoke quietly but firmly.

'Heléna, I'm going to pray now. We need to ask God what the best thing is to do next.'

Without changing her position on the lounge, she continued to hold Heléna's hands as she prayed.

'Our Father, we're your children, and right now we're so distressed and confused! O God, please show us what to do! Give us your wisdom and comfort, we pray! Have mercy on Stefan, Father – you know where he is! Please be close to him and strengthen him!'

They continued sitting together, heads bowed and hands tightly clasped. Suddenly, Heléna lifted her head and opened her eyes.

'I need to contact Uncle Erik straight away!' she said decisively.

Andela had heard so much about Uncle Erik, and knew the important part he had played in her friend's music career. She had met him just once, when he had managed to come to Prague for one of Heléna's early concerts with the Conservatorium orchestra. What he could do for her now, she was unsure, but she trusted her friend's judgment. They had prayed, and both of them felt this was indeed their answer.

'Andela, I'll need you to contact him for me,' Heléna went on to explain. 'I believe Stefan thought it wasn't safe to say much on our phone, so I'll give you his number. Just tell him what's happened! He'll know whom to contact. Tell him I'm safe – and not to worry about me! I'll wait here, Andela. Stefan may contact me, so I need to be here …'

Andela could hear the uncertainty in her friend's voice as she spoke those final words. Heléna hoped with all her heart that Stefan would indeed contact her in some way, but she was realistic enough to know how difficult this would be, even for someone as resourceful as Stefan. Andela hugged her friend tightly, and then quickly jumped to her feet.

'Heléna, I'll go and phone your Uncle Erik immediately, then come back here, because I want to be with you,' she said gently. 'But while I'm gone, please try to eat something, and get some rest!'

Andela was gone then, leaving her violin and music in the hall where she had dropped them on first arriving. Alone in the apartment again, Heléna did as Andela had suggested, making herself some bread and cheese from the supplies she had brought with her. She found it difficult to swallow anything, however, apart from some strong coffee. Sleep proved impossible too. She wandered from one room to another, unable to settle, with thoughts and images of Stefan constantly in the forefront of her mind.

At last she heard Andela's footsteps on the stairs again, and her knock on the door. She had done what Heléna had asked. Uncle Erik, though extremely shocked, had promised to contact those who would know what to do immediately. Heléna, Andela knew, was as dear to him as if she were his own daughter. It was arranged that, as soon as he knew anything, he would phone Andela's home, where her elder brother Miklos, himself a very recent recruit of the underground movement, would wait for his call, since Andela herself could not be there. Miklos promised to bring them any news, good or bad, as soon as it came.

There was nothing more to be done, except wait and pray. Eventually, Andela prepared some lunch, but again Heléna had difficulty eating anything. In the afternoon, after they had again prayed together, Heléna managed to rest for a while, experiencing once more the sensation of being gently cradled by two very strong arms, as she fell into a brief but deep sleep. The two friends talked then, sharing their disappointment at the cancellation of their concerts, and eventually Andela suggested they practise together. By mutual consent, they chose the softer, slower music from Andela's repertoire, Heléna's mind being too preoccupied to play anything which required extra energy and concentration. Dinner time came, with no news from Miklos, and then, around eight, Heléna and Andela heard low voices on the stairs, followed by knocking at the door. Again, Heléna began shaking, her heart in her mouth as she opened the door. Andela's younger brother Milan stood there, and, with him, others from the little group with whom Stefan and Heléna met on Sundays. They moved inside quietly, each embracing Heléna in turn.

'We all wanted to come when we heard, just to be with you,' one of the girls, Zdenka, explained gently. 'We didn't want to overwhelm you, but none of us could decide who should come, so here we all are!'

They moved to the sitting room, making it clear to Heléna as they did, that they would not stay long – just long enough to let her feel their love and support. Apart from Milan and Zdenka, there was a slightly older man, Daniel, and his wife Renata, a younger newly married couple of around Heléna's age, Radim and Irena, and two teenage girls, Johana and Sabina. They talked with Heléna and Andela for a short time, and then, all holding hands in a circle, prayed for her and Stefan – heartfelt prayers that brought such comfort to her spirit, and release for her grief, as the tears flowed unchecked. And before they left, they sang together some wonderful words from a psalm of David for her – reassuring, beautiful words that Heléna loved.

I lift up my eyes to the hills –
   where does my help come from?
My help comes from the Lord,
   the Maker of heaven and earth.

Andela stayed on with Heléna, determined not to leave her alone. Heléna eventually went to her bedroom to lie down, if not to sleep, while Andela curled up on the lounge. The ticking of the grandfather clock in the corner seemed to emphasise the swift passing of time, as Andela lay there wondering what was happening for Stefan, wherever he was. Earnestly she prayed that Uncle Erik's partisan friends would soon ascertain his whereabouts, and somehow be able to rescue him. Even within Gestapo headquarters, her brothers had told her, there were apparently those who were at least somewhat sympathetic to the Czech nation, and the struggles its people were experiencing.

Heléna and Andela must have eventually slept, since they were both woken early in the morning by the sound of knocking at the door. It was Miklos, but only to say that Uncle Erik had phoned with news that some of Stefan's best remaining co-workers had been contacted, and were doing all they could. Miklos thought it best not to pass on the rest of Uncle Erik's message, however, which was that if Stefan had already undergone interrogation, then there was probably little anyone could do. Somehow when he saw Heléna's white face and beautiful, sad, expressive eyes, he could not bring himself to extinguish whatever hope remained in them. Andela planned to return home with him for a short while, and then to shop for a few more provisions, since Heléna could not bring herself to leave the apartment even for a few minutes. Stefan might call, she said, trying to remain hopeful and positive. He might need her. She would wait. Andela left then, promising to return soon.

After they had gone, Heléna wandered back to the sitting room, and seated herself almost automatically at the piano. Her hands wandered over the keys, and although unaware of consciously choosing any particular piece of music, she soon found herself playing the first few notes of 'Nur wer die Sehnsucht kennt'. At first, as soon as she realised what she was playing, she faltered. Then from somewhere within her, a strong surge of emotion rose up, an anger almost white hot in its intensity, similar to what she had experienced that Christmas evening at Tábor before her mother's death, as she had entertained family and friends. It seemed so long ago now, but in the time that had passed since then, so much more suffering had occurred, with so many more people taken from them. Oh Stefan, not you too, her heart cried out in anguish. Please God, not Stefan! She finished playing and sat where she was, feeling somehow suspended in time. She felt so alone, and yet, in some strange way, she knew she was not alone.

Eventually she stirred, and wandered restlessly over to the window. She stood looking down at the empty square, its cobblestones wet and slippery from the early morning drizzle, wondering when Andela would come back. Just as she turned to move to the kitchen, she heard the unmistakeable sound of a motorbike making its way along one of the streets leading to the square. The noise increased, until it stopped directly beneath her window. Soon heavy footsteps sounded on the stairs. Heléna, despite her trembling, had already gone to the door, and was ready to open it by the time the first knock sounded.

There in the little alcove stood a Gestapo officer. Heléna, shocked and wary, realised it was one of the three who had been with her in the apartment. It was the older, heavily built man, the one who had so much liked her music. His blue eyes were still kindly, but also sad, Heléna noticed, and he seemed somewhat ill at ease, as he stood there.

As Heléna stared at him dumbly, the man held out his hand. In it, Heléna saw with a start, was a small, folded piece of paper, with her name written clearly on it. Immediately she recognised Stefan's distinctive, bold handwriting. She reached out and took the note with a shaking hand, aware of a welter of questions and emotions rising up in her. She opened her mouth to speak, but no sound would come. The officer continued to stare at her, before giving an explanation in hurried, rather abrupt tones.

'Frau Marek, your husband wanted me to deliver this to you. It's dangerous to do this – I'm acting against orders! But you played so beautifully, Frau Marek – and you reminded me so much of my wife …'.

He paused, uncertain if, or how, he should continue. Taking a deep breath and looking directly at him, Heléna quickly plied him with questions.

'You brought this from Stefan? Is … is he all right? Where is he? Can you please tell me where he is?'

The officer held up his hand for her to stop, before quickly replying.

'Frau Marek, I can't answer your questions – I shouldn't even be here! But your husband talks to God – I heard him! And he asked me to do this, as if he knew he could trust me! I have to go now. I cannot help your husband any more, but whatever happens, Frau Marek, you must keep playing your music! And you must keep the faith!

Auf Wiederseh'n!'

He turned on his heel and was gone. Heléna was left standing, clutching Stefan's note in her hand. Dimly she was aware of the motorbike starting up, and the sound of its engine receding into the distance. Slowly she made her way inside, curiously reluctant to open the precious note. Somehow it seemed to her that by doing so, she would be admitting to herself that these could possibly be Stefan's last words to her. She walked back to the sitting room and sat in his favourite chair. The minutes ticked by, but still she could not bring herself to open the small folded piece of paper in her lap. She was unsure how long she sat there, oblivious of her surroundings, except for the feel of the note in her hand, as she turned it over and over.

Eventually, another light tap on the front door roused her, but this time it was the little staccato tap that Andela always used. Heléna went dazedly to let her in, still holding the note tightly. Andela, determined to cheer up her friend, carried her various purchases to the kitchen, chattering brightly as she went.

'Heléna, I found some delicious late peaches at the market. Would you like one now? I bet you haven't eaten anything yet, have you? Neither have I – I wanted to get back here as quickly as possible. And we could have some of your special coffee – what do you think? I wonder where Stefan manages to find such superb coffee these days! Do you know, Heléna?'

Finally, Andela's flow of words stopped long enough for her to notice Heléna's silence and stillness, as she stood at the kitchen door staring blankly at her friend. Slowly, Heléna held out her hand with the note in it. As if from a distance, she heard herself explaining how she had come by it.

'Andela, it was the same German soldier, the same man I told you about – the one with the kind eyes and the smile lines! He couldn't tell me, he said, where Stefan was or what would happen to him, but he wanted to give me the note, because he loved my music. And Andela, he heard Stefan praying…'.

At that point, Heléna could not speak any more, or hold back the tears. Andela came to her friend, and they sat down together at the kitchen table.

'So what does the note say, Heléna?' Andela asked breathlessly. 'How's Stefan?'

Slowly Heléna replied, 'I don't know yet – I can't bring myself to read it, for some reason. Andela … I think I might need your help.'

Heléna held out the note to her friend with a trembling hand, and Andela took it, aware as she did so, that her own hand was shaking. Slowly she unfolded it and smoothed it out on the table. Putting her arm around her friend's shoulders, she watched her face, as Heléna's eyes took in the words Stefan had written. They were not many – and even Andela could see that the writing was somewhat shaky in spots. As Heléna read, the tears began to flow, so that soon she had to ask her friend to read it out to her. Taking a deep breath, Andela did as she was asked.

My dear Heléna

I am writing this after interrogation throughout the night and all day today. Heléna, I have not given in! All the time I think of you and call on God's strength to get through this time and to live for him and for you and for my country. It is now night, and I am writing this in some pain and in almost complete darkness, but I want you to know, Heléna, that whatever happens to me, keep trusting God! These things we are going through are hard to understand, but remember our Lord Jesus, 'a man of sorrows and familiar with suffering'! Remember him, Heléna – remember you belong to him! One day, hopefully many years from now, I pray we both, like Paul, will be able to say 'I have fought the good fight, I have finished the race, I have kept the faith.' Keep the faith, Heléna – whatever happens, keep the faith! Stand tall ... and always remember, you belong to him!'

All my love
Stefan

After Andela had finished reading, the two of them sat in painful silence, broken only by the sound of Heléna's crying, and the few words she could manage to get out.

'Oh Andela, I'm so thankful he's still alive, but obviously he's in great pain! And it all sounds so final – as if he doubts he really will see me again!'

Her friend held her close, unable to think of anything to say that would not sound trite. Soon Heléna folded the note, and, holding it firmly in her hand, told Andela she wanted to be alone in her bedroom for a while. The day wore on, Heléna emerging again some time after mid-day, pale but calm. Andela sat with her for a while, and then busied herself in the kitchen, in an effort to make something that might tempt her friend to eat. To her surprise and relief, Heléna did eat a little of the food she had prepared, and also make some effort at conversation. Later, Radim and Irena, the young couple from their Sunday fellowship group, called again, accompanied by Milan and Zdenka. Heléna showed them the note, and together they all held hands again and prayed, for Stefan first, and then for Heléna. Eventually, exhausted by the emotion of the day, Heléna again went to her room. Andela too, worn out and full of sorrow for her friend, curled up under a soft rug on the lounge, and slept.

At around nine o'clock the next morning, just as Andela was wondering if she could risk phoning home to see if Miklos had heard anything, there was a knock at the front door. Andela opened it, to find not only Miklos, but Milan and Zdenka, and also Uncle Erik. One look told her that the news was not good. Ushering them into the sitting room where Heléna was, she went immediately to stand by her friend, who had risen to her feet. Heléna ran to Uncle Erik, holding him close, as he did her. As she stepped back, she noticed the sadness and deep exhaustion etched clearly on his dear old face. Her hand flew to her mouth, and her eyes asked the question for her. Taking her hands in his, Uncle Erik spoke very gently.

'Yes, Heléna, we discovered late last night that Stefan had passed away earlier in the evening. Our sources tell us that he died under interrogation, but he never divulged one single thing about the underground movement! My friend overheard the Gestapo complaining their time had been wasted, and then watched as Stefan's body was placed in a waiting van. My friend is one of our most trusted workers, Heléna – there can be no doubt about the truth of what he told us. I'm so sorry, my dear! I came as quickly as I could – Miklos helped me make the journey in the early hours of this morning. I wanted to be the one to tell you – I'm so sorry, Heléna!'

For a moment Heléna stood rooted to the spot, staring blindly at him, seeing his anguish, but feeling nothing herself. Then before anyone could move, she quietly crumpled to the floor.

Andela stayed on with Heléna, while her own family cared for Uncle Erik. Every day he visited Heléna, urging her to allow him to take her back home to Tábor, until she felt stronger. Berta and Simona would be waiting to care for her, and he and Edita would visit as often as she wanted. One day Simona herself travelled by train to Prague to see her, leaving the children with Berta, to try to persuade Heléna to return with her. At first, Heléna was adamant that she wished to stay on in Prague. Somehow she felt she needed the familiarity of their apartment, and the comfort of Stefan's things around her – his cello, his favourite books, his well-worn Bible, his thick coat hanging in the hallway. It was as if part of her knew he was gone forever, but another part still hoped it was not true. As the days wore on, however, she began to experience a strong desire to be as far away as possible from where everything had occurred, to be with friends who had known her since she was a child, long before she met Stefan. Besides, she wanted to leave Andela free to return home, yet she knew she was not ready to be alone in the empty apartment. Finally, one day when Uncle Erik was visiting her, she agreed to his proposal, informing him, quietly and decisively, that she would leave as soon as he wanted.

The next day, after a tearful farewell to Andela, Miklos drove them down to Tábor in his father's old car. Berta was on the steps to greet her, just as her mother had welcomed her father home so many times, only this time the tears flowed from sadness rather than happiness. Even little Anna, Jan and Simona's eldest, greeted Heléna shyly and gently, her young face sorrowful for her in her grief. Turning to Uncle Erik as he went to get in the car for the short drive to his own home, Heléna clung to him.

'Thank you so much for caring for me, Uncle Erik, exactly like I know my own father would have! Soon, when I'm stronger, we'll talk more, and I'll play again. But not yet – not just yet.'

To Miklos she also said her thanks, noticing momentarily, even in her grief, the warmth of his handclasp, and the depth of feeling in his eyes. But only Stefan filled her mind. She was lost in her grief, unable to imagine how she would live without him. Life must go on – and it would go on eventually, she knew that. She would stand tall, as Stefan had wanted her to, but she needed time to heal, time to think, time to grieve. And time to learn to trust God again.

PART III

When my heart was grieved and my spirit embittered,
I was senseless and ignorant; I was a brute beast before you.
Yet I am always with you; you hold me by my right hand.
You guide me with your counsel, and afterward
you will take me into glory.
Whom have I in heaven but you?
And earth has nothing I desire besides you.
My flesh and my heart may fail,
But God is the strength of my heart and my portion forever.

Psalm 73:21-26

Chapter Eleven

Stefan died early in the evening of 2nd October 1941, two days before his thirty-third birthday. In those first few weeks after his death, Heléna, herself only just twenty-three, could not seem to grasp the enormity of what had happened, or even want to imagine what her life would be like without Stefan. Berta fussed over her, caring for her almost as she cared for her own grandchildren, trying, despite wartime shortages, to cook tasty treats that she knew Heléna liked. Simona tried to be available for her whenever possible, but she took care not to invade the space Heléna seemed to need around her to grieve and to try to come to grips with the reality that was now her life. At first, night times were the worst, and it was then that either Simona or Berta were the greatest help, taking it in turns to comfort her whenever she woke calling out Stefan's name, warning him to run, and then sobbing and begging the Gestapo not to take him away. They would sit with her, holding her as she trembled all over, soothing her until she became calmer. Often, still struggling to wake up fully, she would question them brokenly, unsure what had happened.

'Stefan isn't dead, is he? They didn't take him, did they? I remember – I warned him! He heard our music!'

Then, tears often streaming down their own faces, they would usually hold her and comfort her, until she realised the truth for herself, quietened, and eventually slept again.

During the daytime, Heléna mostly wanted to be left alone. Some days she walked for miles along the riverbank and across the fields, coming home exhausted as the sun set. In the early days of her grief, she took care not to be home too late from these walks, since, in some part of her mind, a voice seemed to say to her that Stefan might come, Stefan might be there, and he would perhaps be worried about her. Then as the weeks went by, she began to stay out as long as the light and the cold of the oncoming winter would let her. It was as if some part of her still expected Stefan to come, but another part did not want to face the disappointment yet again of finding him not there, of coming home to an empty hallway, an empty place at the table, and an empty bed.

In some ways these long, lonely walks were good for Heléna, but in other ways, they hindered her recovery. While she was often aware of the natural beauty around her, she also easily retreated into herself, lost in her own thoughts and her inward battle with God. Some days, the incredible colours of the autumn leaves, trembling and delicately poised on the branches, or the golden shimmer on the surface of the nearby river, as the last rays of the sun reflected from the ripples formed as the ducks took to flight, stirred Heléna's heart deeply, leaving her in awe of a creator who could call forth such beauty. Who was she to question him, to even search for a reason for Stefan's death? On other days, however, the anger that drove her to walk long distances, also blinded her eyes to the majesty and colour and intricacy of nature around her. Then all she could see, with her clouded vision, were the signs that winter was fast approaching, that the leaves on the ground were decaying, that the birds were now silent, that death inevitably followed life. On these days she would return with such an air of hopelessness and lostness about her, that Simona, with her warm, gentle, loving nature, felt her heart almost break inside her. She could not seem to find words to penetrate the blackness that surrounded her friend, and the bitterness that threatened to consume her.

Some days, Heléna's walks took her in a different direction, along the laneways to Uncle Erik's cottage, on the outskirts of Tábor. Heléna could not quite enunciate why, but there was something about these visits that she found so soothing to her shattered spirit. When the weather allowed it, they sat in the sheltered little garden, where often the two of them were joined by Edita, carrying coffee and biscuits, or bread and cheese or perhaps some sausage, depending on the time of day. Or on wet days, and as winter approached, they sat in the cosy little sitting room in front of a fire, sharing Edita's hearty home made soup, and talking quietly. Both brother and sister had seen a lot in their lifetime, Heléna knew. Uncle Erik had been married many years ago, but his wife had died in childbirth. He had never remarried, choosing instead to lose himself in his career and in the world of music. Edita had married too, but her husband, a Lutheran pastor and army chaplain, had been killed in 1917 while serving in France, leaving her with two boys to raise alone. Both boys had emigrated to America over ten years previously, however. While Edita never heard from her younger son, the older one had asked her many times to join him and his American wife and their children – her own grandchildren, whom she had never seen. But the journey seemed too far for Edita, and it was too much for her to envisage leaving her homeland. Besides, she felt she had to look after her brother, who had been so good to her after her husband was killed.

When Heléna was with them, she sensed that they understood her deep sadness. They understood that nothing could be said that would take the pain away, or would somehow make everything right. Both had travelled long journeys full of sadness and loneliness, but both still had a deep sweetness about them, a gentleness of spirit that was like soothing oil to Heléna's own wounded one. When she needed to talk, they listened – and listened well. They heard her out with great empathy, never interrupting with ready answers, but rather patiently waiting for the right moment to share a word in season. And when all she needed was their comforting, unquestioning presence, they were there for her, understanding that sometimes the soul simply cannot speak of its deepest grief and despair.

Sometimes too Heléna accompanied Uncle Erik, as he walked from his cottage along the laneways and through narrow old back streets to the church, where she would arrange herself comfortably on some cushions in a corner pew, and listen as he practised on the wonderful old organ there. Hearing him play his favourite, intricate Bach preludes and fugues so brilliantly, despite his age, left her breathless with admiration, and her own spirit uplifted and refreshed. She was always deeply stirred, too, by his renditions of the more sombre works of Handel or Mendelssohn, hearing in them a melancholy that reflected her own mood, and seemed to give it form or voice. Often, however, it was the simple old hymns he played which touched her most deeply. Songs of faith, Uncle Erik explained, that had fed his own spirit in his darkest times, and that he knew had kept many others grounded in God down through the years. Heléna particularly loved Luther's hymn 'A Mighty Fortress Is Our God'. Somehow the stirring melody line, with its almost defiant tones, echoed something that was there deep in her own spirit – something that refused to be extinguished, that wanted to rise up and fight, despite having been so wounded. She loved the words, too, despite their almost mediaeval feel.

A mighty fortress is our God,
A bulwark never failing;
Our helper he, amid the flood
Of mortal ills prevailing.
For still our ancient foe
Doth seek to work his woe;
His craft and power are great,
And armed with cruel hate –
On earth is not his equal.

....

And though this world with devils filled,
Should threaten to undo us,
We will not fear, for God hath willed
His truth to triumph through us.
Let goods and kindred go,
This mortal life also;
The body they may kill,
God's truth abideth still,
His kingdom is forever.

For Heléna, the 'cruel hate' that Luther wrote about, that scornful and unreasoning hatred held by human beings towards others equally human, had done its devastating work well in her life. It made sense to her, that the depth of cruelty and the destruction to be seen all around her on such a large scale, must have its roots in a greater source of evil far beyond this world. Surely this spoke of dark powers determined to oppose the goodness of God at every turn, and to manipulate and destroy the creatures God had created in his own image and likeness? Heléna could not absolve those who had killed Stefan, or those who had destroyed her father's life, and indirectly her mother's, from personal blame for their own cruel actions. Yet gradually she came to believe that truly there was a madness abroad in the world – a deceitful, cunning spirit that contrived, with man's cooperation, to foster large scale hatred and greed and fear and selfishness. For the first time, she began to understand the absolute enormity of Jesus' prayer from the cross, and to glimpse the deep heart of compassion behind his cry toward heaven: 'Father, forgive them, for they do not know what they are doing.'

Heléna found that, as yet, she could not honestly bring herself to have that heart of compassion for her enemies. Her loss was still too recent, and the pain too raw. To Uncle Erik and Edita, and also Simona and Berta, as they watched and waited and cared for her, it seemed that there was still deep grief within her that needed to find its outward expression, an anger and disappointment that needed to surface before she could move on with her life. Heléna felt that, too. She felt as if she were in some no man's land, from which there seemed to be no escape. Yet she knew, even in the midst of her questioning, that something was stirring in her, that God had not deserted her, that one day she would feel his loving presence with her again. In some deep part of her, she knew that he would continue to be her mighty fortress and her helper, as Luther had expressed, in the midst of the overwhelming tide of grief. Eventually, his light would pierce the darkness, and his truth would prevail. Right now, she was in great pain, but somehow, whenever she reflected on the crucifixion, she knew without a doubt that Jesus understood that pain. He knew, and he cared, just as Uncle Erik and Edita were lovingly showing her. In those early dark weeks, Heléna did not at first believe that, but as the days passed, she found herself wanting to hang on desperately to that truth. After all, as Stefan himself had begged her to remember, she belonged to God. She truly belonged to him, whatever was happening around her and in her.

December arrived, and with it, the long dark winter evenings. Berta usually lit the fire in the sitting room, and she and Simona and the girls often joined Heléna there after dinner, until the children's bedtime. Heléna loved Anna and little Kristina. She often sat curled up on the rug in front of the fire, with Kristina on her lap, and Anna, who was almost five now, sitting next to her and nestling snugly against her, as Heléna read stories to them. Usually Berta sat in her comfortable old armchair, busily mending something, while Simona tried to finish writing yet another letter to Jan, at the small table a little removed from the fire. Sometimes the two of them, looking up from their work, would quietly watch Heléna with the girls. Then their eyes would meet, and in these moments, both Berta and Simona knew their thoughts were the same – if only there had been time for Stefan and Heléna to have children of their own! Heléna had always loved children, something in their innocence and honesty appealing deeply to her. In her current fragile state, she particularly appreciated their simple, warm acceptance of her, whatever mood she was in, and their spontaneous loving hugs, which touched her deeply. Anna, in particular, seemed to know when Heléna was especially sad. Her big brown eyes would brim with compassion on these occasions, as she snuggled even closer to her. She was old enough to understand that 'Uncle Stefan' had gone to be with Jesus, and to know that Heléna therefore needed lots of warm hugs, just like she herself did when she felt scared in the dark.

One evening, Anna, who had been allowed to stay up a little later than Kristina, was sitting on Heléna's lap in one of the armchairs, as she read to her. They were enjoying looking at a new book together, one Anna had received for her birthday the previous week, with particularly beautiful illustrations.

'Oh, look, Aunty Heléna, that man's just like Uncle Stefan!' Anna suddenly exclaimed without thinking.

Heléna looked at where Anna's little finger was pointing, and saw clearly what she meant. There before her was a man with dark hair flecked with grey at the sides, just like Stefan's, unusually clear blue eyes, and smile lines around his mouth like Stefan's. He was the 'Daddy' in the story, playing with his little boy and girl, holding them close and laughing with them. Heléna's heart turned over, as, with a quick intake of breath, she saw the likeness for herself. Then came the agonising thrust of sudden pain at this unexpected, clear reminder of Stefan, and Heléna found her eyes filling with tears, which she could not hold back. She was defenceless, as she sat holding on her lap an equally shocked and distraught little girl.

'Oh, oh, Aunty Heléna, I didn't mean to make you sad! I'm so sorry! I'm really sorry!' Anna managed to gasp out in between her own sobs, which were growing bigger and bigger, as she saw Heléna's tears and grief. 'It was just ... I just thought he looked so like Uncle St...' she wailed, as Simona came swiftly into the room, having finished putting Kristina to bed.

During this exchange, Berta had remained where she was, sensing something holding her back from intervening. With a wisdom born of many years' experience, she quickly signalled to Simona to hold back also. As they watched, Anna flung her little arms around Heléna's neck, and Heléna buried her face in Anna's thick, black curls, each clinging tightly to the other. Anna was inconsolable, her tender spirit stricken with shame that she had so hurt her beloved Aunty. Heléna held her close, not wanting to let her go, trying to convey, as she wound her arms even more tightly around the little girl, that it was okay, but unable, at the same time, to stop her own sobbing. It was as if a dam had burst, huge tears coursing down her cheeks and falling on Anna's shining curls, and shuddering sobs shaking her body. The two of them stayed like that for some time, the sound of their mingled crying bringing tears to Berta's and Simona's eyes, too.

Eventually Anna quietened, but continued to hold on to Heléna, sensing the latter's need of a warm, compassionate little body pressed close to hers, heart touching heart. Berta and Simona let them be, until they could see that Anna was beginning to fall asleep, her eyelids becoming heavy, and her arms beginning to relax their hold. Simona came then and lifted her from Heléna, carrying her upstairs. Heléna leaned back in the armchair, emotionally spent, her eyes red with weeping, while Berta smoothed away the long strands of hair that had fallen across her forehead, and held her gently. After a long interval, Heléna stirred.

'Thank you, Berta,' was all she said softly. 'I'll sleep now, I know.'

'Go in peace, my dear – go in peace,' Berta responded, her hand resting lightly on Heléna's head. 'May God's angels watch over you and comfort you, even as you sleep!'

A few days later, Simona's husband Jan came home for Christmas, having managed to obtain leave from his work with the German army. Most of his time in recent months had been spent in the northwest of the country, nearer the German and Polish borders, often on the move, and often working long hours in the freezing cold. The little family was overjoyed at his return, and preparations were soon in full swing for a special Christmas together, despite wartime restrictions once more.

Heléna had not been looking forward to Christmas without Stefan – it was too painful even to contemplate. However, since the night when Anna's simple, childlike comment had brought her grief to the surface, penetrating the walls she had built around herself, Heléna had felt a softening within her. It was as if some deep festering sore had been lanced, and healing was beginning to come. On Jan's return, she found herself drawn even more lovingly into this little family circle, sheltered in a safe place, from which she could begin to engage more fully with the world again. On Christmas Day, she was surprised at her ability to enter into the children's delight at the little gifts they received, and in the giving of their own simple homemade gifts to the family and to her. She walked to church with them, aware that something of the wonder and joy of the birth of the Saviour was touching her once again, stirring up hope within her. She stood in the old church with head held high, alone, yet not alone, part of her so sad in her loneliness and grief, but another part warmed and comforted in the presence of God and his people. During the service, Heléna remembered Stefan's urgent words to her, encouraging her to stand tall, and, for a short time at least, she consciously did so. It was as if she were planting a stake in the ground, clearly marking the place from which she would move forward. Sometimes, she knew, she would return to this spot, and look back and grieve what she had lost. That was a necessary part of the journey. She felt God reassuring her, however, that she would never go back to the complete hopelessness of it all, to that wild place of grief, where life itself did not seem to matter any more, where nothing could penetrate the black despair around her. The years ahead would bring incredible challenges, but she would stand strong in God, with a firm hold on life, and on his purposes for her. She would grieve, but she would stand tall, just as Stefan had wanted.

As 1942 began to unfold, and the news of ongoing arrests and executions of Czech citizens continued to reach Tábor, Heléna grew increasingly restless, wanting in her heart to help her people, but also knowing she still had a way to go in her own recovery, before she could be of use to others. She continued to visit Uncle Erik and Edita often, pouring out her thoughts and feelings to them, knowing they would understand and not judge. Some days her anger was uppermost, while on others, she was more acquiescent – still sad, but able to focus on moving forward. She was generally somewhat withdrawn, happiest with young children, such as Jan and Simona's girls, or older people, like Uncle Erik and Edita, and able to relax only with those of her own age whom she knew very well. It was as if it were too much of an emotional effort just yet to interact with those she did not know intimately and to try to relate to their particular worlds.

Those close to her were patient and prayerful, and so determined to honour Stefan's memory and care for his young wife to the best of their ability. And gradually, little by little, Heléna found herself emerging from her fragile cocoon, able to engage again with others a little beyond her immediate supportive circle of friends in Tábor. As yet, she had not felt comfortable about returning to Prague, but she knew, from letters and phone calls received, that her friends from their Sunday fellowship had not forgotten her – particularly Andela.

On one of Heléna's visits to Uncle Erik in mid-January, the subject of her future musical career again came up. Usually Heléna intimated that she did not want to return to serious practice as yet. She felt she did not have the emotional energy to pour into her music that she knew was required to do it the justice it deserved. Indeed, she had rarely played during the three months since Stefan's death. When she arrived on this day, Uncle Erik was giving a lesson to a friend's granddaughter on the old upright piano in his study. As Heléna sat across the narrow hallway in the cosy sitting room, she smiled at Uncle Erik's patient, gentle tone, as he encouraged his young pupil.

'Well done, little one! Well done! Now let's try that again, shall we? Yes, that's right! My goodness, fancy you being able to stretch your fingers so wide! Who would have thought it? Let's count this bar out loud together, shall we? One, two, three, four, one, two, three, four … . Now a big stretch up to that top C there – wonderful! Grandpa will be so proud of you!'

Memories came flooding back of the many hours she herself had spent in that very room, and later at the beautiful grand piano in her own home, as Uncle Erik taught her – hours during which she was sure she must often have tried his patience deeply. Now she listened, as he concluded the little girl's lesson, writing down the things to work on for next time, encouraging her to practise each day, telling her how much she had improved.

Soon after, he joined Heléna, just as Edita arrived with coffee and cake. He sighed deeply, as he eased himself rather wearily into his favourite old armchair, greeting her warmly, nevertheless.

'Wonderful to see you again, my dear! Do you remember when you were just a little one, coming for lessons with this fearsome old man who kept wanting you to work harder?' he asked, with a twinkle in his eye. 'I think then I had much more patience and energy! Nowadays, I do find it more difficult to remain enthusiastic and positive with my young students, particularly the lazy ones! I think I'll give up teaching soon, Heléna – I think the time has come. And that's exactly why I'm glad you're here today! I have a proposal to make – but promise me now you'll think about it, and not turn it down immediately! That's all I ask.'

Heléna looked across at him rather apprehensively, knowing in her heart what he was going to say.

'Heléna, I believe you know what I'm going to ask,' he continued. 'I'd like you to think about taking over my piano students as soon as possible! I need time to work on some organ compositions, and also to finish writing my book. Besides, my patience with the younger students is wearing a little thin, as I've said, and I have no desire to turn into an old ogre who takes away their enjoyment of music! You don't have to commit yourself for any specific length of time – we could take it month by month. And don't give me your answer now. Think about it, my dear, and let me know when you've come to a decision. I'll pray it will be the right one – for your sake and mine!'

Heléna was quiet for some time, letting his words sink in. During her years at the Conservatorium, while other students had majored on teaching, such a path had not appealed to her greatly. She wanted to put her heart and soul into performing, to feel the excitement of the concert hall and recital room, to move people deeply through her music. But things had changed. Now it was wartime. Now in her homeland there were no orchestras, no institutions like the Conservatorium – and no concerts. More than that, there was no Anezka to encourage her, no Václav to be so proud of her – and no Stefan to be her rock, the one who would hold her close after each performance and speak the words of reassurance she needed to hear.

Perhaps Uncle Erik was right. Perhaps this was the road to take – for the moment at least. They parted soon after, Heléna promising to think it over carefully.

That evening, Heléna made her way to the music room, seating herself carefully at the grand piano. Softly she began playing – simple melodies that flowed easily from her fingers. Somewhere deep inside her, she was aware that her soul was beginning to stir, like a bud unfurling, as the rays of the sun touched its petals. She played on, eventually aware of a little figure standing close behind her and to her right. She stopped and turned around, holding out her hand to little Anna, standing there in her warm woollen nightdress as if mesmerised, her big brown eyes shining with excitement.

'Oh, Aunty Heléna, it's so beautiful hearing you play – I love it so much!' she burst out, unable to contain herself. 'Will you please, please teach me to play like you? I want to play so much!'

Heléna sat with her arm encircling Anna's waist as she stood beside her, and looked directly into her small, sensitive face. How could she resist such a heartfelt request? It seemed to her that again this little one was God's special messenger, sent to ease the way for her into the next phase of her recovery. Calmly, and with a deep sense of rightness that seemed to come from somewhere outside her, Heléna heard herself reply gently.

'Of course I will, Anna! You'll be my very first pupil here in Tábor! But you'll have to be very patient with me, just as I'll try to be with you! Run to bed now, but let's begin tomorrow!'

Now she knew what her answer to Uncle Erik had to be. This, she realised, was the natural next step – to begin again in a small simple way with her music, to share what she had learnt and been given, and, in the process, to begin to receive the healing that she believed God had for her. Life would never be the same again without Stefan. She herself would never be the same. But she knew the time had come to begin moving out on that journey into whatever lay ahead, into a future without Stefan by her side. And she knew she would only see the next part of the journey clearly, as she faithfully embraced that part open to her in the present moment. How long she would teach in

Tábor was unknown at that point – but she knew her answer to Uncle Erik had to be yes.

And so Heléna began to teach – hesitantly at first, but with ever increasing confidence, and an unexpected sense of fulfilment. Uncle Erik did not have many students, but at first even this small number tired her, as she prepared herself before each lesson to engage emotionally with her young pupils and help them achieve their best. And as she began to focus more intentionally on others, giving of herself to them, and seeking to enable each one to enjoy making music, she found, paradoxically, that this enabled her to cope better with her own grief. Her life had a shape to it, her days were often quite full, and there was always plenty of work to do in preparation for her lessons. And as she played little excerpts from her student's pieces for them, slowly the desire to return to serious playing began. Initially, she was impatient with herself when she was unable to play as she had before, almost allowing the discouragement to overwhelm her, and cause her to give up before she had really started. Yet deep in her heart she knew she had to give herself the grace to stumble and make mistakes. It would take time – time to reach the high standard she demanded of herself, time to be strong enough to stand against the black cloud of depression that threatened to engulf her, when nothing seemed to go right with her playing.

And God was with her in it all, she knew that. He was eternally patient with her, her faithful friend who accepted her fully, despite her weakness and imperfections, and his grace and love would not let her down.

Often when she came to a difficult section in one of the works she had prepared for her concert tour, she would play the notes over and over, until the phrase flowed easily from her fingers once again. In her mind, she could hear the passionate voice of her teacher, Alexandr, urging her on, as he paced restlessly around the room.

'Heléna, it's so true that practice makes perfect! You have to believe you can do it perfectly – just keep persevering and you will do it! Believe in yourself, Heléna – believe in yourself!'

The memory of Alexandr always saddened her, but also spurred her on to persevere and to reach a standard that would have pleased him so much, causing his sad face to light up with hope and joy. She wondered where he was – whether he was in fact even still alive. Possibly he was still in Terezin, or in one of the Polish concentration camps. One thing she was sure of was that wherever he was, there would be no piano to play, no beautiful music even to listen to that might help soothe the sadness in his spirit. Here she still had her freedom, she still had opportunity both to play and to teach. Compared to Alexandr and his fellow Jews, she had so much for which to be thankful. What a tragedy it would be, she began to realise, if the faith he had shown in her, and the brilliance and sensitivity of his teaching were wasted! He may not still be alive, but she could ensure that his memory would live on through her music! She would try her best, being patient with herself in the process, allowing God's gentle voice of encouragement to feed her spirit. In his time, he would show her clearly what the next step would be for her.

By the end of March, as spring began to make its presence felt in the fields and lanes around Tábor, a vague restlessness seemed to well up within Heléna. Recently, Andela had come see her for the first time since Stefan's death. It was a sad but joyful reunion, her arrival bringing back so many memories of those last hours of waiting for news of Stefan. It warmed Heléna's heart to be reminded of the wider circle of friends who were waiting for her in Prague, and whose interests and beliefs she still shared deeply. They had all wanted to visit her, but had respected her wishes to wait until she was stronger. Now, she felt a growing desire to see them again, to return to her apartment, and to pick up the pieces of her life there once more. It would be very difficult, she knew, to stand in the exact spot in the hallway where Stefan had last held her in his arms, to see his cello and his bible and other treasured possessions sitting unused, destined never to be held in his hands again. But her friends would be there to help in any way they could, she was sure of that.

She decided that she would go soon – but not yet. Not quite yet. Her little pupils were gradually giving her the confidence to pick up the threads of her musical career again, but she felt she still needed the comfort of her childhood surroundings and the support of those who had been part of her life for so long.

Uncle Erik was relishing the freedom Heléna's presence gave him to return to his writing and composing. Alongside this, his involvement in the underground movement continued, Stefan's death serving to make him even more committed to the cause. Together with his old friend Jiří, he could be found on many evenings in the tunnels below Tábor, caring for those sought by the Germans for various reasons. For some, their only 'crime' was that they were members of the intelligentsia, others had been too outspoken with their political views – and many, many of them were Jewish. It broke his heart to see the desperate state of these people, and despite his age, he did all he could to make them comfortable, before they began the next stage of their journey.

It was in the tunnels one night that the question of Heléna's future arose. One of the younger partisan leaders was sharing with Uncle Erik and Jiří the pressing need for more workers in Prague itself, and for more temporary places of shelter for those being hunted by the Gestapo.

'It's becoming so hard, because so many of our best workers have now either been captured or killed. The Germans are very vigilant, keeping those of us suspected of underground involvement under very close scrutiny. We do our best, but sometimes, out of sheer exhaustion, we make mistakes that endanger others – and ourselves – unnecessarily. There's a feeling around that things are not going to let up for some time to come. In fact, it's possible things might worsen very soon,' he said wearily. 'We're not about to give up – but we'd certainly welcome reinforcements!'

'Young man, if I were even twenty years younger, I'd be alongside you tomorrow!' Uncle Erik replied. And then he became silent, while the conversation flowed around him. After a while, he spoke up again.

'I've been thinking – do you remember when Stefan Marek was arrested, interrogated by the Gestapo, and killed?'

'Of course,' the young man, David, replied. 'He was a wonderful leader – one of the best!'

'I know his young widow well – Heléna. Of course she's still grieving for him, and has a way yet to go in her recovery, but I wonder … . She came home here after his death, but I know she's aware that she must return to Prague soon. Perhaps she'd consider continuing her husband's work in some way. I'll speak to her, and get a message to you, if she's at all open to the idea.'

It was time then for David to leave, taking with him a young Jewish family, guiding them on the next part of their journey to freedom. Uncle Erik left too, stopping for a short time for some organ practice in the church, to legitimise his being out at night, should anyone ask. His thoughts turned often to Heléna, and her possible response to the proposal he intended to put before her.

The next afternoon, Heléna arrived as usual to teach two of Uncle Erik's pupils who were unable to make the journey each week further out of the town to her own home. Afterwards, she stayed for coffee and cake, at Uncle Erik's request. From the outset, she suspected he had another challenge to put to her, so was not unduly surprised when he eventually cleared his throat and began to share what was on his mind.

'Heléna, I know you feel it's not time yet for you to return to Prague. Besides, I want you here too much for a little while longer! Nevertheless, as I listened to my young friend David last night in the tunnels, your face came clearly to mind.'

Uncle Erik went on to outline his conversation with the young partisan leader, explaining how he had mentioned her name to him.

'No pressure, my dear,' he continued kindly, seeing the unmistakeable signs of tension and fear in her face. 'No one's going to force you to have anything to do with the underground again, if that's your choice. It would be completely understandable if you had no desire to be involved in something that has brought you so much pain and loss – but I had to ask, Heléna! I had to obey the prompting I had to lay this challenge before you. Just think and pray about it, my dear – that's all I ask!'

Later that night, Heléna tossed and turned, unable to sleep. Fear threatened to overwhelm her even at the thought of falling into the hands of the Gestapo again. They had let her go once, since she did not seem to be involved in Stefan's work, but they would certainly not make that mistake a second time. Whether they would be watching her all the more because of Stefan, or whether they would now have no interest in her, she had no idea. As she lay mulling it over in her mind, one clear idea kept coming to her, compelling and insistent – she could teach music in Prague, just as she did in Tábor, and possibly help the partisans at the same time! There were no concert tours about to take place, and neither would they, while the war continued, and cultural organisations remained shut down. She was not ready anyway to begin performing immediately. But with music students coming to her door at various time during the day, it would be much easier to carry on partisan work undetected, to cover the tracks of any who needed help to escape. Gradually the thought of continuing the work for which Stefan had given his life no longer filled her with fear, but rather a feeling almost of wild elation. Perhaps she really could contribute something more, shaking her fist, in the process, at the forces of evil that had threatened to consume her too! In a sense, it would be a constructive channelling of the anger that still surfaced on occasions, and possibly a help rather than a hindrance to her recovery, despite the dangers involved.

In the end, Heléna decided to wait, and not to rush into things. She would take time to pray and think further, to sit with God until his peace came. Then she could move on with confidence that she would be equal to the task, through the strength and courage that he would provide. On that note, she fell into a deep sleep.

Four weeks later, at the end of April, she had come to a decision. She had grown to love her teaching in Tábor, but Uncle Erik had almost finished his writing and composing, and, she suspected, was also beginning to miss his young pupils.

'Yes, Heléna, you're right!' he ruefully admitted, when she confronted him about it. 'My young students may be tiresome, but I do miss them – I do miss them indeed! They keep me young with their conversation and energy, and give me hope for the future of our nation. But please keep teaching them for as long as you feel is right, my dear! I have plenty to keep me occupied, with my writing and partisan work.'

Heléna decided to return to Prague at the end of May, thus giving her time to prepare herself for what lay ahead, and also to enable Uncle Erik to complete his book. Berta and Simona were both sad and happy when Heléna broke the news to them – sad because they would miss her deeply, but happy that she felt sufficiently recovered to take this step. At first, Anna, and little Kristina too, were inconsolable. What would they do without their beloved Aunty Heléna to read to them, play with them and teach them? At that point, Simona took the opportunity to inform them that they would soon have a little brother or sister, their delight in this forthcoming event balancing out, to some degree at least, Heléna's news. But the prospect of not seeing them so much was also sad for Heléna. They had become like her own children – children she felt she would now never have. She promised them she would visit often, for her own sake, as well as theirs.

The weeks flew by. On the last day of May, Miklos and Andela drove down to Tábor to collect Heléna, anxious to make the transition as smooth as possible for her. Tearful farewells had already been said to her young students, as well as to Uncle Erik and Edita. Now it was time for a final goodbye to Berta and Simona and the girls. Heléna attempted to convey to them, in words that seemed so inadequate, how much their love and care had meant to her during the past months of deep mourning. She promised them she would come back soon, but not until she had become a little more established in Prague again. As they drove off, Heléna felt that a dark and difficult chapter of her life was closing, but also that things had been birthed in her in this time that would bear good and lasting fruit, not only in the immediate future, but also in years to come.

Chapter Twelve

The days that followed were a strange mixture of relief and agony for Heléna. While she loved her own family home in Tábor, it was in some ways comforting to be back in the apartment in Prague, surrounded by her familiar things, and supported by her special circle of friends. In other ways, the agony of seeing Stefan's possessions again, constantly being reminded of him wherever she looked, was at times overwhelming. The sight of his shoes in a corner of their bedroom, the familiar smell of the coffee he had particularly loved, the feel of his thick coat, as she brushed against it where it still hung in the hallway – these were among so many things that pierced her deeply, causing the grief and loneliness to rise swiftly to the surface and threaten to undo her at first. Nighttimes were the most difficult. Lying alone in the dark in Stefan's own beautiful, old bed, the worst and most frightening memories would sometimes surface again, as they had at Tábor in the early days after his death. Sometimes she would wake herself up with her screaming and sobbing, only to realise that the scenes in her nightmare were true, that she really was alone, without Stefan beside her, and without even Berta or Simona to comfort her. Usually she would get up, make herself a hot drink, and listen to some quiet music, until she could sense God's comforting presence around her once again. Then she would know she was safe, that she would not be overwhelmed. She was determined to allow herself to feel the pain, to look it fully in the face, and eventually to walk through it, to a place of greater acceptance of her loss – a place of strength and even peace, despite the sadness she knew would always be part of her. With God's help, and the loving care of her friends, she knew she would win through. And she was determined to use whatever influence she had, in the months ahead, and whatever she possessed in the way of gifts and resources, to be of assistance to her homeland, at this dark stage of its history.

Almost as soon as Heléna arrived in Prague, things became even more difficult for her homeland. On 4 June, the SS officer in charge of the protectorate, Reinhard Heydrich, died from injuries inflicted by a Czech paratrooper and partisan leader. It was as if all hell broke loose, as the Germans embarked on a frenzy of revenge. Apparently as a warning to the rest of the nation, the entire small village of Lidice, lying between the capital and Kladno, was utterly wiped out. All the men were executed, the women and older children interned in Ravensbrück concentration camp, and the younger children farmed out to families in Germany. The persecution of Jews became even more ruthless, too, under Heydrich's successor. Mass arrests were ordered, with almost all remaining Jews herded together and transported to the Terezin ghetto, and from there, to camps over the border in Poland, where they were exterminated by the thousands. At the same time, the hunt for partisans became relentless. Many were captured, while those remaining were forced to lie low, hoping to avoid arrest and thus ensure that the Czech underground remained alive – to some degree at least.

While Heléna was shocked and sickened by the sheer scale of the revenge meted out to her people, this did not deter her from seeking to prepare for renewed underground involvement, as soon as it became relatively safe to do so. She knew she would be needed more than ever, as word began to filter through of the loss of so many of their key workers. Apparently the young leader, David, with whom Uncle Erik had spoken recently in the tunnels at Tábor, was safe, having narrowly escaped capture, as was Uncle Erik himself and Jiří. In Prague, Miklos, Andela's brother, had eventually reached home, after several nights on the run, as had Heléna's friends Radim and Irena from the Sunday fellowship group. Others known to them all, however, had not made it back from their various missions, or had been arrested in their homes, leaving behind grieving families – wives, parents, grandparents, children.

Heléna, knowing so well how they felt, grieved along with them. She experienced a huge anger at the desolation and loss all around her, adding to the anger still there within her, as her own personal grief continued to work its way to the surface. She felt its energy surging through her, urging her to cast caution to the wind and take up underground work again immediately, whatever the risk. As she talked with Uncle Erik and other trusted friends, however, reason eventually prevailed, along with the discipline and patience to move by God's agenda, rather than her own. She would wait and pray and prepare. She knew she could be of strategic value to the movement and to her homeland if she moved with caution, taking time to establish herself again in Prague, allowing the remaining partisan leaders time also to regroup, and assess how they could now best work together.

At first Heléna wondered whether, in the midst of such troubled times, anyone would want to begin music lessons with her. She felt that her lack of experience, both in performance and teaching, might very much count against her, as well as her inability to produce an official graduation certificate. Yet she was soon proved wrong on both counts. In no time, despite the non-existence of any official cultural organisations, word began to spread in Prague music circles that Heléna Marek was back, and beginning to take students. Young people from across Prague, many of whom had lost their teachers to the ghetto at Terezin or to the camps in Poland, soon contacted her, eager to continue their studies, even through the summer holiday period. It almost broke Heléna's heart to have to turn down so many, but she knew she could manage only a few students each day.

Trying to decide which students to select was difficult at first. But Heléna soon discovered, as she herself had experienced with her own beloved Alexandr, that with some students, there was an immediate and inexplicable rapport, while with others, that special vital spark or connection was absent. Of those who did become her students, some were unable to pay much, if anything, but this was not an issue for her. These ones, she knew, would work hard, and seeing them achieve their goals and improve so rapidly would mean more to her than any financial reward. Besides, she did not really need a large income from her teaching, since Stefan's companies, while having to manufacture more and more products for the war effort, were still producing good dividends.

While Stefan's factories now belonged to Heléna, she was thankful that she could trust implicitly his good friend of many years, Ivan George, whom she had eventually appointed as company director and chief executive. He had stepped into the breach in the first few weeks after Stefan's death and, without having to be asked, had kept things running smoothly on Heléna's behalf, until she was able to make firm decisions regarding the future. She knew she owed him a great debt, along with all the loyal factory managers and other personnel who had worked with Stefan for many years. They had loved him, trusting his judgment, and valuing his fairness in any personnel issues and crises that had arisen. Each one was now determined not to make things any more difficult for his grieving, young widow, but to serve her well, just as they had Stefan. They were aware she knew nothing about business matters, so for her sake, resolved to be loyal to Ivan George. He soon proved worthy of their respect and trust and Heléna's too, thus taking a load off her shoulders, and leaving her free to enjoy the quite generous income that resulted from the company's dividends.

For the first few weeks after her arrival, Heléna focused on settling in, and establishing good working relationships with her students. This was not difficult, since all were extremely eager to learn – especially from someone so gifted, who they knew had excelled in her studies at the Conservatorium and had begun to make a name as a solo performer, just as her mother had done before her. In fact, Heléna found herself having to encourage some of her students to relax a little and enjoy their music more, rather than work at it with such seriousness. Yet so much around them conspired against fun and laughter, since many had experienced great sadness and loss in their own families, and were confronted with it every day on all sides. For many of the older ones, the fact that their studies had been so disrupted had birthed in them a general sense of hopelessness and frustration, so that their lessons with Heléna became a lifeline for them, both as a way of continuing to pursue their goals, as well as a means through which to express their deep inner feelings. And Heléna understood these feelings well. These days she herself was finding her increased hours of practising, and of playing with and for her students extremely therapeutic, a healthy avenue through which to express the confused mixture of pain and anger and other emotions that still overwhelmed her at times. She was also aware that her playing had matured and improved greatly – perhaps a foretaste or token, she felt, of the good that God would eventually bring out of the devastating events that had occurred in her life.

By mid-July, Heléna felt it was right to investigate further involvement in the underground. Through Uncle Erik, she was put in touch with the young leader, David, who had known and admired Stefan. It was arranged that, although in reality being far from musically gifted, he would visit Heléna, as if he were having normal piano lessons. The first day he arrived at the apartment, Heléna greeted him with mixed feelings. She was able to welcome him warmly, liking his open face and friendly manner, and was eager to begin discussing plans with him, but his very arrival stirred up so many memories for her. And along with that came a very real apprehension that the course of action she was embarking upon would invariably be fraught with danger.

The first time David came, in order to satisfy any curious neighbours, Heléna played several short pieces for him, after which he himself laughingly stumbled through a piece he had learnt many years earlier from his sister.

'I do hope your neighbours aren't too musical,' he grimaced. 'Otherwise it won't take them long to discover the disparity between my ability and that of your other no doubt very talented students!'

Heléna smiled, David's words easing the tension she was feeling inside her a little. Eventually, taking a deep breath, she decided to explain to him exactly how she was feeling.

'David, I can't pretend I'm not nervous at offering my services to our underground once again, after what happened to Stefan. There's not a day that passes that I don't remember how the Gestapo came here, and how I tried to warn him. That's part of my motivation now for choosing to take this step. Somehow, if at all possible, I want to carry on doing what Stefan gave his life for. Somehow I have to try to make sense out of what has happened in our family! I believe in my heart that this is what Stefan would want me to do, despite the danger involved. He loved this country, as I do. And he loved me passionately, even though our time together was so short, as I loved him. I realise I'm still only young, but there'll never be anyone like him for me, I know that. I want to honour his memory with all my heart, and also the personal challenge he left with me – to stand tall and remember that I belong to God! So I'm standing as tall as I can, and trusting God that this is his will for my life right now.'

Heléna had spoken quietly, but her voice was full of passion and determination. David was roughly the same age as she was, but as he listened, he was in awe of her, and humble enough to admit that here, in this beautiful young woman, was a maturity and a steely determination that would take him years to develop. He was moved with both pity and admiration for her, sensing her deep grief, but also her strength and courage, rapidly concluding that Heléna would indeed be an asset to the movement, and a force to be reckoned with in the days to come.

Eventually he stood and shook her hand, concluding their time together.

'Thank you, Heléna,' he said humbly. 'Thank you, on behalf of my co-workers left in our underground at present! I'll come next week at the same time, and we'll see then what your first task will be for us as a partisan in your own right.'

So began a new phase for Heléna in her journey of recovery, involving a return to both the musical world of Prague as well as the underground movement. The following week, David arrived carrying his music case, seemingly for another piano lesson – and Heléna received her first assignment.

'Heléna, after our time together, I'll go to a hiding place not far away and send to you two people, an elderly Jewish woman named Dorota, and her grandson Gustav. They're the only members of their family left, and have managed to survive this far through the kindness of neighbours. But it's getting too dangerous to shelter them any longer where they are, so they need to leave this evening. When they come, pretend you're giving the boy a lesson – he's quite a gifted pianist, I understand. Then keep them here until I return later this evening. After that, we'll try to get them away to the tunnels at Tábor and across the border and on to Switzerland, via our remaining contacts. It's very risky, but there's no alternative now.'

They talked a little more, and then Heléna began taking David through some scales and simple piano exercises, before he played again for her from his very limited repertoire. Heléna helped him with some of the more difficult passages, and then the 'lesson' was over. Only minutes elapsed after his departure, it seemed to Heléna, before there was a rather hesitant knock on the door. Heléna opened it, to find a woman with a pale, thin face and greying hair, standing beside a young boy of around eleven or twelve. Both wore several layers of dark clothes, despite the rather hot, summer weather, and the boy carried a music case that, Heléna noticed, remarkably resembled

David's own battered one. Heléna was moved with compassion when she saw the anxious, hunted look in the woman's eyes, and the fear evident in the boy's face, as he stood with his arm protectively around his grandmother, his body poised for flight. She quickly ushered them inside, trying to allay their fears with her warm smile and gentle manner, and plying them with coffee and biscuits. Haltingly, the woman Dorota began to tell her story.

'My only son and his wife, this boy's parents, were shot before our very eyes, on the footpath just outside our apartment block, during the arrests last month,' she explained brokenly, the tears streaming down her cheeks. 'In the minutes that followed, Gustav here took my hand and also his little sister Magda's, and we ran and ran. Gustav guided us as fast as he could through the alleyways – he knows them well from the games he plays with his neighbourhood friends. Then we came to a main road, and were about to run across, when we were caught up in a crowd who had panicked and were streaming away from another ghetto district. In the sudden crush, Gustav lost hold of little Magda's hand, and she disappeared, swept along by the crowd and away from us! We called and called her name, and searched for her for a long time, but we couldn't find her! Eventually, we were too exhausted to search any more, so had no choice but to find our way back home. The bodies of my son and daughter-in-law had been removed, along with many others. Then we discovered that our apartment had been ransacked, and almost everything destroyed! Our neighbours took us in and hid us in a small back room, but we knew we could shelter there for only a few days at the most. The father of this household is a member of the underground, you see, but it's too dangerous right now for him to be involved – he's constantly under surveillance by the Gestapo. Yet despite the danger, he helped search for our Magda, and also managed to get a message to the young man, David, who showed us the way here to this apartment. He told us your name is Heléna and that you'd help us. That's all we know!'

Heléna comforted them as best she could, explaining, as David already had, that they were to remain with her until around midnight, when he would come for them and guide them to the next safe place. Dorota seemed exhausted, but would not hear of leaving Gustav alone, even for a short time, and going to Heléna's bedroom to sleep. Instead, Heléna made her comfortable on the lounge in the study, encouraging her to rest while she herself entertained Gustav there. At first it was difficult to engage the boy in any conversation, but as soon as Heléna offered to play some music for him, his face brightened a little, and he moved to stand next to her, as she sat at the piano. Then, aware that, as far as her neighbours or anyone else watching were concerned, she was supposedly giving a normal lesson, Heléna asked Gustav if he played, receiving a solemn nod in reply. She stood up, motioning him to sit at the piano, and seated herself in Stefan's old armchair to listen. Without music, Gustav launched into a most difficult sonata, his small face intent, his whole being focused on conveying a passion and depth of feeling through his music normally expressed only by much older musicians. He continued playing, losing himself in his music, something of the weight of grief that was upon him lifting, at least a little, in the process.

Heléna sat stunned, aware of the even more urgent need to get Gustav and his grandmother to freedom. Here was a young boy who played with the brilliance and maturity of an adult, who deserved every opportunity to develop his genius – yet now he was being hunted down, simply because he was Jewish! Her heart went out to him, and, as she listened, she prayed God would protect him, and bring him to a place where somehow he would be enabled to reach his full potential. When he finally stopped playing, Heléna moved over to him, placing her hand on his shoulder.

'Thank you so much for your beautiful music, Gustav,' she said gently. 'I've studied piano myself for many years, and now teach others, as you know – but it was an honour to hear you play today! I pray that some day I'll have the privilege of seeing you perform before thousands! Who taught you so well?'

'My grandfather did,' he explained briefly, 'but he became ill a few weeks ago, and we couldn't find a hospital who would take him. He died in our apartment – I miss him so much!'

At that, the boy's face crumpled, and big sobs began to wrack his thin body. Immediately Dorota woke from the deep sleep into which she had fallen, and held out her arms to her grandson. They clung together, trying to comfort each other, two lonely figures forming an unforgettable tableau, as they sat together opposite Heléna. Wiping the tears from her own eyes, Heléna muttered something about preparing their evening meal, excused herself and moved to the kitchen. When she returned some time later, both her visitors had fallen into an exhausted sleep, their arms still wrapped around each other. She covered them gently with a rug, letting them sleep on for the moment, and returned to the kitchen to eat her solitary dinner.

Eventually, after some hours had passed, she roused them, knowing they would need to eat before David came. They accepted the meal gratefully, eating every morsel put before them. Food had been scarce for them for some time, she was aware – and who knew when they would be able to eat again?

Around midnight, when all three were dozing fitfully, there was a soft knock on the door. Heléna sprang up, her heart in her mouth. Oh God, may this be David and no one else, she prayed, as she quietly opened the door just a fraction. In a moment, David was inside, and the door firmly closed.

'Time to go!' he stated simply.

Heléna went to rouse her guests, who were already awake and alert. In the next few seconds, Dorota, Gustav and David, the latter clutching his battered old music case again, had disappeared silently down the staircase and out into the square below, keeping to the dark patches near the walls until they reached the nearby laneway. Then suddenly they were gone from view. Heléna, watching from the window above, stood there for some time, praying for their safety, wondering where their journey would finally end, hoping beyond hope that somehow Gustav would be given the opportunities he so deserved.

In the weeks that followed, Heléna was to hear stories like Dorota and Gustav's often from those who sought shelter with her. The details varied, but the basic content remained similarly horrifying. They came in their ones and twos to the apartment, mostly towards evening, as Dorota and Gustav had done, to be whisked away around midnight by David. In those intervening hours, Heléna saw her own grief mirrored many times over, etched on the faces and deep into the spirits of people from a wide variety of backgrounds and ages. Many were Jewish, but others were members of the Czech underground, hunted for their alleged part in Heydrich's death, or some uprising against the Germans before then. And now, unlike what had happened in Heléna's case, spouses and children of partisans were also targeted, being considered just as guilty as the worker himself – or occasionally, herself.

Heléna never forgot one girl, married at eighteen, and now widowed at twenty-one, with two little girls to care for, one only a few weeks old. Her husband had been shot dead by the Gestapo as he came home late one night, just after the baby had been born. His wife had found him outside when she woke the next morning, still holding the bunch of flowers he had bought for her. During the few hours this little family spent with Heléna, the young mother held her baby close, unwilling even to lay her down to sleep. She refused too to let go of a small bible that she clutched firmly to her, opening it from time to time to check that she had not lost the flower from her husband's bouquet, which she had lovingly placed between the pages. She would stare numbly at it, touching the petals gently, her hand shaking, and then eventually close the bible again, her eyes filled with such a look of despair that Heléna's heart ached for her. While it was a grief to Heléna that she and Stefan had not had children, she knew in her heart that the time had not been right for them. Now she realised that her situation was in many ways much easier than this young mother's – yet at least this little family would have each other in the years ahead, she was sure, whereas she would have no one. Putting her own feelings aside, however, she tried to comfort the young mother with her own firm belief that somehow, somewhere her little family would make it together – but she was too devastated, too lost in her grief. Heléna could only pray for her, and care for her physical needs as best she could.

It was this family that almost brought disaster to Heléna and to David. With others David had led to Heléna's apartment, it had been relatively easy to give the impression that he or she was another of Heléna's new music students. When an adult and a child were involved, this could easily be seen merely as a parent accompanying a son or daughter to a lesson. Heléna had taken care too, in all instances, to play the piano, at least for a short time, early on in each visit. But suspicion had obviously been aroused in someone's mind during the weeks in which David had come regularly to Heléna's apartment, accompanied by a new and different 'student' on each occasion. Equally puzzling, it seemed, was the fact that these 'students' usually stayed with Heléna much longer than the normal time a lesson would take. Now, when this young family knocked on her door, someone had obviously at last felt it their duty to raise the alarm. When these facts were added to suspicions already held by the Gestapo concerning David's previous activities, not to mention Heléna's own involvement in the movement through Stefan, a heart-stopping visit from the German authorities soon eventuated.

During one of David's 'lessons', Heléna had scarcely begun playing, when there was a loud banging at the door. She sat frozen, vivid memories of the time the Gestapo had come searching for Stefan returning immediately. For a moment, her eyes locked with David's, and then, knowing there was nothing for it except to pray and trust God for his protection, she moved towards the door.

Two Gestapo officers quickly entered, alert and observant, as Heléna conducted them into the study, where her 'lesson' was in progress. The officers came straight to the point.

'We've had reports, Frau Marek, that you're harbouring individuals and families wanted by the authorities, and that you're working with the underground to help them escape! We're here to search your home and also ask you a few questions.'

'By all means,' Heléna managed to answer calmly, so thankful that her little family had escaped only a matter of hours earlier, ' – but you're wasting your time! And as you can see, I'm in the middle of a piano lesson.'

An unbelieving smirk appeared on the officers' faces, as they glanced knowingly at each other.

'We'll be the judges of that, Frau Marek,' the older of the two replied.

He sent his co-officer to search the apartment immediately. When the officer returned, having found no trace of anyone hiding, both began plying Heléna and David with questions that showed an alarming knowledge of their contacts and recent movements. Heléna continued to maintain that those seen coming and going from her apartment were merely her music students.

'Most of them come each week, but some can only afford to come now and again – hence the many new and different faces people have obviously seen at my door,' Heléna explained. 'I wish they could all come more regularly, but, as you're aware, this is not the easiest time economically for our people!'

Eventually the officers produced what they obviously felt was their trump card.

'Frau Marek, we have no doubt you yourself play beautifully. We heard you as we came up the stairs, our contacts have also heard you many times, and I myself even saw you perform on one occasion with your colleagues from the Conservatorium. We seriously doubt, however, that your friend here is truly your student!' the older one continued. 'Therefore, sir, please play something for us!'

Heléna glanced at David, who answered without hesitation.

'I'm happy to play for you, gentlemen, but I'm sure you won't want to listen for long! Especially not after hearing my teacher play! That's exactly why I'm learning from her – I've forgotten almost everything my sister taught me many years ago now. But, if you insist, I'm happy to oblige!'

With that, David seated himself at the piano and began to play his only reasonably presentable piece, stumbling on occasions, but persevering through it, even executing some phrases with something of a defiant flourish. Heléna, while fully aware of the danger they were in, could not help feeling proud of him, as he struggled valiantly with the more difficult sections. She prayed fervently throughout, especially that the officers would not ask him to play anything else, and sighed with relief when the older officer eventually interrupted.

'Enough, enough! You've shown us you can play – at least a little,' he conceded reluctantly, 'but even I can tell you're not very good! Your story might be true – but who knows?'

He glanced at his watch, and, obviously feeling they had wasted too much time on what seemed a fruitless mission, on this occasion at least, rose to his feet, indicating to his co-officer that the interview was over. As Heléna and David stood facing them, he delivered his parting shot.

'Let this be a strong warning to you both! Don't consider for a moment that this is the end of our investigation into the matter! Your students will continue to be of great interest to us, Frau Marek, as will your own activities, young man,' he growled, turning to glare at David.

With a final slam of the door, they were gone. Heléna sank limply into the nearest chair, and stared helplessly at David, who also appeared shaken. After they had recovered a little, David was the first to speak.

'Heléna, unlike you, I don't believe in God – but I think someone truly was watching over us today! It's a miracle we weren't arrested simply on suspicion of underground involvement! Our cover's blown, I'm afraid – it'll be far too dangerous to carry on as we have been. I'd better lie low for a while at least, and then I think someone else should become your main partisan contact, instead of me. In the meantime, Heléna, you must decide whether you want to continue this work at all in the future, or return to teaching only your bona fide students.'

Heléna knew she needed time to process what had just happened, and to think clearly about the way ahead. David respected that, and left her to make her own decision during the coming week, knowing she would contact him via Uncle Erik when she was ready.

In the next few days, Heléna spent as much time alone as she could, thinking and praying, weighing up the risks involved in the various courses of action open to her. Eventually, she concluded that she did not at all want to give up. She had barely started this phase of her underground involvement, and, according to David, and also Uncle Erik, there were many still hiding from the Gestapo who needed help such as she could give. Besides, as she searched her heart, she discovered that the burning desire remained, no doubt still fuelled by her own grief, to carry on Stefan's work, to stand up and be counted for her country in his place.

One evening, as she was wrestling with the best way to do that, she received an unexpected call from Judith, her cousin Edvard's wife. Judith, Heléna knew, had decided to remain in Czechoslovakia at their own delightful home on the northern outskirts of Prague for the duration of the war, since in many ways it now seemed a safer place than her own home country of England. Also, travelling anywhere was dangerous – and even more so for someone who was seven months pregnant, as she was. Besides, while Edvard was often away working, he wanted to be with his wife as much as he could, something that was much easier to do if she were in his own homeland.

'The point is this,' Judith now explained to her. 'I'm finding it harder to travel around even in Prague these days, the closer our baby's birth comes. Over the past eighteen months, since Tomas and Eva's deaths, I've had to make many trips across town to check on their home, which is now Edvard's of course. We want to hold on to it, until this war is over, and see then what the market's like, but these frequent trips are just too tiring for me, and not really very safe either. Then last night, it suddenly crossed my mind to see if you knew anyone reliable who might like to rent it until the end of the war. Hopefully that will be very soon – but who knows? Do you think anyone from your music circles or your Sunday fellowship group would be interested?'

Heléna promised to enquire amongst her friends and let Judith know. Yet even as she put down the receiver, she knew clearly that this was the answer for which she had been waiting. Why not move back herself to her aunt and uncle's? She could still teach, using the old upright piano there! Her students would understand, if she explained that the house needed minding. No doubt some would surmise that living in her own apartment, constantly surrounded by reminders of Stefan, was proving too much for her, and thus was the real reason for the move. She decided to let them think that if they chose to – anything for her move to appear natural and necessary. Tomas and Eva's house was some distance from her apartment, but not far from a train station, so most of her students would be able to get to their lessons relatively easily. She was fairly sure the Gestapo would not think to look for her there, so this move would hopefully enable her continue both her teaching and underground work.

Soon it was all arranged. At the end of the following week – in fact, almost exactly a year after Stefan's death – Heléna, with the help again of Miklos and Andela, quietly moved to what in her mind was still Tomas and Eva's home.

Looking back, Heléna felt that the extra activity and effort this relocating involved was a blessing from God, in that it helped ease the pain and loneliness she felt so acutely, as the anniversary of Stefan's death approached. With more time on her hands, she felt she could easily have sunk back into that deep well of grief and emptiness that she had experienced in the months immediately after his death. She still missed him terribly, but knew she could not, and, with God's help, would not go back to that dark, despairing place out of which he had carried her in more recent times. Immediately after the move, Heléna's old nightmares did surface briefly, no doubt not only because of sleeping in different surroundings, but also because of the emotion that the anniversary of Stefan's death stirred up in her. But she knew better what to do now, when she woke trembling and screaming, and how to receive the help and comfort she needed from God to see her through each episode. She knew that this time would pass, and that she would emerge all the stronger from it. And the kindness and love that Andela and her other friends from their fellowship group showed her also helped greatly. They had not forgotten Stefan's death a year earlier, and Heléna's deep grief, and now all of them took pains to support her in their special, unique ways.

At first, Heléna gave lessons from Tomas and Eva's house to her 'legitimate' students only, waiting until further notification from Uncle Erik before resuming any partisan activities, and always alert for any sign that she was being watched by the Gestapo. Finally, at the beginning of November, a young girl knocked on Heléna's door carrying letters of introduction from Uncle Erik and also David. Jana was a small slip of a girl, around fifteen years old, Heléna guessed. In fact, she turned out to be eighteen. She was also, Heléna soon discovered, deeply in love with David, and he with her. For love of him and also of her country, Jana had become a devoted and very valuable partisan, able to move around freely without attracting nearly as much attention from the Gestapo as the men. Over the weeks leading up to Christmas, she became, to all intents and purposes, another of Heléna's students, in the process leading a number of desperate underground workers and their families to Heléna's for temporary shelter, and then on their way to freedom. Heléna soon grew to love Jana. She admired her alert ways, and the sharpness of her mind, as she grappled with improving her piano playing, and the enthusiastic, almost joyful way she approached life in general, embracing the difficulties she encountered daily in her work, and defiantly overcoming them. Often after her meetings and 'lessons' with Heléna, Jana would give her a quick hug, her eyes alight with the challenge of the next task before her. Then, with a soft goodbye and toss of her head, she would be gone, only to surface again at some unearthly early morning hour to rescue those sheltering with Heléna.

It was inevitable that this activity would not go unnoticed forever, given the extra vigilance of the Gestapo in general, but Heléna was not prepared for it when it happened. One day, Jana did not turn up for her lesson as scheduled. Heléna was concerned, but not overly so, assuming that something unforeseen had occurred. She heard nothing, but decided to wait until Jana's lesson time the following week before making any enquiries. She was sparing with phone calls, always aware that others could be listening in to her conversations. The time for their next lesson arrived, but again no Jana. That evening the doorbell rang, but on answering it, Heléna found no one there. Eventually, as she stood looking out into the empty street, she noticed a crumpled piece of paper on the step at her feet. Glancing swiftly around, she picked it up and moved inside. Unfolding it, she found a hastily scribbled note from David himself.

Jana has disappeared. She's been missing over a week now, but we're still searching, and hopeful of finding her. Have received news of a big crackdown – Gestapo determined to wipe out Czech underground entirely this time. Stay put for now, but be ready to leave as soon as notified. If Jana should come, keep her there with you. Will contact you again soon. David.

Heléna felt her blood freeze. She prayed fervently for Jana, wherever she was, unwilling even to contemplate what may have happened to her.

Two more days passed, during which Heléna tried to give of her best to her music students, and to remain in a place of peace and trust in God, despite the questions and uncertainties in her mind. Then towards evening on the third day, just after she had eaten dinner, the doorbell rang. Heléna opened it cautiously, totally surprised but delighted to see Uncle Erik standing there. Yet even in the dark she could see his tiredness, and knew by his very presence that something must be wrong. She quickly invited him in, helping him take off his heavy coat and scarf.

'My dear, I've come to escort you back to Tábor straight away, if possible,' Uncle Erik explained, as soon as he had caught his breath a little. 'The news isn't good, and we feel it would be wisest for our remaining workers here in Prague to hide in the tunnels immediately – at least for a short while. Come with me tonight, Heléna, I beg you! It was through me that you contemplated this underground work again, therefore I personally feel responsible to see you safely down to the tunnels. David and the other leaders agree too. I understand you're ready to leave at a moment's notice, so there's nothing to keep us.'

For a moment Heléna thought of her students arriving over the coming days, only to find her gone. Somehow she would have to try to contact them, and let them know she would be away for a time. She sighed, realising in her heart the wisdom of Uncle Erik's suggestion, yet reluctant to leave. What if Jana came there that very night, only to find no one there? She was silent for a moment, eventually putting those very thoughts into words.

'I'll come, Uncle Erik, as you wish – but not until morning. You need to rest, and it means I'll be here for a few more hours, if Jana comes seeking shelter. Has she been found yet?'

It was now Uncle Erik's turn to be silent. When he spoke, his voice was heavy with sadness.

'I'm afraid she has, my dear. That's part of the reason we need to leave as soon as possible. David found her himself, in a laneway not far from here. Apparently she was coming for her lesson over a week ago, but the Gestapo waylaid her, took her away for questioning, raped her and beat her over several days, and then dumped her body back where they found her. Someone living nearby who knows them told David what had happened, but they were too afraid of the Germans to try to rescue her. Heléna, it's not safe here – for you, or even for me! Please come with me – right now!'

Chapter Thirteen

Heléna moved in a daze, gathering her things together and preparing to leave as soon as Uncle Erik had quickly had something to eat and drink. She phoned Andela, so that someone at least would know that Uncle Erik had come for her, but refrained from giving her friend any further information. Andela knew enough not to question her, however. She would hear what had happened from Miklos anyway, Heléna knew. Soon after, Uncle Erik and Heléna crept quietly out the front door and into the deserted street, taking a circuitous route to the train station, in case anyone was following them. The last train to Tábor for the evening left just after nine, so they did not have long to wait on the cold, draughty platform. They huddled together, Uncle Erik for the warmth that his tired old body needed, Heléna for the comfort that his close presence gave. Any interested onlooker curious as to their relationship could easily have assumed they were grandfather and granddaughter returning home late after a tiring visit to the city, but no one questioned them. They sat quietly, Heléna too shocked to speak, Uncle Erik too tired for words – too tired, and too sad. Somehow, some day soon surely, he thought, this madness would end, this wrecking of young lives, this grievous, grievous loss for their homeland and for all humanity. Lord, let it come soon, he prayed. It cannot go on much longer! I cannot go on much longer, seeing these young ones suffer and sacrifice themselves like this!

The train came, and fortunately they were able to find an empty carriage, where

Uncle Erik could curl up and sleep a little. Heléna remained wide awake, her thoughts tumbling over an over in her tired brain. In her mind's eye she kept seeing Jana's bright young face, eyes alert, fingers stretched over the keys, as she valiantly tried to master a Chopin Mazurka, and laughing at her own inadequacies. She remembered her last goodbye, head popping around the door for a final cheeky smile and wave, and a cheery 'see you soon'. She grieved for David, hating to think of the moment he had found his sweetheart lying lifeless in the snow. Where would it end, she thought despairingly, for all of them? As the train clattered along through the darkness, the very noise of its wheels seemed to jeer at her and mock her – 'Give up! Give up! Hopeless! Hopeless! Give up! Hopeless! Give up! Hopeless!' – until she felt she could almost scream. Stefan's strained face came to her too, time and time again, as he stood in the hallway of their apartment facing the Gestapo, and then as they drove him away. She must have dozed off at that point, because suddenly she heard again Stefan's voice speaking urgently to her, strong and clear, despite the fog that clouded her brain.

'Heléna, don't give up! You belong to God! Stand tall, little one – stand tall! Remember always, you belong to God!'

She sat up with a start and looked around wildly, trying to get her bearings. Slowly she realised where she was, feeling the swaying of the train, as it hurtled through the darkness. She glanced at her watch, aware that they must not be far from Tábor. Soon after, Uncle Erik woke, knowing, as if through some inbuilt clock, that they were near their destination. Glancing at Heléna's white, strained face, he placed his old wrinkled hand over hers, squeezing it warmly, as if to infuse strength into her. That, combined with Stefan's words still ringing in her ears, was enough to cause Heléna, in the remaining minutes before their arrival, to refocus, gather her strength and determine to move through the days ahead with head held high, honouring Stefan's words, clinging to her faith in God, whatever the chaos and evil around her.

She would need all the strength God could give in the ensuing days, as it turned out. On their arrival in Tábor, Uncle Erik carefully guided her down into the tunnels via the organ loft entrance in the church. In the dim glow of the lamps that were still alight, despite the lateness of the hour, Heléna saw that many of the makeshift beds were already occupied – by whom she could not tell. Uncle Erik took her to the far end of that section of the tunnels, to a little alcove where there was a spare stretcher piled high with quilts and blankets.

'As you can see, my dear, Edita wanted to ensure you were comfortable! When I told her it wouldn't be wise for you to return to your old home just yet, she was determined to have you stay with us. However, that would be too dangerous at this point, even here in Tábor. So we compromised – hence the spare bedding belonging to us that you see here. Go to sleep now, my dear. I'll come back tomorrow, and we'll consult with the others as to the best way ahead.'

To her surprise, Heléna slept, to be woken early by voices and movement a short distance along the tunnel. As she investigated, she discovered, in a wider section of the tunnel system, up to twenty others, mostly young men and women like her, some still washing their faces and hands in buckets of water provided for that purpose, others already seated at small tables or on the floor nearby, eating breakfast and drinking coffee. As she glanced around, it did not really surprise her that, except for David's, all the faces seemed unfamiliar to her. Underground work was secret in nature, but also, while Heléna performed a key role by providing a place of safety for those fleeing, she was not a leader in the movement, as Stefan had been. Soon she noticed that, while some were talking animatedly, others were much more withdrawn, as if lost in their own worlds, eating or drinking rather mechanically. She saw with a pang that David was one of the latter – a much older looking David, his face drawn and pale, eyes staring straight ahead.

Joining those at the buckets, Heléna washed quickly, eventually seating herself a short distance along the table from him, sensing it better not to disturb him immediately. Others around her welcomed her, as the newcomer who had appeared in the night, warmly introducing themselves, and sharing what little food they had willingly with her.

'Eat up,' a friendly but tired looking young girl next to her said, 'who knows where our next meal will be coming from? I must say that the people who set this up have tried their best to care for us well, despite not having much food themselves. Would you like some coffee?'

Heléna accepted gratefully, sipping her coffee and listening in to the general conversation. From time to time she glanced over at David, who seemed to be slowly growing more aware of his surroundings. Eventually she moved closer, putting her hand on his shoulder and speaking gently to him.

'David, I'm so sorry – so sorry about Jana! I heard the news only last night – Uncle Erik told me.'

At first David looked blankly at her, and then she watched as recognition dawned, and tears began to well up in his eyes.

'She was so close to your place – she almost made it!' he whispered brokenly. 'She was so alive and warm and fun to be with. She didn't deserve to die like that! She didn't deserve to be treated like an animal, to be used up and spat out like that!'

He was shaking and sobbing uncontrollably now, tears rolling down his face. The sight of such a strong, vibrant young man so broken and distressed touched Heléna deeply, as it did others nearby. Most knew David as one of their key partisan leaders, but now they grieved for him, as they sat or stood around, heads bowed. Some came up to comfort him, putting their arms around him, as Heléna had. Eventually he became calmer, sitting quietly while the conversation, which had slowly picked up around him, continued on softly. It seemed that those present had been recalled or rescued from various parts of the capital and areas close by, in an effort to protect the leaders and workers still remaining. Now they needed to discuss their next move – whether to regroup, and continue in some form at least, or to rest for a while and recoup their energies. The conversation ebbed and flowed, but to Heléna, newly arrived, it seemed obvious that those who had been there some days already were generally tired and dispirited, many grieving, and some clearly traumatised, as David was. Sometimes they spoke animatedly, spurred on by those a little less weary. But while their words showed hearts still willing to support the partisan cause, little energy remained, in most cases, to translate their passionate beliefs into action. Truly their spirits were willing, but the flesh weak.

Soon Uncle Erik and Jiří arrived, along with two or three other older men whom Heléna recognised from the town. These, she knew, were those largely responsible for maintaining the tunnels, each one deeply committed to his country. They had known both her father and Stefan, and were delighted to see her again, but in turn, sorry that she, along with the others present, needed to be confined where they were for their own safety. After their arrival, the conversation became a little more focused. Representatives from the different sectors within Prague and the surrounding areas were asked to share their thoughts concerning the way ahead, with everyone then discussing the various points made and deciding together. As time went on, one of the main issues that emerged was lack of leadership for the movement, since most of the key leaders had either been killed or captured, while those remaining were well known to the Gestapo, and prime targets in the current crackdown. In turn, many these leaders had trained had also been killed or imprisoned. It soon became obvious that time out was needed for everyone, especially the remaining leaders, who, like David, were almost completely exhausted. When they had rested a little, and when the right moment came, those wishing to do so could regroup, it was suggested, and search out more new recruits to train up and swell their ranks.

No one liked the idea – not even the most exhausted of them – but they could see no alternative. In the end, Uncle Erik summed up the feelings of those present. He did not presume to be their overall leader – someone much younger and more energetic than he was needed for that – but his seniority and experience marked him as the most natural spokesperson.

'It seems we're agreed that all of us need to pull back for a while, to take time to recover our strength and energy, physically and emotionally. We understand that some of you have work and families to return to as soon as possible – but if you do, please be doubly careful! Lie low, and remember – no underground work! If any of you wish to, it should be safe for you to stay here for a few more days. It would be better, however, if you found somewhere further afield where you can stay longer, but make sure you leave a contact address or phone number with us. Then, when it's a little safer, God willing, we'll regroup, stronger and more passionate than ever, determined again to fight for our homeland. May God bless you all, and grant you a time of rest and safety! We older ones are so proud of you all!'

Over the next few hours, the partisans began to move out of the tunnels, quietly and unobtrusively, and away from Tábor, some back to their homes, others to relatives or friends further removed from the capital. Heléna stayed until later in the day, primarily to wait until Uncle Erik returned from ensuring the safe departure of others, but also to contemplate her own future. Of course she could choose to return to her old home at Tábor for a while. No one need even know she was there, if she kept quiet and did not venture out, but undoubtedly it would be the first place the Gestapo would search for her. Indeed, this had apparently already happened once, after she had suddenly disappeared from her apartment in Prague and moved to her uncle and aunt's home. Fortunately, she had not told Berta or Simona where she was going at that point. The Gestapo had apparently searched the family home, but not over thoroughly, believing that the women were indeed telling the truth, when they denied all knowledge of Heléna's whereabouts.

But now it might well be a different story. Now they were even more suspicious of her, and much more determined to squash the underground movement altogether. There was no way Heléna wanted to cause any difficulties for her beloved Berta, nor for Simona and her little family. Neither did she want her childhood home invaded again or damaged in any way by the Gestapo. Uncle Erik's home was not a possibility either. If it had been too dangerous for her and for them to be there the previous night, then nothing would induce her now to put them in any further danger over a longer period. Returning then to her section of the tunnel, Heléna waited and prayed and thought deeply.

As she did so, out of the blue, it seemed to her, memories of her friend Helga and their time together at the Conservatorium surfaced. Since Helga's phone call on the day the Gestapo had been waiting in the apartment for Stefan's return, Heléna had heard from her friend only once. After Stefan's death, she had written a heartfelt note to Heléna, which had been forwarded to her at Tábor. That had been over a year ago, but, as far as Heléna knew, she was still living at the family farm near Domažlice. She remembered Helga's earnest plea to her, both at the conclusion of their years of study together, and then, more recently, during the phone call after the closure of the Conservatorium and the cancellation of her tour. Both times she had begged Heléna to contact her if she ever needed help. Perhaps now Helga could indeed help her, Heléna realised, in a way no one else could. Domažlice was a small town near the Sudetenland border, and Helga's family farm was in a fairly isolated area, she understood. Heléna also remembered that Helga's brothers were away in the German army, and even her father had been conscripted for border patrol work. With only Helga and her mother at home, surely there would be room for her to stay for a short time at least? Heléna also knew that, despite Helga's family being German, they would have no hesitation in offering her hospitality. She and Helga had talked at length about that during their time together in Prague, and she was aware that her friend's family was in many ways more Czech than German. Certainly their sympathies lay equally, if not more so, with their adopted homeland than with the fatherland. Helga's brothers had joined the German Army only because they believed that, if they did not, they would pay a high price for such a decision. Each hoped that he would be posted to some place far away from the Czech border, since none of them had any desire to harm friends they had known since childhood, or cause difficulties for a country they had grown to love. It seemed clear, therefore, that this was her best option, and one, she felt, that had been brought to mind by God, just at the right time. As soon as Uncle Erik returned, she would ask if she could phone her friend from his home.

By dinner time that evening, it was all arranged. Helga herself had answered when Heléna phoned, and been quick to urge her friend to come immediately. They had not talked for long, but Heléna had discovered that at least one of her brothers was home, although Helga stressed that this was no problem – in fact the opposite. Exactly how that could be so, Heléna had to wait to find out.

That night she stayed in the tunnel again. Soon after breakfast the following day, Uncle Erik insisted on accompanying her to the station, in order to see her safely on a train bound for Pisek, south west of Tábor. There, fortunately for her, given the presence of German soldiers everywhere, for whom a very attractive young woman did not go unnoticed, she was able to make a quick connection to Strakönice. An ancient bus then took her a further three hours west to Klatovy, where she then caught a local bus, as per Helga's instructions, to Domažlice itself, at the northern tip of the beautiful Šumava region. This area, known to the locals as the Böhmerwald, was to prove to be a place of freedom and renewal for Heléna in the spring months ahead, with its gentle pine-clad slopes rising higher and higher, until they formed dark, tranquil forests clinging to the sides of the mountain peaks. Now however, it was winter, and her journey in the small, rattly bus was slowed to a crawl by the icy roads.

Finally, they arrived in Domažlice, and there was Helga, waiting eagerly. Heléna had hardly stepped down from the bus, before she was enveloped in a huge hug, and held close for a long time.

'Heléna, it's so good to see you! I can't believe you're here! Oh Heléna, I'm so sorry about Stefan – so very sorry! I so much wanted to come to you when I heard, but I couldn't leave the farm. You did know that, didn't you?'

Heléna returned her friend's hugs, assuring her that she understood. As they made their way to the farm a few kilometres outside the town, Helga briefly explained the circumstances that had led to the younger of her two older brothers being sent home recently from his German army unit stationed in the Ruhr area.

'A few months ago, Franz was wounded in a bombing raid. He spent some time in hospital, where unfortunately the doctors had to amputate one leg. His other leg was also badly injured, but the doctors managed to save it. Now he's in a wheelchair – he needs time to heal and regain some strength, before being assessed for an artificial limb. Hospitals in Germany are really overcrowded and understaffed, so we're not sure how long he'll have to wait. In the meantime …'

Helga did not finish the sentence. Heléna could see that she was deeply worried about her brother, and that tears had begun to well up in her eyes as she spoke about him. Eventually, she was able to continue.

'We're managing quite well at present, even with Vati and my other two brothers still away, because, being winter, there's not so much to do around the farm. So Mutti and I can stay inside and keep Franz entertained a little more. But when spring comes, it will be difficult. When Franz first arrived, he was so depressed, and felt so useless! I know he'd love you to play for him and talk with him, Heléna. So you see, you won't be a burden at all – and apart from the help you'll be with Franz, I'm so looking forward to having you here to talk to myself! Maybe we can even practise together again – that would be so wonderful!'

Heléna arrived at the farm just three days before Christmas. The next morning, after a fitful sleep in her new surroundings, when the old nightmare had again reared its head, she woke late to an almost completely white landscape. There had been unusually heavy falls of snow overnight, so much so that she would not have been able to get to her destination, had she left it one more day. Despite a disturbed sleep, Heléna knew she was safe there, the remoteness of the farm and now the snowfalls enabling her to feel that way for the first time since moving back to Prague. She had become accustomed, she realised, to being constantly vigilant, alert to who may be watching or listening, and careful always of what she said and did. Here, despite the fact that she was with a German family, although in hiding from the German authorities, Heléna felt as if a tight spring inside her was gradually unwinding. Here she could let her guard down and relax a little, at least for a while, and she was very thankful for that.

That Christmas together at Domažlice was of necessity very quiet. Helga's father was unable to make it home in the end, because of the snow, despite being granted leave – a great disappointment to them all. Only Helga, her mother Renate, her brother Franz, and Heléna were therefore present to enjoy the simple treats the family had been able to put together for that day.

'It's so good you could be here, Heléna!' Helga kept exclaiming over and over, as they shared their Christmas meal together.

Renate smiled at her daughter's enthusiasm.

'I'm afraid it's been rather unexciting here for Helga, Heléna, after enjoying three years in Prague, mixing with so many interesting people!' she commented wryly. 'She's missed her music so much, too. Unfortunately neither Franz nor I can accompany her well enough, but we're so looking forward to hearing you girls sing and play together!'

Despite Helga's protestations of being hopelessly out of practice, the two managed a creditable performance later that evening of some of her favourites – songs by Schubert, Brahms and Tschaikovsky, along with one or two Verdi operatic arias. The only difficult moment occurred when Helga chose Heléna's special Tschaikovsky song, 'Nur wer die Sehnsucht kennt', to bring the evening's entertainment to a close. Fortunately Franz rescued her.

'Let's sing this one, Heléna! This has so much feeling in it, and you yourself used to sing and play it so beautifully, I remember!' Helga exclaimed excitedly, as she found the music in the pile beside the piano.

Heléna gazed at it in silence, her heart racing, and her mind bereft of ideas as to how to answer in a way that would not disappoint or embarrass her friend. Just then, Franz, seated beside the piano in his wheelchair, noticed Heléna's sudden pallor and the slight shaking of her hands, as they rested on the keys. Immediately, much to Heléna's relief, he made an alternative suggestion.

'Maybe another day, Helga. Today's Christmas Day, after all, so let's choose something a little more joyful! What do you say to some old-fashioned carol singing? Then we can all join in!'

Helga looked at her mother in amazement. Franz had a very pleasant tenor voice, and used to love to sing as he worked around the farm, but since being injured, they had not heard him sing at all. Indeed it had been difficult to find anything that caused him to be joyful, so the fact that he had now spoken out surprised and delighted them. Yet whatever they might think, Franz knew he had to make every effort to alter the direction of the evening. For an instant, he had seen clearly on Heléna's face his own pain mirrored there – the raw pain of an injured animal, hopelessly trapped and terrified. He recognised it well, and, in that moment, whatever the cost, he wanted to rescue her.

He succeeded very well in the end. All four of them joined in the carol singing with gusto, bringing their Christmas celebrations to a fitting conclusion. And for Franz, it was the beginning of a journey of healing that would change the course of his life.

Between Christmas and New Year, Heléna and Franz had no opportunity to talk privately, as the whole family was housebound because of the snow. In that time, Heléna observed him carefully, as the four of them interacted around the meal table and elsewhere, and as they sang and played together again. She noticed the frequent, bleak look in his eyes, the deep shadows beneath them, and the lines etched on his young face that spoke of days and nights filled with pain. She heard the slight edge of bitterness in his voice, as he talked of his time in the army, and the sharp tone he used one evening when he asked his mother to turn the radio off, so they could not hear the propaganda being broadcast. And above all, she saw the look of shame and distaste that came over him whenever he had to be helped out of his wheelchair and carried to the bathroom, or when he dropped something and could not retrieve it himself. As the snow began to ease, and Helga and her mother became busier again, caring for the animals wintering in the nearby barn, and fetching supplies for the kitchen, Heléna and Franz finally found time to talk. At first, their conversation was somewhat tentative, but Heléna, used to putting her students at ease, eventually took the initiative, broaching the subject of Christmas evening herself.

'Franz, I've been waiting for the opportunity to thank you for rescuing me on Christmas night! There's no way Helga could have known that the song she chose was such a significant one for Stefan and me. She and I haven't talked in detail yet about the things that happened since we studied together, but I'd like to tell you …'

At that point, Franz interrupted her, speaking quietly but firmly.

'Heléna, please don't feel you have to explain anything to me! I acted as I did only because I happened to see the pain that my sister's choice of song had caused you, and I didn't want to be part of prolonging that for you. Believe me, I know what pain feels like these days!'

Silence fell between them.

'Do you want to talk about it?' Heléna asked, after some time. 'You don't have to either, if you don't wish to, but I'd like to listen. My friends have played such an important part in helping me through my grief by letting me talk – and besides, one good turn deserves another!'

It was all the invitation Franz needed, as it turned out. He surprised himself at how eager he was to share his feelings with someone who was a relative stranger, but somehow he had sensed that Heléna was throwing him a lifeline that he really needed to grasp. Soon his story came tumbling out – how he had never wanted to leave the farm, how he did not believe that war solved anything, and especially how torn he had felt to be fighting against a country which had given them a good living for a large part of his life, and which he had grown to love as much as his own homeland.

'Our family moved here when I was only seven, Heléna. Yes, we have relatives in Germany, but I have good friends here as well. At least I *had* good friends here! Many have been killed, or are now wounded and useless like me – and for what gain? Some say we Germans will win this insane war, but I'm not sure. If we don't, then what will be our family's fate? And if we do – well, my future is bleak anyway, so what does it matter? I hate to be helpless! I hate to see my mother and my sister having to work so hard, and care for me as well! Spring will be coming soon, and how can they plant crops and care for the farm alone? Some nights, when the pain in my legs is almost unbearable, I think it would have been better if that British bomb had finished me off altogether!' he ended bitterly.

Heléna noticed the spent look on his face, as the last drops of the pent up emotion that had fuelled his words drained out of him. She was silent, not wanting to offend him with some trite reply that would solve nothing. They sat for a while, Heléna quietly praying, unsure how to proceed with this angry, grieving young man. At that moment, she felt strongly that God had a purpose in her being with this family at this time, and that it had something very much to do with Franz.

Then slowly and hesitantly, she began to speak.

'Franz ... after Stefan was killed by the Gestapo, I thought my world had come to an end. For many months I was in a dark, dark place. I'm still walking out of that place in many ways, but I know I'm moving forward, and that I've journeyed quite a distance. I believe God is making some sense out of what happened to my family, and using it to bring good to others, in some small measure at least. You'll get through this time, Franz – you'll move through it, and better days will come!'

'I wish I could believe that, Heléna,' he sighed. 'I wish I could believe that some good will come of all this. I used to believe in God, but right now he feels very, very far away! So far away, I'm not sure he even exists any more. But enough of me! Will you play something for me?' he asked abruptly, obviously preferring to change the subject.

Heléna played, and Franz listened. As the days wore on, she played for him often, noticing how the pain lines on his face seemed to disappear a little during those times, and how his whole body seemed to relax. It crossed her mind, on several occasions, to wonder if it would help some of his anger and bitterness to be dispersed, if he were able to play himself. For Heléna, expressing her emotions through music was a precious and indispensable lifeline. Not that she played only, or even consciously, for this purpose. But somehow it just happened, and when it did, it was very healing. Heléna sensed, however, that the initiative needed to come from Franz himself. So she waited, and prayed.

Then one evening, as the family was sharing around the meal table, the opening came.

'Heléna, Franz used to play quite well himself,' Helga commented. 'He used to accompany me when I first began singing seriously. What do you say, Franz? Do you think Heléna could give you some lessons while she's here?'

To their surprise, Franz seemed slightly embarrassed, looking down at the floor as he replied.

'Actually I thought about asking you that myself, Heléna, but your talent's so superb! Why would you want to spend time teaching someone like me?'

His sister and mother howled him down immediately, so the next day found Franz with his chair wheeled up to the piano, endeavouring to play the simple Bach etude that

Heléna put before him. Painstakingly, in the weeks ahead, they went over the basics of his piano technique again and again, until slowly his previously learnt skills returned, and he began to improve rapidly. He practised faithfully, mostly when Heléna was outside helping Helga and Renate with farm chores, or when they were shopping in the nearby town. Helga was happy to have Heléna's company during such outings, but the farm chores were another matter, both Helga and her mother adamant that Heléna was not to risk injury to her hands in any way.

'Heléna, the fact that you're helping Franz means so much more to us than anything else!' they both expressed with feeling. 'You're taking such a load off us! He's so much happier – and that gives us more energy and heart to do the farm tasks. Perhaps not quite as well as the men could, but not too badly!'

Weeks turned into months, and soon summer was just around the corner. Franz continued to improve and even excel with his playing, and soon he began accompanying Helga on occasions in the evenings when she sang. His physical wounds began to heal too, so that the constant pain he had become used to gradually lessened. But it was the unseen wounds, the emotional and spiritual turmoil within him that proved to be the greatest challenge on his journey of recovery. Being able to express himself once again through his music helped, but Heléna sensed that there was still much pain and confusion needing to surface.

Realising that this was the way she could best help not only Franz but his whole family, Heléna listened patiently for many hours, as he began to express his thoughts and feelings, as he questioned God, and as he endeavoured to find meaning in his life and come to a place of peace and acceptance. The journey was difficult, but Franz was spurred on by the fact that right before his eyes was someone even younger than he, who, despite enduring so much, still seemed to have a strong hope for the future, and a deep trust in God. Heléna's life and the things she shared with him about God challenged him deeply. Her gentle words and prayers comforted him, and he was immeasurably grateful for the listening, understanding ear she was always willing to provide, whenever he needed it.

Helga also benefited greatly from Heléna's presence. She had almost given up hope of ever returning to her singing career, until Heléna came to inspire her to practise once again.

'The war can't continue forever, Helga!' Heléna used to say often. 'Somehow, some day you'll have the opportunity to perform again, as you so long to do!'

The two talked for hours, sometimes late into the night, about all sorts of things. Helga listened as Heléna told her of the anguish she had experienced in recent times, but she herself shared even more, airing many of her own questions about life in general, and faith in God in particular. Helga had always been drawn to Stefan and Heléna during her time in Prague, simply by the love that seemed to flow out of them, not only towards each other, but to any whose lives they touched. Occasionally, she had accompanied them to their little Sunday fellowship, always feeling so warmed by their friends' acceptance of her, and often deeply challenged by the things she heard and by their strong faith. Helga had been raised in a traditional, German state church environment, which had instilled in her the concept of a powerful but distant God, always to be held in awe and honour. She saw that same high view of God reflected in Stefan and Heléna's lifestyle and words, but also a deeply real and personal belief in his loving care and acceptance, and a strong sense of his presence with them. She saw it clearly – and wanted it herself so much. Now, many times, as she sat cross-legged on her bed talking with Heléna, she, like Franz, was challenged afresh by her friend's firm belief in God's unchanging love for her, despite all the heartache and loss she had experienced.

Heléna had spoken briefly with Uncle Erik a number of times since being at Domažlice, but each time he had encouraged her to stay where she was. Apparently, after a break of around two months, the remaining key partisan leaders had begun meeting secretly again, but had felt it unwise to engage in any actual underground work again at that point. Now, after six months had elapsed, the network was again becoming active, albeit on a smaller scale. Gradually their energies were deliberately being focused towards building up support and training new leaders and members, as they planned and waited for the right moment to challenge the Czech population in general to become more pro-active, and to rise up en masse against the German authorities. Heléna was of one mind with them in this, but could see no immediate role for herself in what they were now undertaking. Uncle Erik obviously felt, too, that it was still not quite safe enough for her to return to Prague – even to her legitimate students. It did not take Heléna long, therefore, after weighing up what seemed to be the situation in Prague with that which currently existed at Domažlice, to come to the conclusion that God wanted her where she was at present. So she stayed on – much to everyone's delight and relief. Even Helga's father, a quiet, reserved man, returning to his border patrol work after his occasional short times of leave, would farewell her warmly, always thanking her for what she was doing for the family.

As time went by and Franz became stronger, Heléna took over more responsibility for the housework and cooking, freeing Helga and Renate further to focus on the work needing to be done in the fields during the summer months. She enjoyed this work, having helped Berta in the kitchen at Tábor many times as she was growing up, but her greatest delight in these days was to listen to Franz and Helga perform together. Franz was becoming more and more confident with his playing, putting his whole self into his music, and even beginning to consider the possibility of becoming a professional musician after the war. Heléna felt such fulfilment within herself as she listened, and such joy for him in his recovery, both emotional and spiritual. And Helga continued to weave her magic with her beautiful soprano voice, increasing her repertoire each week, with her friend's help. Heléna loved the rich, velvety quality of Helga's voice, always feeling so privileged to be part of such superb, intimate performances. One day, she was sure, Helga would thrill audiences of thousands in the concert halls and opera houses all over Europe. As she listened, she prayed earnestly it would be so.

Then two things happened that were to change the course of events drastically, for Franz in particular. Firstly, the terrible news came of the death of his and Helga's older brother, Klaus, somewhere near the Polish border. Heléna watched and grieved, as the whole family reeled under the blow, endeavouring to be there for each of them as needed, in the days and weeks that followed.

Franz felt the loss deeply, to the point that again bitterness and depression threatened to overwhelm him. How could God, whom he had been learning to love and trust again, he asked in an agony of despair, allow this to happen? For a while, Heléna feared he would not recover, as, apart from losing a much loved brother, in his own mind he had been depending on Klaus to come home and take over responsibility for the farm, given that he himself, injured as he was, could not now easily do so. Indeed he did not even want to, having become determined, when the war was over, somehow to pursue his music studies.

Eventually his mother and sister, supported strongly by Heléna, managed to convince him that whatever happened, he must not stay in Domažlice, but move on to the new things God had for him.

'The farm will survive!' Renate told him very definitely. 'Anyway, I have a feeling your young brother Jürgen might wish to remain at Domažlice after the war. And besides, you father will soon be returning, I'm sure!'

The second piece of news was much more positive, and was to affect Franz's future both immediately and in the long term. Finally, after months of waiting for his wounds to heal sufficiently, as well as for resources to become available, he learnt he was to be sent back to a military hospital in the south of Germany, where he would be fitted with an artificial limb, and helped to walk again. He was to leave at the end of September, in just three weeks' time.

After receiving this news, Franz's spirits rose markedly. At the same time, realisation dawned on him that his personal piano tuition with Heléna was almost at an end. He would be undergoing repatriation in Germany for some time, and even when he did make it home again, Heléna would no doubt have long since returned to Tábor or Prague.

At the end of his final lesson, Franz tried to express his thankfulness to Heléna for all she had done for him.

'What can I say to you, Heléna, that would be adequate? You literally saved my life, you know! You've given me, through my music, a reason to live again, here and now – but more than that, you've shown me an altogether deeper and more authentic way ahead for my life, trusting in God for eternity! I might lose sight of him at times in the years ahead, but I know now he'll never lose sight of me! I hope you don't misunderstand me when I say I truly love you, Heléna! As a brother to a sister, I love you from the bottom of my heart!'

'That's the greatest compliment you could ever give me, Franz! I love you too!' she answered gently.

Heléna was more moved than she would care to admit by his words. There was something about him that reminded her quite strongly of Stefan. Perhaps it was his sensitivity, or the direct way he had of looking at her on occasions. Be that as it may, Heléna knew their relationship needed to remain on the level of brother and sister, as Franz had put it. It was, Heléna felt, as if God had ordained theirs to be a special close friendship for a certain time and purpose. That purpose had been achieved, and now it was time for her to let it go.

Heléna stayed on at Domažlice for around two months after Franz left. She and Helga both practised hard, but as Christmas approached, and the cold weather began to set in again, she became more and more restless. In her heart she longed to be home in Tábor, to be preparing to celebrate Christmas again with Berta and Simona and the children, as well as Uncle Erik and Edita. In the end, without even consulting Uncle Erik, she decided it was time to leave the farm, and to return home unobtrusively and unannounced. And once her decision had been made, she acted quickly, first making her travel arrangements, and then informing the others.

Helga was not surprised when told of her plans. She had known Heléna would go soon, and was happy for her friend, but she saw her off with deep sadness, aware of the huge gap she would leave behind in her life.

'Heléna, I'll miss you so, so much, but I've noticed for some time that you're yearning to be home again. I can see it in your face and hear it in your music. We want you to be here out of danger, but we also want you to be happy. Go home, Heléna – and may God protect you! We might have provided you with a place of safety, but you've given us much, much more! I'll thank God for you each day, and pray for you always, Heléna! Whatever happens in this war, I hope and pray we'll meet again soon!'

Chapter Fourteen

Heléna arrived home one cold winter afternoon in early December. Berta had just prepared the vegetables for dinner, and was in the process of placing them in the oven, when she heard a light tap on the door behind her. Turning around, she almost dropped the large baking dish and its contents, in her surprise and delight at seeing Heléna again.

'Heléna! What are you doing here? Oh, is it really you? How did you get here? Did you travel all the way by yourself? Why didn't you let us know you were coming? Oh, I'm so happy to see you, Heléna!'

The words came tumbling out, mingled with tears of joy and relief that she was safely with them again. Heléna found it so comforting to be enveloped in Berta's loving arms and patted and cosseted again like a little child.

When Berta had recovered a little from her initial shock, Heléna explained the reasons for her unexpected arrival.

'I know it was right for me to be in Domažlice for as long as I was, Berta. I was safe there, and I really was needed, as it turned out, in ways I'd never have imagined. But after Franz left, I must admit I felt a little lost. I'm sure Helga and Renate will be able to cope quite easily without my help around the farm, especially during these winter months. I purposely didn't contact Uncle Erik to ask his advice, because I thought he would no doubt encourage me to stay a little longer for my own safety. So here I am, Berta – rightly or wrongly! Somehow though, I think it's rightly – somehow I felt I needed to be home with you all this Christmas, to remember old times, and to celebrate the good things God must have ahead for us in the New Year!'

Berta hugged her warmly, again expressing how glad she was to see her again. Especially, as she shared with Simona later, because she had noticed in Heléna's words and the expression in her eyes, a loneliness that caused her to want to hold her and comfort her in the same way that she often comforted her own grandchildren. Simona decided to reserve judgment, however, until she had opportunity to be alone with Heléna and talk heart to heart. But these days, as Heléna soon discovered, times of quietness were a rarity for Simona – more than a year earlier, she and Jan had welcomed their third child, a boy this time. He had been born on 2nd October, the anniversary of Stefan's death.

Berta and Simona would never forget the moment after dinner that first evening, when Anna and Kristina, delighted to have their beloved Aunty Heléna back, proudly introduced their baby brother to her. Heléna had not yet seen him, since her only visit to Tábor since his birth had been when she was obliged to hide in the tunnels below the town. She had just sat down in her favourite chair near the sitting room fire and was talking to Berta, when Anna came in, carrying her little brother, Simona and Kristina following close behind. With a big smile, Anna carefully placed him in Heléna's lap.

'Aunty Heléna, we'd like you to meet Stefan, our little brother!'

Heléna reacted instinctively, putting her arms round the little fellow, as he sat gazing solemnly up at her with big blue eyes. She held onto him tightly, in an effort to try to stop shaking.

'Did you say his name was Stefan?' she managed to whisper after a moment. 'I... I thought you'd called him Jan!'

'His first name *is* Jan, Heléna, like his father and grandfather before him,' Simona answered gently. 'But since he was born on 2nd October, we felt it would be a fitting way for us all to remember your own wonderful Stefan, by naming him Jan Stefan. Every time my Jan has been home on leave these past months, however, we soon discovered how confusing it is to have two people with the same name in the one household! And besides, as our little man has grown, every time he looks at us, his big blue eyes remind us so much of your Stefan. We've all commented on that – even Jan. So naturally we began calling him Stefan ...'

Simona's voice trailed off, as she looked in consternation at Heléna's face, and saw the tears welling up in her eyes and beginning to trickle down her cheeks. Quickly she went to take Stefan from her, but Heléna held onto him desperately, at the same time leaning her head against Simona's, as she knelt beside her to comfort her.

'Simona, it's a beautiful name, and he's truly a beautiful baby!' Heléna eventually responded. 'I'm very touched that you've named him after my Stefan – I really am! It was just such a surprise to hear the name again! You're so right – his eyes are very like Stefan's. Beautiful, clear, blue eyes that looked into one's very soul, I always thought.'

The tears were still falling, but Heléna continued to hold onto little Stefan, moving him to nestle comfortably in the curve of her arm, and smoothing his fine blonde hair with her free hand. She loved the feel of the soft skin of his little arm as it rested on hers, and the way he reached up with his other arm to touch her face gently. Anna and Kristina remained nearby, both anxious to help. Heléna put her other arm around them as they stood there, and smiled through her tears.

'What a special little brother – and how fortunate he is to have two such wonderful older sisters!' she said at last. 'I think Uncle Stefan would have been proud of you all! I didn't mean to cry and upset you, but it's just that I miss him so very, very much! I've missed you all too – and that's why I knew I had to come back to see you and celebrate Christmas with you again!'

For a while longer all three children played with Heléna on the rug in front of the fire, little Stefan growing sleepier by the minute. Finally Simona carried him off, and the two girls were also shepherded to bed by Berta, after Heléna had promised to read them their favourite stories the following evening. Heléna was not far behind in deciding she needed to sleep, the day's events now taking their toll. For some time she lay awake in her old bed, exhausted, yet unable to detach her mind from the events of the evening and relax her body. She tried to pray, but somehow could not seem to find her way through the fog of emotions which seemed to crowd out everything else. Eventually she fell into a fitful sleep, full of confused dreaming – and then the old nightmare came again. She woke up screaming, and trembling all over, with tears running down her face. Simona, always alert for little Stefan's cries, heard Heléna immediately, and hurried to her side, speaking clearly and firmly to her, soothing her until the tremors subsided.

'Heléna, don't be frightened! It's Simona! You're safe with us. You're home here at Tábor!'

Heléna gradually became aware of her surroundings, and recognised the soothing voice of Simona, immediately embarrassed that she had disturbed her friend's much needed sleep.

'I'll be fine now, Simona, but thank you so much! As soon as I settle here again, the nightmares will go, I know. Perhaps we can talk tomorrow, and I'll also try to see Uncle Erik. Then we should know if I can stay here safely for a while, and not endanger anyone.'

Berta and Simona had known about Heléna's own involvement in the underground, since the day she went to Domažlice. She had sent them a note via Uncle Erik, and since that time they had redoubled their efforts in praying for her each day. Now Simona merely hugged her close, assuring her again they were so glad she was back safely with them.

The next morning, Heléna phoned Uncle Erik and arranged to see him that afternoon. He seemed pleased she was home, and not unduly surprised either, she felt. And after she had greeted him and Edita, and they were seated comfortably before the fire, she began to understand why.

'Heléna, I truly am delighted to see you home again! Fortunately, you're probably quite safe here, since the authorities seem to have other more pressing issues on their minds at present. From what we can make out, the Germans are busy fighting on various fronts, requiring a huge deployment of troops and resources to these places. We're small fry, compared with everything else demanding their attention right now! But we still have to be careful, especially in Prague. If we were to stir up trouble again, there'd be no mercy, I assure you! Some have tried, and paid the price. All that aside however, I've been wondering what's been happening for you, Helena. You've been away from us for quite a while now, and something in your voice when we last spoke made me wonder if you were missing us. Or is that just an old man's wish?' he joked, smiling across at her, his sharp eyes under his bushy eyebrows nevertheless detecting a loneliness in her own, and something of a slightly lost air, he felt.

'I'm fine, Uncle Erik,' Heléna replied, but her words were accompanied by a little sigh, which Uncle Erik did not miss. 'It was right that I stay in Domažlice as long as I did, but I felt it was time to come home now. As I explained to Berta, I found myself useful to Helga's family in ways I never would have imagined. Having opportunity to encourage Helga with her singing was a privilege in itself, and being part of Franz's physical recovery, as well as helping him rediscover his passion for music was a very special experience. But above all, I think the fact that both Franz and Helga have a much stronger faith in God now has made me very happy indeed.'

'I'm so proud of you, my dear, and proud of what you were able to achieve in Domažlice for your friends!' Uncle Erik responded warmly.

Heléna could feel that the tears were not far away, as Uncle Erik spoke so kindly to her. She always sensed the beautiful, healing presence of God when she spent time with Edita and him.

'Domažlice was God's provision of a safe place for me, I'm sure of that,' she said eventually, almost as if she were thinking aloud, 'but I feel so restless again now – so unsettled and unsure of where I fit and what I should do!'

'Heléna, let me ask you something. I don't mean to pry, my dear,' Uncle Erik said carefully, 'but was Franz possibly more than a good friend to you? I'm sensing that his going left a very painful gap indeed.'

'Yes, you're right,' she admitted, after a lengthy pause. 'We spent many hours together, so inevitably became quite close. When he left, he told me he loved me from the bottom of his heart, as a brother loves a sister, and I do love him that way too. Truly I don't believe Franz was ever meant to be more than a good friend and brother to me

– but sometimes he reminded me so much of my Stefan!'

The tears came then – tears of loneliness and sorrow, but also tears of relief, that she could share her heart openly, and know that she would be heard with grace and compassion. They talked on, Uncle Erik listening carefully, as Heléna shared possible plans for her immediate future. Prague, he felt, was still out of the question for her, but he promised to think and pray about it, and to meet with her again soon.

Later that night, Heléna, Simona and Berta also talked, after the children were in bed. Heléna shared her journey of the past year with them, keeping her more personal feelings about Franz to herself, however. Simona, always quietly perceptive, guessed something of Heléna's heart, but kept her thoughts to herself, vowing to do all she could to help fill the void of loneliness that she sensed was there. There was no doubt, Berta and Simona agreed, that Heléna should stay with them again, until she was able to return to her own apartment. Anna and Kristina, and even little Stefan, as he got to know her, would be delighted to have their Aunty Heléna close by again.

'The girls missed you so much when you left,' Simona commented. 'No one could read stories quite the same as Aunty Heléna! Anna has missed her piano lessons with you too. We felt she was a little young yet to learn from Uncle Erik – and besides, he had more than enough students. I know she'll be delighted if you agree to start teaching her again while you're here!'

It was the week leading up to Christmas before Heléna saw Uncle Erik again. He had been making enquiries among his current partisan contacts, her told her, on her behalf.

'They all say it would not be wise to return to Prague yet, Heléna. Only recently, David, and also Miklos, now being trained as a potential leader, apparently narrowly escaped capture, after addressing a group of supporters and possible recruits there. In fact, I've just received news that these two are expected in Tábor this evening, looking for shelter in the tunnels!'

Giving in to Heléna's pleas to see them again, Uncle Erik allowed her to accompany him as he met with them. Jiří had made them comfortable, and despite the fact that both were exhausted, having been on the run for several days, they were delighted to see Heléna again, and eager to talk with her. Both were in complete agreement with Uncle Erik, however, that Prague was not the place for her. David, it seemed, did not want to see the same happen to her, or to any other woman, as had happened to his Jana, while Miklos strongly supported her staying where she was for much more personal reasons, so it appeared to Uncle Erik. Heléna herself noticed the admiring glances Miklos cast her way from time to time, despite his tiredness. She was touched and mildly flattered, remembering his particular care for her even in the early days after Stefan's death, but could hardly imagine a more inopportune moment to be thinking along such lines. Miklos was on the run, and she herself – well, she might not be in immediate physical danger as Miklos was, but emotionally she was not ready yet to trust her own responses and make any important decisions, as far as ongoing relationships were concerned. Heléna, therefore, was warm and caring in her responses to them both equally, as she chatted to them and enquired about other mutual friends and co-workers. In the end, the meeting confirmed her decision to keep a low profile for the time being, until clearly led to do otherwise.

A week later, when everyone was still seated around the big dining table on Christmas evening, Heléna realised afresh how glad she was to be home amongst old friends. This year, Uncle Erik and Edita, and Jiří were present, along with Berta, Simona and Jan, who had again managed to obtain leave for a few days, and of course the three children. Edvard and Judith had also arrived for a brief visit, along with their little son Tomas, now almost a year old. He was so much like the grandfather he would never see, that Heléna felt like crying, the resemblance reminding her so forcefully of two more wonderful people who were no longer with them. Knowing her cousin and his wife had been aware of Stefan's underground activities, Heléna felt she could share her plans openly with everyone present.

'It's so good to be together again!' Heléna began. 'This past year we've certainly been scattered far and wide – but we're here now, and I for one am very thankful to God for that! For me personally, it seems best that I stay here for some months at least, and not resume any partisan work until things are safer in Prague. I hope to use this time to practise and prepare again for my future music career, under Uncle Erik's guidance. Also, I want to take the opportunity to learn more about God, and be better equipped for whatever he has for me.'

After several others had shared their hopes for the new year, Heléna invited them all to move to the sitting room for the usual carol singing around the piano. This year, the children particularly enjoyed this time, little Anna, recently turned seven and, in her eyes, quite grown up, gallantly trying to sing all the words along with the adults. Heléna, seated at the piano, could not help but remember times when the beautiful voices of her father, of Stefan, and also Tomas had swelled the volume of their singing considerably, adding wonderful depth and beauty as they did so. Jan, Edvard, Uncle Erik and Jiří all tried, but despite their enthusiasm, it was not the same. Her eyes caught those of Uncle Erik, and in a break in the singing, when it was bedtime for the children, he put his old hand on her shoulder, just as Stefan used to on occasions, and spoke softly to her.

'Yes, my dear, I'm feeling too that everything has changed so much! Regrettably, we can't turn back the clock, but we can go forward with courage! Remember, Heléna, that "all shall be well, and all manner of things shall be well" eventually!'

So Heléna approached 1944 with determination, yet prepared to take each month as it unfolded. She threw herself into her practice and studies, wanting to reap the most benefit from this time that seemed given to her for a purpose. All around her, in her own country and across Europe, battles raged on many fronts, with so much resultant destruction, and so many families torn apart and grieving. Heléna felt it all, pouring her emotions into her playing, which to Uncle Erik's practised ear, seemed to become more and more exquisite as the weeks went by.

And she filled many journals in this time, with questions to God, deep thoughts, and rich quotations from the bible and other sources that touched her deeply. Many hours were spent with Uncle Erik and Edita, drinking in their wisdom gained from years of journeying with God and their fellow human beings. Heléna's friend, Andela, also visited on occasions, enabling them to enjoy lively discussions, as well as special quiet, sacred moments. Sometimes Andela brought her violin, and then she and Heléna would play together, as they had in the days before Stefan's death. Often Uncle Erik would be their audience, so much enjoying the richness of their talent, yet so sad that others in their homeland could not hear their beautiful music as well.

By the summer of 1944, the Czech underground had gained strength, recruiting more and more members, and quietly enlisting the support of a wider sector of the population. Six months previously, Edvard Beneš, the exiled President, had reportedly travelled to Moscow and made an alliance with the USSR, a move which many in Heléna's homeland deemed very astute, given the might of the Russian army. Perhaps, aided by the Russians, so it was reasoned, they might soon be able to rise up against their enemy, and be free to pursue their own destiny once more. Others, including Uncle Erik and Edvard, had grave doubts about such an alliance, seeing in it seeds of future trouble for the non-socialist intellectuals, as well as the industrialists and landowners of the nation. At the same time, hope gradually began to grow within Czechoslovakia that Germany might in fact soon lose the war. Its resources were now so stretched on every front, that more than thirty thousand Czech citizens had now been dispatched to various parts of the Third Reich to swell its depleted labour force.

Heléna learnt these things from Edvard and Judith, as well as from Uncle Erik and Andela, who were kept informed by their underground contacts. She was as impatient as any of the partisans for the Czech people to rise up and confront the German authorities, yet she understood, as did her fellow workers, that acting too precipitously could bring even greater disaster. Better to wait for the right moment, they argued – a wise decision, in the light of what soon happened in neighbouring Slovakia. In August, sections of the Slovak army and partisans joined forces to bring about a national uprising, in an attempt to rid themselves of their Nazi-backed government. After only two months, the uprising was brutally quashed by German troops, and complete Nazi occupation of the country followed. No one in Czechoslovakia wanted such a thing to happen to their people – yet, while their nation appeared to acquiesce, in reality, many were quietly rallying to the cause, biding their time, waiting and praying for the right moment.

October came, and with it, the third anniversary of Stefan's death. Heléna was working hard at increasing her musical repertoire and fine honing her piano technique, but at the same time, she was delighting in new discoveries in prayer, and in her knowledge of God. Life for her was rich, with daily challenges and a variety of fresh insights. Yet, as the anniversary approached, the old restlessness began to bubble up from beneath the surface. Alert to its signals, Heléna put time aside to walk alone across the fields and along the riverbanks, back to her old childhood haunts, and to reflect. She knew there was anger and frustration inside her that these years during which she would hopefully have begun forging a career and building up a reputation with concertgoers were slipping by. And on an even deeper personal level, the anniversary of Stefan's death was a stark reminder, once again, of the beautiful relationship she had lost, and probably would never find with anyone else, and of the loneliness she still felt daily.

Yet more than this, she realised that the rich input she had received over these months needed an outlet – it needed somehow to be expressed and shared with others. As she sat on the grassy bank of the Lužnice, watching the autumn leaves float slowly down to the water and be carried along by the current, Heléna prayed for guidance, determining to seek advice from Uncle Erik once again.

It came as no surprise to her that, when she broached the subject of this new restlessness with him, he had already perceived it. As he spoke, he lent forward in his chair, his old face lined and craggy, but his eyes still alert and sympathetic.

'Heléna, if you can hold on a little longer, I believe that in the new year, it will be possible for you to return to Prague. I think you need your good friends around you – those more of your own age and interests with whom you can share deeply, and who'll help alleviate the loneliness you're feeling. I know you have Simona, but she's preoccupied with her little family – and as for Berta and Edita and I ... ' Uncle Erik paused, sighing a little, and rubbing his tired eyes, 'well, speaking for myself, I'm beginning to feel very, very old!'

Heléna had already noticed that he was aging. It sent a chill of fear through her, that soon there may be no Uncle Erik to whom she could come for support and guidance. He must be close to seventy-five, she surmised, but he had always been so active and his mind so alert.

'Uncle Erik, you'll always be young at heart,' Heléna responded warmly, taking his old hand in hers. 'People like you never really grow old! I can see you're a little tired – is there anything I can do for you before I return to Prague? Perhaps help with your young students again?'

He did not need much persuasion. Apart from helping him, he was aware this would provide some form of temporary outlet at least for Heléna's restlessness.

'Thank you, my dear,' he said simply. 'I love my students, but I am tired. In the new year, we'll have to find some other permanent arrangement for them, I feel.'

Heléna's spirits rose in the weeks that followed, as she prepared for her move back to Prague. She was looking forward not only to what the future might hold for her career-wise, but also to mixing with her good friends there again. And she felt happy about what she had learnt and accomplished in the past months also. Even without input from those around her like Uncle Erik, she herself knew that her playing had matured and become more polished. And she realised too, with thankfulness, that she had matured in her faith, that the rock beneath her feet had become much firmer, and that her knowledge and experience of God had deepened considerably.

Even though the war still dragged on, that Christmas was special for Heléna's beloved friends and family, as they gathered together once more. There was a sense that an end was in sight, and that, in the coming year they would be able to move on with their lives. So they rejoiced, thankful for God's love and care, and hopeful for a brighter future. On New Year's Day, 1945, Heléna's sixth wedding anniversary, she travelled back to Prague with Edvard and Judith and Tomas. Many fond farewells were said to Berta and Simona, as well as Anna, Kristina and little Stefan, along with promises to visit often. But Heléna reserved her final farewell for Uncle Erik.

'Goodbye, Uncle Erik! Thank you so much for all you've done for me in these months, from the bottom of my heart! I'll do my best for you – and for Stefan! I'll keep the faith, I'll stand tall, and I'll always remember that I belong to God!'

Chapter Fifteen

Back in Prague, Heléna found that two years had indeed brought about many changes. Friends and acquaintances were now absent, some captured and taken no one knew where, some killed by the Gestapo, others conscripted as labourers and sent to various parts of Germany. Still others, women whose husbands had been killed or were missing, had been forced to move in with relatives, along with their children, in order to survive. In her own apartment block, Heléna soon discovered that things had altered considerably. Much to her relief, her old neighbour and suspected Nazi informer from the apartment below was no longer there. Life was noisier as a result, however, since the new occupants were two sisters with young families, waiting for husbands to return from Germany.

Yet some things had not changed. As soon as she walked into her apartment, she felt a great sadness, but also an unmistakeable peace. She was home again – a home without her beloved Stefan, where his tangible presence would never again fill the room and simply light it up for her, but also a special place of so many good memories of precious times together, of deep mutual love, of shared hope and joy in God. She felt God's calming, comforting presence welcoming her, assuring her that his peace would not leave her, whatever lay ahead. Most of Stefan's clothes had been given away before she had moved to Tomas and Eva's, since Heléna was aware how so many families around her were in desperate need of such items. Stefan would have wanted her to do that, she had felt, but many of his special possessions still remained – his cello, his beautiful piano, his bible and other books, his special pen, his favourite chair. Now these reminders brought her comfort as well as sadness, linking her with the past, but also strengthening her to move on into the next part of her journey.

Heléna was particularly delighted to find that friends from her fellowship group had not changed greatly during her time away. She had no sooner arrived in her apartment, than there was a knock on the door, followed by cries of joy, and much hugging, when she went to answer it. Andela was there, closely followed by Milan and Zdenka, Radim and Irena, Daniel and Renata, and also Johana and Sabina. Miklos was absent, still needing to remain in hiding. The group had brought some home cooked treats with them, despite wartime shortages, which they proceeded to share with everyone, as they listened to Heléna's news, and she theirs. Everyone seemed to have a story to tell of God's protection during this time, or his strengthening and provision in various ways. Radim and Irena headed the list, having survived several narrow escapes from the Gestapo in the course of their partisan work. Briefly, Heléna shared something of her own journey, both in Domažlice and back at Tábor, reflecting in her own mind, even as she did, how much she had learnt about God and about herself in that time. Later as everyone went to leave, Daniel spoke for them all.

'Heléna, it's so good to have you with us again! You continue to amaze us! You've grown so much that we can hardly keep up with you! God bless you, Heléna – may your career unfold this year in a wonderful way!'

The demand for good music teachers in Prague seemed to have remained unchanged too. Heléna hardly needed to contact her old students personally, so quickly did the news travel that she had returned, and others clamoured to join their ranks, so that Heléna had to guard her own practice times carefully. She was deeply impressed by the marked improvement she noted in some of her keenest students who, like Heléna, had worked hard by themselves, gleaning whatever advice they could from others in the intervening two-year period. Most were preparing for the day when the Conservatorium would again open its doors and they could begin studies there, just as Heléna had herself over six years earlier. They chafed at the bit, like so many others in Prague, eager for the German authorities to leave, waiting for the right time for their people to take back control of their own city, with or without the help of the Allied forces.

They did not have to wait long. In February and March, word reached them that the German army were sustaining massive losses on all fronts. Liberation had already begun in eastern Slovakia towards the end of the previous year, with the Russians collaborating with combined Czechoslovak troops to free Ruthenia from German control. Then in early April, Beneš travelled from Moscow to Košice, where he set up a provisional Czechoslovak government, made up of a coalition of Social Democrats, Socialists and Communists. The news of Hitler's death on 30th April did not take long either to stir up hope among the Czech people. Then finally, on 5th May, the people of Prague, led by key members of the underground, rose up against the German authorities, liberating most of the city even before reinforcements arrived, in the form of US troops from the west, and the Russians from the east. Three days after the Germans were granted free passage out of the city by the Czech partisans, they began leaving, the day before the arrival of the Russian troops.

Things moved relatively quickly after that, with Beneš welcomed back enthusiastically by the people of Prague a week later. Even then, some of the more politically astute citizens wondered how well this leftist coalition government would eventually be accepted by the general population, and how the Czech industrialists and landowners in particular would fare. But in those early days of liberation, most people simply savoured the moment, thankful that war was finally over, and overjoyed that soon their loved ones would be released from the labour camps, and life would hopefully return to some sort of normality.

Over the summer holidays, colleges and universities across the nation began to prepare for reopening that September, as did the Prague Conservatorium. Yet this task proved extremely difficult, given the massive purge of the nation's intelligentsia that had occurred in the early years of the war. Gradually some came trickling back, vastly changed people, but very determined to be part of rebuilding their homeland and their institutions of higher learning. Gradually, orchestras, choirs, dance companies, and other cultural groups began to reform, eager to meet the demands of a population crying out again for beauty and colour, and all that was to be had from such artistic endeavours.

Heléna could do nothing but rejoice wholeheartedly, as she watched these events unfolding, so happy for those of her students who managed to make it into the Conservatorium's September intake, despite particularly stiff competition. Soon too, exciting and challenging possibilities began to emerge as far as her own career as a concert pianist was concerned, but Heléna did not rush into anything. Apart from wanting to weigh up her options, she needed time to find a teacher – someone who could help her develop into a truly first class performer.

As soon as possible after the Germans left, Heléna began searching for her old teacher, Alexandr Veverka, among the survivors of Terezin, but to no avail. What she did see and hear, however, she could hardly believe or comprehend. Thousands upon thousands of Jews from Bohemia and Moravia alone – more than seventy thousand, it was estimated – had been killed while the Germans were in power, with only about eight thousand surviving the terrible time in Terezin. And thousands more had been lost to their homeland in a different way, she realised, having fled the country to avoid imprisonment in the concentration camps. Heléna followed every lead as best she could, hoping beyond hope that Alexandr and his family were somewhere among the survivors – but without success. All she could discover, from the official information available, and from Jewish friends of the family, was that they had in fact been in Terezin, but were moved, so they had heard, to a concentration camp in Poland, where they would have had little chance of survival.

Heléna was heartbroken for Alexandr and his family – such beautiful people with so much to give. But there was also an enormous sadness in her at what the loss of so many gifted, intelligent and hard working people would mean for her country in general. She personally had known many outstanding Jewish musicians in Prague before the war – how could they ever be replaced? Whole families had been wiped out, and others reduced to one or two members, while many who returned were barely recognisable, so deeply shattered were they, both physically and emotionally. Heléna and her friends in the fellowship grieved for them and with them. They prayed for restoration of minds and spirits, and cared for the physical needs of those known to them, helping them, with what food and resources they had, to try to begin again somehow. With all their hearts, they felt the need to try to right a terrible wrong inflicted on a people simply because of their race and religion, and endeavoured to show compassion and empathy to them, despite their differing faith.

Heléna was also deeply grieved over an entirely different problem that quickly emerged after liberation. She saw with dismay how her own people chose to retaliate against the German population of the Sudetenland and those living elsewhere in her country. Apart from anything else, the same food rationing was now enforced upon them, as the German authorities had enforced on Jews in Czechoslovakia. Heléna's concern grew for Helga and her family in Domažlice, since she had not heard from them for some time. Eventually, she telephoned the farm, relieved to hear Renate answer.

'Heléna, it's so good to hear from you!' she greeted her. 'Yes, Heinz and I are fine, but we're both working very hard on the farm. Actually, Helga is with Franz in Germany now! She left just a few weeks ago. She was going to wait until she was settled there before letting you know, but then with the end of the war here and all the uncertainty …'

Her voice trailed off. Heléna detected some anxiety, and not a little exhaustion in her tone.

'Franz is doing very well, Heléna!' Renate finally continued. 'Recently he moved out of the hospital, but since he had no one to care for him, we felt Helga should join him there. We miss her so much, but now we're so glad she went!'

Again she was silent. This time, before she could begin again, Heléna spoke.

'Renate, is there anything I can do? Is there anything you need? Do you have enough food?'

'Yes Heléna, thankfully we have food. It's not so bad here on the farm – but we know many of our friends nearby in the Sudetenland are starving. It's true they and we are German, but we love this country too! Things have been a little difficult here lately.

Some of our Czech neighbours are quite unfriendly towards us now, and we've heard that soon the government officials will be paying us a visit – and I don't think they'll bring good news. Also, just after Helga left, we heard that our Jürgen is a prisoner of war somewhere in France. We were so relieved, as we hadn't heard from him and didn't know where he was, or even if he were still alive! We hope he'll be released soon and come home – but it depends what happens to us here. Maybe he'd be better off in Germany with Franz, or perhaps he could go to some other relatives in the north near Hamburg. At least it's good that I have my Heinz here with me! He often asks after you – you were such a help to us, Heléna!'

The conversation ended soon after, with Heléna making Renate promise to contact her, if they ever needed help.

That was the last time Heléna ever spoke with her. It was not until later that she discovered that the same fate befell Helga's parents, as befell almost two and a half million of the German speaking population of the Sudetenland over the next two years. Not only were their homes and farms confiscated, with no financial reimbursement, but they were also expelled from Czech lands altogether – 'transferred', as it was described, back to Germany or Austria. Some suffered severe punishment in retaliation for their own treatment of Czechs living within their borders when war broke out, others because they later collaborated with their own countrymen and betrayed Czech friends and neighbours.

But many, like Helga's family, were innocent victims, caught between their two countries. Some fled in fear, while others were killed even before they could begin the long, torturous march back across the border. Heinz and Renate, so she was told, had had their land confiscated soon after her phone conversation, and had been forced to walk south into the Sudetenland, and then, along with hundreds of others, herded towards the Bavarian border. Somewhere during this forced march, they, like so many others, were tortured, beaten and killed – two kind people who had committed no crime, except that of being caught up in issues they could never have envisaged when they had first moved to Czechoslovakia. When Heléna found out their exact fate, she was extremely saddened, but not surprised. Ever since news of President Beneš' 'transfer' policy had swept the country in May, and was greeted with loud applause by the general population, Heléna had feared they would inevitably be among those who would suffer severely.

Yet it was not only the German speaking population of Czechoslovakia who suffered in these first months of peacetime. As Beneš' coalition government began to settle into its role, rumours began to spread that caused great alarm among the country's industrialists and wealthier landowners. The days of large-scale nationalisation appeared to be imminent – something Heléna realised even then could possibly affect her own financial situation. Since the death of both her parents, she, as the sole beneficiary of their wills, had inherited all of Václav's business interests and farming estates, as well as the actual family home at Tábor and its surrounding lands. Then after Stefan's death, with ownership of his factories also passing to her, Heléna financial security was assured, at least assets-wise, if not in terms of actual available cash funds. Now that peace had finally come, she knew that big decisions would have to be made, not only by the board of management of Stefan's company, still capably led by Ivan George, but also those overseeing Václav's farming interests.

To complicate matters further, her father's heavy machinery factories that had been commandeered by the German army after his arrest and managed by their own personnel, were now lying idle. The manufacture of weapons, tanks and other army equipment had ceased, and now important decisions needed to be made concerning future production. If current rumours were correct, Heléna realised that the first of her business interests likely to be affected would, no doubt, be these very factories. In one simple move, they could easily pass into the hands of the state, without any thought of their being returned to her as their rightful owner, or of her receiving any compensation for loss of property or income. All Heléna could do was to wait and pray, and be prepared for whatever should eventuate. She was not penniless by any means, and much better off than so many others around her. Besides, she believed in her heart that, somehow, God would see her through this time and provide for her, whatever happened.

By the end of June, Heléna had to accept the fact that Alexandr would not be returning, and began seeking another teacher. She wanted someone like him – focused and committed, gentle and encouraging, yet also willing to confront and challenge. One evening, at a benefit concert for Jewish families who had lost everything, she was introduced to Sergei Prokov, a Russian musician now married to a Czech woman whom he had met on a visit many years previously. Initially they had returned to his homeland to live, but now, with the ties between the two countries much closer since the war, and with his wife's elderly parents needing someone to care for them, Sergei had responded to an advertisement for a teaching position at the Prague Conservatorium. While his time was more than fully taken up with that role, given the severe shortage of qualified teachers, he nevertheless did not need much persuasion to agree to tutor Heléna as well, after hearing her play that evening.

Heléna would not easily forget this first meeting with Sergei. During supper, Uncle Erik, who had travelled to Prague especially to be present for Heléna's first concert since her return, performed the introductions, since he had known Sergei for many years. As he did so, Heléna could not help noticing how Uncle Erik, quite a large man himself, although now somewhat stooped with age, was almost dwarfed by the Russian. Soon his large hand had clasped hers firmly, and he was shaking it almost violently, all the time gesticulating with the other, and speaking volubly in a mixture of Russian and Czech.

'My dear girl, I am so pleased to meet you! So happy! I enjoy so much your performance this evening – you play with such feeling and passion for a so young woman! But I think somehow you are a little sad, no? I hear it in your music – too much sadness for a little one who look – how you say – like an angel!! Ah, what I would give to teach a one as you! You like much the music of my Russian friend Tschaikovsky, no? I would have you play much Tschaikovsky, I think – yes, much Tschaikovsky, but also much Beethoven. My wife Katerina, she say: "Sergei, when will you stop wanting to teach, teach, teach every young pianist you hear?" But I say to her: 'No, Anna, not every young pianist – just every beautiful young woman pianist!" I say that, but I make joke, you know – she understand that! She still my very favourite young woman, after thirty-two year long our marriage!'

With that, Sergei let out a great roar of laughter that turned heads in the room, causing many to pause and smile in mid-sentence. At first, Heléna was taken aback by this almost larger than life person, but then as she looked into his eyes, she saw clearly in their depths great wisdom and compassion, masked – deliberately so, she came to believe – by the sheer volume of his words and laughter. Immediately she felt a sense of safety and security, and simply of rightness. Everything about him was so different from Alexandr, yet he was the one, she believed, whom she could trust to help her develop further musically and to guide her wisely in her future career.

Thus it was that Heléna entered a new phase of growth in every area of her life. In the midst of the turmoil of post-war activity, of homecomings and of grieving, of political upheaval, of economic uncertainty everywhere, Heléna could almost feel herself growing larger on the inside, as it were. She felt herself constantly being filled, not only with strength and energy that she believed was God's provision for her, but with deep comfort and a sense of being carried by him, despite all the unknowns. She knew that the fulfilment and joy she was deriving from her music, and, in particular, from Sergei's input, was a special timely gift also. It was as if God were lavishing a richness upon her that fed the very depths of her soul, so that whatever happened in the future, this deep well of beauty and creativity he was forming within her would never run dry.

In the hours leading up to her weekly lesson with Sergei, Heléna always eagerly anticipated the treasures that would be unwrapped for her that day – hidden nuances and depths often surfacing unexpectedly in familiar and well-loved compositions, as if another beautiful facet of a diamond were being revealed. New and wonderful discoveries were also made, as Sergei encouraged her to experiment with different composers and a range of musical styles. In this period, she undertook to perform at only a limited number of concerts, aware that she needed time to settle into this new phase of her growth, and to find her own individual style. But on each occasion, to Heléna's delight and relief, her earlier, loyal fans applauded her enthusiastically, as well as those who had never heard the name Heléna Marek before.

One great sadness in this time for Heléna, was that Uncle Erik was no longer able to attend her performances in Prague. Not long after the benefit concert at which she had met Sergei, her old teacher suffered a severe stroke, and had been bedridden ever since. Heléna visited him when she could, and prayed earnestly for him and Edita, for peace of mind amidst the frustration of communication difficulties, and also for his complete recovery.

The first financial blows began to fall for Heléna at the end of October, when, in accordance with decisions made at Košice the previous April, and agreements signed by the various political factions, in one comprehensive move, around sixty per cent of industry across the country was nationalised. Since Heléna had expected her father's factories to be among the first to go, she had taken care to ensure that any dividends owed to her were collected and deposited to her bank account. This had turned out to be small indeed, in the end, because of the disruption of the war years, and also because of Václav's policy of never amassing great profits. Instead, he had always preferred to plough these back into further expansion and design experimentation or, more recently, to use them to fund underground work. Finally, just prior to her leaving on a brief concert tour, Heléna received news, from her family solicitor, that her father's factories had indeed passed into the hands of the state. While she had expected this to occur, and had resigned herself to it, she was nevertheless deeply saddened at the loss of something into which her father had poured so much time and effort.

What Heléna had not expected, however – or at least not so soon – was that this sweeping government takeover would also include Stefan's biscuit factories. Since the time when, newly returned to Prague, she had reaffirmed Ivan George as managing director of Stefan's main company, she had enjoyed the privilege of receiving reasonable financial returns from any profits accrued. Certainly these dividends had decreased towards the end of the war, because of the cost to the company of the diversification of production demanded by the German authorities. Nevertheless, they had arrived at fairly regular intervals, leaving Heléna with no real financial concerns, and no pressing need to earn her own living, unlike many around her. In recent weeks, however, Ivan had become increasingly aware that the company might indeed be included in this first push towards nationalisation, and had sought for a way out of the situation, bargaining with government officials for more time at least. As soon as possible, he had tried to warn Heléna about what was happening, but had been unsuccessful, since she was away on her concert tour. In the end, all he could do was to ensure that any available funds that were rightfully hers were transferred speedily into her own private account.

But officials of the new government, spurred on by their communist ideology and by what they perceived was best for their homeland in this new era, also moved very fast. Within days of Václav's factories being forcibly turned over to the state, Stefan's followed suit. In both instances, workers nearing retirement age were pensioned off, and management level staff were replaced by state appointed personnel and offered, in exchange, factory floor positions, involving long hours of work for low wages. While many stayed, realising that any work was better than none, some chose to begin preparations to leave the country. Ivan, sick at heart, not only for himself, but for all Stefan's faithful workers, was one of the earliest to make this difficult decision.

Meanwhile, his was the task of breaking the terrible news to Heléna. No sooner had she arrived back in Prague late one afternoon than Ivan called to see her. One look at his face, as she answered the door, told her what the news would be.

'Yes, I'm afraid it's not good news, Heléna,' he began, responding to the sign of alarm on her face, and her concerned questions. 'I've hardly slept this past fortnight, thinking of how to break the news to you. We're all aware of what's happening in our country, but unfortunately I didn't think it would happen so quickly to Stefan's company. My dear, it's not Stefan's or yours or ours any longer – it's now state owned, will be run by state appointed personnel, and the profits kept and disposed of as the state sees fit! Whether we like it or not, we've had to relinquish all aspects of ownership and management. I'm so sorry, Heléna! We've worked so hard to manage it on your behalf, and as Stefan would have wanted – and all for nothing, it seems!' he ended bitterly.

Heléna was silent for some time, trying to take in the magnitude of what Ivan was saying. It had been three weeks since she had received the news of the loss of Václav's company, but in her need to keep focused on her concert tour, she had not allowed this news to touch her deeply at that point. Now, before she could even process this first loss, a much greater disaster had taken place – one that hit her like a heavy blow right in the pit of her stomach.

Eventually, when she did not comment, Ivan continued.

'I've placed as much of the money owing to you that I could into your bank account, before we were removed. I hope it's enough for you for some time to come. I've done my best, but I feel I've failed you, Heléna – please forgive me! I only hope that at some future date, it will all be returned to you, as it rightfully should!'

Heléna did her best to reassure him, pointing out that no one could have withstood the onslaught of an egalitarian government with such different ideology from theirs, and such determination to sweep everything before it in its bid to bring about immediate nationwide change. He left dejected, despite Heléna's assurances that he was not to blame.

It was just as well Ivan did not realise the extent of the disaster that had in fact befallen Heléna, or perhaps his courage in breaking the news to her personally would have failed him. What neither of them knew then, was that the money paid into Heléna's account from the company profits was not safe at all. Nor, in fact, were the profits from Václav's company. Nationalisation, Heléna was informed in the days to come, involved not only acquisition of all property and stock belonging to a company, and removal of those in management positions, but also the freezing of all liquid assets amassed by the owner, and the surrender of these to the state. Heléna, along with many other company owners and business partners across the country, was in fact left with very little in the bank at all.

In the months following this catastrophic turn of events, as Heléna tried to come to grips with her new situation, she grieved for the large number of Stefan's managerial level staff who had lost so much, not only in terms of income, but also in job satisfaction. She still had her music career, but they, in contrast, had very little now. She longed for some wise insight and comforting words from Uncle Erik, but he himself was still quite unwell, and only able to take part in the simplest of conversations. Her father's solicitor, a rather stern, reserved, but trustworthy gentleman, while commiserating with Heléna over the loss of Václav's companies, endeavoured to reassure her concerning her future financial security.

'Mrs Marek, I'm extremely sorry about what has occurred for you, but I feel I must point out that the potential income from your father's farming estates is increasing rapidly, as more labourers return to the land, and also as the factories begin producing improved farming equipment, rather than armaments! You have suffered considerable financial loss, but I believe things will come to rights for you very soon!'

Heléna listened, thanking him for the careful way he was watching over her interests, but only half believing the reassurances he gave. After all, she had thought Stefan's factories would be safe, and had soon discovered otherwise.

It was her Sunday fellowship group, in the end, who gave her the perspective she needed. Heléna had continued to meet regularly with them since her return to Prague, unless her concert engagements precluded it. The group had grown in size, some members having returned from months of forced labour, and others, including Miklos, at last able to come out of hiding. Others had recently joined, touched by the loving care shown to them by the group in various ways. Now, as Heléna shared her situation with them all, they were stunned and grieved at her loss, whatever their own political convictions. Andela cried for Heléna, overcome by this latest turn of events, having watched her friend already walk through such devastation and loss in her life.

'Heléna, you know that we love you, and feel deeply for you in this loss,' Daniel said eventually, speaking for them all. 'Many of us remember how hard Stefan worked to build up his company, and also how both he and your father used so much of their profits to support the partisan movement. Both of them were men who loved God, and honoured him in all their words and actions. Do you remember how God said to Samuel in the Old Testament: 'Those who honour me, I will honour'? That's why I believe, Heléna, that however dark things look right now, God will honour them, and you too, as you keep trusting him.'

'And I keep thinking of Stefan's words to you, Heléna,' Andela added, ' – how he urged you to remember that you belong to God. I believe that's what he'd be saying to you now, if he were here, and could see his factories and all that he worked for gone, and his wife not provided for! Stefan would be encouraging you and all of us, Heléna, to stand tall and to continue to hope in God, whatever happens!'

'I know in my heart that God will provide for me, and that life is more than money and material possessions.' Heléna responded quietly. 'They're just things – it's what we do with them that counts. Today you've given me something much more valuable, in your sincere love and heartfelt support, so thank you all!'

They prayed for her then, before going their separate ways to face the week ahead – a week filled for Heléna with practice for upcoming concerts, an important lesson with Sergei, and more of her own music students than she really had time for. Now however, given her changed circumstances, her teaching provided the regular source of income that would keep her head above water. Certainly her concerts provided some financial reward, but even in this area there were rumblings of possible government restrictions, according to Sergei. How long things would continue as they were, Heléna had no idea. All she could do was take each week as it came, and give of her very best in her teaching, and at each and every concert performance.

The spring of 1946 passed quickly for Heléna, as she poured herself into her music, earning the love and respect of each and every one of her students, and also building quite an enviable reputation as a concert pianist, for one so young. At the same time, she was aware that all around her, things were changing rapidly. Across Czechoslovakia, people were joining the Communist Party in droves, responding to its anti-German stance, and also the practical help given by Soviet forces in liberating the nation. These days, Heléna had little time, and no taste for any great involvement in political issues, but she was well aware that many of her friends were becoming more and more attracted to the communist ideology being promoted and played out before their eyes. In the May elections, the Communists managed to snatch a much higher proportion of the vote, resulting in more of their leaders being given positions of authority, and the Communist leader Gottwald himself being installed as Prime Minister. Through friends on both sides of the political fence, Heléna was made aware that increased Communist influence in government in the areas of economics, labour and agriculture could well mean imminent changes in farm ownership and farming methods across the country, despite her family solicitor's recent assurances to the contrary. He had indeed been correct about the increased income from Václav's farming estates, but their potential did not go unnoticed by the newly elected Communist leaders either.

By the end of summer, it was obvious that private ownership of farming land would soon be a thing of the past in Czechoslovakia. Heléna, returning from another concert tour, scarcely had time to consult with Václav's solicitor, before she was required to hand over all title deeds to her father's estates, including the farm at Tábor that had been in her family for generations. For the moment, the family home and the garden immediately surrounding it were to remain in her possession, but that was all – all that would be left of what had been a considerable inheritance from her parents. Everything else was gone, with little or no hope of any recompense.

Heléna had no choice but to bear it well, along with others of her countrymen in a similar situation. During a break in her concert schedule and in her teaching that summer, she travelled home to Tábor one weekend, wandering down to the river alone, and rambling for hours along its banks, as it meandered beside fields that had once been her father's. She remembered how as children and then teenagers, she and Emil had ridden blithely across the fields, so full of plans for the years ahead. Emil, she understood from Simona, had taken over the family farm after his father's recent death, only to lose it soon after, in the same way that Heléna had lost her father's estates. Doing manual labour for the state was not what he envisaged for himself, however, and he, like Jan and Simona, and Edvard and Judith, now had his heart set on resettling overseas. As Heléna sat in the kitchen at Tábor discussing the future with Jan and Simona, she could not help being impressed by their courage and determination, in the face of the huge decisions ahead. Jan, after being conscripted to work for the Germans, had lost his own small car repair business during those war years. Now, faced with the prospect of never being able to own his own business, he and Simona were even more firmly set on migrating.

'We're seriously considering going to Australia, if possible,' they told her. 'We've heard it's a land of great opportunity, where perhaps we can begin again. We want to get right away from Europe and what the war has done to us all. And we want to be free too of this repressive communist government in our own country!'

Heléna asked them many so many questions, but their response was always the same.

'God will take care of us, Heléna! Besides, we won't be alone. We know of others who think the same as us – and anyway, we'll have each other!'

Berta, although getting on in years, was still adamant that she would go with them when the time came. Heléna felt a wave of desolation sweep over her at the thought of being separated from this family, whom she regarded as her own. Already she had visited Uncle Erik that weekend, and faced the realisation that, although he had recovered enough to talk with her for a short time, he would never be his old self again. She did not want to think about a future without him, and without Jan and Simona and Berta as well. True, she had other friends, but, wonderful as they were, they had not known her almost all her life, as her old Tábor friends had. And even some of them, she had heard recently, were considering leaving the country. Radim and Irena were definitely restless, and they in turn were influencing Daniel and Renata along similar lines.

She returned to Prague, bewildered and confused. Where did her own future lie? Was she to remain in Czechoslovakia? She remembered how passionately Stefan had loved their homeland, how he had talked in a way that had shown he could not easily leave it, and how, in the end, he had given his life for it. But things had changed, and Stefan was no longer here. What would he himself want her to do now, she wondered?

Wrung out by the emotion of the weekend, Heléna did not play her best at her lesson that week with Sergei. Eventually he stopped her in mid-phrase, demanding she tell him what was going on inside her. Out it all came – the recent loss of her father's estates, the added financial problems that had brought, her sense of abandonment almost, that so much was changing and so many of those close to her were considering leaving their homeland – even her uncertainly about where she herself belonged now. He let her talk, all the time sitting back in his favourite chair, eyes closed, as if asleep. When she finally stopped, he rose to his full height and then, folding his arms and leaning on the grand piano, looked straight into her eyes as she sat there, his own full of wisdom and compassion.

'My dear girl,' his voice boomed out, his words softened by the kindly look in his eyes, as he waved his finger at her, 'you must stand tall – you must stand full of courage, straight and tall! I, Sergei, who do not believe in your God, he say to me, you belong to him! I know that here in my heart,' he said, leaning even closer to her and tapping his chest. 'This God, he say to me here, "Sergei, help this one to stand tall! Help her! She belong to me!" Ha! He speak to me – old Sergei! Maybe one day I meet him, you know – so I better do what he say, what you think, huh?'

Sergei roared with laughter, his eyes still gentle with compassion, as he concluded, speaking a little softer now.

'So ... you will stay, and I help you play your best, no? For now at least, you stay and play – for me, and for your God!'

Chapter Sixteen

So Heléna stayed, and she played. For the rest of that year, apart from a short break at Christmas, and on into the next, Heléna poured her heart and soul into every performance. She played her best for her God, as Sergei had put it, she played for Sergei himself, she played in memory of her Stefan, and of Anezka and Václav, but she also played for the sheer joy of it, for the delight it gave her to perform well for each member of her audiences. And every time she stood at the end of a performance to receive the enthusiastic applause that inevitably came, she remembered what Stefan had said, and what God had said to her through Sergei – she made sure she stood straight and tall, her head held high. In her teaching too she tried to give of her best, delighted when her students succeeded in their studies, and so rewarded when she listened to their excellent performances.

Yet in her heart, Heléna knew this period of her life would not last, and for that reason she was even more determined to make her mark. By May of 1947, pressure was beginning to mount for those who were not yet members of the Communist Party to join, a decision which Heléna had so far managed to avoid making. And gradually, as Sergei had predicted, cultural organisations were again coming under close government scrutiny, albeit from a different government, with tighter controls being imposed upon them and on all performers. By the end of 1947, when the harvest failed, and the country was obviously suffering economically, many began to lose confidence in those in power, despite the promises they gave of a better future for all. Anyone who spoke out, however, was soon likely to be branded as 'counter-revolutionary', and subsequently arrested. Gradually the government pushed for greater authority, tightening their control across the country, in an attempt to squash any further dissent.

As a result, soon Heléna and others like her began to receive letters containing vague threats of loss of earnings and even loss of property, unless they were to join the Communist Party. At first she ignored them, angered at such coercion.

'I'm not my father's daughter for nothing!' she said to Uncle Erik, on one of the rare occasions when she was able to visit him. 'How dare this government, which has already helped itself to so much of what is rightfully mine, think it can demand anything more from me!'

Although Uncle Erik was still unable to leave the house, and his speech was a little slow and slurred, he loved to have visitors, even if only for a short time. He was always especially delighted to see Heléna, responding to her comment with something of his old strength and passion.

'My dear, Václav would have been so proud of you! If he were prepared to lose his freedom rather than agree to manufacture weapons for the Nazis, then I believe he would not have stopped short at risking his home either, rather than join a political party with whose basic tenets he couldn't possibly agree. These are hard times for you, Heléna. Let's pray that you'll at least be able to keep your remaining property!'

The old man dozed off at this point, and Heléna tiptoed out, so as not to disturb him. His comments stayed with her, as she journeyed back to Prague. She had thought of her father a lot in recent days, wondering what decision he would have made, had he been faced with the possibility of losing his beautiful old home that had been in his family for generations. Now as she pondered Uncle Erik's words, she knew in her heart that he was right. She knew that the only decision she could possibly make was to stand firm and refuse to join the party, come what may. She could remove herself from the spotlight, as some others had done, and turn her back on a blossoming career, so that the party leaders would not concern themselves with her any further, but she felt that was not an option for her – not when she knew that she had to stand tall, to be true to herself, to go on using and growing in the gifts God had given her. He would watch over her, she was sure of that. She belonged to him, and, as Andela had reminded her when Heléna had shared about her financial losses, she must continue, like Job in the bible, to hope in God, whatever happened.

Two weeks later, that hope was severely shaken. Firstly, Heléna received a stern letter from government authorities, demanding she join the Communist Party forthwith, or lose her family home at Tábor within ten days. The very next day, she received a further letter, warning her that she would lose Stefan's apartment within ten days if she did not sign up as a party member.

Heléna knew what she must do, and had prepared herself for such a situation, but this did not lessen the pain she now felt, as reality began to strike home. She knew that this was the end for her in her homeland, and that it was time for her to flee over the border with Jan and Simona and Berta and the children as soon as possible, and for all of them to begin again somewhere far away from Czechoslovakia. She had already discussed it with them, and they had been welcomed her decision to join them, while at the same time feeling deeply for her.

Before she travelled back to Tábor, to pack the few things she could manage to take with her, and to store or give away the rest, she met once again with her friends from the fellowship group. Her mind was made up, but she knew she needed right then the love and support they could give her. They had seen her through so much, it was only fitting that they complete the journey with her.

As Heléna talked and her friends listened, interjecting from time to time to ask questions, she sensed that, while they felt deeply for her, not all saw things quite the same way as she did. She had already discussed her decision with Andela and Daniel and Renata, so it was not a complete surprise to them all, but some obviously felt she had other options. Miklos in particular was clearly upset, and impatient to be heard. Eventually he burst into the conversation, speaking with considerable force.

'Heléna, as you remember, while I was in total agreement with you and Stefan as far as our underground work against the German authorities was concerned, since then we've taken rather different paths politically. I admire you tremendously for your courage in staying true to your principles, and I respect your right to have your own views on communism, but surely this is going too far! Surely you must see that communism is here to stay in our homeland, and that the only way for you to continue to move forward in your career is to become a party member! You believe in equal rights for all! You would want to see wealth distributed fairly, to see that no one starves, while others have more than enough! If you join, surely you can focus on the parts of communism with which you agree, such as these, and forget about the rest! Think how much you'll be able to do for our country if you still have your homes and your income from your teaching and performing! Our country needs you here at this time!'

Miklos ended his impassioned speech abruptly, his face flushed and his eyes now downcast, as the silence lengthened around him. Some of those present knew that he loved Heléna, and had cherished the hope that she might in time begin to regard him as more than just a friend. Heléna had recognised the signs, but had never at any time desired things to be more serious between them, nor had she encouraged him to hold out hope that it might prove otherwise. Now, as he sat there looking so young and wretched, her heart went out to him, she spoke gently, despite the turmoil and indeed antipathy his words stirred up within her.

'Thanks, Miklos, for your concern for me! I know you mean well, and I wish I could take the path you suggest, but everything within me tells me I can't! I wouldn't be being true to myself, and to what I believe Stefan or my parents would have wanted, if I acted in any other way. I believe that this is what God would have me do, but I stress that it's my journey alone, and not necessarily what he has for you! I love you all – we truly are brothers and sisters, united in God's love, I believe! We all desire to obey him and live for him, even though we might not agree on everything – especially when it comes to political issues. So please forgive me, if I have offended or disappointed you! And please pray for me, that I'll be wise in my decisions, and that I'll be true to what God wants me to do. I'll stay here until the end of winter – I have concerts scheduled, apart from anything else. Sergei and Anna have offered to have me live with them for the time being, but I know I'll need your support and prayers so much through this time!'

As Daniel led them all in prayer for Heléna, he wondered how much longer they would be able to meet openly as a fellowship like this, under the current government. Along with recent tighter control of cultural organisations, had come the beginnings of a crackdown on religion – something that concerned him deeply, considering what had happened to the church in Russia. The more idealistic and optimistic ones amongst them, such as Miklos, believed all would be well. The rest wondered just how long any of them could remain in their homeland, if religious restrictions eventuated.

Heléna's final performances were among her best, in Sergei's opinion, but they were personally costly. He and Anna saw that clearly, during those final weeks when she was with them. Yet somehow she found the inner strength to continue to give of her best, despite the deep sadness that had almost overwhelmed her at the loss of her family home and her apartment in Prague. Heléna could not decide which of these experiences had been the most painful – saying goodbye to her beautiful old home at Tábor, filled with so many wonderful memories of her growing up years with her beloved parents, or letting go of the apartment where she and Stefan had shared their brief but idyllic years of marriage, and where there was so much to remind her of him.

At Tábor, Jan, Simona and Berta had helped her sort out her parents' remaining possessions, and decide what was worth selling, and what should be given away. Then with great sensitivity, they left her to say her own quiet goodbye to her home. Slowly, she walked alone from room to room on that last day, lingering for the longest time in her two favourite places – her father's study, and, of course, the music room. Here was where she had first played for Stefan, and where, many times in earlier years, her parents and Uncle Erik had been so proud of her performances. She wandered around the room, now largely empty of its beautiful furniture, gripped by the past, lost in so many memories. For the last time, Heléna sat at the beautiful old grand piano, due to be sold the next day, and began to play – Brahms, Liszt, Schumann, Mendelssohn, and finally, her favourite Beethoven. She did not know she played for a rapt audience of two little girls, Anna and Kristina, as they sat quietly on the floor in the hall outside, hardly daring to move.

As she concluded, she moved quickly to the door, not wanting to prolong her farewell, almost stumbling over them in her haste to leave. They stared up at her, sorrow in their eyes, but childlike love and understanding also. Quickly they scrambled to their feet and hugged her tightly, their little faces pressed into her skirt, as she held them close.

'You play so beautifully, Aunty Heléna!' Anna said tremulously at last. 'You mustn't ever stop playing!'

Kristina wordlessly nodded her agreement.

'Thank you, Anna! Thank you, Kristina!' was all Heléna could say in response, their adoring faces and simple words worth more at that moment than the loudest applause she had received in any concert hall.

A few days later, Heléna repeated the procedure at her own apartment, this time assisted by Andela, Miklos and Milan, as well as Daniel and Renata. Again, while Heléna was able to sell some of the furniture and household items, much had to be given away. In this the men were particularly helpful, transporting Stefan and Heléna's possessions to those who needed them the most. Hardest of all to part with were Stefan's many books, and his piano and cello music. The books she distributed among their closest friends, but some of his music she kept, along with her own favourites, packing it tightly in an old leather satchel that still bulged, whichever way she tried to fit it all in. Stefan's beautiful old baby grand was to be cared for by Sergei and Anna, since Heléna could not bear to part with it any other way. Sergei agreed, on condition that as soon as she settled in her new homeland, she was to send for it. He and Anna would gladly cover the shipping costs involved, he told her.

Stefan's cello was another matter. Heléna could not find it within herself to part with it under any circumstances. She sat for some time running her fingers over its beautiful polished wood, hearing again in her head the way Stefan had played his favourite Saint-Saëns music, 'The Swan', for his guests, on that first night in his apartment. In the end, she placed it lovingly in its thick cloth carry-case, determined to take it with her, however difficult that might prove to be. That way, she would feel that some part of Stefan at least would cross the border with her and go on into her future. Her own personal belongings she kept to a minimum, giving away many of those also. But again there were a few items she refused to part with, such as her mother's beautiful fine jewellery, and her father's special gold fountain pen, which he had sometimes let her play with as a child. One day, she sensed, she would be glad she had kept these treasured possessions.

Finally, by February of 1948, all her concert engagements had been completed, and the moment arrived for her to leave. She would always be thankful for Sergei and Anna – her lifesavers, as she termed them – in those last days and weeks. Both of them understood what it meant to leave one's homeland, and were particularly gentle and compassionate towards her, allowing her space to sit quietly and to grieve when she needed to, yet at other times drawing her into their circle of friends, and generally making her last days in Prague memorable. When Heléna's final day arrived, both were so sad to see her go, although fully understanding why she had to. It had been arranged that Andela and Miklos would drive Heléna to Tábor, where she would join Jan and Simona and their family for the next part of her journey, over the border and into Germany. As Sergei stood to say goodbye to Heléna, his usual geniality and lively manner deserted him, and his voice sounded decidedly gruff.

'This is it, eh, Heléna – my favourite female student running away from old Sergei, just as I knew she would one day! You have been like a daughter to us, my dear – like the daughter we could not have, Anna and I. Ah well, I understand, I know you must go. But such a promising career! Your country is all the poorer that you go – all the poorer, I think for sure. Anna and I, we are since long ago members of the party, as you know, but that does not mean we do not have questions – many, many questions. We are too old to change now, except that more and more I think I like your God, my dear! I help you, just like I think he say to me to do in 1946, and you stayed and played for us and for him, just like I think he say to you to do! Now he say it is time for you to go, Heléna – but you must promise me two things, my dear. Wherever he take you, do not stop playing! And whatever happen, remember you belong to him!'

With tears glistening in his eyes, Sergei enveloped her in his huge bear hug, kissing her on both cheeks before he released her. Anna hugged her too, crying openly, and then it was time to go. Time to close the door on her career, for now at least, time to leave the city that had given her so much. Almost blinded by her tears, Heléna climbed in the car, thankful that Andela and Miklos were understanding enough to let her to sit quietly, lost in her own thoughts and feelings, during the journey to Tábor.

Heléna was to stay with Uncle Erik and Edita overnight, while Berta, Jan and Simona and the children had relocated to the tunnels, after vacating Heléna's home. They had not wished to involve anyone further in their plans, possibly endangering others, with government officials becoming increasingly vigilant and suspicious. The day after Heléna arrived in Tábor, they would make their way very early to the railway station – merely another family heading west, ostensibly to visit grandparents. As for Heléna, although her close friends in Prague knew otherwise, she was simply staying with family friends at Tábor, and then returning to Domažlice for a while. Again through underground sources, they knew the very real dangers of attempting border crossings, aware that around one in five people did not make it. Jan had planned things carefully, however, and all four of the adults involved were confident they would succeed, with God's help. Now, as Miklos pulled up outside Uncle Erik's cottage, Heléna realised that soon she would be on her own, her final ties with her homeland severed.

Miklos farewelled Heléna first, as Andela talked to Edita, seizing the moment to be alone with her, and holding her hands in a firm clasp as he spoke.

'Heléna, it's not too late to change your mind, even now! I'll speak plainly – you must know I love you dearly, and would do everything in my power to make you happy if you were to stay! I want to marry you, Heléna! I know you feel there's no one else for you apart from Stefan – but Heléna, he'd want you to be happy, and I'd take good care of you! Please say you'll reconsider and stay here, where you belong!'

Heléna at first tried to extricate her hands, but then, seeing the sincerity in Miklos' face, and hearing the earnestness in his voice, she took pity on him, letting him continue to hold them, as she spoke the words she knew she had to say.

'I'm so sorry, Miklos, but my answer has to be no. I think in your heart of hearts you sense that too. Please know that I don't take your words lightly – I'm truly touched by what you've expressed! You'll find someone else very soon, I know you will – and I'll pray that you'll be very, very happy! You've been a faithful friend, Miklos – I thank you from the bottom of my heart for everything!'

For a few moments, he continued holding her hands. Then he let them fall, and, looking straight into her eyes, said his final farewell.

'Then it's goodbye, Heléna, and may God bless and keep you!'

His voice shook as he spoke these few words. Heléna could not have felt more miserable, as she turned to say her own farewell to Andela. She and Miklos needed to return almost immediately to Prague, so Heléna was determined to keep her goodbyes to her friend brief. They had already shared so much in the lead up to this moment, but as the two now hugged each other tightly, Heléna whispered a final few words to her friend.

'Andela, I have so much to thank you for! You've been such a special friend to me, ever since our first concerts together, and all through the time of Stefan's capture and death. We've shared so deeply – you've been like a wonderful sister, so trustworthy and loyal, and I'll miss you so much! I'm so sorry, Andela, that I've had to disappoint Miklos with my answer too – but it has to be!'

Andela nodded her understanding, and hugged her friend even closer. There were no more words left to say, so with one final tremulous smile, Heléna climbed into the car and, with a wave of the hand, was gone.

One further farewell lay ahead – perhaps the hardest of all, yet in many ways a beautiful closing of the door. Uncle Erik was confined to his bed most days now, and often, Edita explained, a little confused as to the hour or even the day.

'He's so eager to speak with you one more time, my dear, although he's not good at long conversations,' Edita said softly. 'Every day for the past week he thought you were coming, and has been asking me exactly when you were arriving! And now you're here at last!'

She ushered Heléna into his room, not wanting to delay for his sake. As soon as Uncle Erik saw her, his face lit up, and he reached out his one good hand to greet her. Heléna held it tight and sat down gently on his bed. His voice was very soft and his words even more slurred, as he began speaking. Heléna leaned closer, determined not to miss anything he said.

'I'm so glad we have this opportunity to say goodbye to each other, my dear,' he began, each word spoken slowly and deliberately with some effort. 'I didn't want to think of your going so far away without my blessing. Heléna, I believe you're doing the right thing – the only course open to you, in fact. I think I said this to you before, but I know Václav, and also Anezka, would be so proud of you! And so am I! Many times you've made me proud – when I used to hear you play as a young girl to entertain your parents' guests, when you gained a place at the Conservatorium, that Christmas evening after Václav's arrest when you played so beautifully – so many times! But I've been just as proud of you, Heléna, watching and listening to you as you tried to make sense of Stefan's death, as well as your parents', as you risked your own safety to help the partisans, and now, as you're so determined not to compromise your faith and your deep convictions – and at such cost! You have stood tall, as Stefan wanted you to, my dear – you have stood tall, and paid the price. And I'm so proud of you!'

The old man was very tired then, but as he finished speaking, he withdrew his good hand from Heléna's, and fumbled for a moment under his pillow. After finding what he was looking for, he held out his hand again, and opened it, to reveal a small gold ornament nestling in his palm. As he motioned for Heléna to examine it, she saw that it was an exquisite miniature grand piano, around three centimetres high and the same across, with its lid raised, and a tiny musical score open on a little filigree stand behind the keyboard. Each beautifully fashioned piano leg held a small diamond encrusted on its foot, while the top of the lid was decorated with small precious stones in an ornate design. Heléna gasped at its beauty, as Uncle Erik, his eyes now closed and his voice even weaker, went on to explain.

'Heléna, Edita and I would like you to have this as a parting gift from us. It belonged to our great, great grandfather Josef, a composer and musician in the Bohemian prince's court of his day, and has been handed down through the family since then. I have no children, as you know, and Edita feels that rather than leave it to one of her sons, she would be much happier if it were given to you. I know you'll treasure it, my dear – it is quite valuable. Perhaps it might be some sort of insurance for you, should you ever be in financial need. We'll pray you never will be, Heléna, but it's yours now, to be used in whatever way you feel is right.'

Edita had joined them, and nodded her agreement, also signalling to Heléna that it was time for Uncle Erik to rest. Heléna did not know how to respond. Any words, she knew, would sound inadequate. Quietly she slipped her hand into his again, leaned forward and kissed him gently on the forehead.

'Thank you so much, Uncle Erik – for everything!' she whispered. 'I love you, and I'll treasure this beautiful gift always! I'll never forget you – all my life I'll remember how you have loved me and believed in me and encouraged me! I'll go now – you need to rest, but perhaps you would like me to play for you one last time?'

Uncle Erik nodded weakly, as Edita smiled her approval. Slowly Heléna rose, still cradling the little gold ornament, and moved to the piano in the room across the hall. Without even stopping to reflect, she began to play her favourite – Tschaikovsky's 'Nur wer die Sehnsucht kennt' – softly at the beginning, and then more passionately as it gathered momentum, and then calmly and softly again, as the music came to a close. The tears fell as she played, but through them she could see the little gold ornament, gleaming in the lamplight where she had placed it on top of the piano, reminding her of the past, but also reassuring her and, in some way, signalling hope for the future.

The next morning, before Uncle Erik had stirred, Heléna left early to catch the train, along with the others, for the first part of their journey to Domažlice. She was unaware until weeks later, via a letter from Edita, that he had passed away in his sleep that last night they had been together. Edita had discovered him the next morning, just an hour after Heléna had left Tábor. He had looked so peaceful, she wrote – as if he had completed all he had wanted to do, before taking that final step from this world into his eternal home.

Chapter Seventeen

Certainly that long journey they made together that first day from Tábor to Domažlice was markedly different from the one Heléna had experienced over five years earlier. The route was the same – three hours by train first to Pisek and then on to Strakönice, followed by a further three hours' bus travel west to Klatovy and then on to Domažlice itself – but everything else was vastly different. Then Heléna had been alone. Now there were four adults, and four lively children to care for, as well as so much more luggage to carry and to see safely stowed on board at each changeover. Berta was wonderful, holding little Stefan tightly by the hand, never letting Anna and Kristina out of her sight for a moment. The girls each carried a bag containing their own personal possessions, as did Berta – mostly clothing, but also a few small treasures they could not bear to leave behind. Simona pushed an old pram containing the newest addition to the family – another son, Josef, born twelve months previously, who fortunately slept for most of the train journey. At the same time, she carried a suitcase crammed with clothes for the family, with a basket containing enough food for the trip perched rather precariously on the pram. Heléna had packed only her most necessary clothing and other personal items in a small suitcase, since she had been determined from the beginning to take her bulging music satchel, which she now wore slung over one shoulder. And on her back she carried her most treasured possession – Stefan's cello in its cloth case. While her friends had tried to dissuade her from attempting to take it on what would doubtless be such a difficult journey, she had steadfastly refused to leave it behind. She would manage, she had replied, quietly and firmly. Finally, Jan was responsible for the two larger suitcases crammed with more clothes, sheets, blankets and other household items. Under one arm too, he carried a battered wooden case containing his favourite tools, those he had found most indispensable in his mechanical workshop, and which he hoped would help him begin again in their new homeland.

At Domažlice it had been arranged that they would stay overnight with friends Heléna had made during her time at Helga's parents' farm. It had been over four years since Heléna had last visited them, but their greeting was as warm and loving as if it had been yesterday. Karl was a pastor in the village and also cared for his people in the surrounding areas, while his wife Branka taught at the small village school. They had no children of their own, but had taken into their hearts and lives the young son and daughter of dear friends, partisans killed by the Nazis in the last year of the war. Despite their tiny cottage being overcrowded already, they welcomed Heléna and her friends with open arms, finding space for them to sleep in their sitting room, and in a corner of the church next door. It was there that Heléna heard the news, on the family's battered old radio, of what had transpired after the recent resignation of the remaining non-communist government ministers in Prague. A general strike had been called by the communists, with armed workers taking to the streets to ward off any 'counter-revolutionary' threats. Finally, only the day before, a huge demonstration, the largest the country had ever seen, had taken place in the capital, with thousands of Czechs showing their support of Gottwald and his all-communist cabinet. President Beneš, who had been unwell for some time, was apparently unable to protest, and so at last the coup that many had wanted had taken place, giving the communists complete control of Czechoslovakia. That month, February of 1948, so the announcer said, would be declared 'Victorious February', in honour of such a momentous time in the nation's history.

Heléna and the others listened in silence. The news was not unexpected, but it was the swiftness and apparent ease with which it had occurred that stunned them momentarily. When they did speak, they were all in agreement that the months ahead would be even more difficult for any who opposed the communist regime, especially those in positions of authority. They thanked God they were already on their way – surely now there would be many, many more refugees seeking to flee their homeland, in the light of this final takeover.

As it turned out, they were among the first of thousands of their fellow countrymen and women to attempt to flee into Germany or Austria. At the time of their escape, while border crossings were certainly illegal, with patrols constantly on the alert for such attempts, they were definitely more likely to succeed than in later months. Not that their own journey was free from danger and difficulty. In fact, at times over the next few days, Heléna wondered if they would ever make it. Karl and Branka cared for them lovingly, sending them on their way with what food they could find, further up into the foothills nearby to an even smaller village, by means of an old local bus that had definitely seen better days. There they linked up with a key partisan leader who had known both Uncle Erik and Stefan, and who now was equally eager to play his part in resisting the communists. Viktor lived alone in a two-roomed cabin on the very edge of the village, but was more than happy to accommodate Heléna and the whole family overnight on his living room floor. In the remaining daylight hours, he took Jan to an old barn close by, where he had hidden a German army van built for travelling over rough terrain, captured by partisans during the war. He had been tinkering with it for some time, trying to restore it to working order. Now he put a proposition to Jan.

'My friend, I understand you're a good mechanic. If you can fix this engine, I'll drive you as close to the border as I can! There are some dirt roads in these mountains that only a few locals like me know about, which are quite accessible – if you have the right vehicle. I think we'll all fit. Surely that will be better than walking, especially for the children!'

Jan did not need to be asked twice. There were still a few hours of daylight remaining, and the pair of them got to work immediately. For most of that time, all the women and children could see was their legs sticking out from under the vehicle, or the backs of their heads bent over the engine, as they worked frantically. When they finally emerged hours later, their faces and hands were black with grease. Not long after, the sound of a powerful engine suddenly roaring to life split the air, to cries of delight from the children and sighs of relief all round.

'Praise God!' was Berta's heartfelt response, as the engine coughed a few times, and then settled down to a steady rhythm.

Simona and Heléna echoed this in their own hearts. There would, they knew, still be long distances to walk, and some tiring climbs ahead, so to be able to cover an unexpectedly large part of the journey by car was a wonderful gift.

The next morning they loaded themselves and all their possessions on board, minus the old pram, which Simona had decided to leave with Branka, along with some of their clothes, thus lightening the suitcases a little. The van, while not built for comfort, was at least relatively roomy, with enough space in the front cabin for Viktor, Jan and Berta, with little Josef on her lap. Simona, Heléna and the three children climbed into the back, arranging themselves as best they could among the luggage, Heléna holding tightly to Stefan's cello, as they bumped over the rough ground. That day, they drove along a web of narrow dirt roads, up sloping hillsides and down into rocky valleys, across beautiful rolling wooded hills and on into more densely forested regions, until the road Viktor was following simply petered out, and the van could go no further. They had stopped in a small clearing, and the children thankfully jumped out, feeling slightly carsick from the bumpy ride in such an enclosed space.

'Aunty Heléna, are we in Germany yet?' Kristina asked, for around the sixth time that day.

'Not yet, dear,' Heléna answered patiently, 'but soon we will be. Just a little walk ahead of us now!'

Heléna was not sure how the adults, let alone the children, would manage the next stage of their journey, but she thanked God for Viktor, who seemed unperturbed about the difficulties, indeed even enjoying his role in helping them escape.

'Time for us all to walk a bit now,' he announced cheerfully, after they had eaten their lunch. 'Let's see how far we can get this afternoon, eh, children?'

With that, he helped haul the luggage from the van, laying claim to two of the suitcases himself, so as to lighten the load for Simona in particular, who now had Josef perched on her back, in a little canvas seat that fitted over her shoulders. This also enabled Jan to pick up little Stefan and help him over the more difficult stretches. Kristina held on tightly to Berta's hand, each of them helping the other, while Anna marched with determination beside Heléna. Viktor led the way along forest paths that, he explained, were rarely visited even by the most avid hikers, gradually climbing higher and higher. Most of the conversation had ceased long ago, as they focused their energies on keeping close to their leader.

At last they reached a rocky outcrop high up on the skyline. Viktor skirted this, and there before them, stretching into the distance, they could see not only more wooded hills and valleys, but also, in the foreground, two parallel rows of barbed wire fencing, with a strip of rocky bare earth between them.

'There you have it,' he said somewhat triumphantly. 'The border at last! Now you see below you not Czech, but German forest! Soon we'll be walking on Bavarian soil rather than Bohemian – but perhaps we should wait until tomorrow, do you think?'

Viktor had taken in at a glance their exhausted appearance. He himself was used to such expeditions, but he had known it would be an arduous journey for them. The little group stood gazing in shocked fascination at the two fences that formed the border, and then back at him in puzzlement at his suggestion to spend the night where they were.

'Don't worry! I'll show you where you'll sleep!' he laughingly explained. 'Also, there are ways of crossing this border that neither the Germans nor the communists in our own country know anything about! Follow me!'

Eventually he led them to the mouth of a small cave in the side of the rocky outcrop, which widened out into a space the size of a large room. Piles of sacking lay here and there on the floor, as did some basic cooking utensils and the remains of a fire. Viktor soon answered their curious looks.

'There are just a handful of partisans who know about this cave, and also about something else I'll show you soon. We often camped here during the war, either going to or coming from our forays into Germany on our missions for the Allied forces. Recently we've begun to use it for people such as you, and, if I'm not wrong, I think we'll be using it more and more in the days ahead. But come and let me show you where we'll go!'

He moved to the back of the cave, and they saw that a tunnel led on from there into the darkness beyond.

'My friends and I, by using some German explosives we found abandoned towards the end of the war, and by digging as often as we could, ever since the border fence was built, have managed to tunnel through these rocks and under the border itself right into Germany!' he explained. 'It will be safe for you to walk through tomorrow. I've travelled it many times, and I'll light the way for you.'

With that he pointed to a miner's helmet stored at the back of the cave, as well as some other large torches. The weather had gradually become colder as they had climbed. Now, as they stood in the cave, trying to take in all Viktor had said, they shivered from the cold as well as from anticipation of what the next day would hold. But soon there was a fire going, and it was not long before the children were curled up on the sacks provided, with others covering them, sleeping soundly after the exertion of the day. The adults sat together for a while longer, staring into the fire, so thankful that they had come this far, yet all, apart from Viktor, feeling the strangeness of this last night in their homeland.

Eventually, Heléna felt compelled to speak.

'Let's pray for our country as we leave, shall we? I feel relieved that we're so close to crossing the border, but also very sad. We've left so much behind, and so many people we love! What will their future be? We don't know ours either, but let's trust ourselves and our families and friends again to God!'

They prayed together, Viktor, who had not thought to do such a thing in years, deeply touched by the moment. Then like the children, they curled up and slept the sleep of exhaustion.

In the early hours of the next morning, Viktor led them through the tunnel, carefully negotiating the first section that sloped down a little way, and then helping each one climb the incline of the second section. Eventually they emerged on the German side of the border, where the tunnel entrance was well camouflaged by strategically placed boulders and a thick clump of bushes. Viktor himself made a quick second trip to retrieve some of the luggage that had been too difficult for them to carry, and then it was time for him to return home. Briefly he gave them their final instructions.

'Make your way around these bushes to that large tree there,' he said to Jan, pointing in a westerly direction. 'You'll find an old hiking trail there. Follow that down to the next valley, until it joins a dirt road along the edge of the stream. That will take you several kilometres until it in turn joins a wider road that leads down towards Schwandorf.

Most of Schwandorf was destroyed in the bombing at the end of the war, but my old friend Heinrich and his wife are still there. They live on the edge of the town, in the first cottage on the right hand side, and they'll be watching out for you. He'll tell you what to do next. Take care, all of you! I wish you much happiness in your new life!'

He smiled in acknowledgement of their thanks, and with a wave of his hand, was gone.

Only a matter of weeks later, Heléna heard from other partisan friends who joined them at the displaced persons' camp in Germany, that Viktor's tunnel had been discovered in a routine search of the border area, and he himself had been arrested and imprisoned in Prague.

That day, however, Jan led them on, past the tree Viktor had pointed out, along the trail and down to the dirt road beside the stream. Eventually, after frequent stops, they reached the end of that road and made their way, a tired, straggling little band, laden down with their suitcases and other possessions, towards the town below. They had not seen another soul since farewelling Viktor, but now, as they neared the first of the cottages, Heléna was gripped with apprehension as to how they would be received.

She need not have worried. Soon they saw an old tractor approaching them, with a large empty trailer attached. An elderly man was at the wheel, and soon he lifted his cap, and called out to them in German, a broad smile lighting up his brown, weather-beaten face.

'Guten Tag, meine Freunde! Wilkommen! Ich heisse Heinrich! Bitte steigen Sie auf!'

Heléna translated for them all, and soon they and their luggage were piled into Heinrich's trailer. They bumped along the road towards the town, pulling up with a flourish in the farmyard behind the first cottage on the right. Heinrich's wife was there to greet them at the kitchen door, a big smile on her face also, as she gestured for them to come inside and eat. After a wonderful lunch of warm soup and freshly baked bread rolls, Heinrich suggested that they remain quietly at their farm for the remainder of that day, to rest and recover a little. The next day he would take them to the nearest police station, and from there they would be allocated to a displaced persons' camp somewhere in Germany. Heléna again translated all he said, although Jan also knew German quite well, from his enforced labour for the Nazis during the war, as did Berta and Simona from German friends back in their homeland.

As they journeyed into Schwandorf the next day, bouncing along once again in Heinrich's trailer, they encountered many smiles and waves from interested onlookers. Later they discovered that these locals were beginning to get used to the strange assortment of men, women and children whom Heinrich seemed to 'happen' to find, as he worked his farm on the edge of the town. At the police station, Heléna and Jan briefly explained that they were Czech refugees seeking temporary asylum in Germany before emigrating. The local police officer, puzzled as to what to do with such a large group of new arrivals, asked them to wait, as he spoke volubly to his superior. Eventually, a van was dispatched from elsewhere in the town to pick them up, and soon all eight of them, along with their possessions, were loaded into the back, and taken further south to Regensburg.

They barely caught a glimpse of the beautiful old city on that first day, as they quickly alighted from the van, loaded themselves up with their possessions once again, and were immediately herded into a large reception room at the town hall. There the local German authorities questioned them at length, before taking them to a nearby church hall, where they were greeted kindly by the old pastor, and given food to eat. Eventually they bedded down for the night on mattresses provided by the occupation forces, for the ever-increasing stream of refugees beginning to appear in these German border towns.

They faced further questioning the next day, this time by representatives of the occupation forces in the area. Heléna could not help but be proud of the children, as they waited so patiently and politely through hours of discussions and negotiations in a language unknown to them, before the various authorities involved were able to decide where they should be temporarily housed. Berta and Simona did their best to occupy them, with little games and quiet conversation, reassuring them with lots of hugs that they were safe, despite the presence of so many officials in army uniform. Finally, it was decided that they would be sent to Augsburg, around eighty kilometres to the southwest, where plans were under way to establish a large refugee camp. The United Nations, they were told, were currently putting in place an arm of their organisation to deal with the particular needs of the increasing numbers of refugees flooding across the border on a daily basis. Until then, members of the occupation forces would be seconded to care for them.

Eventually, they again climbed into the back of a large army van, their luggage piled in after them by soldiers with strange accents but smiling faces, and transported to Augsburg.

The following days and weeks seemed to be filled with constant movement, many interviews, and a sea of new faces from different parts of Europe, and indeed from across the globe. At first, Heléna and the others were housed in various temporary places of shelter, and then, when the International Refugee Organisation began to coordinate activities in March, they were moved to a large old building that had been used as German army barracks. Officials of the IRO, along with native German speakers, attempted to interview carefully the growing tide of homeless people, those 'displaced' for various reasons, soon flooding in. These were mainly from Czechoslovakia and Poland, but also from countries such as the Ukraine and Latvia. Initially there was plenty of room for them all, so that Heléna and Berta were able to have their own room at the barracks, while Jan and Simona the children occupied another large room. That soon changed, however, as more and more refugees arrived, so that eventually they all slept in the one room, double bunks close together, sometimes even sharing this space with other families, as the need arose.

Heléna's heart often went out to these fellow refugees, many of them Jewish. Some had survived the horrors of the Warsaw ghetto and Nazi prison camps, while others had sat out the war hidden away in back rooms, afraid to show their faces. She and Jan and Simona and Berta were so much better off in comparison. Many had lost whole families, and their own health had suffered greatly, as a result of such deprivation and ill treatment. Heléna felt deeply for them – these traumatised ones with sad, sad eyes, and broken hearts. Surely God cared for them, his chosen people from long ago? Surely he would give them a hope and a future somewhere?

At nights, Heléna often found it hard to sleep, as the grief of others stirred her deeply, sometimes causing her own old nightmares to surface again. Then she would wake herself and others up with her sobbing, as she again heard in her dream Stefan's footsteps on the stairs outside their apartment, his key in the door, and her own voice crying out to him to run. Usually Berta, sleeping below her, would patiently and lovingly quieten her, soothing her as she had when she was a little child, and pray softly for her, as they tried not to disturb the others in the room any further.

It was around then that Edita's letter finally caught up with Heléna, informing her of Uncle Erik's death. While she was saddened by the news, and grieved for Edita in her loneliness, his death felt like the severing of the deepest remaining emotional tie to her homeland, confirming that her decision to leave had been right. With the last of those who had been dearest to her – Anezka, Václav, Stefan, and now Uncle Erik – all gone, she felt that this indeed was a final closing of the door to the past. She was now twenty-nine, still quite young, yet in some ways she felt so very old. She had seen and experienced so much, and all of it would invariably shape her forever. Yet she must go on, she knew, trusting God to lead her through the next stage of her journey, and on into whatever he had for her in her new homeland.

As the year progressed, gradually some order was achieved, the IRO workers sorting out, as best they could, the needs of such a varied cross-section of humanity. Jan, Simon, Berta, and Heléna, after being duly screened, were classed as 'eligible' for IRO help, and each allocated a 'Displaced Person's Card', which they guarded jealously. This, they knew, was their ticket to freedom, to a new life somewhere far away from Germany and from Europe itself. For now, it entitled them to stay in their barracks accommodation, and to food and any other personal or medical care they required. They were also told that, as the opportunity arose, they could select a country to which to emigrate, and that the IRO would be responsible for their transport costs.

The four of them talked and prayed together often about where they felt their future lay. Meanwhile, although food was not so plentiful, they were cared for as well as possible in the camp, and the children were relatively happy, as they played with other children and made new friends, despite language barriers. But Jan in particular was eager to move on with their lives, to start afresh, to become established again in a new country and begin providing for his little family. Simona also longed for a settled place where she could again care for her family and for those like Heléna, who needed to be drawn into their loving circle. Berta suffered too, needing somewhere quieter, away from so many people. Yet she was at peace, prepared to wait, with a patience born of a long life of hard work and trust in God, until the way ahead became clear.

Heléna kept most of her feelings hidden deep down these days, she realised. So much inside her longed to be expressed, certainly through her music, but also in other ways. She prayed often, and faithfully read the small bible Stefan had given her when they were married, and that she had carefully carried inside her coat all the way from Tábor. She tried to be patient, like Berta, but time was passing, and she, like Jan, felt the frustration mounting within her, as the weeks and then months passed.

One aspect of life in the Augsburg camp that did help to dispel some of the frustration Heléna felt was the concert program organised by the IRO staff. Through this, they attempted to showcase the talents of the refugees themselves, many of whom were gifted musicians. Heléna took part in these, her performances always being greeted by enthusiastic applause, and even standing ovations. She loved to bring comfort to the wounded spirits of many in her audience through her music, always trying to give of her best, despite the limitations of the only piano available, an old upright Wertheim that had long seen better days. She sang too, as did others – mostly the old folksongs of their homeland, tears often welling up in the eyes of listeners and singers alike, as the memories came flooding back. Sometimes, guest artists would volunteer their time and talent to entertain the refugees. On these occasions, Heléna would often play to accompany the violinists or flautists or singers who came, a challenge she found both interesting and exciting.

It was during one of these visits that Heléna met Franz again. She had gone early as usual to the camp's community hall, where the concert was to be held, to see if anyone needed her to accompany them. As the musicians were unpacking their instruments and sorting through their music, she suddenly heard a familiar voice behind her. She turned quickly, recognising Franz instantly, despite the fact that he was no longer in his wheelchair. He was standing tall and straight, moving freely without any problems it seemed, as he talked to a pretty girl with a smiling face unpacking her music beside him. The next moment he looked across at Heléna, pausing in mid-sentence, and staring at her in disbelief.

'Heléna! What ... what are you doing here?' he stuttered, lost for words. 'It is you, isn't it? I can't believe it!'

Eventually he recovered himself enough to hold out his arms to her and then kiss her excitedly on both cheeks. Heléna returned his greeting enthusiastically, aware even as she did, of her great delight at seeing him again, and the warm feeling that seemed to be spreading around her heart.

'Oh Franz! Yes, I'm really here ... it's a long story! But you ... what about you? How wonderful to see you standing and walking! You look so well! And where's Helga? Is she here with you in Augsburg?'

The questions came tumbling out, but before he tried to answer them, Franz remembered the girl beside him, and quickly introduced her to Heléna.

'I'm sorry – I was so surprised, I've forgotten to introduce you two! Brigitte, this is Heléna – you remember, I've talked about her often! She was such a big part of my recovery back home at Domažlice, after I was wounded and lost my leg. She managed to get me to play again, and taught me so much! Heléna, this is Brigitte, my fiancée!' he ended proudly.

Brigitte smiled warmly at Heléna, and held out her hand. Heléna took it, liking her immediately, but aware too of a hollow feeling of disappointment deep inside her. Quickly she steeled herself – she and Franz had only ever been like brother and sister, and, if she did harbour any deeper feelings towards him, then it was only because somehow he reminded her so much of Stefan. All of these thoughts tumbled through her mind, as she heard Franz explaining that he was there to accompany some of the others who were performing that day. Brigitte and he would also be singing together, he went on to say.

'I still can't believe it, Heléna! After all this time and in such an unexpected place! We must meet and talk more after the concert – I can hardly wait! But we have to get ready to perform now. Our group has had very little time to practise, but hopefully everyone will enjoy what we do.'

The puzzlement showed clearly on his face, as he tried to take in the fact that Heléna was indeed one of the 'displaced persons' they had come to entertain. Explanations had to wait, however. Heléna disciplined her mind to accompany well those who needed her, and then relaxed to listen carefully to Franz as he played, and then as he and Brigitte sang together. There was no doubt Franz performed with great gentleness and sensitivity. Heléna felt so proud of him, and such personal reward for the hours spent with him at the farm, nurturing his talent. She loved his singing too, his fine tenor voice blending beautifully with Brigitte's light soprano one, as they sang a classical duet together, followed by some well-known old hymns, much to Heléna's delight. Finally, the concert was over, and there was just time for them, in the remainder of their visit, to find a quiet corner and catch up on all that had happened.

Apparently Franz now lived about forty kilometres away in Munich, where he had almost finished his music studies, but he was soon to relocate to Augsburg, where Brigitte lived, and where he himself would teach piano. The army hospital where he had been sent for his new artificial limb was in Munich, and when the war finished, he decided to stay there to study, not only because of what had happened to his parents and their farm at Domažlice, but also because by then he had met Brigitte, a fellow music student. Helga had initially joined him there to help care for him, as Heléna knew already from her phone conversation with Renate, but she was now pursuing her own further studies in singing in Berlin. Heléna was pleased to hear that, but disappointed she would most likely be unable to see her friend again before they left Germany. Sadly there had been no further news of his younger brother Jürgen, missing, presumed killed in action, somewhere in France. Heléna grieved for him in that, but even more when she saw the shadow cross his face at the mention of his parents and the way they had been thrown off their farm and so cruelly treated after the Nazis were defeated.

'After my parents died, I found I had no desire and indeed no reason to return to Czechoslovakia, even if I could have! But I should be very thankful that my own wounds have healed so well – I'm completely used to my artificial limb now. And at least I survived the war, which is more than many of the soldiers in my regiment did, and many of my friends back at Domažlice. And if it hadn't been for my injury, I wouldn't have met you, wouldn't have taken up my music again, and also, at least as far as I know, wouldn't have come to the place of acceptance, and of renewed faith in God that I now have! Do you remember the many long talks we had about God? I had so many questions, but, like you, Heléna, I've had to learn to trust him, even if I don't understand everything. One day, perhaps we'll know why. But what about you, Heléna?' he asked, obviously wanting to shift the focus from himself. 'I know you returned to Tábor after I left, and then to Prague, but how is it that you're here now?'

Heléna briefly told him and Brigitte about the loss, firstly of both Václav's companies, and then Stefan's, following by all their the farming estates.

'And then on top of that, I was put under great pressure, as were others, to join the Communist Party. If I didn't, then our apartment, as well as the family home at Tábor would be taken from me. And that's what happened in the end. I really felt I had no choice but to flee then – apart from anything else, I would have had very little future there as a concert pianist. So, as you see, here I am,' she concluded, 'complete with only a few possessions, but with a strong hope in God that he'll enable me to begin in a new country and to stand tall for him! He's brought me through so much – and I know he'll continue to watch over me, wherever I go!'

Franz and Brigitte promised to come and visit Heléna again as soon as possible after the move to Augsburg, and to bring some friends from their student fellowship group. They were to be married not long after the move, so Heléna knew it would be some time before they could fulfil that promise. She wished them well, and waved them goodbye, wondering even as she did, whether she herself would know anything more of her own future by then.

As August arrived, more advertisements began to appear on the camp noticeboards listing emigration prospects in various countries willing to accept refugees. As the refugees made their choices, they then faced more screening and a battery of interviews, before finally being accepted for their chosen destination. Eventually, the Australian Immigration Commission, the main body processing applications from refugees wishing to resettle in Australia, set up its headquarters in the Augsburg camp itself. Heléna had thought many times about her cousin Edvard's words that Christmas evening so long ago now, it seemed. He had mentioned Australia as a possible destination, should he and Judith emigrate, and although they had later decided to join Edvard's sister in New Zealand, the prospect of settling in Australia had stayed in the back of Heléna's mind. She and Stefan had had no interest in pursuing the idea then, but now, looking back, she wondered if God had indeed been planting a seed in her heart and mind, which one day would germinate just at the right time. Eventually, after further discussion, Heléna, Jan, Simona and Berta decided to apply to the Australian Immigration Commission for assessment, and to trust God that the outcome would be right for them.

Having made the choice, Heléna felt much more at peace. Medical examinations followed for all of them, along with security checks for the adults, and a personal interview with the Australian Consul, a genial fellow whom Heléna liked immediately, and who put them very much at ease. Australia was looking in particular, he explained carefully, for single and married immigrants up to forty-five years of age. Berta did not fit that requirement, he realised, but would be considered as part of their family unit, since she could not return to her homeland, and had no means of support there anyway. As far as Heléna and Jan in particular were concerned, each would be required, after their arrival in Australia, to complete a two year contract working at whatever job the Australian Government provided for them and for which they considered them qualified. After that, they were free to pursue whatever career they chose. The possibilities were endless in Australia, the Consul informed them.

'Besides, my dear,' he continued, as he concluded his interview with Heléna, 'you're such a beautiful young woman that you'll no doubt be married before those first two years are completed! There are plenty of eligible men in Australia. Then you'll be busy with a family of your own before you know it!'

He laughed heartily, and Heléna smiled politely, knowing he meant to be kind. Inwardly, she was sceptical. If she ever did marry again, she needed to be able to accept her husband for who he was, and not continually compare him with Stefan. She knew that, but right now she knew she still clung too much to his memory to be able to judge any others who showed interest in her fairly. Only time would change that, she felt. Time, and God's hand of healing – and possibly her new country of Australia.

After that, things moved swiftly. The following week, they were informed that they had been accepted for emigration to Australia. Around four weeks later, in the middle of October, they learnt of their departure date from the Augsburg refugee camp – 15th November, only four weeks' time. Along with many others from the camp, they would travel by train to Munich, south over the border into Austria, and then finally into Italy, bound for a town near Naples, where they would remain in a holding camp until a suitable ship arrived to take them to Australia.

During those weeks, excitement naturally began to mount concerning their future in their new country. But Heléna was aware that her excitement was still somewhat tinged with regret for the things she was leaving behind in Europe, and apprehension about what lay ahead. She knew little about Australia, apart from some information about the climate, and the strange animals unique to that continent. It was an ancient land, with a rich aboriginal history, she had been told, but a young country as far as European settlement was concerned, the British having arrived only in 1788. How strange this seemed to her, coming from a European heritage that stretched back hundreds and hundreds of years! Perhaps this would mean that many of the political problems and issues now dividing Europe would seem insignificant in such a setting, she mused. Hopefully too she would have enough familiarity in her surroundings, and enough friends around her, to be able to survive any homesickness she might suffer.

Throughout this strange waiting period, much to her joy and relief, she received unexpected solace and support from Franz and Brigitte and their friends. They visited her regularly, sometimes in a group, and sometimes just the two of them. Always there were lively discussions, and much music and laughter, as they enjoyed one another's company. Franz and Brigitte were deeply committed to God, despite the many questions the war had brought, as were their friends. Together they shared rich times of fellowship, always focused on encouraging Heléna and the others in some way.

During one of these times, Heléna discovered that Brigitte not only sang beautifully, but had also studied the cello for many years.

'The cello's my first love in fact – even ahead of singing!' she explained. 'But I don't play regularly at present. Unfortunately, my cello was damaged beyond repair when our home was hit during an air raid, along with many of my parents' possessions. I borrowed a cello to complete my studies in Munich, but since then that's been difficult to do.'

She stopped talking then, and turned her head to one side, but before she did, Heléna noticed the quick welling up of tears, and the convulsive swallowing in her throat, as she tried to control her emotions. Franz, seated beside her, had seen what was happening, and squeezed her hand reassuringly, guiding the conversation in another direction. But Heléna sat silent, her mind in a whirl.

Her heart went out to Brigitte. She understood well how frustrating it was for an artist to want desperately to play, yet to have no means by which to express what was inside. For a week after the conversation with Brigitte, Heléna struggled deeply. She had never mentioned the fact to either of them that she had Stefan's cello with her. But she knew clearly what she should do – as clearly as if God had appeared and spoken to her face to face. And yet she struggled. She liked Brigitte, but something within her rebelled at contemplating giving her beloved cello to anyone – let alone someone who was to marry Franz! She knew herself well enough to recognise she was undoubtedly jealous, yet at the same time, she wanted to justify how she was feeling. After all, Franz had been very special to her, and she to him. Eventually, however, after a long tussle, Heléna dismissed these thoughts as unworthy, but still she hesitated. She had persevered in carrying Stefan's cello all that distance over kilometres of rough terrain, guarding it carefully the entire journey. Why give it away now? It reminded her so much of Stefan – but was it wise or even right to carry it on to her new country, especially when here before her was someone who needed it so desperately?

On their last day in Augsburg, when Franz and Brigitte visited her to say a final goodbye, Heléna won the battle. She excused herself briefly and returned to her dormitory, emerging with Stefan's cello held tightly to her. Silently, and with an effort, she held it out to Brigitte.

'Heléna ... what is this? Whose is it? Are you saying it's for me?'

Brigitte could not believe her eyes.

'Yes, it's yours, Brigitte,' Heléna said gently, willing her voice not to quaver. 'I believe it's right to give it to you, so please accept it! It belonged to my husband Stefan, who as you know was killed by the Nazis during the war – he gave himself up for me. I wanted to take it with me when we left our homeland. I couldn't bear to part with it, as it reminded me so much of him. It's a little battered now, since I've carried it so far – by train, in the back of vans, and on foot through the mountains – but it's still a beautiful instrument. For me it will be a comfort to know it's being played wonderfully somewhere in Europe, that something that was so close to Stefan's heart is still enriching and blessing others here. I think it's important for me to let go of it now. Somehow I feel it will be a symbol of the old being left behind, and the new being welcomed. Please take it – and may it give you and others many hours of pleasure!'

Heléna handed it over with tears in her eyes. Brigitte did not know what to say, but Franz, with tears in his own, rose to his feet and, stumbling a little, moved towards Heléna. She too rose, and the two hugged each other tightly, their tears not only for the personal cost to Heléna of this gift, but for all the pain of times past, and also, she sensed, for what might have been. Eventually, Franz drew Brigitte into the circle of their arms, and after they had prayed together, said his final goodbye, his voice filled with emotion.

'Our thanks are so inadequate, Heléna, so I won't try to say anything! Goodbye, dear friend! God bless you so much – we'll never forget you! One day, I believe God will make this up to you!'

Heléna was glad that the rest of that day was so full of last minute preparations, and of farewelling others at the camp. That way, she had no time to think about her action and possibly regret it. During that night, her nightmare returned with great vividness – this time, much to her embarrassment, she woke up screaming loudly. Berta eventually managed to settle her with the little German lullaby she had often sung to her as a child when she was particularly ill, but she still lay awake for hours. Oh God, she prayed silently, I need you so much! I miss Stefan so much! Please give me an extra portion of your strength for this next part of my journey!'

Early the next day, all refugees bound for Australia boarded a train in Augsburg, each one carrying the pitifully small piles of luggage that were their only remaining possessions. At the main Munich station, where they were to change to the long distance train that would take them south through the mountains into Italy, the children were disappointed to hear that they had not yet arrived in Naples. A long journey lay ahead, they were warned – hours and hours of tedious travel in tightly packed compartments. Yet somehow the adults managed to keep the children occupied and their spirits high, as they sped through the ever changing landscape, further and further south through Bologna and Rome and on down to Naples – towns none of them had ever seen before. On arriving in Naples, they were taken once more to a camp, this time to the Embarkation Centre at Bagnoli, where they knew they had to wait for a ship to transport them to Australia.

After the barracks at Augsburg, the centre at Bagnoli was poorly equipped, to say the least, with overcrowded sleeping quarters, and bunks packed tightly together There was little to do in the weeks they were forced to remain there, apart from swap stories with some of the hundreds of other refugees from many different parts of Europe, hold impromptu concerts, and try to learn what English they could. Disappointingly, it was not even possible for them to leave the camp to see anything of the beauty of this southern part of Italy, an area most would never see again. Nevertheless, spirits were high, the children in particular waiting with great anticipation for their 'big boat' to arrive.

Christmas came and went, marking a stay in Bagnoli for them of almost six weeks. Eventually, on the last day of 1948, their 'big boat' did in fact arrive – an old ex-German troop ship, ironically enough, now owned and operated by a Norwegian company. Heléna, Jan, Simona, and Berta, each holding a child, walked joyfully on board, delighted at last to be on their way.

On New Year's Day, 1949, they finally set sail for Australia.

Heléna stood on deck staring down at the ever-widening expanse of water as the ship left port, aware with mixed feelings still, that she was watching her last link with Europe and her old life being severed before her eyes. Turning, she grasped little Stefan's hand even more tightly, and followed the others, head held high, down to the cabins below.

As she lay in her bunk that night, feeling the unfamiliar swaying of the ship beneath her, she prayed silently. Oh God, thank you that you hold me firmly by the hand, that you are still my refuge and fortress, the strength of my heart, and my portion forever! I'll stand tall for you in my new country, and keep the faith! I'll remember that I belong to you – always!

Heléna's story continues in Jo-Anne Berthelsen's second novel

'All The Days Of My Life',

available early 2008.

For further information about the author and her novels, or to contact her, please visit her website,
www.jo-anneberthelsen.com

Lose yourself in another Ark House book...

www.arkhousepress.com